ONLY FOR A KNIGHT

"Hooked me from the first page . . . larger-than-life characters and excellent descriptions bring this story . . . to vivid life."
—*Rendezvous*

"Captivating . . . fast-moving . . . steamy, sensual, and utterly breathtaking . . . will win your heart."
—FreshFiction.com

"Four-and-a-half stars! Enthralling . . . Welfonder brings the Highlands to life with her vibrant characters, impassioned stories, and vivid descriptions."
—*Romantic Times BOOKclub Magazine*

"Wonderful . . . Kept me glued to the pages."
—RomanceJunkies.com

"A book I highly recommend for those who enjoy sexy Scotsmen. A wonderful tale of love."
—TheRomanceReadersConnection.com

"Terrific . . . [a] fine tale."
—*Midwest Book Review*

"As usual, Welfonder gives her many fans another memorable historical read."
—ReadertoReader.com

"Such a sensually romantic read . . . enticing."
—HistoricalRomanceWriters.com

WEDDING FOR A KNIGHT

"TOP PICK! You couldn't ask for a more joyous, loving, smile-inducing read . . . Will win your heart!"
—Romantic Times BOOKclub Magazine

"With history and beautiful details of Scotland, this book provides romance, spunk, mystery, and courtship . . . a must-read!"
—Rendezvous

"A very romantic story . . . extremely sexy. I recommend this book to anyone who loves the era and Scotland."
—TheBestReviews.com

MASTER OF THE HIGHLANDS

"Welfonder does it again, bringing readers another powerful, emotional, highly romantic medieval that steals your heart and keeps you turning the pages."
—Romantic Times BOOKclub Magazine

"Vastly entertaining and deeply sensual medieval romance . . . for those of us who like our heroes moody, *ultrahot*, and *sexy* . . . this is the one for you!"
—HistoricalRomanceWriters.com

"Yet another bonny Scottish romance to snuggle up with and inspire pleasantly sinful dreams . . . a sweetly compelling love story . . . [with a] super-abundance of sexual tension."
—Heartstrings

more . . .

BRIDE OF THE BEAST

"Larger-than-life characters and a scenic setting . . . Welfonder pens some steamy scenes."
—Publishers Weekly

"A wonderful story . . . well-told . . . a delightful mix of characters."
—RomanticReviews.com

"Thrilling . . . so sensual at times, it gives you goose bumps . . . Welfonder spins pure magic with her vibrant characters."
—ReaderToReader.com

"Four-and-a-half stars! . . . A top pick . . . powerful emotions, strong and believable characters, snappy dialogue, and some humorous moments add depth to the plotline and make this a nonstop read. Ms. Welfonder is on her way to stardom."
—Romantic Times BOOKclub Magazine

KNIGHT IN MY BED

"Exciting, action-packed . . . a strong tale that thoroughly entertains."
—Midwest Book Review

"Steamy . . . sensual . . . readers will enjoy this book."
—*Booklist*

"Ripe with sexual tension . . . breathtaking!"
—**RoadtoRomance.dhs.org**

DEVIL IN A KILT

"A lovely gem of a book. Wonderful characters and a true sense of place make this a keeper. If you love Scottish tales, you'll treasure this one."
—**Patricia Potter, author of *The Heart Queen***

"As captivating as a spider's web, and the reader can't get free until the last word . . . tense, fast-moving."
—*Rendezvous*

"Four-and-a-half stars! This dynamic debut has plenty of steaming sensuality . . . [and] a dusting of mystery. You'll be glued to the pages by the fresh, vibrant voice and strong emotional intensity . . . will catapult Welfonder onto 'must-read' lists."
—*Romantic Times BOOKclub Magazine*

"Engaging . . . very fast-paced with fascinating characters and several interesting plot twists . . . a keeper."
—**Writers Club Romance Group on AOL**

Bride for a Knight

SUE-ELLEN WELFONDER

FOREVER

NEW YORK   BOSTON

Cover design by Diane Luger
Typography by Ron Zinn
Illustration by Craig White
Book design by Giorgetta Bell McRee

Forever is an imprint of Grand Central Publishing.

The Forever name and logo is a trademark of Hachette Book Group USA, Inc.

Forever
Hachette Book Group USA
237 Park Avenue
New York, NY 10017
Visit our Web site at www.HachetteBookGroupUSA.com

Printed in the United States of America

First Printing: September 2007

10 9 8 7 6 5 4 3 2 1

In loving memory of Elizabeth "Lizzy" Benway.
Passionate reader, enthusiastic supporter of romance,
and much-loved friend to many authors,
a hurricane tragedy ended her life way too soon.
Lizzy loved Duncan, the hero of DEVIL IN A KILT,
and I will never forget the fun we had when she launched a
contest for that book on her popular John DeSalvo Web site.
Above all, Lizzy will be remembered for her big-hearted
goodness and the unbridled joy she poured into
everything she did.
I miss you, Lizzy, and thank you for making
my early-author-days so very special.
A brilliant light went out in the romance community
the day we lost you.

Acknowledgments

Scotland is a land of great beauty where ancient tradition, legends, and lore are still alive and appreciated. Those who dwell there are privileged; those who visit are enchanted, forever spellbound by Scotland's magic. No place is more soul-claiming, more difficult to leave. Scotland is also my secret elixir, the wellspring of my inspiration, and every time I visit, I am renewed. Repeatedly awed by how easy it is to walk there and feel and glimpse the past. Or, too, to believe that in such a special place, dreams truly might come true.

While researching this book, I happened across quite a few heroic James Macphersons, each one larger-than-life and leaving their own bold legacy on Scotland's past. One in particular touched my heart for he lost his life unjustly, succumbing to a corrupt hangman's noose in the very moments a racing horseman arrived waving a pardon.

Known as the "Gypsy Outlaw," this James Macpherson was a gifted fiddler. Like the Jamie in this book, he was also said to have been quite tall and of incomparable strength. Roguish, dashing, and full of charm, he was only twenty-four when he died, his dream of rescue shattered when the town clock was set forward, sneakily enabling his execution before salvation could reach him.

The charming young fiddler should not be forgotten and perhaps some of Scotland's magic blessed him after all, for he outwitted the authorities one final time, his legacy living on in his music, appreciated to this day whenever "The Macpherson's Rant" and his other beautiful tunes are played.

I would also like to remember three women who lend their own special magic to my work, offering much appreciated advice and encouragement. Roberta M. Brown, my best friend, agent, and greatest champion. My wonderful editor, Karen Kosztolnyik, whose insight and guidance I appreciate so much. And Michele Bidelspach, who I have adored since *Devil in a Kilt*.

As always, my deepest love and appreciation to my very handsome husband, Manfred, for not complaining (too much) each time I run off to Scotland. His support and enthusiasm means so much. And my little dog, Em, faithful companion and much-loved friend, the whole of my world revolves around him.

Bride
for a
Knight

BALDREAGAN CASTLE
THE WESTERN HIGHLANDS, 1325

Devil take your tsk-tsks and head-shakings." Munro Macpherson, a lesser Highland chieftain of scarce renown, clenched his fists and glowered at Morag the midwife. He refused to look at the wraith on his bed, focusing his fury on the bloody-handed old woman. "Dinna think to tell me she's dying. No-o-o, I willna hear it!"

He took two steps forward, another when the midwife cast him a sorrow-filled stare. The same kind she'd been sending his way ever since he'd burst into the birthing chamber.

A stare that said more than words.

Told him things he didn't want to accept.

Shuddering, he glared denial at her, willed the sympathy off her lined, age-pitted face. " 'Tis you and no other who'll be meeting your Maker this night if you do not soon restore my wife's vigor!"

" 'Tis God's will, sir." Morag sighed, made the sign of the cross.

"Then call on the old gods!" Munro shouted, his mouth twisting. "All in these hills know you're familiar with 'em!"

The old woman pressed her lips together and rubbed more herbed oil onto her hands. "Your own eyes saw the piece of cold iron I laid in her bed. And I told you the water my niece is using to blot the sweat from her brow comes from St. Bride's own well."

"Then use devilry!" Munro all but choked. "Try anything!"

He narrowed a scorching stare on Morag's timid-faced niece, the dripping rag clutched in her hand. Rage scalded him that such a pale wee mouse of a female could live and breathe while his lady, so lush, golden, and until yestereve, so alive, could lay dying.

Consumed by fever, already long out of her senses.

Unable to bear it, he whirled away from the two women, the pathetic shadow that was his life. All that remained of her were incoherent moans and the tangled spill of her glorious hair across the soiled bedsheets. A magnificent cascade of rippling bronze, but already matted and losing its luster. Just as her creamy, rose-tinged skin, always her pride, had drained of all color.

Haggard and spent, she no longer even thrashed when the birth pangs gripped her. She simply lay there, her sunken eyes and the waxy sheen of death signaling her fate.

Her destiny, and Munro's doom.

Entirely too aware of his inability to do aught about it, he planted himself before an unshuttered window and frowned out on the bleak autumn night. Hot tears rolled down his cheeks, but he fought them, drew in a great breath of the chill, damp air.

But no matter how hard he stared into the rain-washed darkness, or welcomed the furious thunder cracking in the distance, he felt impotent. Small and inept, as if he were no longer the tall, powerfully built man who strode so boldly across the hills, but a quivering nithling ready to drop to his knees if only pleading might help.

Instead, his blood iced and his entire body went so taut he wondered it didn't crack and shatter into thousands of tiny ne'er to be retrieved pieces.

Tight-lipped, he kept his gaze riveted on the dark of the hills, his hands curled around his sword belt. "Hear me, Morag," he said, his tone as humble as one such as he could make it, "for all my moods and rantings, I love my wife. I canna bear to lose her."

The words spoken, he turned, his gut knotting to see the old woman peering beneath his wife's red-splotched skirts, her wizened face drawn into a worse scowl than his own.

Munro swallowed, tightened his fingers on his belt. "Name your price if you save her. Whate'er it is. I will be ever in your debt, and gladly."

But the midwife only shook her head again. "The babe is too big," she said, easing his lady's thighs farther apart. "And she's lost too much blood."

"Meaning?" Munro's temper resurfaced, his eyes began to bulge. "Speak the truth, woman, lest I pitch you and your sniveling niece out the window!"

"Your wife will die, sir," Morag answered him, "but

there's a chance the bairn will live. His head is already emerging. Strong shoulders, too. Be thankful—"

"*Thankful?*" Munro thrust out an enraged hand, yanking up his wife's blood-drenched skirts in time to see a large, coppery-haired man-child slip from between her lifeless thighs.

"Thankful for a tenth son?" he roared, glaring at the wailing babe. "The child who killed my Iona?"

"He is your son, my lord." Morag cradled the babe against her chest, splayed gnarled fingers across his wet-glistening back. "And a fine, strapping lad, he is. He will make you forget. In time—"

"I will never forget," Munro vowed, staring past her, watching the horrible glaze coat his wife's vacant eyes. "And I dinna need a tenth mouth to feed. I didna even want this one! Nine healthy sons are enough for any man."

"Sir, please . . ." The midwife handed the babe to her niece, hastened after him when he made for the door. "You must at least name him."

"I must do naught!" Munro swung around; he would have hit her were she not so old and bent. "But if you would have a name then call the lad Jamie—James of the Heather!"

The midwife blinked. "*'Of the Heather'?*"

"So I have said," Munro confirmed, already stepping out the door. "'Tis there **he** was spawned in a moment I'll e'er regret, and 'tis there he can return. So soon as he's old enough. Baldreagan has no room for him."

Chapter One

✦

FAIRMAIDEN CASTLE
NEAR BALDREAGAN, AUTUMN 1347

"*The tenth son?*"

Aveline Matheson paced the length of the high table, her father's startling news echoing in her ears. Equally distressing, her sister's red-rimmed gaze followed her and that made her feel unpleasantly guilty.

She took a deep breath, trying hard to ignore the sensation that her world was spinning out of control.

"To be sure, I remember there was a younger son, but . . ." She paused, finding it hard to speak with Sorcha's teary-eyed stare boring holes in her.

Indeed, not just her oldest sister, but every kinsman crowding the great hall. All of them were staring at her. Swiveling heads and narrowing eyes. Measuring her reaction as if the entire future and fortune of Clan Matheson rested upon her shoulders.

And from what she'd heard, it did.

Wincing inwardly, she stopped in front of her father's

laird's chair and stood as tall as her diminutive stature would allow.

That, and Alan Mor Matheson's fierce countenance. A look her plaid-hung, bushy-bearded father wielded with as much skill as he swung his sword.

Seeing that look now, she swallowed, wanting only to escape the hall. Instead, she held her ground. "For truth, I am sore grieved for Laird Macpherson," she began, scarce able to grasp the horror of losing nine sons at once, "but if you mean to insist upon a union between our houses, shouldn't Sorcha be the bride?"

Upon her words, Sorcha gave an audible gasp.

Alan Mor's face hardened, his large hands splaying on the high table. "Saints of glory!" he boomed, his choler causing his eldest daughter to jump as if he'd struck her.

Ignoring her distress, he leaned forward, kept his attention on Aveline. "Your sister was to be the bride. She was to wed Macpherson's eldest son, Neill. As well you know. Now, with Neill and the others dead, only Jamie remains."

He paused, letting the last two words hang in the smoke-hazed air. "Sorcha is more than fifteen summers the lad's senior and your other three sisters are wed. I willna risk the alliance with Macpherson by denying his only remaining son the most suitable bride I can offer."

Aveline lifted her chin. "Be that as it may—"

"It doesn't matter. Not now." Sorcha touched her arm, blinking back the brightness in her eyes. "'Twas Neill who should've been mine. I-I . . . would have followed him to the ends of this earth, even through the gates of hell," she vowed, her voice thick. "I've no wish to wed Young Jamie."

"Even so, I still grieve for you." Aveline released an uneven breath, a surge of pity tightening her chest. "And my heart breaks for the Macphersons."

Alan Mor hooted. "Your sister is a well-made young woman with fine prospects. Another husband will be found for her," he declared, glancing around as if he expected someone to gainsay him. "As for that cross-grained old goat, Macpherson, that one has e'er claimed the devil's own luck. His hurts will lessen once he remembers the bonny bit of glen he'll be getting to graze his precious cattle. Not to mention the well-filled coffers he wheedled out of me."

A chill slid down Aveline's spine. She said nothing.

If her father had brimming coffers to offer Munro Macpherson, he'd likely filled them with stones—or empty words and bluster.

Sure of it, she watched Sorcha whirl away and move toward the hearth fire. With her shoulders and back painfully straight, the older girl's face looked pale in the torchlight, her eyes shadowed and puffy. Worse, her stony expression voiced what every Matheson knew.

Neill Macpherson had been her last chance to wed.

Few were the suitors willing to accept Sorcha's large-boned, overly tall form for well made. And even Alan Mor's most cunning double-dealing and swagger couldn't transform her plain face into a pleasing one.

Indeed, not few were those who shook their heads over Neill's acceptance of her.

But he'd agreed for the sake of an alliance.

And now he was dead.

Shuddering, Aveline curled her fingers into her skirts, the image of the MacPherson brothers' last moments flashing across her mind.

Not that she'd been there.

But everyone born of these hills knew the treacheries of the white-water cauldron known as Garbh Uisge, the Rough Waters. They filled the deep, birch-lined gorge that divided Matheson and Macpherson lands.

A danger-fraught chasm, alive with a wildly plunging waterfall and splashing, boulder-strewn burn, the surging cataracts and clouds of spume now posed a forever reminder of nature's wrath. Leastways when served by the splintering of damp, age-warped wood.

The unexpected collapse of a narrow footbridge neither clan had been willing to refurbish, each laird insisting his neighbor made more use of the bridge and ought to dole out the coin for its repair.

A hotheaded foolhardiness that had taken a grim toll, and now sent Aveline striding across the hall, away from her father's black-browed arrogance.

"You err," she said, keeping her back to him as she wrenched open the shutters of the nearest window. "Naught in this world will ease Laird Macpherson's pain."

"Mayhap not," Alan Mor shot back, "but the man's a good deal more daft than I thought if he isn't at least comforted by the boons he'll reap through this alliance."

To Aveline's dismay, an immediate ripple of assent swept the hall. Murmured agreement swiftly followed by the clinking of ale cups and boisterous cheer. Alan Mor's own self-pleased grunt.

Aveline tightened her jaw and stared out at the misty, rain-sodden night, the outline of rugged black hills and the glimmer of distant stars twinkling through gray, wind-torn clouds.

"God grant you have the rights of it," she said at last, welcoming the evening's chill on her face. "Nevertheless, I would speak out against taking advantage of a man who is down and foundering."

"'Taking advantage'?" Alan Mor's deep voice shook the hall. "You'd best speak plain, lass. And hie yourself away from that window."

Stiffening, Aveline kept her gaze on the silvery glint of the river winding through the trees not far from Fairmaiden Castle's curtain walls. Older than time, the slow-moving river gave itself much more placid than the white-watered Garbh Uisge that had claimed so many innocent lives.

And brought others to this unexpected pass.

Herself included.

Her temples beginning to throb, she turned from the window. Sorcha now stood in a darkened corner, her ravaged, tear-stained face shielded from the reach of torchlight. Everyone else was turned her way, her father's face wearing an even darker scowl than before.

Aveline squared her shoulders, then took a step forward.

"Well?" Alan Mor demanded, his stare almost searing the air. "Are you accusing me of trying to deceive Macpherson?"

"Nay, I—" Aveline broke off, unable to lie. Her father's famed sleights of hand and well-oiled words were known throughout the Highlands.

Coming forward, she sought a way to cushion her suspicions. "I would not accuse you of aught," she ventured, hoping only she heard the cynicism in her tone. "And to be sure, I am willing to wed, am even eager for the day I might have a husband and household of my own."

"Then why are you looking as if you've just bit into something bitter?"

"Because," Aveline admitted, "I do not think Munro Macpherson will appreciate us meddling—"

"So now I'm a meddler?" Alan Mor shot to his feet, the movement scattering the parchments spread before him. "Helping the old fool is what I'm doing! Did you not hear me say tongue-waggers claim he's taken to his bed? That he fears leaving his privy chambers because he thinks the ghosts of his sons have returned to Baldreagan? Are haunting him?"

Alan Mor glared at her, his nostrils flaring. "Munro isn't yet in his dotage, but he soon will be if no one takes him in hand. He needs Jamie."

"Since when have you cared about Macpherson's well-doing?" Aveline challenged, stepping onto the dais. "You and Munro were ne'er friends."

"We are neighbors." Her father looked down, took a sudden interest in examining the colored string tied around a rolled parchment. "Knowing he's right in his head is a lesser evil than annoying the bastard."

"I vow you'll vex him mightily if you persist in this fool plan of yours." Aveline snatched the parchment scroll from her father's hand and held it out of his reach. "Munro Macpherson ne'er spoke fondly of Jamie. He's even been heard to call him a dirk thrust beneath his ribs."

Alan Mor sucked in his breath, his surprise at her bluntness all the answer Aveline needed.

Neither the Macpherson nor Young Jamie knew her father still meant to uphold the proposed alliance.

"Word is, Jamie's grown into a fine, strapping lad. A knight." Alan Mor recovered quickly, thrusting out his chin. "He even fought alongside King David at Neville's Cross last autumn, his bravery and valor earning him much acclaim. Munro will change his mind about the lad once he's home."

"Still . . ." Aveline tightened her grip on the parchment. "I do not think this should be sent to Jamie until Laird Macpherson is fit enough to decide if he, too, still wishes a union between our houses."

To her horror, her father laughed.

As did his inky-fingered scribe.

"Too late!" Alan Mor's eyes lit with mischief. "That scroll in your hand is naught but a letter to your sister in Inverness, asking of her health and thanking her for the casks of wine her husband sent to us. The many jars of their heather-tasting honey."

Aveline dropped the parchment. "You mean you've already sent word to Jamie? Without informing Macpherson?"

The look on her father's face turned smug. "Someday you'll thank me. You, and that blethering fool, Macpherson."

"And Jamie?"

Alan Mor snorted. "Him most of all—once he sets eyes on you!"

His foul temper forgotten, he beamed on her. "What young loon wouldn't be pleased with such a delicate bloom?"

But Aveline wasn't so sure.

Glancing down, her gaze skimmed over her thick braid, not acknowledging how it gleamed like gold in the candlelight, but rather settling on her tiny hands and feet, the smallness of her breasts. Anything but a full woman, lushly curved and ripe, she doubted any man would find favor with her.

Or the distasteful circumstance that would propel her and Young Jamie into a marriage bed.

No man liked being duped.

Long-lost son, or no.

Across miles of darkling hills and empty moorland, thick with bracken and winter-browned heather, Clan MacKenzie's Cuidrach Castle loomed above the silent waters of Loch Hourn, the stronghold's proud towers and that great sentinel, the Bastard Stone, silhouetted against a cold, frosty sky.

A chill night; icy stars glittered in the heavens and knifing winds whistled past the windows, rattling shutters and making those within glad for the leaping flames of the great hall's well-doing log fire. Eager-to-please squires circulated with trays of hot, spiced wine and steaming mounds of fresh-baked meat pasties. Men crowded benches drawn close to the hearth, jesting and jostling amongst themselves, their rich masculine laughter rising to the ceiling rafters, bawdy good cheer ringing in every ear.

Only one of Cuidrach's residents shunned the comforts and warmth of the hall this night, seeking instead the privacy of a tiny storeroom filled with wine casks, blessed torchlight, and James Macpherson's mounting frustration.

Holding back an oath that would surely curl the devil's own toes, Young James of the Heather, sometimes teasingly called Jamie the Small, glared at the tiny red bead of blood on his thumb.

The fifth such jab wound he'd inflicted on himself in under an hour.

And, he suspected, most likely not the last. Not if he meant to complete his task.

Sighing, he licked the blood off his finger, then shoved his stool closer to the best-burning wall torch. Perhaps with brighter light, he'd have a better chance of restitching the let-out seams of his new linen tunic.

A birthday gift from his liege lord's lady.

And the finest tunic he'd e'er possessed. Softer than rose petals and with a bold Nordic design embroidered around the neck opening; just looking at it brought a flush a pleasure to his cheeks, and even made his heart thump if he thought about the long hours Lady Mariota had spent crafting such a gift for him. A gift he was determined to wear to his birthday revelries later that night.

He would, too.

If only the tunic weren't so tight across the shoulders, the sleeves a mite too short. And his fool fingers so damnably clumsy.

Frowning, he picked up his needle and set to work again. Truth be told, there was nothing wrong with the tunic . . . it was him.

Always had been him.

He was simply too big.

And, he decided a short while later, his hearing a bit too sharp. Leastways keen enough to note the sudden silence pressing against the closed storeroom door.

He tilted his head, listening.

But his instincts hadn't lied.

Gone indeed were the muffled bursts of laughter and ribald song, the occasional barks of the castle dogs. The high-pitched skirls of female delight. Utter stillness held Cuidrach's great hall in a firm grip, the strange hush smothering all sound.

A deep kind of quiet that didn't bode well and even held sinister significance—if he were to trust the way the fine hairs on his nape were lifting. Or the cold chill spilling down his spine.

Curious, he set aside the unfinished tunic and his needle and stood. But before he could cross the tiny storeroom, the door swung open. His liege lord, Sir Kenneth MacKenzie, stood in the doorway, flanked by Sir Lachlan, the Cuidrach garrison captain, and a travel-stained man Jamie had never seen.

The stranger's rain-dampened cloak hung about his shoulders and his wind-tangled hair bespoke a hard ride. But it was more than the man's muddied boots and bleary-eyed fatigue that made Jamie's mouth run dry.

It was the look on the stranger's face.

The undeniable impression of strain and pity that

poured off him and filled the little storeroom until Jamie thought he might choke on its rankness.

Especially when he caught the same wary sadness mirrored in Sir Kenneth's and Sir Lachlan's eyes.

Jamie froze. "What is it?" he asked, his gaze moving from face to face. "Tell me straight away for I can see that something dire has happened."

"Aye, lad, I'm afraid that is so. Would that I could make it otherwise, but . . ." Kenneth glanced at the stranger, cleared his throat. "See you, this man comes from Carnach in the north of Kintail. Alan Mor Matheson of Fairmaiden Castle sent him. He brings ill tidings. Your father—"

"Of a mercy!" Jamie stared at them. "Dinna tell me he is dead?"

None of the three men spoke a word, but the tautness of their grim-set expressions said everything.

Jamie blinked, a wave of black dizziness washing over him. Sakes, even the floor seemed to dip and heave beneath his feet. It couldn't be true. Naught could have struck down his indomitable father. Munro Macpherson was honed from coldest iron, had steel running in his veins. And after a lifetime of the man's indifference, Jamie shouldn't care what fate befell him.

But he did.

More than he would have believed. So much, the roar of his own blood in his ears kept him from hearing what Kenneth was saying. He could only see the other man's mouth moving, the sad way Sir Lachlan and the courier shook their heads.

Jamie swallowed, pressed cold fingers against his temples. "Tell me that again, sir. I-I didna hear you."

"I said your father is not dead, though he is faring poorly and has taken to his bed. That's why Laird Matheson sent his man to us." Kenneth came forward to grip Jamie's arms. "And there has been a tragedy, aye."

Jamie's heart stopped. He could scarce speak. Breaking away from Kenneth's grasp, he searched the men's faces. "If not my father, then who? One of my brothers?"

The three men exchanged glances.

Telling glances.

And so damning they filled Jamie with more dread than if someone had leveled a sword at his throat. For one sickening moment, the faces of his nine brothers flashed before his eyes and he thought he might faint. But before he could, Sir Lachlan unfastened the hip flask at his belt and thrust the flagon into Jamie's hand.

"Drink this," he urged, his face grim. "All of it if you can."

And Jamie did, gulping down the fiery *uisge beatha* so quickly the strong Highland spirits burned his throat and watered his eyes.

The last softly-burning droplets still on his tongue, he squared his shoulders. Prepared for the worst. "Tell me true," he entreated, his fingers clenching around the flask. "Which one of my brothers is dead?"

"It grieves me to tell you, lad." Kenneth drew a long breath, slid another glance at the courier. " 'Tis not one of your brothers, but all of them. They drowned in the swollen waters of the Garbh Uisge when the footbridge collapsed beneath them."

"Christ God, no-o-o!" Shock and horror slammed into Jamie, crashing over him in hot and cold waves as eerie silence swelled anew, its damning weight blotting all sound but a high-pitched buzzing in his ears and the keening wind.

A low, unearthly moan he only recognized as his own when lancing pain closed his throat and the wailing ceased.

And so soon as it did, he staggered backward and sagged against the stacked wine casks, disbelief laming him. His knees began to tremble and his vision blurred, his entire world contracting to a whirling black void.

A spinning darkness made all the more terrifying because it taunted him with glimpses of his brothers' faces, cold and gray in death, but also as they'd been in life.

Neill, the oldest, with auburn hair bright as Jamie's own and the same hazel eyes. Confident and proud, he was the most hot-tempered of Jamie's brothers. After Neill, came Kendrick, the most dashing with his roguish grin and easy wit, his ability to create a stir amongst the ladies simply by entering a room.

Then there was Hamish, the dreamer. A secret romantic, good-natured, quiet, and most content when left alone to ponder great chivalric myths and tales of ancient Gaelic heroism. And six others, all dear to him, brothers who'd been his lifeblood in the years his father had shunned him.

His heart's joy and only solace right up to the day he'd struck out across the heather, found a new home and purpose as squire to Duncan MacKenzie, the Black Stag of Kintail, his liege lord's uncle.

And now his brothers were gone.

Jamie closed his eyes and swallowed. He couldn't believe it; wouldn't be able to accept the loss so long as he had breath in his body. But when he opened his eyes and looked into the troubled faces of the three men standing just inside the storeroom's threshold, he knew it was true.

Still, he tried to deny it.

"It canna be. My brothers knew every clump of heather, every peat bog and lochan, every stone and hill face of our land," he said, willing the room to stop spinning. "They crossed that footbridge every day, would have known if it was near to collapsing."

The courier shrugged, looking uncomfortable. " 'Tis thought the recurrent rains of late weakened the wood. The planks were aged and warped, some of them rotted. My pardon, sir, but you've not been to Baldreagan in years. The bridge truly was in need of repair."

Jamie struggled against his pain, gave the courier a long, probing look. "You are certain they are dead? All nine? There can be no mistake?"

"Nay, son, I am sorry." The man shook his head, his words squelching Jamie's last shimmer of hope. "I saw the bodies with my own eyes, was there when they were pulled from the river."

Jamie nodded, unable to speak.

The words tore a hole in his heart, stirring up images he couldn't bear. With great effort, he pushed away from the wine casks and moved to the storeroom's narrow-slit window, welcomed the blast of chill air, the heavy scent of rain on the raw, wet wind.

He curled his fingers around his sword belt, held tight as he looked out on the night mist, the dark belt of pines crouching so near to Cuidrach's walls. Swallowing hard, he fixed his gaze on the silent hills, willing their peace to soothe him. But this night, the beauty of Kintail failed him.

Indeed, he doubted that even the sweetest stretch of heather could calm him. Wondered how moments ago his only concern had been restitching his birthday tunic, and now. . . . He tightened his grip on his belt, let out a long, unsteady breath just as Cuillin, his aged dog, nudged his leg, whimpering until he reached down to stroke the beast's shaggy head.

In return, Cuillin looked up at him with concern-filled eyes and thumped his scraggly tail on the floor rushes. Neill had given him the dog, Jamie recalled, a shudder ripping through him at the memory. But so soon as the tremor passed, he turned back to the room, his decision made.

He cleared his throat. "I've ne'er been one to thrust myself into places where I am not welcome," he began, standing as straight as he could, "but I shall ride to Baldreagan, whether my presence suits my father or no. I must pay my respects to my brothers. 'Tis a debt I owe them."

To his surprise, the courier's mouth quirked in an awkward smile. " 'Tis glad I am to hear you say that," he said, stepping forward. "See you, as it happens, I've brought more than ill tidings."

He paused, puffing his chest a bit. "Truth be told, I have something that might prove of great interest to you."

Jamie cocked a brow, said nothing.

Undaunted, the courier fished inside his cloak, withdrawing a rolled parchment tied with colorful string and sealed with wax. "Something that might give a lift to your aching heart. See here, I've a letter from—"

"My father?" Jamie asked, incredulous.

The courier shook his head. "Och, goodness, nay. Your da is in no form to be dashing off letters. 'Tis from my liege, Laird Matheson. But he sends it in your father's name, and out of his own wish to do well by you."

Jamie eyed the letter, suspicion making him wary. "My father and Alan Mor were e'er at odds. It is one thing for Matheson, as our nearest neighbor, to send word of my brothers' deaths if my father was unable. But to pen a letter in my da's name? And out of courtesy to me? Nay, I canna believe it."

"On my soul, it is true." The courier held out the parchment. "Much has changed in the years you've been away. As the letter will prove. You might even be pleasantly surprised."

Jamie bit back an oath, not wanting to take out his pain on a hapless courier. "I'd say this day has brought enough surprises." He folded his arms. "I'm not sure I wish to be privy to any more."

But after a moment he took the parchment, ran his thumb over the seal. "Though I will admit to being curious."

"Then read the letter," Kenneth urged him. "What the man says makes sense, Jamie. Now might be a good time to mend the breach with your sire and put the past behind you."

I have tried to do that the whole of my life, Jamie almost blurted. Instead, he found himself breaking the wax seal, unrolling the parchment. He stepped close to a wall torch, scanned the squiggly lines of ink, an odd mix of astonishment and dismay welling inside him.

A brief flare of anger, too. That he should be welcomed home only now, under such grievous circumstances. As for the rest . . . he looked up from the parchment, shoved a quick hand through his hair.

He started to speak, but the words caught in his throat, trapped there by the irony of his plight. If Alan Mor weren't playing some nefarious game, everything he'd ever wanted now lay within his reach.

If he did what was asked of him.

Seemingly in high favor for the first time in his life, he turned to the courier, trying not to frown. "You know what is in here?" And when the man nodded, "Is it true that my father and Alan Mor have entered into an alliance? One they meant to seal with the marriage of my brother Neill and Alan Mor's eldest daughter?"

The man bobbed his head again. "'Tis the God's truth, aye. So sure as I'm standing here." He accepted the ale cup Sir Lachlan offered him, taking a sip before he went on, "Your father is in sore need, asks daily if you've arrived. He's failing by the day and won't even set foot outside his bedchamber. 'Tis hoped your return will revive him."

Pausing, the man stepped closer, laid a conspiratorial

hand on Jamie's arm. "That, and seeing the alliance between the clans upheld."

"Through my marriage to this Aveline?"

"Tchach, lad, which other lass would you have?" The
courier drew himself up, looked mildly affronted. "Poor
Sorcha is heartbroken o'er the loss of her Neill, and too
old for you by years. The other daughters are already
wed. It has to be Aveline—she's the youngest. And still a
maid."

Jamie eyed the man askance, would've sworn he could
feel an iron yoke settling on his shoulders.

It scarce mattered to him if Aveline Matheson was tender of years. The state of her maidenhood concerned him
even less.

He remembered the lassies of Fairmaiden Castle.
Regrettably, not by name. If memory served, there wasn't
a one amongst the brood he'd care to meet on a moonless
night. And with surety nary a one he'd wish to bed.

One nearly equaled him in height and build. Another
sported a mustache some men would envy. And one e'er
smelled of onions. Truth be told, he couldn't recall a single redeeming feature amongst the lot of them.

Binding himself to such a female would prove the
surest and quickest route to misery.

But he did want to see his father. Help him if he could.

Jamie sighed, felt the yoke tightening around his neck.
"I ne'er thought to see my father again in this life. For
certes, not because he claims to need me. As for taking
one of Matheson's daughters to wife—"

"Och, but Aveline is more than pleasing. And spirited."
The courier stepped in front of him, blocking the way

when Jamie would have paced back to the window. "She brings a healthy marriage portion, too. Prime grazing lands for your da's cattle. I say you, you willna be sorry. I swear it on the souls of my sons."

"I will think on it," Jamie offered, doing his best to hide his discomfiture.

"Why don't you hie yourself into the hall to get a meal and some sleep?" Kenneth clamped a hand on the courier's elbow, steered him to the door. "Jamie will give you his decision on the morrow."

Turning back to Jamie, he arched a raven brow. "For someone who spent his life yearning to win his father's favor, tell me why you lost all color upon hearing of the man's sudden need for you? Surely you aren't troubled by this talk of a desired marriage?"

Jamie folded his arms over his chest again, felt heat creeping up the back of his neck. Damn him for a chivalrous fool, but he couldn't bring himself to voice his misgivings.

Admit he'd rather have his tender parts shrivel and fall off before he'd find himself obliged to bed one of Alan Mor's daughters.

If he even could!

"Ach, dinna look so glum." Sir Lachlan took the letter, glanced at it. "There is nothing writ here that binds you," he said, looking up from the parchment. "You needn't do aught you find displeasing."

And that was Jamie's problem.

Returning home, even now, *would* please him. So much, his heart nearly burst at the thought. And once there, he'd be hard-pressed to disappoint his father.

Or Aveline Matheson.

If indeed such an alliance required his compliance. Truth was, he lived by a strict code of honor. One that forbade him to shame an innocent maid.

Even if sparing her feelings came at the cost of his own.

And besides, arranged marriages were more common than not. With few exceptions, only the lowest-born enjoyed the luxury of wedding for love.

Heaving a sigh, he snatched up his new tunic and donned it, unfinished seams or no. "We all ken I shall wed the lass if my da wishes it," he said, moving to the door. "I'll ride for Baldreagan at first light, and visit Alan Mor so soon as I've seen my father."

His intentions stated, he stepped into the great hall, pausing to appreciate its smoky, torch-lit warmth. The comfort of kith and kin, a crackling hearth fire. Everyday pleasures his brothers would never again enjoy. Indeed, compared to their fate, his own struck him as more than palatable.

So long as Aveline wasn't the sister almost his own size, he'd find some way to tolerate her.

Or so he hoped.

Chapter Two

✦

Jamie knew he was in trouble the moment he drew rein on a lofty, gorse-covered ridge and surveyed the dark hills spreading out all around him. Mist curled in the higher corries, the sight stirring his spirit and squeezing his heart.

Welcoming him with arms flung wide.

An embrace in the old way of the hills and one that clutched fiercely, holding fast until his breath caught and he would've sworn he'd only left these northern reaches of Kintail that very morn.

Wishing that were so, he blinked against the heat stinging the backs of his eyes. Now as never before, he recognized how the lure of hill and moor could make even the deepest cares seem far away.

Behind him, his dog, Cuillin, stirred in his wicker saddle basket, almost as if the ancient beast also sensed a subtle change in the air.

Knew, like Jamie, that they were home at last.

And for certes, they were.

Already deepening twilight, he could just make out the distant yellow-gleaming lights of Baldreagan. Little more than weaving pinpricks of brightness from his vantage point, but home all the same.

The one place on earth he'd ne'er thought to see again. The place he'd expected to miss till his dying day.

"God in heaven," he breathed, a strong sense of belonging sliding around him.

Duthchas, the feeling was called. A Highlander's fierce attachment to his home glen, a soul-deep sense of oneness with the land of his blood.

A pull Jamie now felt to the bone.

His chest tightening, he found himself sorely tempted to swing down from his saddle and kiss the peaty, moss-covered ground. He might have, too, but did not wish to frighten Cuillin.

Instead, he simply looked round, wishing his reason for returning had been a happy one.

But even here, a good distance from the Garbh Uisge, the roar of the rapids tainted the night. A dread sound that hollowed him, gouging an emptiness he doubted could ever be filled again.

Blocking his ears, he swore.

Then he clenched the reins so tightly his knuckles gleamed white.

As did the moonlight spilling across the dark roll of the hills. Bright, slanting bands of shimmering silver, rippling on the night breeze, the beauty stilling his heart.

Especially when one of the iridescent silvery bands proved to have a most pleasing feminine form.

Jamie blinked.

Ne'er had he seen the like.

But he wouldn't be a Highlander if he didn't recognize the wonder before him. A sight as ancient as the rocks and heather, but so rare, his whole world tilted.

His breath catching, he slid a hand behind him, curling his fingers into the scruffy fur at Cuillin's shoulders. "Saints o' mercy!" he marveled, his eyes widening. "A faery!"

There could be no doubt.

Only one of the *Daoine Sithe* could be so delicate and fair.

More exquisite than any female of this earth, the fey beauty slipped through a moon-silvered glade, her dainty feet not seeming to touch the ground.

Saints, she looked so tiny he doubted she'd come up to his chest were he to stand before her. Small-breasted and slight, she moved with a grace that bespoke lithe, slender legs. And she wore her hair unbound and flowing, a glistening sheaf of palest silk so beautiful he would've groaned did he not wish to risk drawing her attention.

But he did catch her scent on the chill night air.

A fragrance reminiscent of summer, violets, and fresh, dew-kissed green.

Truth tell, she must've bespelled him.

Even watching her from a distance, Jamie was seized by an irresistible urge to ride after her and touch her moonlit hair. To tangle his fingers in its silkiness, seeing for himself if the shimmering strands felt as soft and glossy as they looked.

See if her eyes really were the deep sapphire he

suspected. And if the tips of her eyelashes would appear as if dipped in gold.

Perhaps he'd kiss her, too. If a mortal man could even touch such a creature.

Jamie's brows snapped together at once, the spell broken.

A hot flush swept up his neck and the racing of his heart began to slow. Big as he was and fragile as she looked, his very breath would likely bruise her.

And his cheek for having such thoughts about a *Sithe* maid would surely land him in the depths of some faery knowe, bound by inescapable golden bonds. Or, equally unpleasant, see him plunged into a charmed sleep for a hundred years or more.

Such things were known to happen.

He shuddered, reached up to rub the back of his neck.

But then the moon vanished behind a cloud and when it reemerged, the broad sweeps of moor and hill loomed empty, the night still and quiet as it'd been.

"By glory!" He released his breath, peering hard at the little glade, but the faery was truly gone.

Nothing moved through the shadowy birches and scrub but the dark ribbon of a tumbling burn.

"Och, mercy me—did you see her, Cuillin?" He twisted around in the saddle and ruffled the old dog's ears, not missing that Cuillin's rheumy gaze remained on the very spot where the *Sithe* maid had disappeared.

Or that the old dog's tail was wagging.

Not that Jamie needed proof of what he'd seen.

Nor did he blame Cuillin for being smitten. The faery had been a vision of loveliness. Truth be told, she couldn't have been more beautiful had she been wrapped in cloth of gold and moonbeams, her shimmering hair dusted with stars.

And thinking about it, he decided that was a reasonable description of her.

He'd also wager she tasted of nectar and moon-spun temptation. He wasn't a man known for pretty words, only his great size and the skill of his sword arm. Yet this faery inspired him to such courtly verse.

Even so, he released her from his mind, his gaze falling on another glimmer of brightness. This one as earthy and real as the Highlands, welcome enough to flood him with memories. Bringing salvation, and again, the eye-stinging tightness of chest and throat that had plagued him every heather mile since leaving Cuidrach.

A malaise that worsened the farther north he'd ridden.

Setting his jaw, he sat up straighter and swiped the dampness from his cheeks, his stare fixed on the thick, whitewashed walls of a small, hump-backed cot house just visible through a copse of ancient Caledonian pines a bit farther down the long, rock-strewn slope. Peat smoke curled in thin blue tendrils from the cottage's stone-hung thatched roof and if he listened hard, he was certain he'd hear the bleating of sheep. Perhaps even a few faint strains of fiddle music.

And if he really concentrated, he might even catch a savory whiff of beef marrow broth or mutton stew.

For the cot-house was Hughie Mac's. A man already older than stone in Jamie's youth, Hughie Mac's gnome-like body was as twisted and gnarled as the Scots pines sheltering his cottage. But Hughie also had twinkling, smiling eyes. And he'd once been Jamie's grandfather's favored herd boy; a lad prized for his herding talent, but even more for the magic he could make on the strings of a fiddle.

The warm welcome and ready smile he'd always had for Jamie, especially when his world had seemed at its darkest.

For two pins, Jamie would ride there now, hammer on Hughie's door, and if the grizzled herder answered, he'd crush him in a hug that lasted till the morrow.

Hughie would greet him kindly.

His da's reception remained to be seen.

And it made him mighty edgy. Especially since glimpsing the faery. So he squared his shoulders and rode on, eager to be done with it. Digging in his heels, he sent his garron plunging down the rough, broken hillside and straight through his da's cattle, his passage startling the lumbering beasts.

A tall, hooded figure stared at him in horror from the edge of the protesting, scattering herd.

A tall, hooded *female* figure.

Jamie's jaw slipped and for one crazy mad moment, he wondered if she, too, was of the fey. Or if Hughie Mac still had a way with bonny lassies. But as he spurred toward the woman, he could see she was mortal as the day.

And without doubt the plainest creature he'd e'er set eyes on.

She was also the most terrified.

"Dinna come near me!" she shrieked, backing away. "No closer—I pray you!"

Jamie prayed, too.

His heart thundering as the most unchivalrous corner of his soul pleaded the saints that this Valkyrie wouldn't prove to be Aveline Matheson.

The proximity of Fairmaiden Castle made it a distinct possibility.

Nevertheless, he pulled up in front of her and swung down from the saddle. His honor demanded no less. But to his amazement, her eyes flew even wider and she flung up a hand as if warding off a horde of flying banshees.

"Have mercy!" she wailed this time, her face blanching in the light of the rising moon. "I—"

"You must be one of the Fairmaiden lasses." Jamie took her by the arms, seeking to soothe her. "You've no need to fear me. See you" —he jerked his head in Cuillin's direction—"what fiend o' the hills would ride about with an aged, half-blind dog? I am James of the Heather, come home to—"

"Praise God!" She blinked at him, her color slowly returning. "I-I thought you were Neill."

Jamie swallowed hard on hearing his brother's name. He'd been thinking about his brothers ever since crossing onto Macpherson land.

Speaking about them, even just one, was something he wasn't sure he could do.

Not yet.

But his knightly vows and Valkyrie's misted eyes had him reaching to brush the tears from her face.

"You knew Neill?" he probed, the name costing him dearly.

She flinched and bit down on her lip as she nodded.

Then her eyes filled anew, her reaction suggesting her identity.

"I am Sorcha," she said, confirming his guess. "I was Neill's betrothed and until a short while ago, the most light-hearted maid in these hills."

She looked at him, her eyes dark pools. "He was tall and bonny. A bold, forthright man who should have had all his days before him. But who could have foreseen . . ." She clapped a hand over her mouth, unable to finish.

Jamie drew a deep breath. "Saints aid me, lass, I dinna ken what to say to you." Having never mastered the courtly skills of proper wooing or even comforting distressed damsels, he did think to take her elbow and pull her with him to his garron. "I'll see you to your sire's keep," he suggested, trying to avert any further talk of his brother. "You can ride and I'll walk alongside."

But she backed away when Cuillin lunged forward to sniff her, his tail thumping against the wicker of his basket. "You are as goodly as Neill e'er said you were, but I wish to be alone. Fairmaiden is not far and the walking is a comfort to me. I've already come from Baldreagan this e'en, a few more paces willna—"

"From Baldreagan?" Jamie stared at her. "But that's well more than a few paces," he said, striding after her as she moved toward the trees. "And no journey for a maid unescorted. 'Tis nigh dark and the Rough Waters . . ."

He left the warning tail off, but she must've understood because she stopped, turning around to face him. "I know better than to go near the rapids. They are still in spate and there are ghosts there," she said, a dull flush spreading up her cheeks. "Only a fool would set foot there of a night."

She lifted her chin, fixed him with a piercing stare. "Truth be told, I doubt I'd even go there by day. The ghosts have been seen by many, they—"

"*Ghosts?*" Jamie looked at her, hoping he'd misunderstood.

She nodded. "Your brothers' spirits, aye. 'Tis why I thought you were Neill. He's been seen down at the cataracts. They all have."

Jamie folded his arms. "I dinna believe in ghosts."

The *Sithe*, aye. There wasn't a Gael born and walking who'd deny the existence of the Good People.

But bogles?

And of his own brothers?

Nay, he couldn't believe it.

Frowning, he drew himself to his full height and put back his shoulders—just to emphasize his denial. "Nay, lass," he repeated, shaking his head, "that canna be. Not Neill. Not any o' my brothers, saints rest their souls."

"I canna say I've seen them, but others have." The Valkyrie gave him a long look. "At the rapids and up at Baldreagan," she added, brushing at her cloak. "Your da sees them most often and they frighten him. That's why I was there tonight. My sister and I take turns looking in on him."

Jamie rubbed a hand down over his face. "The sister you mention, is she Aveline?" he asked, looking back at her.

But she was gone.

Or rather, he could just make out the dark swirl of her

cloak as she disappeared through the trees in the direction of Fairmaiden Castle.

Her father's keep, a sister bound to him by an alliance he had yet to fully believe, and a tangle he wasn't sure he cared to unravel.

But at least Aveline wasn't the Valkyrie.

And nary a jealous *Sithe* princeling had yet appeared, enchanted blade flashing and ready to escort him to his doom.

His plight could have been worse.

Or so he thought until a short while later the vast sprawl of Baldreagan loomed before him. A proud demesne, its sturdy towers rose dark against the surrounding hills. And, as at Hughie Mac's cottage, curling threads of bluish smoke drifted from the tower chimneys. No one could be seen on the parapet walk, nor did anyone shout a challenge as he drew near, yet he could feel wary eyes watching him.

And with reason, for lights shone from some of the higher windows, including the one he knew to be his da's private bedchamber.

But the welcoming effect of the flickering torchlight and the earthy-sweet scent of peat proved sorely dampened by the sprays of red-berried rowan branches affixed to the castle gatehouse.

Red-ribboned and ridiculously large, the rowan clusters stared back at him. A mute warning of what he'd find within, for red-ribboned rowan was his family's special charm.

An ancient cure bestowed on the Macphersons by

Devorgilla, the most respected wise woman in all the Isles and Western Highlands.

A charm the cailleach had assured would safeguard the clan's prized cattle, keeping them fat and hardy throughout the long Highland winters.

But also a talisman said to repel evil of any kind.

Including bogles.

Ghosts.

Jamie frowned. Thinking of his brothers thusly was not the homecoming he'd envisioned.

Even the weather was less than desirable, for the night had turned foul, with a thin drizzle chilling him and thick fog sliding down the braes to creep round Baldreagan's walls. An eerie, shifting gray shroud that minded all too easily of his reason for being there.

Refusing to be daunted, Jamie pulled his plaid more closely around him and peered at his father's empty-seeming gatehouse. Not surprising, the portcullis was lowered soundly into place. And since his brothers had e'er taken turns at sharing the castle watch, there'd be no telling on whose shoulders such a duty now rested.

He found out when the shutter of one of the gatehouse windows flew open and a less-than-friendly face glared down at him.

A young face, and one Jamie didn't recognize.

Even though the lad's freckles and shock of red hair marked him as a Macpherson.

A herder laddie, Jamie was certain, for when the boy leaned farther out the tower window, a distinct smell wafted on the night breeze. As if the lad had just returned from mucking out the cow byre.

"Who goes there?" the stripling demanded, his suspicious tone lacking all Highland warm-heartedness. "You're chapping unannounced at the door of a house in mourning and I've orders not to open to any."

"Not even to a son of this house?" Jamie rode beneath the window. "I am James of the Heather," he called up to the lad. "I've come to see my father. And pay my respects to my brothers. God rest their souls!"

The herd boy stared at him, disbelief in his eyes. "My laird's youngest son occupies himself in the far south of Kintail, in the service of a MacKenzie, last we heard. He hasn't been to these parts in years."

"That may be, but I am here now and would have entry to my home," Jamie returned, his temples beginning to throb. "It is cold, dark, and wet down here. Too wet for the old bones of the dog I have with me." He reached around and patted Cuillin's head. "We are both weary from traveling."

The boy hesitated, his gaze flicking to Cuillin then back to Jamie.

"You do have the look o' Neill about you," he allowed, still sounding doubtful. "What if you're his bogle?"

"His—" Jamie began, then snapped his mouth shut, unwilling to discuss ghosts twice in the same evening.

Instead, he cleared his throat. "I am my father's son James, so true as I'm here," he said, his head aching in earnest. "Now raise the portcullis and let me in. I would see my da before he sleeps. I was told he's ailing."

"Hah!" came a second voice as a stern-faced old woman appeared at the window. "Aye, and so he is unwell," she confirmed, peering down at Jamie. "He's in a bad way and he willna be troubled this late of an e'en. These are dark times with many ill things afoot. We canna trust—"

She broke off, her eyes rounding. "Jesus wept—it *is* you!" she cried, clapping her hands to her face. "Wee Jamie come home at last. Ach dia, how I've prayed for the day."

Jamie blinked, staring open-mouthed. He scarce trusted his eyes. But the silver-gray curls framing the well-loved face and the sharp, all-seeing eyes were the same.

His indulgent childhood nurse, a woman who'd filled every hour of his earliest years, shielding him from his da's temper and spleen. Soft-hearted for all her bluster, she'd been the mainstay of his youth, lavishing him with warmth and love, salving his boyhood hurts.

And now she stood clutching the window ledge and gawping at him with such moony-eyed astonishment, Jamie felt a surge of warmth and pleasure.

He shook his head, his heart clenching.

"Ach, Morag, is it yourself?" he managed, but then his throat closed and her beloved face blurred before him.

Not that he minded, for in that moment, she whirled from the window and, almost at once, the great spike-tipped portcullis began rattling upward.

That sweet sound ringing in his ears, he spurred beneath, riding straight through the gatehouse arch and into the torch-lit bailey, the chill, cloudy night and even the red-ribboned rowan promptly forgotten.

He was home.

Nothing else mattered.

And if his father's welcome stood in question, Morag was clearly pleased to see him.

Swinging down off his garron, he lifted Cuillin from his basket, then caught the old woman to him in a close embrace.

"Holy saints, Morag, you do not look a day older," he vowed, holding her tight until she pulled away to beam at him, tears spilling down her face.

"Come away in," she urged, dabbing at her eyes, then grabbing his arm and pulling him toward the keep where the massive double doors stood wide. "Praise God, you came," she added as they entered the great hall. "Your da grows more muddle-headed by the day and all in this hall would agree with me."

She squeezed his arm. "'Tis more than his fool ghost talk and losing your brothers that ails him," she confided, lowering her voice. "He's old and knows he split this clan asunder the day he sent you away. He yearns to make peace with you, even if he doesn't know it."

Jamie stopped.

He drew a deep breath and let it out slowly. Across the hall, on the wall above the high table, two well-flaming torches framed the Horn of Days, his clan's most prized treasure, and he had the most uncomfortable sensation that the thing was staring at him.

Waiting.

Or, better said, assessing and challenging him.

Exquisitely carved and banded with jewels, the ivory horn had been given to Jamie's grandfather by Robert the Bruce after the great Scottish victory at Bannockburn. A gift made in appreciation of the clan's support and loyalty.

A celebration of days spent in faithful service to the crown and days filled with prosperity in the clan's future.

Recognition, too, of each new clan chieftain, with the horn now passing with great ceremony from one laird to his successor.

A family tradition that should have honored Neill.

Now the horn would be Jamie's.

Staring at it now, its gleaming jewels still seeming to bore holes into him, Jamie put back his shoulders. He'd accept the horn's challenge and prove himself worthy.

Even, no *especially,* to his father.

Turning back to Morag, he addressed his first hurdle. "So it's as I thought?" he pressed, not forgetting she'd stated his father wished reconciliation even if he didn't know it. "My father did not send for me?"

Morag glanced down, fussed at her skirts.

The clansman crowding around them averted their gazes and even those clustered before the hearth looked elsewhere. Those sitting at the nearest trestle table busied themselves making a fuss over Cuillin. Others took great interest in their ale cups or the wisps of smoke curling along the blackened ceiling rafters.

No one met Jamie's eye. But, he would've sworn their cheeks flushed crimson.

He lifted a brow. "So it was Matheson's doing?"

To his surprise, his kinsmen's bearded faces turned an even brighter shade of red.

Only Morag had the steel to look at him.

"His doing and ours," she admitted, leaning heavily on

her crummock, the same hazel walking stick Jamie was sure she'd used in his youth. "Alan Mor had the idea after your brothers . . . *er* . . . when his eldest daughter no longer had a betrothed. And we"—she waved a hand at the clansmen suddenly hanging on her every word—"agreed for your da."

Jamie's eyes flew wide. "You agreed for him?"

Morag nodded, a touch of belligerence tightening her jaw.

"What else were we to do?" She tilted her head. "Your da isn't by his wits and willna leave his bed. So we held a clan council. God kens, he'd reached a fine alliance with the Mathesons and he needs the grazing grounds that would've been Sorcha's bride portion. Alan Mor offered a way to uphold the agreement—"

"By seeing me wed to Matheson's youngest daughter?" Jamie stared at her. "Da knows nothing of this?"

"He does now," Morag owned, still looking too uncomfortable for Jamie's liking. "He's agreed to honor the alliance."

"And I wouldn't be standing here were I not willing to meet my obligations," Jamie returned, his gaze sliding again to the Horn of Days, the great looping swath of his grandfather's plaid hanging so proudly above it. "He needn't worry I would unsay his sacred word."

Rather than answer him, Morag fidgeted. "A man of your da's ilk is ne'er so easily pleased."

Jamie looked at her with narrowed eyes, but she'd clamped her lips together and he knew the futility of trying to pry them apart.

So he glanced about the smoke-hazed hall, keenly

aware of his kinsmen's speculative stares and the telltale shifting of their feet. The revealing way the tense silence throbbed in the air.

Curling his fingers around his sword belt, he frowned against his suspicions. Morag was keeping something from him and there was only one way to find out what it was. Not that he should care, all things considered.

But another glance at the dais end of the hall, this time at the empty laird's chair, twisted his heart. Much as he didn't care to admit any such weakness.

Sentiment was a dangerous thing.

A pitfall he'd learned to avoid whenever his father crossed his mind.

Giving in to other emotions, he grabbed Morag one more time and planted a smacking kiss on her cheek. "Dinna you worry," he said, lifting his voice so all could hear him. "I am not here to set Da's plan to naught. And I'll do my best to mend the rift between us."

His declaration made, he snatched up a platter of hot, cheese-filled pasties—a savory favorite of his da's—and strode from the hall, swiftly mounting the spiraling stone steps to his father's bedchamber.

A room steeped in darkness and shadows for the shutters were securely fastened and none of the torches or cresset lamps had yet been lit. The only light came from a large log fire blazing on the hearth and a lone night candle.

Munro Macpherson lay asleep in his bed, the covers pulled to his chin, one arm flung over his head.

And the longer Jamie hovered on the threshold gaping at him, the harder he found it to breathe.

So he stalked into the room and plunked down his peace offering on a table beside the hearth. "Cheese pasties just as you like them," he said, his da's snores telling him he hadn't been heard.

"You're looking fine," he lied, wondering when his great stirk of an irritable, cross-grained father had grown so old and frail. "A bit of sustenance in your belly, a hot bath, and you'll be looking even better."

"I dinna want a bath and I told the lot of you I'm not hungry!" Munro's eyes popped open and he glared at Jamie. "I only want—holy saints!" he cried, diving beneath the covers. "Would you jump out of the dark at me again?"

"I'm no ghost." Jamie crossed the room and pulled the covers from his father's head. "I'm James of the Heather, come home to help you set things aright."

"You!" Munro pushed up on his elbows, color flooding back into his face. "I gave orders you weren't to come anywhere near me," he snapped. "And that trumpet-tongued she-goat of a seneschal and every man below-stairs knows it!"

Jamie sat down on the bed and folded his arms. "Mayhap if you'd eat more than the untouched gruel and watered-down wine on yon table, you'd have the strength to better enforce your wishes?"

"I don't have any wishes." Munro glowered at him. "Or can you bring back my sons? And I dinna mean as bogles!"

I am your son.

Jamie left the words unspoken, knowing now what had troubled Morag and his kinsmen.

His da may well have aligned him in marriage to Alan Mor's daughter, but he did so believing he'd be spared any contact with the son he'd e'er considered a bone in his throat.

Even so, a wave of pity for the man swept Jamie.

Pushing to his feet, he crossed the room in three quick strides, pausing before the nearest window. "Fresh air will chase the bogles from your mind," he said, sliding back the latch and throwing wide the shutters.

A blast of cold air rushed inside, but Jamie welcomed its bite. He braced his hands on the window's stone ledge and stared out at the rain-chilled night.

A quiet night cloaked in drifting mist so thick even the hills beyond Baldreagan's walls were little more than dark smudges in the swirling gray.

Somewhere out there Aveline Matheson slept.

Or perhaps she stood at her own window, wondering about him.

Just as chivalry deemed he ought to be thinking of her. If not with eagerness, at least kindly.

Instead, it was a single glimpse of a dazzling will-o'-the-wisp he couldn't get from his mind. A faery maid so delicate and fine he knew he'd barter his soul if only he could touch a single finger to her shimmering flaxen hair.

Jamie frowned, shaking the notion from his mind.

Other, more serious matters, weighed on his shoulders and in the hope of tending them, he turned from the window and plucked a cheese pastie off the platter on the table and returned to his father's side.

"Eat," he said, thrusting the savory into the old man's hand. "Bogles are more likely to come a-visiting those with empty, growling stomachs than a man well fed and sated."

Munro sniffed. "Dinna you make light of what I see nearly every e'en afore I sleep," he grumbled, scowling fiercely. "And my wits aren't addled as a certain clack-tongued scold surely told you."

"I am glad to hear it," Jamie returned, pleased when his da took a bite of the cheese savory. "Finish that pastie and I'll leave you to your peace. Eat two more and I'll send up a fresh ewer of ale to replace that watery wine."

"Had I known what a thrawn devil you've grown into, I'd have ne'er agreed to Alan Mor's plan," Munro carped, between bites. "Broken alliance or no. And to be sure not to satisfy a snaggle-toothed old woman and a pack o' lackwits who call themselves a council."

"Then why did you?"

Munro tightened his lips and glanced aside. He'd finished the cheese pastie so Jamie went back to the table and retrieved two more.

"Can it be you agreed for the pleasure of seeing me yoked to a Fairmaiden lass?" Jamie lifted a brow, betting he'd latched on to the truth. "'Tis no secret those sisters—"

"The Lady Aveline deserves far better than the likes o' you!" Munro blurted, snatching a savory from Jamie's hand. "And I was cozened into the match, led to believe a groom would be chosen from your cousins. The *council* only saw fit to tell me yestermorn that Alan Mor specified you!"

He all but choked on the savory.

His eyes bugging, he leaned forward. "I'll not besmirch my name by having Matheson and his ring-tailed minions claim I reneged on my word," he vowed, wagging a cheese-flecked finger. "And, to be sure, you're the lesser evil, much as it pains me to say it. I'm right fond of the wee lassie and I'd see her away from her da. He's a scourge on the heather and I dinna like how he treats her."

Jamie stared at him, his mind whirling.

All knew Munro Macpherson had little time for women, save bickering with Morag or shouting orders at serving wenches. Tongue-waggers even claimed he hadn't once lifted a skirt since losing Jamie's mother.

Yet his agitation indicated he genuinely liked Jamie's intended bride.

"Dinna gawp at me like a landed fish," he groused, reaching for the third savory. "Now keep your word and leave me be."

"As you wish," Jamie agreed, moving to the door. He looked back over his shoulder, not at all surprised to see his father still frowning at him.

But at least he was eating.

Jamie smiled. "I'll send up someone with the promised ale. See that you drink it."

But as he made his way back to the hall, the victory in getting sustenance into his da's belly warred with the revelation that his cantankerous, hard-bitten father had a soft spot for Aveline Matheson.

It remained only to be seen why.

Chapter Three

✦

Jamie's good humor lasted until almost noontide the next day. But every shred deserted him as soon as he arrived at Fairmaiden Castle and two of Alan Mor Matheson's burly stalwarts escorted him into the stronghold's great hall. Whether the louts appeared friendly or not, he stopped just inside the shadowed entry arch, planting his feet firmly in the rushes and folding his arms over his chest.

The back of his neck was prickling and that was never a good sign.

Indeed, it was all he could do not to put his hand on the hilt of his sword. Perhaps even draw his steel with a flourish. But he'd come to Fairmaiden as a friend and had thus far seen no true reason for wariness.

Even so, the fine hairs on his nape were stirring and it wasn't the two fool-grinning loons crowding him that caused his discomfiture.

Big as he was, he towered over them and every other

clansman milling about the aisles between the hall's well-filled trestle tables.

Truth was, he'd surely stand head and shoulders over the table-sitters, too.

Though were he to heed the urge to wheel about and leave, he knew he'd be pounced on. Not that he minded a good, manly stramash. Even if Alan Mor's underlings weren't known for fair fighting.

Minions his da called them and Jamie had to agree.

Ne'er had he seen so many different plaids under one roof. Or such a large assemblage of wild-eyed, lawless-looking caterans. Broken and landless men, some were even said to hail from Pabay, a tiny islet off the Isle of Skye and home to any Highland undesirable able to make it safely to that isle's ill-famed shores.

But with generations of Fairmaiden lairds proving unable to sire more than overlarge clutches of daughters, there were few in Kintail who'd rumple a nose at where each new Matheson laird harvested his men.

"Ho, lad! You look like a doomed man standing before the gallows and trying to ignore the dangling noose!" The crooked-nosed giant to Jamie's left clapped him on the shoulder, flashed a roguish smile.

Leaning closer, the brute lowered his voice, "You've no need to fear dipping your wick in aught unsavory," he said, wriggling his brows. "There isn't a man in this hall save Alan Mor himself who'd not give his very breath for one hour with the Lady Aveline beneath him."

Jamie frowned. A nigh irresistible urge to rearrange the oaf's already crooked nose seized him.

But he'd rather not start a melee in Fairmaiden's hall

before he'd even come face-to-face with its laird, so he ignored the temptation.

A word of warning, however, was certainly due.

"I'll own Laird Matheson wouldna take kindly to any fool who'd attempt to dishonor his daughter," he said, flipping back his plaid to display the stout, double-edged battle-ax thrust beneath his belt, the hilt of his equally impressive sword. "Nor, my friend, would I."

His threat set the men back; his way now clear to enter the smoke-hazed hall.

He strode forward through the throng, the back of his neck prickling more with every step he took.

And then he knew.

It was the *hall* that unnerved him; not Alan Mor's milling horde of cutthroats. Nor was it the reason for his visit—a neighborly call to confirm the alliance and to meet his intended bride.

Nay, it was Alan Mor's hall.

A hall like any other, if notably filled with boisterous, weapon-hung men. And with nary a skirt in sight. Not the sad-eyed Sorcha or any of her sisters so far as he could see. Truth be told, Fairmaiden's hall could be anywhere and anyone's. Its lime-washed walls were well-hung with the usual banners, weaponry, and a few moth-eaten stags' heads, and was filled with enough peat smoke to mist the eyes of noble and baseborn alike.

The expected number of dogs scrounged beneath the trestle tables and a well-doing fire of birch logs blazed in the massive double hearth. And speaking for his host, the floor rushes appeared newly spread, their freshness giving the black-raftered chamber a cleaner appearance than most.

Alan Mor clearly appreciated his comforts.

But something bothered Jamie all the same.

A queer sense of familiarity he couldn't put his finger on. Something faint and elusive that slid around him, teasing his senses and making his pulse race, his breath come rapid and uneven.

An indescribable something that unsettled him so much he didn't realize he'd returned to the hall's heavy, iron-studded door until his fingers closed over the latch.

And other, equally determined fingers clamped on to his elbow. "Young James Macpherson, I'll wager," boomed a voice deeper than sin. "If you're looking to refresh yourself after your journey, you'll find what you need just off the first landing of the stair tower to your left."

Releasing him, Alan Mor eyed him with mock reproach. "Or were you after leaving before even meeting my daughter?"

"Och, I wasna going anywhere," Jamie lied, stepping away from the door. "I just thought to retrieve my betrothal gift for Lady Aveline," he improvised, remembering the silver gilt mirror and comb his liege lord's friend, Sir Marmaduke, had once pressed on him.

Gewgaws, Kenneth had called the gifts, but Jamie liked them. And he praised the saints he'd been so gripped by his arrival at Baldreagan, that he'd forgotten to fetch them from his saddle pouch.

An oversight that salvaged the moment for Alan Mor slapped his thigh, beaming approval. "So you are the gallant I heard tell you were," the man said, and with fervor. "Not at all like your ill-winded, stiff-necked father."

"My da says much the same of you," Jamie returned, measuring the other. "He—"

"Your lout of a father is blessed to have a son with a more honest tongue than his own!" Alan Mor barked a laugh, then threw an arm around Jamie's shoulders. "Come, lad, and meet your bride. You can fetch whate'er bauble you've brought her later."

Setting off toward the raised dais at the far end of the hall, he shot a sidelong look at Jamie. "If there even is a bauble?"

"Och, aye, that there is," Jamie confirmed. "A mirror and comb of finest silver," he extolled, hoping the other man wouldn't guess he'd had no intention of making the items a betrothal gift.

Truth be told, he'd thought to present them to Baldreagan's cook—in the hope of securing extra portions. A necessity for a man of his size and appetite.

"The mirror is well crafted," he offered, maneuvering around a sleeping dog. "It's thought to be from an ancient Celtic horde or perhaps of Viking origin. The silver is—"

"*A silvered mirror!*" Alan Mor enthused, his voice ringing as they stepped onto the dais. "Heigh-ho! Did you hear that, lass? I told you Young James would do you proud. Such finery! Now what do you say?"

"I say him welcome," came a quiet voice from the far end of the high table.

A softly melodious voice, calm and steady, but edged with a definite trace of reserve.

Jamie's brow furrowed.

Alan Mor barged forward, seemingly oblivious.

"And you, lad?" He nudged Jamie toward the lass. "What do you think of my Aveline?" he boomed, waving an expansive hand. "Is she not fine?"

Jamie looked at her and drew a sharp breath, his world upending.

Aveline Matheson was more than fine.

She was his faery.

And recognizing her almost stopped his heart. As did her perfume of violets and sun-washed summer meadows. A sweet, fresh scent that went to his head so quickly he'd swear it was making him drunk.

It also let him know what had bothered him upon entering Fairmaiden's hall.

It'd been her scent.

He'd recognized it.

Jamie swallowed. Saints, he felt so light-headed the floor seemed to roll and dip beneath his feet, letting him feel almost as unsteady on his legs as the one time he'd had the misfortune to cross the Irish Sea.

Even worse, his birthday tunic, donned especially for his visit to Alan Mor, seemed to have grown even tighter. So uncomfortably tight, he was tempted to slip a relief-spending finger beneath his shirt's fancily embroidered neck opening.

And all the while the Lady Aveline sat watching him, an unreadable expression on her beautiful face.

Her unblinking eyes the very sapphire shade he'd imagined.

Not that it mattered whether she blinked or not.

He was surely blinking enough for the both of them.

And, the saints pity him, the whole of his great, hulking body tingled beneath her steady gaze.

Alan Mor grinned. "Well?"

"She is beyond lovely," Jamie managed, his heart thudding. "A vision."

He started to reach for her hand, but thought better of it and gave her a low bow instead.

He'd crushed more than one knightly bravo's fingers with the firm grip of his overlarge hand. His intended bride had the tiniest, most delicate-looking hands he'd ever seen.

Unthinkable should he forget himself and clasp hers too tightly.

Nor was it wise to touch her silky smooth skin, however innocently. Not with that blue gaze locked on him and her bewitching scent of summer violets wafting so sweetly beneath his nose.

"Lady, you bedazzle me," he said, powerless but to speak the truth.

Her lashes—gold-tipped as he'd suspected—fluttered in surprise. "And you, sir, should have allowed yourself time to catch your breath before coming here." She slid a glance at her father and her lips tightened ever so slightly. "My sorrow that we could not have met under more auspicious circumstances."

She stood then, placing her dainty fingers on Jamie's arm. "I am ever so sorry for your loss."

Jamie nodded, her sympathy warming him.

She stood proud before him, for all that she barely reached his shoulders and that the wildly flickering pulse at the hollow of her throat revealed the nervousness she strove so well to hide.

An edginess her father dismissed with a loud *hrumph*.

"'Fore God! An auspicious meeting!" He clapped a hand on her shoulder, pushing her back onto the trestle bench. "What more favorable way could the man begin his return home than coming here to meet you?"

To Jamie's astonishment, a flash of hot anger flared in her eyes and she lifted her chin, the stare she fixed on her da every bit as challenging as any foe he'd e'er faced down on a field of battle.

"Aside from some quiet time to mourn his brothers, some might say a more propitious beginning might have been to count the coin in those coffers you delivered to his sire," she declared, holding her father's gaze. "My marriage portion, you'll recall?"

Jamie arched a brow, her cheek secretly pleasing him.

Alan Mor laughed. "Ne'er you worry about Munro and his siller. That old he-devil e'er gets what's a-coming to him and he cares far more about the sweet grass in our grazing lands than what's in those strongboxes."

Jamie looked from his intended bride to her father and back again.

He cleared his throat. "If several large, iron-bound chests in my da's bedchamber are meant, I dinna believe he's opened them."

"Hah! Just what I meant!" Alan Mor hooted another laugh. "The man has other worries these days and that's why I'm of a mind to help him turn his thoughts elsewhere."

The words spoken, he thrust a hand beneath his plaid,

fumbling inside its folds until he produced a small leather pouch.

"Let no one say I'm no' letting this alliance cost me," he announced, slapping the pouch onto the table with a flourish. "I sent clear to Inverness for these, had them fashioned by the most skilled goldsmith known to do business in that den of robbers and money-pinchers."

The Lady Aveline turned scarlet.

Jamie eyed the small leather pouch, suspicion beating through him.

Alan Mor turned a pop-eyed stare on them both. "Well, it *would* be inauspicious to use the rings meant for Sorcha and Neill now, wouldn't it?" Grinning, he snatched up the pouch and opened it, letting two gold and sapphire rings tumble into his hand.

Jamie stared at him, his amazement only greater when Alan Mor plunked his treasure on the table and beckoned to a man hovering in the shadows of a nearby window embrasure.

A man Jamie hadn't noticed until now.

A dark, heavy-set man with hooded eyes and garbed in the robes of a monk.

He strode forward, his intent writ all o'er him.

"Baldric of Barevan," he announced, inclining his head to Jamie. "I am well acquainted with your sire. He's gifted our humble church with more than one fine stirk down the years."

"Has he now?" Jamie folded his arms.

"Och, aye." The monk flicked a glance at Jamie's bride, his slitty-eyed gaze holding a shade more appreciation than suited a man of God. He returned his attention to Jamie. "Your union with the Lady Aveline will surely raise your sire's spirits."

"Say you?"

"Ahhh, to be sure." Brother Baldric lifted his face heavenward, made the sign of the cross. "He knows God's hand is in the match. Why, just the other e'en he told me how much he's looking forward to grandsons."

Jamie arched a brow.

The man was a bald-faced liar.

And if Barevan church in distant Moray did lay claim to a Macpherson bull, they'd paid out their noses for the privilege. Like as not double what Jamie's da usually wheedled out of cattle buyers.

"Good sir," he began, "everyone in these hills knows my father has gone out of his way to avoid churchmen since my mother's unfortunate passing, claiming he'd prayed his last and lost his faith that ill-fated night."

Baldric of Barevan shifted from one foot to the other.

He said nothing.

Jamie went on, regardless. "See you, my father would sooner walk naked through a blizzard before he'd gift a wee church clear across the Highlands with one of his prized stirks. Truth be told, before he'd make *any* church such a gift."

This time the monk slid an uncomfortable glance at Alan Mor, but that one only shrugged. "I've no idea what Munro does with his cattle," Alan Mor claimed, settling back in his laird's chair. "I only know he agreed to this alliance."

"Aye, that he did," Jamie confirmed, if only for the sake of Lady Aveline.

Honor and tact forbid him to add that his father was anything but pleased about seeing the lass tied to him. 'Twas a match with one of Jamie's many cousins he'd agreed to.

Munro Macpherson had been cozened.

Just as the smooth-tongued, hand-rubbing monk and Alan Mor were now attempting to do to him.

So he wasn't about to argue about bulls, or his feelings about his sainted mother's death. Not with two such obvious blackguards.

And with other serious matters bearing down on him. Namely which sensation plagued him more—the one that felt like a noose slipping over his head or that his knightly spurs seemed to be getting weightier by the moment.

Putting back his shoulders, he eyed the monk and his smug-looking host. The ever-growing circle of grinning, sword-hung Matheson henchmen crowding around them. Most especially, the Lady Aveline. Saints, the maid was tiny enough to ride a milkweed for a steed. And she had the most lustrous hair he'd ever seen.

Jamie took a deep breath, deliberately turning his mind from her beauty. At the moment he needed his wits about him.

Refusal or chivalric duty.

Those were his choices.

And if his guess about the holy man's presence proved accurate, he'd need to decide soon.

Unfortunately, his annoyance at being duped must've shown because his bride-to-be's eyes rounded as her gaze flitted between him, her da, and the monk. And unless his own eyes were failing him, she even looked a little faint, all color draining from her face.

Worse, she'd begun to tremble.

But she surprised him by leaping to her feet and wheeling on her father. "You swore he knew the betrothal ceremony was this noon!" she accused him. "You've made a fool of me—letting me dress in my best gown and braid silver ribbons into my hair! You looked on when Sorcha left the hall, telling her you understood why she couldn't bear to be a witness, reminded of the day she pledged herself to Neill."

"Now, lass." Her father raised a hand. "You ken I ne'er do aught without good reason."

Ignoring him, Aveline jammed her hands on her hips and aimed an equally livid glare on Brother Baldric. Likewise the rough-looking clansmen who'd crowded onto the dais.

"All of you knew!" she railed, her blue eyes snapping. "Everyone knew save the most important soul beneath this roof. James of the Heather!"

She glanced at him then, both sympathy and agitation pouring off her.

"He wasn't told. Just look at him. 'Tis plain to see he knew naught of this." She pressed a hand to her breast, drew a great breath. "I will not be party to such a deception! I—"

"You are beset by the womanly fears that seize every bride on such a day," Jamie declared, her distress making his decision for him.

That, and the endlessly heavy weight of his spurs.

Feeling that weight pressing on him, he stepped closer

to her, using the width of his back and shoulders to shield her from curious stares. If there was one thing he couldn't tolerate it was seeing a woman mistreated or shamed. Blessedly, in this instance, he had the means to salve her embarrassment.

He straightened his back, steeling himself to lie for the second time since entering Fairmaiden's hall.

"For truth, I swear to you I knew about the betrothed ceremony," he vowed, certain a lightning bolt would strike him dead on his ride back to Baldreagan. "My da told me of it when I arrived yestereve."

She looked at him, disbelief clouding her eyes.

Jamie slid a finger beneath her chin, lifting her face toward his. "Think, lass. Why else would I have brought you a fine mirror and comb as betrothal gifts?"

On his words, she bit her lip and blinked, clearly struggling to keep tears from spilling down her cheeks.

And just looking at her, Jamie knew himself lost.

Knew he'd made the right choice.

Even if the lie someday found him sharing a pool o' brimstone with Alan Mor and his shifty-eyed monk.

He narrowed his eyes on them now, not at all surprised when they squirmed. For truth, they had good reason to do so. If either of them e'er exposed him for speaking falsely, he'd forget his size and strength and give them such a pounding they'd wish they'd ne'er been born.

Unfortunately, Lady Aveline still looked doubtful.

And more than a shade unhappy.

"Is this true?" She slipped from Jamie's grasp and turned back to her father. "He did know the ceremony was set for today? This is not one of your schemes to force him into a plight troth he doesn't want?"

Before Alan Mor could respond, James Macpherson stepped close and placed his hand on her shoulder. "I would not be here did I not wish to bind myself to you, my lady. Dinna you think to doubt it, for I have ne'er spoken truer words," he said, his voice soft and low, the warmth of his fingers spilling all through her.

"You don't even know me," Aveline couldn't help but protest, his touch unsettling her. "And I do not know you. We have ne'er even seen each other before this day. We—"

"We both know that isn't true," he said, his fingers tightening ever so slightly on her shoulder. "I *do* want you."

Aveline's breath caught, his words setting her heart to fluttering for he'd dipped his head to her ear and spoken them just for her.

Equally pleasing, he kept his hand on her shoulder in a reassuring way, his touch more welcome and pleasurable than she would have believed. Especially when his thumb began moving in ever so light circles up and down the side of her neck, each tender caress soothing and melting her.

"Hah!" Alan Mor slapped the monk's back with a resounding whack. "Will you look at that?" he cried, his mirth scarce contained. "I coulda searched miles through the rock and heather to find the best husband for my wee lassie and here's my arch-fiend's youngest, smitten as the day is long!"

He rocked back on his heels, his face splitting in a

grin. "Suffering saints! And to think the girl doubted me!"

"There is e'er reason to doubt you," Aveline grumbled beneath her breath, watching her da's mummery with suspicion.

But she couldn't deny that he appeared genuinely pleased.

And like as not, he was. Even if his reasons would be his own self-serving ones and not his professed concern for Munro Macpherson and that one's well-doing.

To be sure, he didn't care a jot if Laird Macpherson's strapping son found favor with her or nay.

Even less that she thought he was the most powerfully handsome man she'd e'er set eyes upon. His great size and similarity of feature revealed his kinship to his brothers, but she was quite sure he'd top even Neill by an inch or more were they to stand side by side.

His shoulders looked wider, too. Definitely more impressively muscled. And though Neill had been a pleasure for any lass to rest her eyes upon, he'd worn his pride and station like a crown and Aveline had ne'er felt wholly at ease beneath his stern, sometimes arrogant stares.

No matter that Sorcha e'er insisted there hadn't been a vainglorious bone in his undeniably comely body.

But *this* Macpherson had his clan's far-famed looks and a good heart. That, she could already tell. It'd been especially apparent in the way his voice had softened when he'd spoken of his mother. And she'd seen it, too, in his readiness to comfort her.

She suspected he had a dimple, too. Something she'd

watch for as soon as he ceased frowning at her father and Brother Baldric.

And, saints preserve her, but she was certain she'd also caught glimpses of glistening, coppery-colored chest hair at the neck opening of his tunic.

Aveline moistened her lips, the notion exciting her. Would such hairs prove as soft and glossy as they'd looked? Or would she find them wiry and crisp?

That she even wanted to know astounded her.

As did the tingling warmth that spooled through her the longer she thought about such things. Aye, she decided, watching him, he was the finest, most magnificent man she'd ever seen.

And the most valiant from what she could tell.

Proving it, he stepped forward and took the two rings from the table, lifting them in the air. "Let it be known that this betrothal ceremony is both binding and desired," he said, raising his voice so all could hear.

Saying the words before his good sense kicked in and sent him hastening from the hall to seek a bride not burdened by a sire he knew to be more slippery than an eel.

Instead, he cleared his throat and concentrated only on her beautiful sapphire eyes, the scent of summer violets.

"I, James of the Heather, take you, Aveline of Fairmaiden, as my betrothed bride," he said, a burst of boisterous approval rising in the hall as he slid the smaller of the two gold-and-sapphire rings onto her finger.

Not surprising, so soon as the ruckus died down, Brother Baldric began rattling off his assets. And one quick glance at Alan Mor's beaming countenance told him where the monk had gleaned such knowledge.

But before he could comment, the second ring was gleaming on his own finger, his *Sithe* maid's soft voice accepting his plight troth and offering her own.

And then the deed was done.

The faery was his bride.

About the same time but across a few mist-draped hills and the wild torrent of water known as the Garbh Uisge, Munro Macpherson tossed in his curtained bed, trying to decide between the perils of falling asleep and risking another fearing dream or staying awake and listening for the heavy breathing that always heralded the arrival of his sons' ghosts.

"Ach—for guidsakes!" Scowling fiercely, he punched down his pillows for what had to be the hundredth time since chasing Morag and her fool meal tray from the room. "Beset by bogles and bowls of gruel in my own bedchamber!"

Flipping onto his stomach, he squeezed shut his eyes and resisted the temptation to jam his fingers into his ears. Whether or not anyone could see him, sequestered as he was behind his tightly drawn bed curtains, scarce mattered.

He was still a man of power and consequence and should maintain at least a semblance of lairdly dignity.

And to that effect, fearing dreams seemed less treacherous than staring into the gloom of his enclosed bed, his ears peeled for any sound he shouldn't be hearing.

Not comfortably ensconced in his own well-shuttered and barricaded privy chamber.

Pursing his lips, he reached to part the bed curtains just

a wee bit. Only to make certain that fox Alan Mor's strongboxes of stones were still piled against the bolted door. Blessedly, they were. And they provided sound proof against further intrusions from his long-nosed she-bat of a seneschal and any lackeys she might send abovestairs to pester and annoy him.

He almost snorted. That was something they all seemed ever good at, bedeviling him.

Alan Mor, by thinking him so simpleminded he'd be fooled by a thin layer o' coin spread oe'r a coffer filled with rocks.

Morag and his kinsmen, by repeatedly sneaking into his bedchamber when he slept to throw open the shutters, nigh blinding him. Or expecting him to eat pig's swill they called gruel and believe such a sorry excuse for vict-uals would replenish his strength.

His strength, a goat's arse!

He hooted his scorn, sending a last glance at the iron-bound coffers. Saints, he would've smiled were he not so concerned about bogles.

But he was, so he let the bed curtains fall shut again and frowned into his pillow.

Truth was, a whole teetering tower of strongboxes wouldn't keep out a ghost. But the three heavy chests he'd managed to pile on top of each other at the door did prove he hadn't lost his muscle.

That he knew the coffers' contents without peeking in-side showed his wits were still with him as well.

If Alan—*fox-brained*—Mor possessed even half his own cunning, the lout would know the Fairmaiden graz-ing ground was more than enough to satisfy him.

That, and the flap-tongued fool's precious wee lassie.

And thinking about her brought a smile to his tired, angst-fraught heart, so he snuggled more deeply into his bedcovers, certain that, for once, his sleep would prove untroubled.

Regrettably, instead of dreaming about sitting before the fire, his feet up and a bouncing, red-cheeked grandson on his lap, it was the sound of water that invaded his sleep.

Swift, swirling water plunging wildly over tumbled rocks. A churning cauldron of froth and spume, its thunderous roar echoed inside the confines of Munro's curtained bed.

A refuge no longer framed by the dark oak of his great bed's canopy but the wind-tossed branches of the skeletal birches rimming the Rough Waters.

The dread Garbh Uisge.

The cataract-filled gorge where his sons had lost their lives.

Sons he could see now, their broken bodies shooting over the rapids, their death cries carried on the wind. Some of them already bobbed lifelessly in deeper, more quiet pools near the gorge's end.

But others still suffered, their battered bodies crashing against the rocks, their flailing arms splashing him with icy, deadly water.

Munro groaned in his sleep, his fingers digging into the bedcovers as his heart began to race. Sweat beaded his forehead, damping his pillow.

The tangled sheets and plaiding of his bed.

Mist and spray surrounded him, its chill wetness making him shiver and quake. And then the rushing water surged across him, carrying him ever closer to his sons' reaching arms. The facedown, floating bodies of the ones already claimed by their watery fates.

"No-o-o!" Munro cried, his eyes snapping open.

He pulled in a great gulp of air, noticing at once the pool of water he'd been wallowing in.

How wet he was.

And that someone had ripped open the bed curtains.

"Of a mercy!" He sat up, dashing his streaming wet hair from his eyes.

He swiped a hand across his water-speckled beard, peering into the gloom and shadows. Sodden or nay, he wasn't about to throw off the covers. Only a spirit could've brought the Garbh Uisge into his room and experience warned him he'd soon see that ghost.

And he did, recognizing Neill despite the dripping wet cloak he wore, the dark cowl pulled low over his white, hollow-eyed face.

An accusing face, filled with recrimination.

"You did this," his eldest son decried, pointing at him. "You and your insatiable greed."

Munro scrabbled backward on the bed. "Begone, I beg you!" he wailed, his teeth chattering. "I had naught to do with—"

"Aye, you did naught. But you could have repaired the bridge." Neill backed into the shadows, his tall form already beginning to waver and fade. "Now it is too late."

And then the shadows closed around him just as the rushing waters of Munro's fearing dream had swirled around and over him, pulling him ever deeper into the horrors he couldn't flee even in sleep.

Trembling uncontrollably, he somehow crawled from his bed and tapped his way across the chamber, making for his chair. Hard-backed and sturdy as befitted a Highland laird's dignity, the chair was anything but comfortable.

But with a dry plaid draped around him and another spread over his knees, it would suffice as a resting place until his bedding dried.

Loud as he'd roared at Morag the last time she'd poked her grizzled head around his door, she wouldn't be coming abovestairs to see to his comforts for a while. A good long while, like as not. And his pride kept him from calling out for her.

So he dropped down onto his chair, tucked himself into his plaids as best he could, and frowned, in especial at the pile of Alan Mor's strongboxes blocking his door. Weak-kneed as he was at the moment, he doubted he could move them even if he did wish to go seeking a sympathetic ear.

Truth be told, there was only one soul he knew whose strength could push open his barricaded door. Munro's brows snapped together. Och, aye, unnerved as he was just now, he might even be glad to see his youngest son.

Infuriated by the notion, he sat back and turned his face toward the fire.

Then he did his lairdly best to pretend such a fool thought had ne'er entered his mind.

Chapter Four

✤

Jamie stood before the arched windows of Alan Mor's hall, for all intents and purposes legally bound to the Fairmaiden laird's faery-like daughter and about to perform his first act as her personal champion.

Once the jostling buffoons crowding around her drew her away from the high table, he'd have words with Alan Mor. Words that needn't reach her gentle ears.

Some things were best kept between men.

A muscle twitched in Jamie's jaw and he flexed his fingers, waiting.

Her composure regained, his new lady accepted her father's men's well wishes with perfect poise. She joined in their laughter and met their cheers and jesting with a dazzling smile, her sapphire eyes alight and glittering in the glow of the torches.

And the longer Jamie watched her, the more she pleased him.

Her voice carried to him, its low-pitch beguiling, its

smoothness flowing over him like honeyed wine. Saints, but he wanted to touch her. Indeed, just looking at her was almost like a physical touching and he burned to cross swiftly to her and pull her into his arms, holding her close and letting her spill soft, sweet words all over him until he fair drowned in them.

But someone had appeared with a generously heaped platter of fried apple fritters and spiced pears, the tempting delicacies drawing enough attention for Jamie to seize his chance.

The time was nigh.

Leaving the shadows of the window embrasure, he strode purposely toward the high table, his plaid thrown back to reveal the many-notched haft of his Norseman's ax and the leather-wrapped hilt of his steel.

Upon seeing him, Alan Mor grinned and reached for the ale jug, making to pour Jamie a cup of the frothy brew. But Jamie took the cup before his good-father could fill it, setting it deliberately out of reach.

Alan Mor's smile faded.

"Ho! What's this?" he queried, one brow arcing. "Refusing my ale? I'd think you'd be after quenching your thirst on such a notable day?"

"Notable, aye," Jamie allowed. "'Tis also a day for plain speaking."

Alan Mor eyed him. "My ears are open," he said, sliding a glance to where Aveline stood in the midst of a crush of apple-fritter-eating clansmen. "Dinna tell me you are displeased with my daughter?"

Jamie took the ale jug and poured himself a portion,

not taking his gaze off the other man as he downed the ale.

"Displeased with her?" he echoed at last, returning the cup to the table. "With surety, nay. But I am mightily vexed to have been duped. See that it ne'er happens again."

To Jamie's surprise, his words only earned him another smile.

"I would hope to stand higher in your favor, having arranged for you to have such a prize." Alan Mor cast another quick glance in his daughter's direction. "She—"

"Is too great a treasure to be publicly shamed," Jamie cut him off, his voice pitched for Alan Mor alone. "Embarrass her e'er again and be warned that you shall answer to me and there'd be no escaping." Jamie let his fingers curl demonstrably around his sword hilt. "I would be after you in a thrice, on your heels as relentlessly as yon greyhounds curled before your hearth fire."

Again to Jamie's surprise, the older man's smile deepened and he slapped the table, this time even barking a laugh. "Saints, had I known you'd take such umbrage, lad, I'd have been more subtle," he vowed, pushing to his feet. "But I am an auld, gruff man, unused to courtly airs and fine ways."

Unmoved, Jamie plucked a fine-looking morsel of roasted meat off the table and tossed the tidbit to a nearby dog. "Forget what I said about your greyhounds," he said, wiping his hands. "Cause yon lassie a single moment of grief from this day forward and I shall be your shadow."

"'Grief'?" The older man grabbed Jamie's arm, turning him toward the cluster of revelers mid-hall. "Say me she doesn't look happier than any maid you've e'er seen."

And she did.

Jamie couldn't deny it.

"All the same," he said, shaking off the other's grasp, "I would that she remains that way. And I'd have a private word with her now. Somewhere away from your hall and where she may speak freely."

Alan Mor dropped back down into his laird's chair, then waved a casual hand. "Auld and gruff I may be, but no' thoughtless. My privy solar has already been readied for you, and with all the comforts of my house."

Jamie nodded, then turned on his heel. He needed but a few long strides to reach Aveline's side. When he did, he brought her hand to his lips and kissed it.

A privilege entirely his, but dangerous.

Just breathing in her violet scent stirred him. Feeling the softness of her skin beneath his lips proved a greater temptation than he'd expected.

Or needed.

Especially now, when he wished to speak earnest words with her.

"Come," she said, twining her fingers with his and leading him from the hall, "I saw you exchange words with my father and understand you'll wish to speak with me." She looked up at him then, her sapphire eyes long-lashed and luminous. "I would speak privily with you, too. My father's solar has been prepared and awaits us."

And it did indeed, Jamie observed when, a short while later, she led him into the quiet chamber, closing the door soundly behind them.

Little more than a small, low-vaulted chamber just above Fairmaiden's great hall, the room held all the comforts Alan Mor could boast. As belowstairs, the floor rushes appeared freshly strewn and sweet smelling and the walls were recently limed, their whiteness holding nary a trace of soot from the pleasant little peat fire glowing on the hearth grate.

A settle near the door invited with finely embroidered cushions and a fur-lined coverlet, while a small table held a light repast of green cheese, cold beef slices, and honeyed almonds.

And Jamie knew without sampling, that the beckoning ewer of wine would prove as heady as any he'd e'er sampled.

Above all, it was the room's smallness that undid him. Close as it was, the tidy little chamber captured and held his bride's bewitching scent. Even the chill, damp air pouring in through the narrow window arches couldn't dispel her pleasing essence.

Her perfume swirled around him, its hint of summer sun and violets teasing his senses. Truth tell, everything about her was proving almost more an enchantment than he could bear.

Especially when she rested a hand on his arm and peered up at him with such concern that his heart skittered.

"I know what's troubling you," she said, lifting her chin. "But you've no cause to harbor such doubts."

Jamie looked at her. "Doubts?"

She nodded, sure of it. "I told you—I saw you speaking with my father. Your displeasure was plain to see."

"My displeasure had naught to—"

"Hear me out, please," she cut in, touching her fingers to his lips. "If it is my size giving you pause, be assured that just because I may look delicate doesn't mean I cannot run a household."

She peered up him, well aware at least two past suitors had rejected her because she didn't appear robust enough. And equally aware she didn't want such concerns clouding her union with James Macpherson.

But he surprised her by looking at her as if he could hardly believe his ears.

Relief sluiced through her, hot and swift.

Especially when he waved aside her worries. "Sweet lady, nothing is farther from the truth," he declared, and her heart gave a lurch. "I've seen the comforts of your home and know you and your lady sister are responsible. Anyone who'd question your abilities is a fool."

Pleased as well as a bit nervous beneath the intensity of his gaze, Aveline crossed the little chamber and flicked the edge of a wall hanging. Truly exquisite, the colors were jewel-bright, the hunting scene depicted of a quality Jamie hadn't seen since leaving Eilean Creag, the isle-girt castle belonging to his first liege laird, Duncan MacKenzie.

"I stitched every thread of this tapestry," his bride revealed, the touching blend of her pride and vulnerability piercing his heart. "And the pillows piled high on the settle by the door."

"Lass, you needn't prove yourself—"

"I can read and Sorcha and I share the task of keeping Father's household accounts," she plunged on as if he hadn't spoken. "Sorcha and I have even run Fairmaiden on our own, in dire times, when my father and his men have been off warring or visiting allies. And"—she fixed him with a level stare—"I am knowledgeable in the healing arts and do not grow faint at the sight of blood and broken limbs. I—"

"You are everything a man could hope for, and more than this one e'er dreamed of making his own," Jamie vowed, three quick strides taking him to her. "You misread my displeasure in the hall. Your father and I had manly matters to discuss. They had naught to do with your lady skills."

She blinked. "Then you weren't speaking of me?"

Jamie pulled a hand down over his chin. "Och, we had other issues to resolve," he said, hoping she'd leave it at that. "But you were on my mind, aye."

"If not my abilities, then what were you thinking of?"

"This," Jamie said, leaning down to kiss her.

A gentle kiss, so soft and light as he could make it. Until she melted into him and sighed with what could only be called pleasure. Clinging to him, she parted her lips—lips every bit as luscious and honeyed as he'd known they'd be.

Unable to help himself, he angled his head, deepening the kiss he'd been burning to give her ever since glimpsing her in the wood. He let his tongue tease hers, his heart hammering when she slid her arms around him, holding fast to his shoulders and tangling her fingers in his hair.

Hair just as thick, rich, and silky as she'd imagined. Falling free to his shoulders, the cool, smooth strands spilled through her fingers as seductively as the slow, sensual glides of his tongue against hers. Fine, liquid heat began streaming through her, making her feel dizzy and yet wondrously alive.

Shivery and breathless.

Her heart began to pound and she pressed closer, welcoming his kiss, her own greedy woman's need reveling in how she could feel every thundering beat of his heart echoing through her entire body.

Her nipples tightened against his chest and her knees quivered, the hot strokings of his tongue unleashing a maddeningly delicious swirl of fluttery sensation deep inside her.

A wicked, incredibly pleasurable pulsing she was quite certain she shouldn't be enjoying.

Not here, in her father's privy solar and the door not even bolted.

But he was her plight-trothed husband and his sapphire ring did wink on the fourth finger of her left hand. So she took courage from that ring and gave in to the wonderment, letting her tongue tease and tangle with his, again and again until such white-hot fire raced through her she was certain she'd find herself singed when the kiss ended.

There could be no harm in allowing him to kiss her.

Or in kissing him back.

After all, wasn't this what she'd yearned for when she'd slipped away to St. Bride's Well the other night? Hadn't she stripped naked in the wood? Bathed in sacred water and moonbeams just to ensure a pleasing, passionate match?

And hadn't St. Bride rewarded her with a glimpse of him?

Though, at the time, she'd thought the handsome, strapping knight she'd seen sitting on his horse and staring at her had been a figment of Highland magic.

A moonlit whim of St. Bride to console her lonely, aching heart.

Indeed, garbed in naught but the night mist, his wind-tossed plaid, and gleaming mail, he'd looked too resplendent for her to mistake him for aught else.

Yet now he was here and kissing her. Aveline sighed into his mouth, opening her own wider, silently willing him not to stop, to keep up his bone-melting assault of her senses until she could no longer bear the exquisite friction of her naked breasts rubbing against the rough warmth of his plaid.

Her naked breasts?

Her eyes popped open, the languorous heat that had been pulsing through her gone in a flash. "Oh, no," she gasped, looking down to see her left breast peeking over the top edge of her bodice.

Not the whole of her left breast, but her nipple was fully exposed.

Dusky pink, tightly ruched, and pressed flush against James Macpherson's chest.

"Ach, dia!" She reached to adjust her gown, but he moved with lightning speed, gently capturing her wrist and lowering her hand to her side.

"Dinna fash yourself," he said, touching just the tip of his finger to her thrusting nipple. "I have ne'er seen a more fetching sight and willna have this day end with you distressed. I want you e'er certain in the knowledge of how beautiful I find you."

Holding her gaze, he brought his hand to his mouth and licked his fingers. He returned them to her breast, toying so lightly with her still-puckered nipple that the sensations stirred by his touch almost made her swoon.

Her knees were certainly weakening.

But she was so small. Her breasts nothing at all like the swelling globes her sisters flaunted so proudly. Or the even larger, great-nippled teats she'd seen on a few of the kitchen wenches.

She knew how often the garrison knights begged those kitchen bawds to pull down their bodices. And she knew, too, the kind of slack-jawed, glazed-eyed letch that always overcame the men in the hall when, with a bold wink and a smile, the kitchen maids complied.

Men favored large breasts.

Big, well-fleshed women. Curvaceous and buxom.

Hot-eyed, robust creatures whose hips swayed when they walked, their bosoms all a-jiggle, and who were wont to throw back their heads and laugh heartily. Brazens who drew manly eyes, inspired lust, and were everything she was not.

Imagining those women now, Aveline swallowed, her pulse racing. But Jamie only smiled at her, so much appreciation shining in his twinkling blue eyes that for a moment she would've sworn he stood not in the fire-lit solar, but in the midst of a grassy summer meadow with bright sunlight glancing off his coppery-red hair.

A stiff breeze coming in the windows riffled that hair, lifting the red-gold strands about his brow and Aveline moistened her lips as she looked at him, certain she'd never seen a man who appealed to her more.

With surety she couldn't imagine anyone rivaling his great height. And the width of his shoulders stole her breath. But it was his warmth and natural exuberance that undid her. The irresistible sparkle of humor that lit his whole face when he smiled.

Even so, she flushed, knew intense relief when he eased up her bodice, smoothing the cloth over her breast until her decency was fully restored.

"You do not believe me," he said, his smile fading. "You doubt me when I say how beautiful you are."

"I am—"

"You are lovely," Jamie declared, seeking to soothe her.

He may not have been blessed with sisters, but he'd spent enough years squiring beneath Duncan MacKenzie's roof to observe that puissant laird's two daughters at their best and at their worst.

If his wee sweet bride hadn't been about to bemoan the smallness of her breasts, he'd eat a brick of peat.

Jamie leaned down, dropping a light kiss to the top of her head. "You have enchanted me and I've meant every word I've said to you. I do want you."

But she continued to look unconvinced. "You have ties to the MacKenzies," she argued, her chin lifting. "They have broad connections and influence. You could have had a maid of higher blood. The Black Stag of Kintail would have done you proud."

"Done me proud?" Jamie could only gape at her.

Her hair alone would be the pride of any husband. Adorned with silver ribbons and reaching to her hips, her thick braid could well be plaited of moonbeams, so fair and bright were the strands.

The privilege of being the man allowed to undo such fine tresses, then run his fingers through the rippling, silken mass, swelled his heart with a feeling so close to wonder, he'd almost believe she really did possess a touch of the *Sithe*.

"Sweet lass, you do me proud," he vowed, lifting her braid to his lips. "If you do not believe me, then I must ask if you have ne'er peered into a looking glass?"

Her blush deepened, but she held his gaze. "Considering how I was foisted on you, I am pleased if you are content."

Frowning, Jamie scooped her up into his arms and carried her across the room, lowering her onto the settle by the door.

"Precious lass," he began, pulling up a stool for himself, "I am more than content—I am ensorcelled, and I have been since I first set eyes on you. And I dinna mean belowstairs in your father's hall."

She considered. "You mean when you saw me in the wood."

Jamie nodded. "I thought you were a faery. And I lost my heart to you there and then, thought you were the most beautiful creature I'd e'er seen."

"But you were frowning." She leaned back and looked at him. "I could see your face in the moonlight."

Jamie grinned. "Lady, I can see I shall not be able to hide much from you!" Leaning forward, he brushed a light kiss across her lips. "I've said you enchanted me, and that is the truth of it. But I did hold you for a *Sithe* maid. And, as such," he added, lowering his voice to make her smile, "I feared the wrath of a handsome faery prince. An outraged soul ready to leap out of the heather, fiery sword to hand and swinging."

She pulled a cushion onto her lap, her fingers curling into its tasseled edge. "Why did you think a faery prince would be wroth with you?"

"Because everyone knows the fey can see into the hearts of men and he would have known how smitten I was with you."

"And now that you know I am not of the fair folk?" she pressed. "Now that you have seen—"

"Your loveliness?" Jamie's brow shot upward. "What I saw just now only proved that you are even more beautiful than I'd thought. For certes, finer than any faery!"

Her eyes widened at that, but she looked pleased.

And seeing her face brighten pleased him. Truth be told, everything about her was pleasing.

In his mind, he could still see her nipple, was even tempted to tell her so, likening its sweetness to a pink rosebud. But he didn't want to frighten her so he simply twisted around on the stool, taking the wine jug and filling two chalices with the bloodred wine.

She angled her head, appraising him through her lashes. "I am thinking you could make a crone believe she was a sight to fill manly eyes, but I am aware of my limitations," she challenged, now meeting his gaze directly. "There are some who might say you would be better served by a stout maid of the north. A wide-hipped lass able to bear you fine, strapping sons!"

Jamie almost choked.

And promptly downed the wine he'd just poured for her.

"I ken many a warring mates whose wives are just as wee as you and who've birthed scores of braw and healthy bairns," he lied, now certain beyond all doubt that he'd spouted enough falsehoods to spend eternity just there where he didn't wish to land.

"I am glad." She reached to touch his face, letting her fingers glide down his cheek and along his jaw, across the curve of his lips. "Other suitors have objected to a match because of my size and I'd feared you'd wished time alone with me to discuss similar concerns."

Jamie bristled. His fist itched to smash the nose of any lout who'd so insulted or hurt her.

"That was ne'er my intent," he began, seeking the best words. "I wanted us to speak privately because I wished to tell you I'd seen you in the wood. I wanted to reassure you that I desired this match because of you and not because of any alliance arranged between our fathers."

She lifted a brow. "But you would have agreed to the union all the same."

Jamie nodded, unable to lie.

"Such is the way of things," he reminded her, pleased when she took a sip of the wine. "I would have done my duty. Now, I am eager for the match."

"I am pleased, too." She looked at him, her words stroking dark places in his heart, soothing hurts he'd forgotten plagued him. "If you thought I was a faery, I would have sworn you were one of the great Fingal's mythical Celtic warriors. Ne'er would I have believed such a fine, braw man would ride up out o' the mist!" She finished her wine, but kept her fingers tightened around the stem of the chalice. "See you, I thought St. Bride of the Waters had summoned you. That she'd sent an ancient Gaelic hero to—"

"St. Bride of the Waters?" Jamie stood, began pacing.

He knew better than most who St. Bride was. And it cost him all his strength to keep from crossing himself. Not to see ill omens in Aveline's mention of the Celtic saint's name.

His mother's brow had been rinsed with water from St. Bride's well on the night of his birth.

And one of his earliest memories was of his da's rantings about the saint. His threats to single-handedly dismantle the well and sink so many stones into its spring that nary a trickle e'er again saw the light of day.

Tobar na Slainte was the well's true name.

The Well of Health.

A chill shot through Jamie and he stopped in front of the settle to look down at his bride, remembering now how close the well was to Hughie Mac's cottage.

"What made you think St. Bride sent me? Had you been to fetch water from the well that night?"

"I'd been to bathe in the well," Aveline admitted, not liking the way his face had lost color. "I—

"You bathed in it?"

She nodded. "I bathed and washed my hair. Why else would I have been hurrying through the wood of a night? Half-dressed and my hair unbound?"

"Why else indeed?" He stared at her, his face even more pale than before. "But that still does not tell me why you mistook me for a Fingalian hero."

"A Fingalian warrior or . . . Highland magic," Aveline said in a rush, watching him.

She stood, squaring her shoulders. "See you, I'd asked St. Bride to bless our union. I knew you were coming and feared you'd be displeased. So I took her an offering of oatcakes and honey and asked for harmony in return."

"Naught else?"

"You must appreciate the suitors I've been presented with," she tried again, not quite able to suppress a shudder. "Whether they withdrew their offers or nay, I would ne'er have consented to wedding them!"

Jamie hid a smile. "That bad?"

"Worse."

"Yet you agreed to the match with me?"

She looked down, flicking her skirts as she dropped back onto the settle. "I am no longer so young as I was," she said, looking up again, a spark of defiance in her eyes. "And I'd grown weary of waiting for a hearth and family of my own."

Jamie sat back onto the stool. "I have ne'er seen the wish for hearth and home put such fire in a maid's eyes," he observed, taking her hands between his own. "What are you keeping from me?"

He wasn't surprised when she pressed her lips together.

Truth be told, he would've sworn she put back her shoulders as well. But wee and delicate as she was, it was difficult to tell.

So he did what he could, lacing his fingers with hers and leaning forward, one brow raised until the resistance went out of her and she blew out a hasty breath.

"That's better," Jamie approved, sitting back and smiling at her. "No shame and no secrets."

"As you wish," she agreed, her cheeks glowing.

Jamie released her hands and topped their wine, clinking his chalice against hers. "So, lass, what other favors did you ask of St. Bride?"

"Only one," she supplied, taking a sip of wine. "Something I suspect all maids yearn for if they are bold enough to admit it."

Jamie smiled at her. "And are you a bold lass?"

She nodded.

"Then what did you ask?"

"For a pleasing and passionate match," she said, the blaze in her eyes melting him. "A new life with a man who loves me and will let my heart meld with his."

A man who will teach me the meaning of mindless rapture and fill my days with joy.

Jamie looked at her, not sure he'd heard her say that last—or if he'd only imagined the words. Either way, he'd heard enough.

His bride was a hot-blooded faery.

And of Fairmaiden stock.

Whoe'er in all the hills would've believed it? His heart took up a slow, hard thumping, a thousand provocative images whirling across his mind. But before an appreciative smile could spread across his face, the door swung open and he swiveled round, glancing toward the threshold.

"Sir James, my father would know if you'll be staying for the evening meal?" Sorcha inquired. "He says he'll open a cask of celebratory wine if you are."

Jamie rose, going forward to greet the lass properly.

Not that he knew what to say to her. Hovering on the threshold, she clutched a rush light in her hand, its upcast light turning her long, sallow face into an even more sorrowful image.

"Lady Sorcha." He made her a quick bow. "You were missed earlier," he said, regretting the words immediately, remembering her reason for avoiding the hall.

But she only nodded, her gaze going past him to Aveline. "Father has ordered Cook to prepare your favorite savories. I vow he is ready to plunder the castle larder just to set a grand table."

"He'll be feeling guilty then," Aveline observed, rising. "He's played with the fates of too many people in recent times and will be wanting to make amends." Coming forward, she touched a hand to her sister's sleeve. "I am sorry, Sorcha, he should not be arranging such a feast. Not with you—"

"I do not mind," Sorcha said with quiet dignity. "The revel will keep my mind from straying where it ought not." Turning back to Jamie, she waited. "Will you stay?"

"My sorrow, but there will not be time for suchlike this e'en," he spoke true. "I would be back at Baldreagan before dusk and I'm hoping to pay my respects to my brothers along the way."

Sorcha inclined her head. "To be sure, my lord. I will inform my father and he will welcome you to our table another time."

"I shall look forward to it."

Sorcha nodded again and retreated, closing the door softly behind her. Jamie almost followed after her, her plight compelling him to comfort her, if only with a few awkward words and a gentle pat or two upon her shoulder.

But by the time he stirred himself to open the door and step onto the landing, the narrow turnpike stair loomed empty. His bride's unhappy sister was already gone.

Turning back to the solar, he was heartened to see that the sky seemed to have lightened. He'd be well served to be on his way before the clouds lowered and the cold rains returned.

His bride had other ideas.

"May I go with you?" she blurted, suddenly standing in front of him.

Jamie blinked. "To Baldreagan?"

She nodded. "I have some wax candles for your father," she said, indicating a cloth-covered basket he hadn't noticed. "He keeps them burning of a night and needs more than Morag can supply him."

Jamie tightened his lips and retrieved the basket, not too keen on catering to his da's fool whims. Like as not, if he'd burn fewer candles, he'd sleep better and imagine less ghostly visitations.

But what was one basket of candles when it meant more time spent in his faery's company?

And even if she weren't a true *Sithe* maid, she certainly had the grace of one. She bedazzled him, standing there limned by the hearth glow and with her violet scent rising up between them, teasing his senses.

For one unsettling moment, she appeared clothed in sparkling, misty glitter and Jamie nigh dropped the basket, but then the image cleared and he realized she'd only flashed him a smile.

"I thank you," she said, touching his chest, and despite the cloud-cast afternoon, he would've sworn the sun itself burst into the tiny chamber. "I know your father can be vexing, but the candles soothe him."

"I suspect it is you who comforts him." Jamie stepped away from her, making long-strided for the door.

His father was a sore subject and other, grievous duties lay ahead of him.

But as his bride slipped past him out the door, his father's scowling face rose up before him and he shot out a hand, circling his fingers around her arm.

"My father is overfond of you," he said, looking down at her. "I doubt it's because you take him candles. Yet"— he paused to angle his head—"so far as I know, he hasn't had a pleasant word for any female in years."

Aveline shrugged. "Perhaps he likes me because of the alliance between our clans?" she suggested, lying out her nose.

Jamie could tell because of the way she avoided his eyes, looking down to flick invisible lint from her gown.

Folding his arms, he drew himself up to his fullest height, fairly or unfairly employing his great bulk as his only self-defense against wee, fetching faery lasses, his over-sized body making escape impossible.

"Could it be you treat him too softly?" Jamie lifted a brow, watching her carefully. "Perhaps listening too long to his blabbering and, through your well-meant sympathy, encouraging his foolery?"

She sniffed. "Some might say you treat him too harshly. He is old and should not be made to pay for past sins or regrets. For myself, I would never do aught that would encourage him to frighten himself."

"Hah!" Jamie grinned. "And there we have it."

"Have what?" Her chin took on a defensive tilt.

"You listen to his prattle about my brothers' ghosts. That is why he is so fond of you."

"Nay, that is not the reason," she said, shaking her head. "Leastways I do not think so."

"Then what do you think?"

"That he likes me because I am the only one who believes him."

Jamie stared at her, his brows shooting upward.

And then he laughed.

"Ah, well, letting him think you believe him may well be it," he agreed, pleased to have solved the riddle.

"You do not understand," she said, the look on her face sending shivers down his spine. "I do not let him think I believe, I honestly do."

Jamie blinked at her. "You believe he sees my brothers' ghosts?"

She nodded. "I know that he does."

"And how do you know?" he asked, feeling the walls beginning to close in on him.

"Because I have seen them, too."

Chapter Five

✦

It wasn't just his father.

His bride had seen the ghosts, too. And her words kept gnawing at Jamie. Especially when they reached his family's chapel and churchyard and he spied all the richly carved grave slabs, the tall Celtic crosses, and other signs of lives long past. Each ancient, moss-covered stone bearing tales and stories.

And some, like the mounded stones covering his brothers' graves, weren't moss-grown at all.

Jamie's breath caught as he drew rein and swung down, reaching out at once to help his bride dismount.

He tried to steel himself, striving to appreciate the beauty and stillness of this sacred place, but it was no use. Telling the sun not to rise in the morning would have been easier.

His brows snapped together in a fierce scowl and his mouth went dry.

His heart split.

"We can leave now." A small hand touched his plaid. "It will make no difference to your brothers if you visit them this night or another," she said, the same note of sympathy in her voice that had so touched him earlier, in her father's hall. "Truth be told, I vow it would please them more if you'd spend the time getting to know your father better. He is not the ogre I know you think he is. He—"

"He ought to have repaired the bridge," Jamie said, still frowning. "Had he not been so tightfisted mayhap my brothers—"

"Do you not think he suffers every night for such a remiss?" Aveline took her hand from his plaid, the warm look of understanding in her eyes cooling. "Can you not think more kindly of him?"

Jamie compressed his lips and ran a hand through his hair. He *was* trying to mend things with his da. Leastways, he was trying to help the man.

But at the moment, the nine burial cairns hit him like a fist in the gut. Nine hard-hitting fists cutting off his air and knifing through him like fire lances. His insides churned and he would've sworn hot, smoldering coals burned in his chest.

Now he knew why he'd put off coming here.

The pain was worse than he'd expected. Far worse. Cold rain and blustery winds were sweeping in from the west, but he paid scarce heed to the rough night.

Even so, the finality of the combined scent of rich damp earth, leaf mold, and regret, almost knocked him to the ground. As did the unspoken echoes of words he wished he'd said and now would ne'er have the chance.

"Holy saints." He blew out a breath, more aware of his bride's pitying glances than was good for him. "If only I'd told them how much I loved them."

"They knew," she said, her voice revealing the thickness in her own throat. She stepped closer, reaching to touch him again, this time smoothing a fold of his plaid. "Their fondness for you was one of the reasons I knew I needn't fear our betrothal."

She raised her head and looked at him. "Your father loves you, too. He hides it well, but he does."

Jamie shrugged. Were they anywhere else, he might have hooted his disbelief. Or questioned her, for the possibility did give his heart a jolt.

But here, in the windy dark of the churchyard, he could see only his brothers' graves. He stared at them, feeling the weight of his sorrow bearing down on his shoulders.

A fierce, searing pain he'd endure gladly if only such suffering would undo the cause.

Certain his soul was ripping, he stared up at the heavens, seeking answers but finding only a scattering of cold, frosty stars and drifting, wind-torn clouds.

The night sky stared back at him with all the chill silence of the hills and the thick-growing whin and broom bushes hemming the churchyard. The dread row of low, piled stones he knew held his brothers' bodies until their fine granite tombs and effigies had been readied for them.

Only he couldn't feel them here.

Not his nine full-of-swagger brothers who should have come strolling forward to welcome him home, their eyes alight and their arms spread wide.

Loud, boisterous, and alive as he remembered them.

Jamie's mouth twisted and he clenched his hands, the hot tightness in his chest stopping his breath. He could think on his brothers all he wished, hearing their voices and seeing their smiles. But still they'd be gone.

Already *were* gone—and well beyond where'er he might reach them.

Nothing but oppressive silence greeted him as he forced himself to approach the graves. A black and eerie quiet marred only by the howling of the wind and the drumming of rain on the dark, wet stones.

That, and as a glance across the deserted churchyard proved, fat clusters of red-berried rowan bedecking the narrow chapel door.

He frowned.

His bride curled her fingers around his elbow, gently squeezing. "Your father thought it best," she explained, once again playing his da's wee champion. "What can be the harm if such safeguards soothe him?"

Jamie tamped down the urge to scowl at her. The *harm* was in allowing his da to sink deeper into his delusions. "My father is close to losing his wits," he finally said. "That is the danger."

The maid's chin shot up. "I told you, I have seen the ghosts, too," she reminded him. "And so have others. Just the other day, one of my father's squires swore he saw Neill and Kendrick in the wood near St. Bride's Well."

This time Jamie did scowl.

But he held his silence, not trusting himself to comment on such foolery.

Neill and Kendrick, his two favorite brothers, were

just as dead as the others. Alan Mor's squire had likely seen morning mist drifting near the sacred well.

Not his brothers' bogles.

" 'Tis true," his bride persisted, almost as if she'd read his mind. "I saw how upset the lad was when he came in."

But Jamie scarce heard her. He was looking past her to the chapel, his stomach knotting.

Someone had even draped rowan around the splendid carved standing stone that guarded the entrance to his family's ancient, half-ruined sanctuary. Supposedly built many centuries before by a follower of Skye's far-wandering saint, Maelrhuba, the tiny chapel stood on the site of an even older stone circle.

Clan belief held that the remaining standing stone marked the burial place of the chapel's sainted builder. But some graybeards and local henwives insisted the magnificent Pictish stone was all that survived of the original pagan circle, claiming early Christians destroyed the sacred stones, renaming them Na Clachan Breugach, the Lying Stones.

An intended slur against stones once believed to have been prized as the Stones of Wisdom because of their ability to foretell the future. Tradition claimed that anyone stepping within the stones' charmed inner sanctum on the nights of certain moons would be blessed with brief glimpses of events yet to transpire.

Jamie didn't know which version of the remaining stone's past he believed and, truth be told, he didn't really care.

At the moment, he could only think of his brothers as

he'd last seen them. Bold, brash, and mirthful, each one bursting with spirit and vigor.

"'Fore God," he swore again, blinking hard.

The wind surged then, splattering his face with icy rain droplets, but he made no move to dash at them. Instead, he let them track down his face, rolling over his cheeks like the tears he could no longer shed.

He did narrow his eyes on the little chapel and its hoary sentinel, fixing his gaze on the rowan garland wrapped round the proud stone's venerable height.

Wind whipped at his plaid and tossed his hair, but he stood rooted beside the burial cairns, his fingers swiping at raindrops that suddenly felt hot on his skin, salty on his lips.

Whether or not the stone was a true remnant of the Na Clachan Breugach, the handsomely carved relic didn't need the rowan's protection.

The monolith held magic of its own.

And so far back as he could remember, deference alone would have kept any Macpherson from even touching a finger to such a sacred relic of the clan's dimmest, haziest past.

"Thunder of heaven," he breathed, his heart drumming against his ribs.

He flashed another glance at the chapel door's rowan-draped lintel. In keeping with old Devorgilla's erstwhile instructions, he could see bright red ribbon winding through the berry-rich branches.

Like as not, he'd find the interior of the church equally festooned; the whole wee chapel brimming with charms and foolery designed to scare away his brothers' souls.

Jamie's jaw tightened. He kicked at a clump of rain-speckled, knee-high deer grass. Then he stooped to snatch up a small rock, hurling it into the moon-glinting waters of a nearby burn. Only Aveline's presence and his damned knight's spurs kept him from muttering an oath that would've blistered the night's chill.

An oath that would've made his brothers roar with laughter and jab each other with their elbows as they wriggled their brows at him, challenging him to do better.

But he couldn't.

Not this night.

Not standing in the wind and rain, heart-stricken, and knowing he'd still be missing them even after he'd drawn his last breath.

Then make me proud and prove you have at least a bit o' my charm by seeing your lady out o' the rain. Now, before it's her last breath that concerns you.

Kendrick!

Jamie started, glancing around.

The words still shimmered in the darkness. They'd come from nowhere and everywhere, yet echoed in his ears so real as if his brother stood right beside him. Glowing with vitality and strength, too handsome by a stretch, and ready as ever to boast about how easily he turned female heads.

Make haste. The voice came again, more urgent but fainter. *Do you not see how the lass shivers?*

But to Jamie's mind, he was the one shivering.

His Fairmaiden bride graced the night composed as always, even if she was staring at the Na Clachan Breugach stone with eyes as wide as if she'd not only heard Kendrick, but seen him as well.

Not that he was going to ask her.

He did coil a quick arm around her and sweep her up against his chest, flipping his plaid over her to shield her from the gusting wind.

But as he strode toward the chapel, a rash of shivers spilled through him. And just when he nudged open the narrow, rowan-bedecked door, he thought he caught a glimpse of something flitting through the trees.

A faintly luminous something, moving away from the cairns and aglow with soft iridescent light.

Until he blinked and nothing but mist-wraiths and empty wind curled through the wood and the only glow in sight proved the glimmer of the moon, peering down at him through the clouds.

The strange light was gone.

And for that reason, he left the chapel door open, preferring a clear view of the churchyard and the surrounding wood of birches and oaks. But he did not fear his brothers' bogles. Truth be told, he'd be keen to see them. But he trusted his instincts.

With all respect to his bride, Fairmaiden Castle was known to attract unsavory men. Broken, clanless caterans well adept at hiding in bracken and heather. Brigands he'd trust to skulk through the gusty night, swinging lanterns and rattling chains, whate'er their nefarious purpose.

A possibility he wasn't about to share with Alan Mor's daughter.

But cold chills such as the ones still slithering down

his spine were the only reason he'd come away whole
from the slaughter at Neville's Cross. He doubted there
was any danger of an English arrow storm descending
upon his family's tiny chapel and churchyard, but something equally unpleasant lurked in the nearby wood.

He was sure of it.

And whatever it was, it wasn't his brothers.

They rested quietly beneath their mounded stones. The
only sign of life within the dank, incense-steeped chapel
squirmed and wriggled in his arms. Soft, warm, and far
too tempting for his current mood. Impatient, too, for she
shoved back the hood of her cloak and looked up at him
the moment he set her on her feet on the rough, stone-
flagged floor.

"You needn't peer about with such caution," she said,
watching him scan the church's dim interior. "They aren't
here. Not now."

"Not now?" He arched a brow at her.

Aveline shook her head.

Jamie folded his arms. " 'Not now implies no longer,' "
he said, uncomfortably aware of the many recumbent effigies of his long-dead ancestors.

Proud Macpherson knights, their tombs lined the
chapel walls and crowded the deeper shadows. Colorful
paint gleamed on their armor and shields, making their
stone helms and swords look startlingly real and bringing
their cold, chiseled features to such vivid life that he
crossed himself.

"And 'no longer' implies they once were here," he finished, trying not to feel his ancestors' stony-eyed stares.

Trying especially to forget that farther back in the

chapel, his mother slept as well. She slumbered deeply, hidden away behind the high altar, well beyond his sword-swinging, shield-carrying forebears, her beautiful marble tomb tucked deliberately out of sight.

As if secreting her sculpted likeness from view might undo its reason for being.

"They were here, aye." His bride's words echoed in the half-dark of the chapel, bringing his thoughts back to the present.

She looked down, flicked a raindrop from her cloak. "Leastways, two of them."

" 'Two of them'?" Jamie could feel the back of his neck heating. "Which two?"

"Neill and Kendrick."

Jamie put back his shoulders, looking at her. "See you, lass, since I'm fairly certain my father would rather roll naked in a patch of stinging nettles before he'd set foot in this chapel, I canna believe he's seen any of my brothers here. Not Neill, not Kend—"

"He didn't. I saw them here." She lifted her chin, her sapphire gaze challenging him.

"You saw Neill and Kendrick?"

She nodded. "Here, and other places, as I told you. But it was outside, in the churchyard where I first saw them. I told your father and he ordered your cousins to bring the rowan charms."

"Then my cousins are as addled as my da."

She looked at him for a moment. "They are devoted to him. And, like me, only sought to ease his cares."

Jamie opened his mouth, but no words came out.

Reminding her that there were some who had good

reason to doubt Munro Macpherson had a caring bone in his body struck him as sounding too unchivalrous to risk.

But his temples throbbed at the thought of his wild and unruly cousins descending on the clan chapel, their burly arms filled with rowan and red ribbon; his family's cattle charms.

But he didn't want to think on such buffoonery or his cousins just now.

Not when he'd just learned that this was where Aveline had seen his brothers. His two favorite brothers.

Especially Kendrick.

Kendrick. The name alone gutted him and he glanced aside, his gaze falling on the holy water stoup set into the chapel wall. He jerked, but before he could look away he felt his jaw slide down and his eyes widen as the pathetic layer of stone dust lining the empty basin suddenly vanished beneath clear, sparkling water.

Holy water teeming with a black mass of squiggly tadpoles, the whole gelatinous lot swimming in the sacred stoup.

A boyish prank Kendrick once played on Morag—much to the amusement of his brothers.

And Jamie as well.

But he wasn't amused now. He was frightened; worried his brain was going as soft as his da's.

A notion that instantly banished the tadpoles.

All saints be praised!

"Kendrick and Neill," he began, studying his bride's face. "Were they . . . did they . . ." He let the words tail off, unable to voice what he burned to know.

Just thinking of them dead undid him.

Talking about their ghosts was beyond his strength.

Saints, he still couldn't quite believe in . . . bogles.

But he did have questions.

He began to pace, rubbing the back of his neck as he went. "Were you not afraid? When you saw them?" he asked, shooting her a glance. "Not afeared to come here tonight?"

"Afeared? Of your brothers?" Aveline smiled before she could catch herself. "Och, nay, they do not frighten me. I feel blessed to have seen them."

So soon as the admission left her lips, he stopped beside one of the narrow window slits. "My father doesn't feel blessed when he sees them," he said, looking skeptical. And so handsome in the moonlight streaming in through the window, that her breath caught.

His coppery hair shimmered like burnished gold against the cold wall, the raindrops caught in the glossy strands gilded silver and glittering like diamonds. And with his great height and size, he made the tiny, vaulted chapel seem even smaller. Almost insignificant, with its dank stone and shadows, while throbbing vitality and rich, glowing warmth seemed to pour off him.

She started forward, then hesitated, not certain she trusted herself not to blush if she stepped too close to him.

Even standing where she was, she could breathe in his scent, a heady masculine blend of clean leather and linen. Chill blustery winds and the freshness of rain.

A heady mixture she inhaled with pleasure, especially when she recalled the more unsavory smells that had swirled around some of her less appealing suitors in the past.

Shuddering, she rubbed her arms. Truth was, she'd always known her husband would be chosen for her, but she'd never expected him to be so dashing.

Or so valiant, she admitted, remembering how he'd sheltered her from curious stares in her father's hall. How he'd leaned close and lowered his voice, whispering soothing words to reassure her.

She swallowed, half-afraid to trust the emotions he kindled inside her.

The hope that he might be the answer to her most secret dreams, her deepest longings.

The kind of things she shouldn't be thinking about now. Not here in his family's chapel with him peering into the gloom, his jaw clenched and a frown creasing his brow.

Almost as if he expected one of his stone-hewn ancestors to leap up and challenge him for daring to intrude on their eternal slumber.

But then his gaze snapped back to her, his eyes narrowed and assessing. "How can you be so at ease about having seen my brothers when my father—a man many times your size and strength—cowers in his bed at the mere mention of their names?"

She lifted her chin. "He has reason to fear them. They are angry when they appear to him."

"So I have heard." He folded his arms, eyeing her. "Yet they were not wroth with you when you saw them?"

"They did not visit me," Aveline explained. "I simply happened to see them. There is a difference."

She moved to one of the tombs, tracing the sculpted edge of the effigy knight's sword.

She wanted to speak of her dreams.

Her hopes for a harmonious future, one filled with family and sharing. Mutual respect and, if they were blessed, love.

Love and passion. Those were the things she burned to explore with him. Not talk of bogles and things neither one of them could change.

But he was striding around the chapel again, clearly bent on a lengthy discourse. "My brothers did not appear ill-humored when you saw them?" he asked, proving it.

Aveline sighed.

"I have seen Neill and Kendrick twice," she admitted, drawing her cloak tighter about her. "Once near the Garbh Uisge, but at such a distance I canna say whether they looked grieved or nay. And the time I saw them here, in the churchyard, they were anything but angry."

She paused to look at him. "If you would know the truth of it, they were dancing."

"Dancing?" Jamie halted abruptly. "You saw Neill and Kendrick dancing? In the churchyard?"

She nodded. "Aye, in the churchyard. With Hughie Mac."

Jamie stared at her, his astonishment complete. "But Hughie isn't dead. I've not yet seen him, but I asked of his health as soon as I arrived. Morag swore he's fit as his fiddle strings."

She shrugged. "I can only tell you what I saw."

"And what exactly did you see?"

She went to one of the windows, looked out at the

rainy night. "I told you. They were in good cheer and dancing. And Hughie Mac, he was standing in the moonlight, playing his fiddle."

"But Hughie—"

"Och, he's fine," she confirmed. "I went to look in on him the next day. He said naught of your brothers, so I didn't ask. It was enough to know him hale and well."

Jamie shook his head. "You must've been dreamwalking."

"Like as not," she agreed. "But whether I dreamed your brothers or nay, I am glad I saw them happy. I was able to share the tale with your father and I believe it comforted him to know I'd seen them in good heart."

But Jamie only made a noncommittal *humph* and started walking away from her, his entire attention on one of his stone-cast ancestors.

A particularly lifelike ancestor, for even in the chapel's dimness, the vibrant paint decorating the carved stone effigy made him appear jauntily swathed in plaid.

"Ach—for guidsakes!" He stopped before the tomb, his eyes rounding.

His knightly ancestor *was* wearing plaid.

In all his days and a lifetime of Highland weather, he'd ne'er seen a Macpherson plaid as sopping wet and dripping as this one.

"What in the name of glory?" He stared down at it, blinking, but there could be no mistaking.

It was definitely a dripping wet Macpherson plaid.

And on a closer inspection, the thing wasn't draped artfully over the effigy as he'd surmised.

It'd been carelessly flung there.

Half the plaid hung down the side of the tomb, its end pooling in a soggy heap on the chapel floor.

An insult to his name even his wild-eyed and rowdy cousins wouldn't allow themselves.

Anger swelling in his breast, Jamie stared at the puddle of water spreading away from the base of the tomb. He clenched his fists, unable to think who would do such a thing.

He'd e'er suspected some of his randier cousins used the secluded little sanctuary for a trysting place with light-skirted kitchen lasses, but even if a kinsman had indulged in such bed sport inside the darkened chapel, he didn't ken a one of them who'd spread his plaid on the uneven stone floor and leave it there.

And to be sure, he didn't ken a soul who'd toss a wet plaid across the solemn form of a sleeping forebear.

Frowning, he stepped closer, touching a finger to the sodden wool. His suspicious warrior nose noted, too, that the plaid didn't stink.

Its drenching was recent.

Yet the slanting rain now lashing against the chapel walls had only begun after he'd carried his bride inside. The rain that had dampened them in the churchyard at the burial cairns had been little more than a Highland shower.

A wetting rain, aye, but not near enough for the voluminous folds of a many-elled great plaid to absorb such a huge amount of water.

A startled gasp sounded behind him and he whirled around to see Aveline hurrying toward him, her gaze fastened on the plaid-draped effigy, her feet flying all too quickly over the wet floor.

"Dia!" she cried, looking aghast. "What is—"

"Slow, lass! There's a puddle," Jamie warned too late.

"*Ei-eeee!*" Her foot slipped on the slick stone flags and she went flying, her arms flailing wildly. But only for the instant it took Jamie to leap forward and catch her before she could fall.

His heart pounding, he clutched her to him, cradling her in his arms and holding her head against his shoulder. "Saints o' mercy," he breathed, not wanting to think of what might have happened if he hadn't caught her.

If she'd slammed down onto the hard, wet stones of the floor.

Or worse, hit her head on the edge of a tomb.

"Dinna e'er run across a wet floor again," he said, well aware he was squeezing her too tightly but somehow unable to hold her gently.

She twisted to peer up at him, the movement bringing her face dangerously close to his. "I didn't know the flags were wet," she said, her soft breath warm on his neck. "I couldn't see the puddle in the dark."

Jamie frowned. "Then dinna do that, either," he warned, releasing her. "Flying about in the shadows!"

She shook out her skirts. "I wanted to see what was bothering you."

You and all your enchantments are bothering me, Jamie almost roared.

Instead, he allowed himself another *humph*.

Then he looked at her, astounded she didn't know how perilously close he was to forgetting the wet floor and even his dripping-tartan-hung ancestor.

He could ponder such mysteries later.

For now, she looked too fetching and dear for him to care about much else.

Especially considering her skirts had hitched to a delightful degree, plainly exposing her slim, shapely legs and even a glimpse of pale, satiny hip.

And, saints preserve him, for one heart-stopping moment, he'd caught an intimate enough flash of nakedness to know the curls betwixt her thighs looked so silky and tempting he burned to devour her whole.

"You know I shall not be taking you back to Fairmaiden tonight," he said when he trusted himself to speak. "The hall at Baldreagan should be nigh empty by the time we return and I would enjoy sitting with you in a quiet corner, perhaps before the hearth fire."

If the hall proved as private as he hoped.

And above all, if he wasn't mistaking the meaning of the flush staining her cheeks. The wonderment in her soft, wide-eyed expression and the way she kept moistening her lips.

How pliant she'd gone in his arms.

All soft and womanly.

As if she'd welcome another kiss, perhaps even some gentle stroking.

"Sorcha and I have slept at Baldreagan before," she said, watching him. "On nights when your father was restless and wished to talk."

Jamie drew a breath and let it out slowly. "Your sister's plight weighs heavy on my mind," he said, picking up the wet plaid with his free hand. "So soon as things settle and she is in better spirits, I will do what I can to find a husband for her. Perhaps—"

"My sister loved Neill," she cut in, letting him lead her from the water-stained tomb. "She truly grieves for him. I do not think she will wish to wed another."

No one will have her.

Some even whisper that losing Neill has turned her mind.

The unspoken words hung between them, loud and troubling as if they echoed off the chapel walls.

Frowning, Jamie cleared his throat, seeking a solution.

"Even if she does not desire a husband," he began, hoping he'd found one, "perhaps she will warm to the thought of a family? A marriage to a widowed clansman? One with wee bairns in need of a mother?"

To his relief, Aveline smiled. "Oh, aye, that might please her," she said, her eyes sparkling. "Do you have anyone in particular in mind?"

"Och, a cousin or two," Jamie offered, thinking of Beardie.

Recently widowed and a bit of a lackwit, but left with five snot-nosed, bawling sons. Wee mischievous devils ranging in age from less than a year to seven summers if Jamie's memory served.

But even good-natured Beardie might balk at the prospect of taking Sorcha Matheson to wife.

A superstitious soul, the widowed Beardie might worry that ill luck clings to the maid. That fear alone would deter the most ardent Highland suitor.

"I don't think we should say anything to Sorcha for a while," Aveline said, and Jamie almost leaned back against the nearest tomb in relief.

Truth was, his bride's sister posed a devil's brew and

he couldn't imagine what to do about her, much as he'd like to help the lass.

So he did what seemed natural and slid his arms around *his* Fairmaiden lass, pulling her to him and kissing her until she melted against him. And even then, he kept kissing her, absorbing her sweetness and reveling in the way she tunneled her fingers through his hair, clutching him to her as if she, too, craved the intimacy and closeness.

Maybe even needed or welcomed his kiss.

And outside the chapel, the squally wind and rain dwindled and the moon sailed from behind the clouds, its silvery light spilling across the little churchyard with its burial cairns and ancient Pictish stone.

Illuminating, too, the tightly entwined young couple standing just inside the open chapel door and kissing so feverishly.

Feverishly enough to send a shiver through the watching hills.

A cold and deadly shiver.

Chapter Six

❧

In a world far beyond Clan Macpherson's little church-yard, more specifically in the isle-girt castle known as Eilean Creag, just off the shores of Kintail's Loch Duich, Lady Linnet MacKenzie sat near the hearth fire of her well-appointed lady's solar and frowned at the untidy stitches of her embroidery.

Clumsy, careless stitches.

And were she honest, the worst she'd made in a good long while. Though, with her needlework gracing count-less cushions, bed drapings, and tapestries throughout her home, everyone within the MacKenzie stronghold's proud walls knew she'd ne'er mastered a lady's skill of being able to make tiny, nigh invisible stitches.

Her stitches fell crooked and large, easily identifiable at ten or more paces.

A lacking her puissant husband, Duncan MacKenzie, the Black Stag of Kintail, accepted with notable toler-ance. E'er a man apart, he even complimented her most inept efforts, never letting on that her skills were anything but splendiferous.

Forbearance she did not expect when he returned from paying a call to Kenneth, their nephew, and discovered that her dread *taibhsearachd* had once again visited her.

Linnet glanced at the hearth fire and sighed. Even after a long and happy marriage, her otherwise fearless husband still felt ill at ease when it came to her special gift.

Her second sight.

As seventh daughter of a seventh daughter, the *taibhsearachd* was something she'd lived with since birth. And while it was ofttimes a blessing, it was more often a curse.

"Aye, a curse," she muttered, letting out a shaky breath.

Shuddering, she set aside her needlework and wriggled her stiff and tired fingers. It was no use sitting on her hearthside stool, jabbing her needle into the hapless cloth. Her gift had unleashed a nightmare this time, and all her usual distractions were failing her.

She couldn't forget what she'd seen.

Or undo its truth.

The action she'd set into motion because of it; a bold undertaking sure to unleash her husband's wrath.

"O-o-oh, he'll be sore vexed," she admitted, speaking to Mungo, a tiny brown-and-white dog curled at her feet and who belonged to her stepson, Robbie, and his lady wife, Juliana.

Biting her lip, she reached down and tousled the dog's floppy ears, gladly obliging when he rolled onto his back to have his belly rubbed.

With Robbie off with Duncan at Kenneth's recently restored Cuidrach Castle, and Juliana gone at Linnet's own behest, wee Mungo was in her care.

And from the way the little dog trotted after her, never leaving her side, she could almost believe that he, too, possessed a touch of her gift. That he knew how much trouble would soon descend upon her.

Sure of it, she moistened her lips and stood, grateful to stretch her legs and move about the lady's solar. Even if she would've preferred awaiting Duncan's return on the wall walk of Eilean Creag's high-towered battlements, as was her usual wont. A habit she doubted she'd allow herself to indulge for a good, long while.

Not after such a fright.

Shuddering again, she hugged herself, rubbing her arms until the gooseflesh receded.

Only then did she glance at the carefully bolted window shutters, wishing she could risk opening them to the brisk evening breeze.

But she didn't dare.

Sparing herself a repetition of the grim vision she'd seen the last time she'd looked upon the still, shining waters of Loch Duich was more important than filling her lungs with fresh night air.

Air she knew she'd need as soon as the door flew wide and she came face-to-face with Duncan wearing his most thunderous expression.

An unpleasantness that was about to crash down upon her, for she could hear angry voices and the sound of hurrying feet pounding up the turnpike stair.

Two sets of heavy, masculine feet.

Accompanied by two identical glares, for Robbie would be with him and equally displeased.

Then, before she could even smooth a hand over her hair or shake out her skirts, the door burst open and the two men swept into the room. Chill night wind from the stairwell's arrow slit windows gusted in as well, its rushing draught gutting a few candles and making the torch flames flicker wildly.

But not near so wild as her husband looked.

Frowning darkly, he strode forward, sword-clanking and windblown, his eyes blazing. "Saints, Maria, and Joseph!" he roared, staring at her. "Tell me you haven't sent my daughters to the north. *To anywhere.* And without my consent!"

Looking equally mud-stained and disheveled, Robbie shook his head, his expression more of disbelief than fury. "Surely we misheard." He glanced at his father. "Juliana would ne'er ride off without telling me. If she had need to make a journey, she would've waited until I returned from my own."

"She went because I asked her. She—" Linnet broke off when Mungo streaked past her to hurtle himself at Robbie's legs.

Scooping him up, her stepson clasped the little dog to his chest, some of the darkness slipping from his face, washed away by Mungo's excited wags and yippings, his wet slurpy kisses.

Duncan snorted.

His brow black as his tangled, shoulder-length hair, he ignored his son and the squirming dog and glanced around the fire-lit room before heading straight to a table set with cheese and oatcakes, an ewer of heather ale. Helping himself to a brimming cup of the frothy brew, he downed it in one long gulp, then swung back around, looking no less fierce for having refreshed himself.

"God's wounds, woman, I have loved you for long." He narrowed his eyes on her, his stare piercing. "But this is beyond all. I canna say what I will do if aught happens to either of my girls."

Linnet clasped her hands before her and lifted her chin. "Our daughters are well able to look after themselves," she returned, meeting his glare. "They are escorted by a company of your best guardsmen. Juliana"—she glanced at Robbie— "accompanied them for propriety's sake."

"That doesn't tell me why they are gone," Duncan shot back, looking at her long and hard.

"You know I would have known if danger awaited them."

"Faugh." He folded his arms. " 'Tis still a bad business."

Linnet held her ground, flicked at her skirts. "I sent them away for a reason."

Duncan arched a brow. "And would that be the same reason you've barricaded yourself in here with all the shutters drawn tight? You, with your love of fresh air and open windows?"

"To be sure, I would rather have the shutters flung wide," Linnet admitted, lowering herself onto her stool. "I—"

"By the saints!" Robbie's voice echoed in her ears, already sounding distant, hollow. "Father, do you not see?"

Vaguely, Linnet was aware of Robbie setting down Mungo, then grabbing his father's arm, shaking him. "She's closed the shutters to block the view of the loch! Like as not, she's had another one of her spells. The *taibhsearachd . . .*"

But Linnet heard no more.

Truth be told, she wasn't even in the lady's solar anymore, but standing on the parapet walk of Eilean Creag's battlements, enjoying the wind in her face and a splendid Highland sunset.

A glorious one, with the still waters of Loch Duich reflecting the jagged cliffs and headlands, the long line of heather and bracken-clad hills rolling away beyond the loch's narrow, shingled shore.

Only then the open moors and rolling hills trembled and shook, drawing ever nearer until the vastness of Loch Duich narrowed to a treacherous defile. A deep, black-rimmed gorge hemming a rushing, raging torrent, all white water, rocks, and spume.

Linnet cried out and reached for support, her legs threatening to buckle as she clung to the parapet wall and stared down at the vision before her, the most-times tranquil loch's dim-shining waters nowhere to be seen.

She saw only the steep-sided ravine and the churning, boiling water. The deadly, racing cataracts and the black, glistening rocks lining the water's edge and thrusting upward through the flying spray.

The tall, well-built Highlander caught in the furious cauldron, his strapping body crashing against the rocks, then shooting onward, downstream, tossing and rolling in the wicked current, his plaid and streaming auburn hair the only notable color in a whirl of frothing, life-stealing white.

But then the white narrowed further, becoming nothing more ominous than the whiteness of her own bright-gleaming knuckles as she held tight to the cold stone of a merlon in the battlements' crenellated walling.

The horror was past.

Linnet drew a great quivering breath and blinked, half-expecting to find herself slumped against the stone merlon, a chill night wind tearing across the ramparts, buffeting her trembling body and whipping her hair. But she was in her tapestry-hung lady's solar, the window shutters still securely latched and the hearth fire crackling pleasantly as if nothing had happened.

Sadly, she knew otherwise.

And from the looks of them, so did her husband and her stepson.

"Holy Christ, Linnet," Duncan swore, proving it.

He knelt before her, holding her hands in a bone-crunching grip, all vexation gone from his handsome face. "Why didn't you tell us straightaway why you were holing yourself up in here?"

He glanced at Robbie, took the ale cup he offered him and pressed it against her lips. "Drink," he urged, looking almost as shaken as she felt. "Then tell us what this has to do with Arabella and Gelis."

"And Juliana," Robbie added, likewise dropping to his knees in the floor rushes.

Linnet blinked again, still dimly aware of the tragedy she'd just seen. And for the second time. She shivered, gratefully taking another swallow of the heather ale.

Seeing the vision twice only underscored its in-evitability.

"Our girls and Juliana will be fine," she said when she could speak. "'Tis Young Jamie that concerns me. He is the reason I sent them to Baldreagan. To—"

"'Baldreagan'?" Duncan's jaw slipped. "Every clapper-tongued kinsman belowstairs claimed you'd sent them to visit Juliana's Strathnaver kin and then on to Assynt, to spend time with Archibald Macnicol and his sons at Dunach."

"That you'd hoped Kenneth's wife's father might know of suitable husbands," Robbie put in.

"I may have said something of like," she owned, a bit of color returning to her cheeks. "Archibald is a great northern chieftain and his sons are making distinguished names for themselves."

She sat up straighter on her stool. "The girls are of marriageable age," she said, her tone and the jut of her chin revealing she was now fully recovered. "Some might even say past marriageable age."

Duncan sniffed.

His foul mood returning, he pushed to his feet. "What do my daughters' tender ages have to do with James Macpherson?" He stared down at her, his hands fisted around his sword belt. "You know he quit service with Kenneth to return home to wed, if Kenneth had the rights of it."

To his surprise, his wife shook her head. "He returned home to die," she said, her voice catching.

"To die?" Duncan could feel his eyes bugging out.

His wife nodded. "I've seen his death," she said,

sounding so sure of it, his nape prickled. "He is going to drown in the Rough Waters, just like his brothers. That's why I sent the girls. On a pretense to order a new stirk for you, but, in truth, to urge Jamie to be careful."

Duncan's head began to ache. "Have you not always told me naught could be done to alter such things as you sometimes see?"

"Aye, that is the way of it," she admitted, looking miserable. "And I warned the girls not to let on to Jamie what they know. Such knowledge might bring on his doom with greater rapidity."

"Then why send them in the first place?"

"Because they are sensitive enough to know who at Baldreagan they can trust," she said, looking at him as if he were a simpleton. "They'll find the right soul to warn."

Duncan grunted. "If a warning was all you hoped to accomplish, why didn't you just send word to old Devorgilla of Doon? She could have worked a spell or winked at the moon and sped a message to Baldreagan without my daughters needing to traipse clear across Kintail."

His wife pressed her lips together, clearly annoyed. "Devorgilla knows without messengers when her aid is needed," she finally said. "Just as I know some action is required of me when I am visited by my gift."

Getting slowly to her feet, she walked past him to the little table spread with oatcakes, cheese, and ale. "If Devorgilla is meant to help Jamie, she will," she added, looking down at the table but touching nothing. "For myself, I have done all I could."

"And if neither your help nor Devorgilla's is needed?"

Robbie joined her at the table, helping himself to a good-sized chunk of cheese. "What if it wasn't Jamie you saw? But one of his already drowned brothers?"

"By God, he's right!" Duncan flashed an admiring glance at his son. "Those Macpherson lads all looked alike."

Replenishing his ale cup, he drank deeply. "Aye, that will be the way of it," he declared, looking immensely pleased.

"Nay, that was not the way of it." Linnet glanced up from the table; she could feel the heat flooding her face. "It was definitely Jamie. There can be no mistaking."

"No mistaking?" Duncan and Robbie chorused.

She shook her head. "None whatsoever."

Duncan stepped closer. "And how can you be so sure?"

"Jamie squired here," Linnet reminded him, unable to meet his eyes.

"Jamie, Lachlan, and a goodly number of others as well," he shot back, eyeing her significantly. "I dinna see what that has to do with it."

It had everything to do with it—and was something she just couldn't push past her lips.

"Squires and young knights often take their baths in the kitchens," she blurted at last, hoping they'd understand.

But they didn't.

Both her husband and her son stood gawping at her, slack-jawed and owl-eyed.

Totally uncomprehending.

Certain her flaming face would soon burn brighter

than the hearth log, she blew out an agitated breath and said the only other thing remaining: "Jamie is a big lad."

Duncan and Robbie exchanged glances.

Neither spoke.

But after a moment, a pink tinge began to bloom onto Robbie's cheeks. "Oh," he said.

"Exactly," Linnet agreed, grateful at least one of them understood. "And that is how I know it was him. By the time his body reached the deep pools at the end of the rapids, his plaid had been torn from him and he was naked."

"Naked?" Duncan echoed, making it worse.

Linnet nodded. "Naked and tossed about often enough in the water for me to know without a doubt that I was looking at James Macpherson. Young James of the Heather."

The image still branded in her memory, she paced to the nearest window and yanked open the shutters, at last breathing in the brisk, strengthening air she so sorely needed.

"And," she added, staring down at the night-blackened waters of Loch Duich, "if naught can be done to prevent it, he will soon be as dead as his brothers."

Jamie's hope for a pleasant evening spent wooing Aveline Matheson before the hearth fire vanished the instant they rode into Baldreagan's bailey and he spied the chaos.

Anything but emptied and quiet—the castle inhabitants tucked in and snug for the night—the supposed house of mourning appeared under siege.

And he and his bride seemed to have arrived right smack in the middle of the assault.

An invasion by MacKenzies!

Jamie's brow furrowed, but there could be no doubt. He'd spent half his life at Eilean Creag, squiring for the castle's formidable laird. He'd recognize these bearded, plaid-hung clansmen anywhere.

As would any Highlander; leastways those of a warrior bent. The MacKenzies were amongst the most fierce fighting men to stride the heather, commanding respect and awe where'er they went. As generous and open-handed to their friends as they struck dread into the hearts of their foes.

And Jamie knew them as friends. The very best of friends.

"Suffering saints," he breathed, their presence transporting him to another, larger and more imposing bailey.

His heart clenched and at once a flood of memories crashed over him.

Good memories.

These men weren't just any MacKenzies. They were the Black Stag's men, and some of his best, if Jamie's eyes weren't lying to him.

Braw stalwarts to a man. Kintail's pride.

Swinging down onto the cobbles, Jamie looked around. The whole of the moonlit courtyard teemed with men, skittish horses and excited, barking dogs.

He even caught sight of his own beast, Cuillin. Ever in the thick of things, the old dog's shuffling gait and milky eyes didn't stop him from joining in the revel and din.

But the MacKenzies caused the greatest commotion.

There were scores of them and they hastened hither and thither, some hefting heavy travel bags on their shoulders, others helping Baldreagan's stable lads carry extra hay and grain into the stables lining the far wall of the bailey.

Stables with room to house at least sixty horses, though considering the ruckus coming from that direction, he guessed a good many more were now squeezed into its stalls. A few had even been crammed into the sheep pens near the postern gate and if that wasn't surprising enough, light blazed from every window of his father's five- toried keep.

But before he could wonder about the unexpected visit, he felt a touch on his arm. Aveline stood peering up at him, her eyes round and luminous. Her pale, flaxen hair shimmered in the moonlight and she looked so beautiful he almost forgot to breathe.

He *had* forgotten to help her dismount.

Already a stable lad was running forward to see to her riderless steed.

Jamie bit back a curse. "My apologies," he said, jamming a hand through his hair. "I meant to lift you down, but I was so surprised—"

"I don't need apologies." She leaned into him, a fetching twinkle in her eyes. "Just as I didn't melt in the rain back at the cairns, neither will I shatter if I slide off a horse unaided."

She stood on her toes, pressing a quick kiss to his lips.

A quick, soft kiss, and with just enough hint of tongue to make him wish they were still in the sheltering dark of St. Maelrhuba's chapel and not the crowded bailey.

But already she was pulling away.

"Of course, you were surprised," she said, glancing around at the bustle. "Who would have thought we'd find Baldreagan overrun with MacKenzies?"

Jamie looked at her. "You know them?"

Aveline smoothed her cloak, suddenly uncomfortable.

"Ach . . . ," she stalled, her gaze going to the keep's forebuilding with its steep stone steps up to the great hall. "See you, the truth is, men from Eilean Creag have visited Fairmaiden a time or two over the years," she finally explained. "They always came for the same reason—claiming your father's asking price for his cattle was too high and wanting to know if my da could make them a better offer."

"And did he?"

"Oh, aye. Every time." She waited until two gear-toting MacKenzies hastened past, then lowered her voice, "He'd tell them they could have all the cattle they desired and for nary a coin."

"For nothing?" Jamie couldn't believe it.

"Not exactly nothing," she hedged, still avoiding his eye. "There was a catch. They could have the cattle if they took one of my sisters as well."

Jamie almost choked.

The only thing that saved him from laughing out loud at his good father's gall was the sudden appearance of a creature almost as ill-starred as his bride's sundry sisters.

"Jamie! You'll ne'er guess who's sitting in our hall, and why!" Beardie came panting up to them, his broad, pox-marked face flushed with excitement. "Och, nay, you'll ne'er guess," he repeated, his great red beard jigging.

Jamie winked at Aveline then looked back at his cousin. "Could it be MacKenzies?" he ventured, feigning ignorance.

"O-o-oh, aye! To be sure, but *what* MacKenzies!" Beardie rocked back on his heels, gave Jamie a sly wink. "Your jaw will hit the rushes, I say you."

"Then do." Jamie folded his arms. "Say me who is here and causing such a stir."

"The Black Stag's womenfolk! His son Robbie's wife, Lady Juliana, and"—Beardie's eyes lit—"his own two girls!"

Jamie's jaw did drop. "Arabella and Gelis are here? And with the Lady Juliana?"

Beardie nodded. "Who would've thought it? They're looking for husbands." Leaning closer, he lowered his voice. "I think they have me in mind for one of 'em. They've been making moon eyes at me."

"That may well be," Jamie agreed, thwacking the other man on the arm, knowing he couldn't bring himself to dash his bumbling, bushy-bearded cousin's hopes for a new wife. A mother for his five bairns.

A female he suspected would be found amongst the lesser kin of an allied laird. A toothsome, big-hearted lass willing to mother Beardie's brood, but with surety not so fine a catch as Duncan MacKenzie's maidenly daughters.

Lively, beautiful, and high-spirited, the well-dowered MacKenzie lasses were destined for only the highest-ranking husbands.

As Beardie would know if he had even a jot of sense.

Instead, he stood preening. Brushing at his plaid and hitching his wide, leather belt to a more advantageous sit across his round and impressive girth.

"I'm off to fetch my great-great-grandda's winged helmet," he confided, speaking again into Jamie's ear. "The fiery lass, Gelis, was impressed when I told her I had a touch o' Norse blood!"

Jamie opened his mouth to tell him there was nary a Highlander who didn't have a few drops of Viking blood in his veins, but Beardie was already running off, barreling a path through the throng, clearly bent on retrieving his rusted treasure.

A relic the likes of which could be found aplenty at Eilean Creag.

Jamie blew out a breath, looking after him.

The moment Beardie vanished from view, he reached for Aveline's hand, pulling her with him toward the keep stairs. Something was sorely amiss and the sooner he found out what it was, the better.

Lady Juliana might well be escorting Duncan MacKenzie's daughters across the Highlands, but the reason wasn't to find them husbands.

Especially not at Baldreagan.

That Jamie knew so sure as the morrow.

He was doubly sure when they neared the top of the forebuilding's steps and a small, grizzled woman materialized out of the shadows to block their way.

"Saints be praised, you've returned!" She swooped down on them like a black-garbed crow, her eyes glinting in the moonlight. "The whole world's a-falling apart and I'm running out o' ways to hold it together!"

"Ach, Morag." Jamie flashed her his most disarming smile. "I've seen you ready the hall for far more illustrious hosts than two wee lassies and Lady Juliana." He reached to ruffle her iron-gray curls. "Dinna tell me—"

"It isn't them troubling me." Morag grabbed his arm, drawing him into the deeper shadows of the door arch. "It's your da. He's in the hall now, at the high table, making merry with the MacKenzie lasses—"

"He's left his room then?" Aveline stepped forward, the notion pleasing her. "Praise be," she said, smiling at the old woman. "These are good tidings. We've been trying to get him to come belowstairs for days."

She paused, sliding a glance at Jamie.

He'd stiffened beside her and whether it suited him or nay, she was determined to help bridge the gap between them.

"Your da has been missed, see you. Especially of an evening," she tried to explain. "No one feels spirited enough to tell tales or even enjoy their ale, and his hounds mope about with hanging ears and sad eyes."

Jamie surprised her by nodding.

"Aye, his presence in the hall is naught to be fretting over," he agreed.

Morag pursed her lips. "It is when I tell you he's only in the hall because he's vowed ne'er to set foot elsewhere!" she said, wagging a finger at him. "He's *pretending* to be at ease. In truth, he's in a greater dither than he's been since I can remember."

Aveline's smile froze.

Jamie's expression hardened. A muscle began jerking in his jaw.

Seeing it, Aveline edged closer to him. "Did Munro have another visitation?" she asked, lacing her fingers with Jamie's and squeezing. "Was it Neill again?"

Morag nodded.

"Aye, that's the rights of it," she confirmed, her head still bobbing. "And the poor laird took such a fright, he barricaded himself in his room. We found him huddled in his chair, talking gibberish."

She sent a wary look over her shoulder. "Like as not, he'd still be there if four clansmen hadn't put their shoulders to the door," she said, lowering her voice. "And if the MacKenzie lasses hadn't arrived when they did. They're the reason he came belowstairs."

Jamie raised his brows. "And now he's vowing to stay there? In the hall?"

"So he says."

Aveline frowned. "He canna sleep in the hall," she objected, the image of the old laird passing the night wrapped in his plaid in the draughty cold of the hall making her shiver. "For all his bluster, he's old. And not himself of late."

Jamie bit back a snort.

So far as he'd seen, with the exception of his newfound fear of bogles, Munro Macpherson was still very much his crafty, cantankerous self.

But his bride seemed to have tucked him into her heart, so he gave her the most reassuring look he could muster. "Ne'er you worry," he said. "I willna let him bed down in the hall. He'll sleep abovestairs as befits him."

"Tchach! We shall see." Morag clucked her tongue.

"That old goat is as thrawn and unyielding as the day is long. Nay, I canna see him going back to his room."

Jamie shook his head. "Last time I spoke with him, he was vowing ne'er to leave his bed."

"Aye, he was all for hiding beneath the covers," Morag agreed, stepping closer. "But that was before Neill's ghost came a-calling, all wet and dripping from the grave."

Jamie's heart stopped.

Aveline grabbed his arm, holding tight.

"What are you saying?" Jamie stared at the old woman, the fine hairs on the back of his neck lifting. "What do you mean Neill was *'wet and dripping'*?"

"Just what I said." Morag put back her bony shoulders. "Your da won't be going back to his bed because he's afraid of drowning in it. If we want to believe his rantings, the last time Neill appeared to him, he was dripping wet and the very waters of the Garbh Uisge were flowing all around him."

"That canna be," Jamie argued.

Morag shrugged. "Be that as it may, his bedding and the floor rushes were drenched when we found him."

"You saw this?" Jamie asked, though, in truth, he already knew.

The icy chills sweeping down his spine answered him.

Indeed, he didn't even hear Morag's reply. The blood was roaring too loud in his ears. And in his mind's eye, he was seeing only one thing.

The sopping wet plaid flung across his ancestor's tomb.

Chapter Seven

❖

Jamie paused just inside the hall door and immediately found himself surrounded by jostling, rowdy clansmen. Clearly in good cheer, they pushed, shoved, and wrestled in the aisles between the trestle tables. Others stood apart, indulging in that favored Highland pastime of story-telling, the more golden-tongued among the visitors re-galing circles of listeners with rousing tales about their ancestors.

But it was another MacKenzie who caught Jamie's eye.

Burly and bearded, the man stood nearby, thrusting a great drinking horn in the air and claiming he'd filled it to the brim with *uisge beatha*. Grinning broadly, he chal-lenged any who'd dare to gulp down the fiery Highland spirits in a single draught.

Jamie frowned at him, thinking he'd borrowed the clan's famed Horn of Days. A treasure only touched when the reigning Macpherson chieftain relinquishes his authority to his successor. Certain the man didn't know the horn's significance, Jamie started forward. But on closer look, the reveler's drinking horn was only a common ox horn.

The man simply enjoyed the carouse—as Gaels are wont to do.

Even so, his ringing voice added to the mayhem, the whole commotion proving so crushing Jamie slid an arm around his bride, keeping her close as he blinked against the thick, smoke-hazed air. But it took a few moments for his eyes to adjust to the shadows and torchlight, his ears to grow accustomed to the raised voices and laughter.

Boisterous laughter, clamor, and song.

A stir and tumult the likes of which he doubted Baldreagan had seen in years.

Truth be told, the din and disorder almost matched the chaos in the bailey. And ne'er in all his days had he been more grateful to lose himself in such a raucous swirl of noise and confusion.

Every blessed distraction took his mind off the wet plaid and a nagging suspicion so disturbing it felt like an iron yoke settling around his neck.

The morrow would be soon enough to ponder such troubling matters.

For the now, he'd force a smile and the best spirits he could summon. And for good measure, he'd watch his back and keep a wary eye on over-dark corners.

Including *corners* well known to him, much as such a notion displeased him.

But as Kenneth MacKenzie once said, pigs aren't likely to sing from trees. And neither did sopping wet plaids sail into dark and empty chapels and fling themselves across stone-faced Highland knights.

Jamie drew a deep breath and let it out slowly. He also tightened his arm around Aveline.

Och, aye, something was amiss.

And until he solved the riddle, his new lady wasn't leaving his side.

"O-o-oh, I see the trumpet tongues spoke true," chimed a female voice just to his left. "You *have* found yourself a beautiful *Sithe* maid!"

Jamie swung about, almost colliding with a glowing-eyed, flame-haired lassie no one would dare call a faery.

"Gelis!" he greeted Duncan MacKenzie's youngest daughter. "Saints, but you've grown."

He looked down at her, amazed at how womanly she'd become in the short months since he'd last visited Eilean Creag. "You are a fury unbound—sneaking up on us when I'd hoped to escort my lady to the dais in style."

The girl tossed her bright head and whirled to face Aveline, eyeing her with open curiosity, but a warm and teasing smile lighting her face.

"Ah, well, then I shall take her," she trilled, grabbing Aveline's hand and leading her away, pulling her deeper into the hall, straight through the milling, carousing throng and up onto the dais.

"He will catch up, dinna you fear." She gave Aveline a conspiratorial wink. "That one needs a jolt now and then," she added, urging Aveline to take a seat at the high table. "He worries too much about propriety."

"And you do not?" Aveline looked at her, certain she'd never seen a more vivid, breathtaking creature.

All burnished coppery hair, sparkling eyes, and dimples, she breathed charm and enchantment.

She was worldly as well. Aveline could see it in her eyes. "You do not care what the glen wives say?"

Gelis laughed and dropped onto the trestle bench beside her. "Not if I can help it!" she said, settling herself. "Worrying is for graybeards and . . . Jamie!"

"Hah! And the moon just fell from the sky," a raven-haired beauty put in from across the table. "My sister worries all the time. Regrettably, too often about things that do not concern her."

Lifting her wine cup, she smiled. "I am Arabella," she said, as serene and self-assured as her sister brimmed with gaiety. "And"—she indicated an older, equally stunning woman farther down the table—"that is the Lady Juliana, our brother Robbie's wife. Like myself, she is along to keep young Gelis out of mischief."

" 'Young'?" Gelis leaned forward, her plump breasts swelling against her low-cut bodice. "I am not so young that certain braw eyes haven't been admiring my charms!"

Arabella set down her wine cup. "As you can see, she is overly modest as well."

Gelis gave a light shrug. "If you weren't so swaddled in the folds of your arisaid, I vow you'd have a few manly eyes looking your way, too," she quipped, picking up the end of her braid and wriggling it in her sister's direction. "We both know your *charms* are even bigger than mine."

Running a finger up and down the side of her wine cup, she looked through her lashes at a passing MacKenzie.

An especially bonnie one.

"Yours jiggle more, too," Gelis observed, returning her attention to her sister. "Or they would if you'd put them to better advantage," she added, her fiery hair bright in the hearth glow.

Arabella flushed. "We did not come here to flash smiles at hot-eyed guardsmen," she minded her sister, something in her tone sending a shiver down Aveline's spine.

But the dark beauty's face revealed nothing. She sat ramrod straight, the image of polished dignity, her sole attention on the bannock she was smearing with Morag's special heather honey.

Only her flame-haired sister seemed fidgety.

Gelis squirmed on the trestle bench and kept sliding cheeky glances into the main area of the hall, her gaze going repeatedly to a long table crowded with young MacKenzie guardsmen.

And, Aveline knew, several of Jamie's bolder cousins.

She also knew no man had ever looked so hungrily at her.

Unlike the MacKenzie women, she had tiny breasts that would never strain and swell against her bodice, threatening to spill over the edging in a provocation that had surely delighted and stirred men since the beginnings of time.

And in her case, a pitiful lacking that clamped white-hot fire tongs around her heart, squeezing hard and jabbing sharp little green needles into soft and hurtful places she didn't care to examine.

Until she heard someone mention Jamie's name and

remembered how his eyes had darkened with passion when they'd kissed in her father's solar and her gown had slipped, baring her left nipple.

She remembered, too, how gently he'd touched her.

At once, a pleasurable heat bloomed inside her making her almost ache with the need to feel his hands on her again. She'd never imagined a man's touch could be so exquisite. Just remembering sent tingly warmth sweeping across her woman's parts and a deliciously weighty sensation to her belly. She shifted on the bench, hoping no one would guess the reason for her restlessness.

Hoping, too, she might later have the chance to explore such tingles in earnest.

"Baldreagan cattle, eh?"

Munro's booming voice cut into her reverie, and she glanced down the table to see him in deep conversation with Lady Juliana. To Aveline's relief, he looked anything but feeble or frightened. Indeed, she recognized the glint in his eyes. It was a look she knew from her father, as well, but the MacKenzie woman appeared Munro's match.

Well made and exceedingly comely, she had fine glowing skin and a wealth of reddish-gold hair that glistened in the torchlight. And like her two young charges, she'd been blessed with one of the fullest, most alluring bosoms Aveline had ever seen.

"My good father, Duncan MacKenzie, wishes a new stirk come the spring," she was saying, watching Munro over her wine cup as she spoke. "He might even take two if the conditions are amenable."

" *'Amenable'?*" Munro slapped the table and hooted. "My conditions—"

"Will be more than amenable," Jamie announced, his voice brooking no argument. "They will be fair and good."

Munro glared at him. "What do you know of cattle dealing?"

"I know more than you suspect."

Striding up to the table, Jamie nodded to Lady Juliana, then poured himself a healthy measure of ale, draining it in one long draw before setting down the cup with a loud *clack*.

He dragged the back of his hand over his mouth, his gaze fixed firmly on his father.

His bride looked far too fetching in the soft glow cast by the well-doing dais fire and he couldn't allow such a tempting distraction—not with the image of that dread wet plaid looming in his mind.

But he did wish to distract his father. Only so could he squeeze more than rants, splutters, and snorts out of the man.

So he took a seat, snitching a bit of cheese from a platter and tossing it to Cuillin. Then he got comfortable and launched his assault.

"Anyone who can afford blazing log fires in every hearth can also allow a bit of openhandedness when selling cattle to a long-time ally."

Just as he'd expected, his father tightened his lips and frowned at him.

And said not a word.

"I hope, too," Jamie went on, circling a finger around

the rim of his ale cup, "that you've laid an equally fine fire in your bedchamber? It's a chill night and I wouldn't want you catching an ague."

Munro gripped the table edge and leaned forward. "Since I willna be sleeping in that room again, there's no danger of me taking ill there."

Gesturing for Morag to replenish his ale, he sat back in his throne-like laird's chair and treated Jamie to a rare smile.

A smug smile.

Tight-lipped and defiant.

"Indeed," he continued, his self-pleased stare still riveted on Jamie, "I just decided I shall sleep in your chamber. You can have mine."

Refusing to be baited, Jamie didn't even blink. "As you will. Truth be told, I am much relieved as I'd heard you'd meant to make your bed in the hall and I would not have allowed that. Too many men spread their pallets here and I'd not see your night's rest disturbed."

Not when one amongst those men might wear two faces.

And a sopping wet plaid.

Sure of it, Jamie reached across the table, laid strong fingers atop his father's age-spotted hand. "Tell me," he said, speaking low, "when Neill came to you this last time, was he swathed in his burial shroud or wearing his plaid?"

"His plaid, you buffoon!" Munro snapped, yanking back his hand. "His drenched and dripping plaid." He twisted around and shot a glare at Morag. "As everyone in this hall knows!"

"Then I shall offer him a new and dry one if he dares make a repeat visit," Jamie declared, bracing himself for his da's next outburst. "And you shall indeed quarter in my bedchamber. You and two trusted guardsman."

" *'Two trusted guardsmen'!*" Munro mimicked, glancing around. "There's not a soul under the heavens can hold back a flood once the waters start rushing. I near drowned in my bed, and no muscle-armed, smirking guardsmen woulda been able to help me had the waters not receded when they did."

"But such treacherous waters as the Garbh Uisge can be rendered harmless if one avoids them." Lady Juliana picked up a platter of jam-filled wafers, setting it in front of Munro, but turning a sharp eye on Jamie. "There are many who would sleep with greater ease if you vowed to avoid the Rough Waters," she said, something in her expression making Jamie tense.

"Trust me," he said, "I've no wish to go there. If e'er an ill wind blew through these hills, that's where it is. But I do mean to examine the damaged footbridge," he added, feeling every eye at the high table upon him. "The bridge will have to be repaired."

"That devil-damned monstrosity canna be repaired," Munro grumbled, and bit into a wafer. "I've sent every last bit of it to the flames o' hell where it belongs!"

" *'The flames o' hell'?*" Jamie exchanged glances with Aveline, but she looked equally perplexed.

"Och, aye. Straight to Lucifer himself," Munro snipped, reaching for a second wafer.

"He means he's burned it," Beardie gibed, elbowing

his way through the throng. "The whole footbridge. Every last piece."

Burned it. Every last piece.

The words circled in Jamie's head, an unpleasant inkling taking seed as Beardie came closer and the red, pulsing glow from the dais fire edged his great, bumbling form.

Jamie looked from his cousin to his father and back again. "Dinna tell me the logs blazing on every hearth grate are bits of the footbridge?"

Munro sucked in his breath and spluttered something unintelligible. But the annoyance sparking in his eyes proved Jamie's suspicions.

His tightfisted da hadn't spent a coin laying in fuel for Baldreagan's scores of fireplaces. The bright gleam Jamie had noticed lighting every tower window were the flames of his brothers' death weapon.

Beardie's beard-shaking nod confirmed it.

Looking pleased to be the bearer of as-yet-unknown tidings, he drew up behind Gelis, his tarnished Viking helmet clutched in his hand.

"Where do you think we've been these last days?" He cocked a bushy brow, indicating a few other kinsmen milling about in the shadows.

Death lurked in those shadows, Jamie would've sworn someone whispered. Someone close behind him, their voice pitched low and full of warning. But when he twisted around and glanced over his shoulder, no one stood near enough to have flustered the words.

Hughie Mac held court on the far side of the hall, playing his fiddle with gusto and flourish. And one of Jamie's cousins had drawn a fulsome kitchen lass into the semi-privacy of a nearby window embrasure, the flickering torchlight revealing the white gleam of her naked breasts and that his cousin's hand was groping deep beneath the lassie's skirts. Other cousins occupied themselves shouting encouragement to two MacKenzie guardsmen enjoying a vigorous round of arm-wrestling at one of the long tables.

And Morag hovered close by the dais steps, her sharp gaze on Beardie's older lads as they chased a few of the more playful castle dogs around the oaken partition that made up the hall's screens passage.

Everything appeared as it should.

Yet he'd swear he could feel malignant eyes watching him.

"Those were dark hours, down at the Garbh Uisge," Beardie was saying, and a few listening kinsmen nodded in shuddery agreement. "Tearing apart what remained o' the bridge and fishing the rest from the water. I wouldn't want to do the like again."

Jamie tipped back his head and stared up at the smoke-blackened ceiling, blew out a frustrated breath.

Wouldn't want to do the like again, Beardie had quipped. A muscle in Jamie's jaw twitched.

Would that it hadn't been done at all.

Wishing that were so, he put back his shoulders and straightened his spine against the chill creeping over him. Ever since discovering the wet plaid, he'd wanted to examine the fallen bridge.

Scour each and every inch of splintered, shattered wood for hints of foul play.

But now the best he could do would be sweeping the bridge's ashes from Baldreagan's hearth grates.

And making certain that the misbegotten sod who was staring such angry holes into him was kept well away from his lady and his da.

Well prepared for a clash of wills with the latter, he reached across the table and slid the platter of jam-filled wafers away from his father's grasp.

"Whose idea was it to burn the bridge's remains?"

"The bogles," Beardie answered him, claiming a seat beside Gelis. "Neill was furious with your da because o' what happened and warned he wanted no reminder left o' the tragedy."

"The idea was my own," Munro insisted, fisting his hands on the table. "Mine, and Alan Mor's. I'm paying for a new bridge to be built and he's seeing to the sculpting of my sons' effigies and tombs."

He glanced at Jamie. "'Tis part of our agreement. A way to appease the bogles."

Jamie frowned and bit his tongue.

Beardie looked doubtful. "But you said they're wroth—"

"And so they are!" Munro shot back, glaring down the table. "Though why they dinna plague Alan Mor as well is beyond me. He bears equal blame for letting the footbridge fall into disrepair. God kens we both made use o' the thing!"

"And did anyone examine the bridge before you turned it into firewood?" Jamie asked, his persistence reaping another of his da's dark frowns.

When nothing but the scowl answered him, he pushed to his feet.

"I'll see Lady Aveline to Kendrick's old chamber," he said, already moving to help her rise. "It's closest to yours, and since I'd relish a visit from Neill or whoe'er else might wish to call, I'll gladly accept your offer that we exchange rooms."

Munro grunted and reached for his ale cup. "You'll be sorry you're jesting about your brothers' ghosts," he warned, tossing down a swig. "They *are* afoot and they willna be pleased with your mockery."

Jamie shrugged. "And I willna be pleased if I visit the Garbh Uisge and uncover one sign of fiddling—and I dinna mean yon Hughie Mac and his music!"

Sliding his arm around Aveline's waist, he drew her against him, feeling a need to shield her. "Whether the bridge is gone or not, there might yet be something left that the *bogles* dinna want us to see. If so, I mean to find it."

He glanced round at his kinsmen and friends, making sure everyone had heard him.

Hoping any *un*-friends who might be about, heard as well.

"And when I do, it won't be me who'll be the sorry one," he added, pulling Aveline along with him as he strode for the tower stair.

But their exit was marred by a feminine gasp, a rustling flurry of skirts as Gelis leapt to her feet and dashed after them.

"O-o-oh, you canna go near the cataracts," she cried, grabbing Jamie's arm. "Say you will not!"

He swung around and looked down at her, the fear in her eyes and the paleness of her face making him all the more determined to go indeed. Especially since she was Linnet MacKenzie's daughter.

He knew better than to discount warnings coming from that direction, but he also recognized the need for caution. So he patted her hand and forced a reassuring smile.

"Ne'er you worry," he lied, telling a falsehood to an unsuspecting female for what was surely the hundredth time in just the last few days. "I willna go near the Rough Waters."

But I might poke around a bit on the braeside over-looking them.

That last, of course, he left unsaid.

"I did not like the way she looked at you."

Aveline blurted her concern the moment they topped the turnpike stair head.

"Gelis?" Jamie shot her a bemused look. "The Black Stag's sassy wee gel?"

Aveline nodded.

She smoothed her hands on her skirts, annoyed by their dampness. Truth was, she hadn't seen anything *wee* on the MacKenzie lass.

Not that it mattered.

She'd liked the girl. And Jamie—clearly hearing with a man's ears—had totally misunderstood her.

Even so, she wished the words unsaid. But that was impossible, so she let him lead her down the dimly lit passage and into the empty bedchamber that had been his brother Kendrick's.

She bit her lip as they crossed the threshold, her own agitation immediately forgotten. Faith, but the room's silence twisted her heart.

Truth be told, she'd liked Kendrick tremendously. Though like her sisters and any female with a whit of sense, she'd known not to take him seriously. A notorious skirt-chaser; laughing-eyed, full of himself, and e'er amusing, he'd been the most dashing of the Macpherson brothers.

Quick to smile, outrageously flirtatious, and able to make even the most withered stick of a crone feel beautiful.

Aveline swallowed, fighting against the thickness in her throat.

Even the few times she'd glimpsed his ghost, he'd looked, well, larger than life.

Anything but . . . dead.

"Come, lass." Jamie looked at her over his shoulder. "You needn't fret o'er Gelis. Or fear this room. Kendrick isn't here."

But Aveline wasn't so sure.

Gelis didn't really bother her, but traces of Kendrick's zest lingered in the chamber and it was all she could do to keep from glancing about, looking for him.

Half-expecting him to swagger over to them, offering refreshments and a lusty, wicked tale, she shivered and clasped her hands before her, looking on as Jamie closed and bolted the door.

He *humphed* as soon as the drawbar slid into place, but

other than that noncommittal grunt, he gave no sign of intending to say more.

Far from it, he strode across the chamber, taking the night candle from the table beside the bed, then lighting it at the hearth. A charcoal brazier already hissed and glowed in one corner and a few of the wall sconces had been lit and were throwing off their light as well, but Jamie continued to move about with the burning taper, tipping its flame to the wick of every candle in the room.

"To better see the *bogles*," Aveline thought she heard him say.

But she'd been listening for other voices, finding it so hard to imagine Kendrick gone. And feeling not quite at ease claiming his quarters. The notion sent chills sliding up and down her spine no matter how many candles Jamie set to blazing.

An unnecessary extravagance, for enough moonlight streamed into the chamber to stretch deep into the room, silver-gilding the elegant trappings, illuminating the sumptuousness.

And the room was sumptuous.

Looking round, Aveline knew she'd seldom seen anything quite so fine.

Rather than the usual rushes, furred skins covered the wood-planked floor and still more furs, softer looking and more luxuriant, made the room's great four-poster bed an almost irresistible enticement.

Her heart thumping, she went to one of the arched windows and breathed deep of the chill damp air. The night smelled of rain, wet stone, wood ash, a soul-lifting hint of heather and Caledonian pine.

Soft mist and dark, lowering clouds.

The silvery sheen of the moon.

Night scents familiar to all Highlanders and not at all unlike she knew from Fairmaiden. But here, in this grand-seeming chamber with its heavy oaken furnishings and arras-hung walls, intoxications that caressed and stirred.

Rousing her deepest, most elemental yearnings. Desires even Kendrick's ghost couldn't squelch. Not with James of the Heather striding toward her, the look in his eyes melting her.

"You needn't fret o'er Gelis," he said again, stopping not a handsbreath away from her. Lowering his head, he brushed his lips ever so gently across hers. "I think you saw in the wood that night just who enchanted me."

He pulled away to look at her and she drew a shaky breath, the taste of him still heady and sweet on her lips.

"I did not mean—"

"I ken what you meant." He smoothed his knuckles down her cheek. "But you're worrying for naught. Duncan MacKenzie's daughters are like sisters to me. I could ne'er think of them otherwise. Though I'll admit they make fair gazing!"

Aveline glanced aside.

He caught hold of her chin, tilting her head for another kiss. A slow, soft one this time, with just a hint of tongue. "See you," he went on, ending the kiss, "those girls have been spoken for since birth."

He slid his arms around her, drawing her closer. "Leastways, it stands clear that they'll wed highborn husbands. If their father doesn't stop hiding them away behind his stout castle walls."

Aveline blinked. "I thought they were traveling north to seek possible matches?"

"Och, nay, sweetness. They came here for a different reason." Jamie splayed his hands across her back, rubbing her gently. Soothing her. "A reason that has little to do with their weddings, whene'er their da allows the like."

"You know the reason?"

Jamie looked aside, his gaze on the windows and the darkness beyond. "I have guessed, aye."

"And will you tell me?"

He was silent, but a muscle jerked in his jaw and Aveline would've sworn she felt him stiffen.

Och, aye, she could feel the ill ease thrumming all through him. A taut wariness she could almost taste, and troubling enough to make her own heart skitter.

So she circled her arms around his neck and twined her fingers in his hair, determined to hold fast until he told her what she wanted to know.

Needed to know.

"Can the reason have anything to do with the way Lady Gelis was looking at you in the hall?" She peered up at him. "When she ran up to us as we were leaving?"

"So that was the look you meant?" Jamie reached to caress her hair. "You were not jealous? Only concerned about her warning?"

"So it was a warning?"

He shrugged. "I can only guess, but I would say aye. Those three women came here for one reason. To warn me away from the Rough Waters."

Aveline shivered.

He disentangled himself from her grasp and began pacing about the room, peering into corners, eyeing the locked and bolted door.

The air around them seemed to darken, the very shadows drawing near. Until, watching him stride past a window, Aveline caught a glimpse of the moon sailing from behind a cloud and its silvery glow returned, once more filling the room with soft, shimmering light.

A cold light, for even the fine-burning log fire seemed to have lost its warmth.

Biting her lip, she rubbed her arms against the room's sudden chill. "Surely they cannot think something bad might happen to you, too?"

Jamie turned to face her. "Sweet lass, I'll own they *know* something unpleasant will happen," he said, not wanting to frighten her, but thinking it best she hear the truth. "The lassies' mother has the *taibhsearachd*. Her gift is unfailing and so true as I'm standing here. I have seen the proof of her abilities many times."

Aveline's heart stopped. "And you think she's seen something?"

"I can think of no other reason for them to come here." Jamie rubbed the back of his neck. "Even their excuse about the Black Stag wanting to haggle with my da over a stirk or two rings false."

"Because he's always sent his men to do the like?"

"Exactly."

"Then you must make them tell you what they know." She hurried over to him, clutching at him. "If they know you've guessed, they will not keep it from you."

Jamie shook his head. "They've already revealed

more than is wise," he said, catching one of her hands and bringing it to his lips. "Highland as you are, you ought to know it isn't wise to poke and prod into what's revealed to those with second sight. They've given me a warning and I'm accepting it gladly."

Aveline frowned. "But—"

"It is enough. And more help than many receive."

He turned her hand and dropped a kiss into her palm, folding her fingers over it. "You keep that kiss to yourself and let it soothe you when you worry," he said, smiling at her. "And keep whate'er we discuss between us."

Her eyes flew wide. "You fear treachery?"

Jamie put his hands on her shoulders. "After seeing the sky darken with English cloth-yards at Neville's Cross, there is not much left to fear," he said, meaning it. "Least of all anyone cowardly enough to drape themselves in a wet plaid and try to frighten an old man."

But I do fear what such a miscreant might do to you.

Leaving that concern unspoken, he went to stand before the hearth, trying hard not think about what burned so merrily on its grate.

"I do not doubt what you've told me, lass." He raked a hand through his hair and hoped she'd believe him. "I am sure you did see Neill and Kendrick at the cairns, dancing with Hughie Mac. And down at the Garbh Uisge, too. Even so—"

"I did see them. I swear it," she insisted. "And they had to have been bogles. They vanished right before my eyes. Even as I was staring right at them."

She came to him then and he gathered her close.

"Leastways that was the way of it in the churchyard. At the cataracts, they just sort of drifted off into the trees."

"Ah, well." Jamie stroked her hair. "'Tis not my brothers' spirits that concern me. 'Tis the bastard masquerading as a ghost that's plaguing me."

She looked doubtful. "You truly think someone is?"

Jamie cocked a brow at her. "Can you truly think someone isn't? After what we found in the chapel and then discovered upon returning here?"

And to his relief, she shook her head.

"But what do you mean to do about it?"

Jamie grinned. "What I do best when the need arises," he said, flipping back his plaid to reveal the many-notched haft of his Norseman's ax and the leather-wrapped hilt of his sword. "Assure the safety of those I care about."

"And what about those I care about?" she returned, touching his cheek. "Those I know your father cares about. You are the one who received Lady Linnet's warning."

Jamie captured her hand, kissing her fingertips. "Och, I shall be careful, ne'er you worry."

He smiled again, pleased with the precautions he'd arranged.

"Even as we speak, Beardie and another cousin should be taking up position outside this chamber's door. And" —he winked— "Beardie wields an even deadlier Viking ax than I do. If you haven't yet noticed, he's rather proud of his Norse granddaddies. And he doesn't take kindly to anyone even glancing cross-eyed at a woman."

She peered up at him through her gold-tipped lashes, looking more confused than reassured. "You've set two guardsmen to protect me? Just like the two you ordered to see to your da?"

Jamie grinned again. "I've set two trusted men to guard the door. I shall protect you."

"Oh!" Her gaze flew to the large, fur-covered bed. "So you will be sleeping here?"

Jamie followed her gaze and immediately began to harden.

The very reason he would not spend the night in the same room with her. Especially not in his brother's sumptuous love nest of a bed.

Not just yet, anyway.

Clearing his throat he stepped to the side of the hearth, glad for a means to distract himself before the tightening at his loins overrode his good sense.

"I shall sleep in my da's chamber, as he wished," he told her, whipping aside a heavy tapestry to reveal an oaken door. "This room was once my mother's, see you. That is the true reason for its opulence. And you will be safe here, I promise."

She blinked, her jaw slipping when he opened the door to reveal a small anteroom. And, clearly visible on the other side of the wee chamber, a second closed door.

"The bedchambers are connected," he said, taking a wall torch from its bracket and ducking into the little room. "We'll leave the doors open and the torches burning."

"To scare away the bogles?"

Jamie cocked a brow but said nothing. He knew

enough of lasses to let her think what she would if doing so soothed her womanly mind.

Truth be told, he was the one in need of soothing.

She'd followed him to the open doorway, her beguiling violet scent and the proximity of her soft feminine warmth almost making him regret he'd mentioned the connecting doors.

He could easily have stayed with her in Kendrick's chamber. If only wrapped in his plaid before the fire. The saints knew he'd slept in more uncomfortable places than on his late brother's fur-strewn floor.

Hovering on the threshold of the anteroom, she watched him with great, luminous eyes.

"And you will know if something stirs?"

Jamie jerked as if she'd reached out and curled her fingers around him. If she knew the kind of stirrings her mere presence was causing him, she'd wish him back belowstairs—no matter how passionately she kissed.

She was yet a maid and he meant to go gently with her.

"Lass," he said, his voice thick, "I will know if the night wind shifts a raindrop on your window ledge."

His most courtly reassurance spoken, he touched the smoking torch to the anteroom's two wall sconces, satisfied when they caught flame and the little room filled with the same golden light as Kendrick's chamber.

In a matter of moments, his da's room would be awash with light as well.

But not to frighten bogles.

O-o-h, nay, he hoped they'd come.

Leastways the one who favored dripping plaid.

And if the lout did make an appearance, Jamie would be ready for him.

Him, his Norseman's ax, and his trusty blade—whiche'er death the *ghost* preferred.

Chapter Eight

✤

A sennight later, Aveline paused on the landing outside Jamie's former bedchamber, a well-laden dinner tray clutched in her hands. Munro's dinner tray, for he alone whiled behind the chamber's closed oaken door.

And judging by the silence from within, Aveline suspected he slept.

But when she shifted the tray onto her hip and eased open the door, she found him sitting up in bed, propped against his pillows and rummaging through a great iron-bound chest.

A scuffed and somewhat rusty strongbox that looked very much like the one her father had sent Munro as her bride price, but that she knew contained only stones.

And sure enough, a scattering of stones were strewn across the bedcovers.

Stones and a few rolls of ancient-looking parchments.

Aveline took a deep breath, debating whether to retreat or stay.

"Sir," she finally called. "I've brought—"

"For mercy!" Munro looked up, jerking as if he'd been stung.

He slammed shut the chest's lid and grabbed for the parchments, crumpling one in his hand but sending two others fluttering to the floor.

"Saints, lass," he said, his brow furrowing, "I wasna expecting a meal this e'en." He eyed the steaming bowl of stewed beef and fresh-baked bannocks, but his mind was clearly elsewhere. "Morag said she'd be away, a-seeing to some ailing glen wife and Jam—er, ah . . . *that one* claimed he had business of his own."

Aveline forced a smile. "You should have known I wouldn't let you go without aught to eat," she said, trying not to look at her father's damning strongbox.

Embarrassment heating her cheeks, she approached the bed with the tray. "I know Morag or Jamie usually bring your victuals, but I thought you wouldn't mind if I did in their absence?" she asked, placing the food on a table beside the bed. "I can sit with you while you eat—"

She broke off, a whirl of doubts rushing her.

Her father's chest sat on the floor opposite the bed, its heavy iron lock undisturbed.

"I thought you were looking in my father's strongbox," she said, only now seeing that the chest on the bed appeared much older than the one containing her *bride stones*.

Following her gaze, Munro swore and scrambled to his feet. "This has naught to do with Alan Mor and dinna you tell a soul what you've seen," he said, snatching the fallen parchments off the floor, then trying to scoop up the stones spread across the bedcovers.

Lovely stones.

And as Aveline now recognized, each one was beautifully smooth and rounded, and in an array of striking colors. Some green, some reddish, with a few black ones shot through with sparkling ribbons of quartz.

The kind of stones she and her sisters had collected as children, up on the high moors. Treasures, the pretty little stones had been. And from the way Munro was clutching his, she had a sneaking suspicion he cherished these as highly.

Likewise the tattered-edged scrolls he'd jammed under a pillow.

"Not a word," he warned again, this time inching up the lid of the chest just enough to drop the stones inside. "I willna have that old she-goat belowstairs laughing at me and young Jamie needn't ken—"

"Needn't ken what?" Aveline turned to the table and poured a measure of ale into a cup. "I don't understand," she added, handing him the brew.

"No one would understand." Munro seated himself on the edge of his bed and took a deep swallow. "Not after all these years."

"All these years?"

Munro *humphed*.

Then he pressed his lips together and glanced aside.

Aveline looked closely at him, seeing not only the stubborn set to his jaw but the over-brightness of his eyes.

She also caught a faint whiff of something she hadn't

noticed until now. Not until he'd reopened the lid of his chest.

It was the pungent tang of heather.

Old heather.

Puzzled, she sniffed again, certain the distinctive smell came from the old laird's strongbox.

And then she knew.

Between the scent and the stones, anyone with even a shred of sentimentality would have guessed. Especially anyone from these parts—folk who knew how fond Munro was of walking the high moors.

Especially the heather-grown moor known locally as *Iona's Heath.*

The rumored trysting place of Munro and his late lady wife, Iona, in the long ago days of their youth.

The woman who'd died birthing Jamie.

And, as the tongue-waggers also claimed, Munro was never able to forget.

"Och, nay." Aveline's heart clenched. She took the empty ale cup from him and returned it to the table. "Dinna tell me you've filled that chest with—"

"All I have," he blurted, the stubbornness going out of his jaw, but the brightness in his eyes now damping his cheeks. "My memories," he added, reaching to lift the lid of the chest. "One handful of heather and one stone for each year she's been gone. I collect them every year up on the moors, on the eve of her passing."

"Jamie's birthday." Aveline's own eyes misted as she peered into the chest at the clumps of dead and dried heather, Munro's collection of colored stones.

Swallowing against the sudden thickness in her throat,

she sat beside Munro and hugged him. "It wasn't his fault," she said, hoping she wasn't making it worse, but feeling compelled to speak. "Jamie cares about you. I suspect he always has. Perhaps if you—"

"I'm no dried-up husk without a heart." Twisting round, Munro yanked one of his parchments from beneath the pillow and thrust it at her. "I've kept abreast o' the lad o'er the years."

Her own heart thumping, Aveline unrolled the scrunched-up missive and began reading. Sent by a man she knew to be one of Munro's allies, the parchment was dated about a year before and detailed Jamie's valor during the tragic Scots defeat at the battle of Neville's Cross near the English city of Durham.

She looked at Munro, not knowing what to say.

He humphed again and reached into his strongbox, fishing deep into the clumps of heather until he withdrew another handful of squished and yellowed scrolls.

"There are others—as you can see." He stuck out his chin, his eyes now glinting with a touch of belligerence. "Years' worth."

Aveline set down the Neville's Cross parchment and took a deep breath.

Munro stared at her, his mouth set in a straight, hard line.

"You must show the scrolls to Jamie," she said, disappointed when the old laird's expression didn't soften.

"That they exist ought to be enough," he said. "And you'll say naught about them. I'll have your word on that."

Aveline sighed, but finally nodded.

"As you will," she agreed, her heart aching for Jamie. And his father.

Munro Macpherson was wrong. The mere existence of his scrolls wasn't enough to smooth the rift between him and his only surviving son.

But it was a beginning.

A notion that would not have pleased the shrouded figure standing in the swirling mist high above the Garbh Uisge and peering down at the racing, roaring cataracts.

Healing, justice-bringing rapids. Quiet now, save for the deafening rush of the water; the fitful winds rattling the birches and bog myrtle clustered so thickly on the steep braesides.

Nothing else stirred.

The curses and shouts that had shattered the gorge's peace on a certain fateful day were silent now and those who'd deserved to die slept cold and stiff in their graves.

All save one.

And he, too, would soon be no more.

His father, bluster-headed coward that he was, would do himself in. Fear and guilt were his enemies. No great effort would be required to rid the hills of him.

A few others might follow as well.

If a greater atonement proved necessary.

The beginnings of a most satisfying smile twitched at the corner of the figure's lips. A soft, much-deserved laugh was also allowed. There was no need not to savor the moment. The darkening woods and the frothy white gleam of the water. The pleasure that deepened with each return to the scene of the figure's shining triumph.

Aye, it was a moment to be relished.

And with the exception of the figure's dark and flowing cloak and its shielding hood, there was no need for caution. Enough mist and rain had descended on Kintail in recent days for there to be ample cover to slip inside one of gorge's deep, mist-filled corries should any fool risk a visit to this devil-damned defile.

The figure sniffed. Nay, unexpected intruders were not a concern.

Neither from Baldreagan or Fairmaiden.

The winding deer track from Fairmaiden, especially, was choked with drifting curtains of thick, creeping mist. No one from that holding of reformed cutthroats and new-to-the-soft-life caterans would desire to bestir themselves on such a gray and clammy afternoon.

And if they did, it wouldn't be to trek through chill, impenetrable mist just to gain the treacherous confines of the Rough Waters. Those who dwelt at Fairmaiden relished their comfort too greatly to brave the gorge's steep, rock-lined shoulders save on fair, sun-filled days.

And the fools cowering within Baldreagan's blighted, hell-born walls were too busy poking about elsewhere to pose a serious threat. Too occupied switching bedchambers and lighting candles, thinking smoking pitch-pine torches and bolted doors would protect them.

The figure stared out over the Garbh Uisge, admiring the gloom and flexing eager fingers. Truth was, all the heather and stone in Scotland wouldn't hide them if a *bogle* wished to find them.

Whether they paid a visit to the ravine again or nay.

Though it could be surmised that *he* stayed away because his silly bride dogged his every breath and step.

His faery.

The figure scowled and clenched angry fists.

Only the great flat-footed James of the Heather would come up with such a ludicrous endearment.

Och, aye, that one was too chivalrous for his own good and wouldn't want to take a chance on the wee one trailing after him into the mist and twisting her precious ankle on a leaf-covered tree root.

Or worse.

Like watching a puff of wind blow her away.

Perhaps looking on in horror as she lost her footing on the slippery, streaming slopes and plunged headlong into the icy, tossing waters. Hitting her fair head on one of the many waiting rocks.

Black and jagged rocks.

So deadly.

And utterly innocent. Who could foist blame upon the dark, serrated edges of a rock if a soul was careless enough to fall atop it?

Certainly not the fools who'd gathered the remains of the footbridge and then been empty-headed enough to burn the wood without even noticing the saw marks and gouges it'd taken to cause the worm-eaten, weather-warped old bridge to collapse.

The figure smiled again.

And moved closer to the edge of the ravine.

If one leaned forward a bit and looked carefully enough into the foaming cauldron, it was almost possible to imagine a swirl of pale, streaming hair caught in the tossing waters. A dainty hand, reaching out for a rescuer that would never appear.

Or, even more pleasing, a flash of bright auburn hair and a quick glimpse of a bonnie male face, the eyes wide with terror and the mouth roaring a silent, water-filled scream.

But all the cries and thrashings would prove for naught.

Just as they hadn't helped his brothers when the footbridge had given way beneath them. The figure's lips began to quirk again and a warm, pleasant sense of satisfaction banished the afternoon's chill.

The Macpherson brothers had dropped like stones.

And most of them hadn't even struggled, for all their swagger and boasting in life. Their black-hearted gall and deceit. They'd sputtered and gasped for breath, flopping about like hapless flotsam, letting the current speed them to their deaths.

A few had fought fiercely, kicking their legs and flailing their arms, wild-eyed and shouting, cursing down the sun.

But the sun hadn't cared.

And neither had the lone figure standing high above them, looking on with an approving smile.

A smile that had soured just over a sennight ago when happenchance allowed the figure to witness an act of infuriating passion.

A kiss so shamelessly heated even the memory scalded.

And in a holy place, standing on the threshold of St.

Maelrhuba's chapel and in clear view of the Na Clachan Breugach stone.

The figure shivered and stepped back from the lip of the gorge. Not wanting to invoke the older, darker powers that might frown on taking such justice into one's own hands, the figure adjusted the folds of its great, voluminous cloak and slipped back into the mists and shadows.

While St. Maelrhuba's influence might be a bit watered down after so many long centuries, there wasn't a Highlander walking who'd doubt the lingering sway of the ancients.

The mysterious Picts and others.

Shadow folk one would be wise not to rile.

Passing by the Na Clachan Breugach stone each time a visit to the ruinous chapel was required was daunting enough. Kissing in the shadow of such a stone, and then so lustily, was to call up a thousand devils.

Never mind that in the days of the ancients more lascivious acts than kissing had surely gone on within the sacred circle of those hoary stones.

Stones of Wisdom or the Lying Stones, only one remained and the figure was sure it hadn't been pleased to witness such a kiss.

Such passion.

And so, the figure decided, moving stealthily through the trees, measures would need to be taken to ensure such passion didn't flame again.

Only then would the stone be appeased.

And the figure's grievances well met and avenged.

*   *   *

About the same time and not all that far from the swirling waters of the Garbh Uisge, Jamie followed Alan Mor into his privy solar at Fairmaiden Castle. Once again, he marveled at the little room's cheery warmth and beauty. This time he also wondered if he hadn't misjudged his host.

Perhaps placed unwarranted suspicion on his doorstep.

Truth was, whether he found it hard to believe or not, the Matheson laird looked genuinely outraged and appalled.

And, Jamie couldn't deny, exceedingly innocent.

Leastways of having had anything to do with the deaths of Jamie's brothers.

Alan Mor's indrawn breath and the way he'd leapt from his seat at the high table when Jamie stated his reason for visiting was testament enough to his surprise. Even now, his bushy-bearded face was visibly pale.

Clearly shaken, he raked a hand through his hair and strode to the shuttered windows, then wheeled back around almost as quickly. "I would not be party to such a black deed if my own life depended on it," he vowed. "Or the lives of my fair daughters."

"But you understand I had to come here?"

"Och, aye," Alan Mor owned. "I just canna think who would do such an evil thing."

He started pacing, rubbing the back of his neck as he stalked around the solar. "I'll admit your da and I have had our bones to chew, but any feuding we carried on has e'er been amiable feuding. Anyone in these hills will tell you that. Though I willna deny we keep a wary eye on each other. But see Munro's lads done in?"

He stopped in front of the hearth fire and shook his bearded head. "Nay, lad, I had naught to do with the like."

Jamie frowned.

Ne'er had he accused any man of such a vile deed.

Even by association.

But he'd seen and heard what he had.

His brothers were as dead as dead can be. He couldn't back down. If he hadn't been able to save them, he could at least honor them now with his persistence in uncovering their murderer.

And hopefully, in the doing, prevent more tragedies.

Someone had appeared in his father's bedchamber draped in a dripping plaid—a plaid that selfsame someone later tossed onto the effigy of one of Jamie's long-dead forebears.

Although he'd not discount Aveline's insistence that she and others have seen his brothers' ghosts, Jamie was certain the *bogle* plaguing Munro was a flesh-and-blood man.

Someone well capable of tampering with an age-worn footbridge.

And, he suspected, equally guilty of recently mixing fish bones in a kettle of porridge meant for consumption at Baldreagan's high table.

A near disaster he'd learned of just recently, the almost-tragedy, averted thanks to Cook's watchful eye.

Just now, though, Alan Mor's eyes were on him, waiting. So Jamie put back his shoulders and plunged on.

"In truth, sir, I canna think who would have done it either," he said, speaking true. "I—" He broke off when the door opened and Sorcha entered with a large flagon of warmed, spiced wine.

Jamie nodded to her, gladly accepting the cup she offered him. He also tried not to frown again. But it proved difficult for her presence made him keenly aware of the loss of his brothers.

His reason for visiting Alan Mor.

Taking a sip of the wine, he turned back to his host. "After what I've told you, surely you must see that someone is responsible?"

"So it would seem," Alan Mor agreed after a few moments of brow-furrowing. "But" —he whipped out his dirk and thrust it at Jamie, hilt first—"I'd sooner have you ram my own blade into my heart if you think my hands are stained with your brothers' blood."

Jamie took the dirk and tucked it carefully back beneath the older man's thick leather belt. "I can see it was not your doing," he said, meaning it.

But the matter remained unresolved.

He slid an uncomfortable glance at Sorcha, not wanting to besmirch her father's house and his associations in her presence. But she didn't seem to be paying them any heed.

She was seeing to the fire, jabbing a long iron poker into the flames, and he couldn't help thinking of the hearth fires at Baldreagan, each grate well laid with smoldering pieces of the footbridge.

The notion called his brothers' nine faces to mind and

he could almost feel their stares. They wanted and deserved their deaths avenged.

Something he'd never see accomplished if he fretted about offending those who might have answers.

So he took a deep breath and cleared his throat. "Your men," he began, watching Alan Mor closely, "can there be one amongst them who'd carry such hatred against my clan?"

"My men of Pabay? The reformed cutthroats as the glen wives call them?" Alan Mor waved a dismissing hand. "There's not a one o' them I'd trust to commit such a barbarous act."

"But they wouldn't have come to you from Pabay—the robbers' isle—if they didn't carry a good share of dark deeds on their shoulders."

"Dark deeds, aye. But there are degrees of villainy."

Jamie cocked a brow. "I've ne'er heard the like."

To his surprise, Alan Mor grinned and thwacked him on the shoulder. "Lad, now you see why I've trusted my wee lassie to your care. One look at you and a man knows you'd ne'er do ought to hurt her."

Jamie almost choked on his wine. "To be sure I'd ne'er harm her. I'd kill any man who tried."

"Well, now! Isn't that what I just meant?" Alan Mor grinned at him. "And, aye, there are degrees of villainy, but my Pabay men have put their days of thieving and deceit behind them. Though a few are scoundrels. I willna deny that."

He paused and jerked his head meaningfully at his daughter, waiting until she left the solar and the door closed softly behind her.

"Nevertheless, there isn't a murderer amongst my men," he continued, folding his arms. "That's always been a line I refused to cross. If you knew aught about such men as call Fairmaiden their home, you'd know they'd ne'er do aught to lose their welcome here."

He fixed Jamie with a piercing stare. "See you, I give them a chance to make a new life. They'd be fools to vex me."

Jamie returned the stare. "There's something you aren't telling me," he said, certain of it.

Alan Mor blew out a breath. "Only that there are some in these parts who do bear grievances against your da."

"Who?" Jamie took a step forward. "Name them if you know."

"Ach, laddie, would that I could," Alan Mor returned. "But doing so would mean naming every laird and chieftain e'er to purchase cattle from your father."

Jamie stared at him. "You mean men vexed o'er his cattle prices."

Alan Mor nodded and poured them both new cups of wine. "Munro's haggling and scheming to squeeze the last coin out of his buyers has earned bad blood," he said, handing Jamie one of the replenished cups. "Likewise his gloating when he succeeds. If you'd e'er seen him preen and squawk as he tucks away his money pouches, you'd understand."

"Och, I understand," Jamie assured him.

His da *was* filled with wind and bluster. And he did relish trumpeting his own horn.

"I'm glad you do understand," Alan Mor said.

"Though I still canna see one of those up-backed cattle lairds going to such extremes to vent their spleen. Highland honor forbids such low-stooping, whether a man is rightly grieved or no."

He paused for a sip of wine, then dragged his sleeve across his mouth. "Nay, laddie, I dinna think you'll find the murderer amongst Munro's cattle buyers."

"Neither do I." Jamie took his own wine and went to stand at the window.

Setting down his cup, he unlatched the shutters and opened them wide. The air held a biting chill and full darkness would soon claim the eerie half-light, so filled with shadows and damp, sighing wind.

He stood rigid, staring out at the gray pall of mist. Thick, drifting sheets of it curled across Fairmaiden's bailey and the surrounding woods.

Woods that bordered on some of the finest, most lush grazing grounds in Kintail. Fairmaiden's greatest prize and a treasure he could scarce believe would soon be his.

Leastways a goodly portion of it.

He was quite sure his da wouldn't have parted with an inch of such sweet, rich pasturing lands. No matter how many daughters he might have had to dower.

And that was another question he had to put to Alan Mor.

Once and for all time.

He turned from the hushed silence beyond the window. "I will find my brothers' murderer," he said, willing it so. "No darkness will be black enough for the bastard to hide in for long. But I would ask one more question of you."

Alan Mor shrugged. "I've naught to hide."

"Save the stones weighting down the bride price coffers you gave my da."

To Jamie's surprise, the older man laughed. "A private jest," he said, sounding not at all put out that Jamie knew. "Call it repayment for all the years your da has fleeced me to the bone each time I've been fool enough to buy a stirk or two from him."

He wagged a finger at Jamie. "That'll be the reason the pop-eyed lout hasn't complained. He knows he owes me."

Jamie folded his arms. "What I would know is why the alliance in the first place? Both your daughter Sorcha to Neill, and now giving Aveline to me?"

He glanced at the closed door, wishing it were bolted. Or perhaps even better, opened wide. Simply to ensure curious ears weren't pressed against the wood.

Especially Sorcha's for he had no desire to stoke the maid's sorrow.

"Aye," he went on, looking back at Alan Mor, "I canna wrap my mind around your willingness to forge a bond between our houses. It's bothered me since I first received your missive at Cuidrach Castle, and it still plagues me. Though I am more than pleased to have Aveline as my bride."

"Why shouldn't I wish peace between our houses? A lasting bond?" Alan Mor jutted his chin. "Mayhap I've grown weary of feuding?"

"Amiable feuding," Jamie reminded him.

"So I have said."

"You have the better grazing lands," Jamie pointed out. "By your own admission, you must've bought enough Baldreagan bulls o'er the years to have enriched and strengthened the blood of your own herd."

"Would you believe because your cattle are protected by old Devorgilla's rowan charms?"

Jamie shook his head. "Not for a heartbeat."

Alan Mor curled his fingers around his belt. "Suffering saints, laddie, I hope my wee daughter ne'er gets on your wrong side!" he said, but his tone was amused. "If you'd have the truth of it, there is another reason I sought this alliance. But it has naught to do with your brothers. That I swear."

"Then what is it?"

Alan Mor pressed his lips together, scratched his bearded chin.

And said nothing.

But the faint tinge staining his cheeks assured Jamie he did have something to say.

Jamie waited. "Well?"

"Ach, simply this." Alan Mor swept his arm in a great arc to take in the splendor of his privy solar. The fine tapestries dressing the walls and the costly standing candelabrum with its pleasantly-scented beeswax tapers. The richly carved settle by the door with its sea of welcoming cushions.

Even the flagon of heady spiced wine they'd been sipping. The generously-laden platters of cheese, confits, and sweetmeats spread on a table near the window.

Alan Mor enjoyed his comforts and Jamie couldn't

fathom what the man's high taste had to do with making peace with his long-time feuding partner.

Good-natured bickering or no.

Unless . . .

Jamie's brows drew together. The notion forming in his mind was too preposterous to put in words.

"I canna believe you feel threatened by my da?" he asked, regardless. "Dinna tell me you feared he'd seize Fairmaiden? Take your riches from you?"

"Sure as I'm standing here, that's the reason I wished an alliance with the cross-grained devil," Alan Mor admitted, his face coloring a deeper red. "Though it was ne'er Munro himself who concerned me. The saints know he hasn't roused himself to raid a neighboring keep in more years than I can count!"

Jamie frowned. "That still doesn't explain the alliance."

"Nay?" Alan Mor guffawed. "I'm a-thinking it does well enough. If you think about it! See you, I'm a man who appreciates his leisure. I had my share of warring in my younger days, even traipsed across the land and the Isles with the good King Robert Bruce in his fraught and hungry years before he won his crown."

He started pacing again. "And I've done my own share of devilry, cattle stealing and the like. Why do you think I open my doors to the men of Pabay and other souls like them? Broken men can find a home here, warm themselves at my hearth and drink my ale. They are welcome to make their pallets in my hall."

He threw Jamie a challenging look. "So long as they've put their roving days and banditry behind them.

I want no cause to lose what I've worked so hard to gain. My peace of a night" —he paused to plump one of the settle cushions—"and my comforts."

"Begging pardon," Jamie said, "but I doubt my da cares whether Fairmaiden is filled with luxuries or if you and your men sleep on straw."

I doubt he cares where and how I sleep.

But he kept that last to himself.

"I told you—it isn't your da," Alan Mor said, helping himself to a sugared sweetmeat. "It's his fool cattle dealing and the enemies he's made because of it. High-placed enemies in some cases and I canna afford to have such long-nosed snoopers poking around hereabouts."

Taking a handful of the sweetmeats, he dropped onto the settle, looking suddenly tired. "See you, even though my men have ceased spreading havoc across the heather, there isn't a one o' them whose name wouldn't perk ears in certain lawful places. So it's been my concern that your father's dealings might cause the wrong souls to come swarming into these parts one o' these years."

Jamie's brows shot up. "So that's why you wished an alliance? To keep away the law?"

Alan Mor nodded. "I willna have a grieved cattle laird sending a sheriff across my land to get to yours and, by happenchance, discovering how many reformed cutthroats dine at my table!"

"But how would an alliance prevent such a thing?"

"Because," Alan Mor wiped his mouth and leaned forward, "your brother Neill had a far sounder head on his shoulders and knew how to settle a fair deal. I'd hoped the marriage of Munro's eldest son would see him managing more of your da's lairdly duties. He would've tempered the dangers and grievances your father seems to stir whene'er he opens his mouth."

"I see," Jamie said, understanding at last. "And you think my marriage to Aveline will bring the same benefits?"

"That is my hope." Alan Mor stood. "Aye, there you have it."

"Then I shall do my best not to disappoint you," Jamie said, the words surprising him.

Ne'er would he have imagined he'd one day be offering a hand of peace to Baldreagan's bristling bear of a neighbor.

And a well-meant hand of peace, at that.

The door swung open then and Sorcha stepped inside. "'Tis almost vespers," she said, glancing at the now darkened window arches. "The evening meal is set in the hall if you care to come belowstairs? And" —she looked from her father to Jamie and back again— "I need to know if an extra bed needs to be prepared for the night?"

"You are kind, but I must return to Baldreagan," Jamie told her, already making for the door. "I've already tarried too long. Though I will stay for a quick bread and ale, aye."

But a short while later, as he pushed back from Alan Mor's table, his words kept circling in his head, haunting him.

. . . *Tarried too long.*

He could think of something else that had lasted too long.

Namely the rift between himself and his sire.

A matter he needed to devote more attention to and would, as soon as he'd rid Baldreagan of bogus bogles and avenged his brothers' deaths.

Hopefully the coming days would bring success.

And since the alternative wasn't acceptable, he'd simply have to ensure that they did.

Chapter Nine

❧

"Gunna of the Glen?"

Aveline's fingers stilled, her needle poised over her handiwork. Her question hovered in the hall's smoke-hazed air, almost alive, definitely taunting her. Worse, she could feel her pulse beating in her throat, and so rapidly she was sure the others would notice.

But she'd had to ask.

Something about the way Gelis had said the woman's name struck dread into her heart.

As did the pointed glances Arabella and Lady Juliana turned on the girl. Not to mention the high color now staining Gelis's cheeks and how she promptly lost the ability to meet Aveline's eye.

"Who is she?" Aveline's gaze flitted between the three MacKenzie women.

"She is no one," Lady Arabella finally said, glancing up from her own needlework, but not without sliding an-other chastising look at her younger sister. "Gunna of the

Glen is a widow, naught else. She dwells in a side glen near our cousin Kenneth's holding, Cuidrach Castle, and is best known for her golden herrings."

Gelis sniffed and began jabbing at her embroidery work with particular relish. "Herrings—bah!"

Ignoring her, Arabella set her stitching aside and stood, pressing a hand against the small of her back. "Prized smoked herrings," she intoned, glancing round as if to dare anyone in Baldreagan's crowded great hall to deny it.

"Smoked herrings and her skill in bed." Gelis lifted her chin, accepting the challenge. "Our own father admits there isn't a man in Kintail who hasn't enjoyed her charms! She has masses of long, silky hair the color of soot and breasts said to bring even the most fierce Highland warrior to his knees at just a glance. Some even say she keeps herself e'er naked and that her voice alone is enough to—"

"You have ne'er seen her," Arabella quipped. "Mother says she has a kind heart."

Gelis snorted. "Mother likes everyone. Have you ne'er heard the glen folk call her St. Linnet?"

"Hush," Lady Juliana admonished them, her own needlework long finished and set aside. "I am sure Lady Aveline has no wish to hear of a Glenelg joy woman."

But Aveline did.

Especially since Gelis had let slip that Jamie had been known to pay calls to the voluptuous beauty. A creature said to be irresistible. Whether Linnet MacKenzie found her kind or no, Aveline didn't like the sound of her.

But the matter appeared closed, as the other three

women had clamped their lips together as tightly as if they'd bitten into something sour.

"Now you see why we must leave on the morrow," Lady Juliana said after a few uncomfortable moments. "Our purpose in coming here has been met. Jamie now knows it would not be wise to visit the Garbh Uisge and you've promised to encourage him to be cautious if he does venture there."

Aveline bit her lip. Having grown up with a bevy of sisters, all of them save Sorcha married and away, she'd relished the company of the MacKenzie women. Even if their stay meant finding out about a well-made joy woman in some faraway side glen, she'd be sad to see them leave.

She slid a glance across the hall to the high table where Munro sat eating his meal. He, too, would regret the women's departure. Even now, occupied as he was enjoying cheese pasties and roasted chicken, no one could miss how his gaze repeatedly sought the lively MacKenzies. The pleasure he took in their company.

Pleasure that meant a much-deserved distraction.

Aveline's heart dipped.

"I will miss you," she said, returning her attention to the visitors. "Everyone will. You've only been here a short while—"

"Trust me," Lady Juliana interrupted, glancing at Gelis, "it is better for us to leave before our welcome frays. A boiling cauldron can be cooled, but once it spills over, the damage is done."

Standing, she brushed at her skirts. "Indeed, we should

retire now and see to our packing. The way north is long and difficult. An early night will serve us well."

"I am not yet tired," Gelis objected, making no move to budge from her stool. "We've not yet told Aveline about our marriage stone ceremony. With her own wedding celebrations set for the spring and Jamie having squired at Eilean Creag, mayhap she'd like to hear of it?"

Clearly warming to the idea, she leaned forward, her eyes lighting. "Perhaps she'd even wish to come to Eilean Creag for the wedding? Use the stone—"

"Only MacKenzies can use the stone," Arabella reminded her. "Jamie squiring at Eilean Creag does not make him a MacKenzie, much as we love him."

Aveline tried to look interested, but what she wanted was to hear more about Gunna of the Glen.

More specifically, Jamie's visits to her.

"Marriage stone ceremony?" she asked, her heart not in the words.

Gelis nodded. "'Tis a more romantic tale than any French ballad."

But Aveline scarce heard her.

Her ears still rang with the girl's earlier chatter about the raven-haired joy woman with her sultry voice and magnificent breasts. More discomfited than she wished to show, she stole another look across the hall, this time scanning the torch-lit entry for a particularly broad set of shoulders and a familiar flash of bright auburn hair.

But she only saw Hughie Mac making his hunched way toward her, his own auburn hair age-faded and streaked with gray.

He clutched his fiddle in one hand and his horn-handled crummock in the other, using the long walking stick to propel himself to where the women had claimed a reasonably warm and well-lit corner to do their stitching patterns.

That, and engage in female babble.

The latter being an occupation Aveline now wished they'd ne'er embarked upon.

But Hughie Mac had a way about him, with his laughing eyes and good humor. Older than stone and many claimed just as wise, he hobbled forward, his hazel stick *tap-tapping* through the floor rushes, his grizzled appearance somehow lost in the warmth of his smile.

Aveline sprang to her feet, quickly fetching an extra stool and setting it in the warm glow of a nearby brazier.

"The MacKenzies' marriage stone?" Hughie Mac looked round as he lowered himself onto the stool. "I've seen it once," he said, resting his fiddle across his knees and leaning his crummock against the wall. " 'Tis a beautiful and mysterious stone."

"Mysterious?" Aveline echoed, reclaiming her seat on one of the twin facing benches of a window embrasure. "I thought it was a marriage stone?"

"And so it is. In truth, a swearing stone like so many others scattered around our hills and glens," Hughie Mac revealed, stretching his legs toward the warmth of the brazier. "A good-sized standing stone of a fine bluish cast and carved with ancient Celtic runes, the MacKenzie stone is more fair than most such stones but it shares the usual hole through its middle."

"It's the centerpiece of every MacKenzie wedding feast," Gelis enthused, plopping down beside Aveline.

She curled her legs beneath her and grabbed a pillow, hugging it close. "At the height of the feast, four of our brawniest warriors carry the stone into the hall and parade it about for all to admire while our seneschal approaches the high table with a ceremonial chalice of hippocras for the bride and groom to share."

"The happy twain and certain young lasses who have no business sipping such a potent concoction!" Arabella put in, claiming a seat on the window bench facing them.

Gelis rolled her eyes. "Father himself gives me my own wee cup—as you well know!"

"Our father would pluck down the moon if you asked him," Arabella returned, flicking her dark braid over her shoulder. "Like as not, the sun, too. Even if fetching it down would mean forever branding his hands."

Gelis flashed a grin. "Do not fault me if he loves me best."

"He loves you both and none more than the other," Juliana interceded, turning to Hughie Mac with an apologetic shrug. "They are young," she said, and Hughie nodded, looking young as well, for the space of a breath.

His hair thick and rich-gleaming in the torchlight, his weather-worn face smooth and almost bonnie, and his crooked legs straight once more.

"Aye, they are young," he agreed, the moment passed. "They also left out the most exciting part of their clan's marriage stone ceremony."

Aveline looked at him. "The mysterious part?"

Hughie shook his head. "The mystery is the stone's origin," he said, nodding to the clansmen who'd gathered near to listen. One handed him a brimming ale cup and he took it gladly, tipping back a healthy swig.

"The exciting part is the kissing." Gelis leaned forward and swatted her sister with a tasseled cushion. "Is that not right?"

Arabella flushed. "You would enjoy the kissing part."

Gelis stuck out her tongue. "'Tis the best part," she said, smoothing her skirts. "Even if the silly legend has to be recited first."

"Silly legend?" Aveline lifted a brow.

"The tale of how our clan came to possess the marriage stone," Gelis told her. "But the kiss is better." She turned to Hughie Mac, smiling. "Do you know the kissing part?"

"To be sure, and I do," he said, taking up his fiddle. "After the ceremonial drink-sharing and the telling of the legend, the stone is carried thrice around the high table before the clansmen carrying it stop behind the laird's chair. The newlyweds then join hands through the hole in stone. They vow to honor the old gods and ask for their blessing."

He paused to wink at Gelis, playing a few lively notes clearly meant for her. "Then the groom takes his bride in his arms and the couple kiss—"

"Then they're escorted abovestairs for the bedding!" Gelis exclaimed, her eyes alight and her cheeks dimpling. "Mother won't allow us to join in that part," she admitted, fluffing her skirts.

"Och, indeed." Arabella rolled her eyes. "You've not missed a single bedding at Eilean Creag since you were old enough to realize everyone in the bedding chamber would be too ale-headed to notice you sneaking into the back of the room to watch!"

Gelis wriggled her braid at her sister. "At least I have learned about . . . things! 'Tis more than you can say."

"I am content to learn such things when it is time for my own bedding ceremony," Arabella snipped, her face scarlet.

"What is the stone's mystery?" Aveline asked, noting Lady Juliana's thinned lips and wanting to steer the conversation in a safer direction.

She glanced at Hughie, not surprised when he began playing a slower, almost heart-rending tune. "You said it's stone's origin?"

Hughie nodded. "No one knows the stone's true history or where it came from. There is a legend, aye."

Pausing, he waited until the hall quieted. "Magnificent as the stone is, its base is ragged and cracked as if it was wrested from its original location. All that is known is that the stone washed ashore at Eilean Creag and has been blessing MacKenzie marriages e'er since. 'Tis believed the power and beneficence of the old gods is vested in the stone."

"Then tell the tale," one of the younger MacKenzie guardsmen encouraged Hughie. Pushing through the crowd, he sat at the old man's feet, and soon a few others joined him.

Even Munro looked on from the high table, though he made no move to leave the dais.

"Ah, well . . ." Hughie glanced at Lady Juliana and raised a scraggly brow. "If it is not too late, my lady?"

Lady Juliana looked about to protest, but then smiled

and shrugged. "Those lasses would not sleep now even if I chained them to their beds," she said, the affection in her voice taking the sting out of her words.

Looking pleased, Hughie set down his fiddle and flexed his fingers before he started playing a soft, poignant tune.

"The legend of the MacKenzies' marriage stone hails from a distant time," he began, his voice seeming to swell and deepen on each word. "A time when Scotland was young and the old gods still held sway."

The hush in the hall thickened and those who'd gathered near edged closer. "Some claim the stone comes from the Land of Shadows, the hither side. If so, its true background will ne'er come to light," he said, his words falling sweet now, flowing and golden as his music. "Others say that Mananan, the old Celtic sea god sent the stone as reward for the MacKenzies' valor in battle. But most believe the stone has a more tragic past and that it is the version recited at MacKenzie wedding feasts."

Reaching down to stroke Cuillin's head when the old dog came to lie at his feet, he waited a few moments before he took up the tale again.

"Long ago, in an age before time was counted, a proud Celtic king dwelt not far from where Eilean Creag stands today," he said, his voice carrying to all corners of the hall. "A powerful and bold man, no enemy dared challenge him and 'tis even said the devil avoided him, knowing even he couldn't best such a formidable foe.

"The king had four daughters and they, too, stood in awe of him. Some might even say they feared him. Only his youngest lass laughed at his bluster, doing as she

pleased and so sure of his love, she saw no reason to hide
her wish to marry a young man she knew her father
would deem unworthy."

Hughie slid a glance at Gelis. "This daughter was his
favorite. She was also his destruction. So great was his
love for her that he raged for seven days and nights upon
learning of her betrayal. For even though the maid's
sweetheart was a braw and pure-hearted lad, his bonnie
face and strapping build would ne'er make up for his lack
of prospects; the empty future which was all he could
offer a bride of such noble birth."

Aveline slid a glance at Gelis, not surprised to see the
girl's stare fixed on Hughie.

He had that kind of effect on his listeners and his ability to weave a tale only seemed to grow richer with age.
Only Cuillin appeared restless, but with all eyes on
Hughie, that was understandable. Rapt tale-listeners do
not usually dole out tasty tidbits to hungry dogs.

Aveline, too, spared him only a moment's glance, then
looked back at Hughie, sorry to have missed even a few
words of his tale.

"Devastated to see how gravely she'd misjudged her
father's favor, the lass and her braw laddie ran away, fleeing to the marriage stone, certain its sanctuary would save
them.

"And it would have, for the stone's magic was powerful and true. Anyone gaining the sacred ground on which
it stood and then joining hands through the stone's hole,
would be blessed, their union sanctioned by the Old
Ones." Hughie set down his fiddle, his voice music
enough to finish the tale. "Sadly, the father was warned

and he chased after them, coming upon them the very moment the young lovers thrust their hands through the stone."

He paused again, looking satisfied by the thick quiet that had descended over the hall.

"The king's rage overcame him and he rushed forward, his fury giving him the strength to tear the stone from its cliff-side base and hurl it into the sea—his daughter's lover with it." Hughie pushed to his feet, using his long hazel stick to lean on. "The deed stopped the old king's heart as he'd ne'er meant to kill the young man, howe'er livid he'd been. Truly repenting, he fell to his knees, pleading his daughter's forgiveness. But the girl's pain went too deep. Not even looking at her father, she followed her sweetheart into death, calmly stepping off the cliff edge to claim in the netherworld the love she'd been denied in life."

"So furious were the old gods by the king's disregard for the stone's sanctuary," Gelis finished for him, "that they took away all he held dear, destroying his stronghold so thoroughly that not even a stone remained to mark where he'd once ruled."

"But all was not lost," Arabella supplied, "for many centuries later the stone washed up onto our little island and has been in our safekeeping ever since." She lifted her chin, looking round. "We believe the stone's magic is even more potent today and we guard it well, considering it our most prized possession. Every newlywed MacKenzie pair clasps hands through the stone and makes the ritual oath, thus pleasing the Ancient Ones and guaranteeing themselves a bond that no mortal man can destroy for the old gods watch o'er them, granting them their forever favor."

"I told you the tale was romantic." Gelis beamed at Aveline. "'Tis the stone's honest history. I feel it here," she declared, pressing a hand against her heart. "There really was an ancient king who threw our stone into the sea after killing his daughter's one true love and seeing her leap to her death. I am sure that was the way of it."

"The stone could have come from anywhere," Arabella countered. "We are blessed to have it at Eilean Creag and that is enough."

But Aveline doubted anyone outside the window embrasure had heard her, for ear-splitting applause suddenly erupted to chants of *"Hughie Mac! Another tale!"*

But Hughie simply smiled and shuffled back to his stool, his energy for the evening clearly spent.

"Another day," he promised, gratefully accepting the hot meat pastie and fresh cup of heather ale one of the MacKenzie guardsmen brought him. "I am glad I had the chance to be present at a MacKenzie wedding many years past. Were that not so, I could not have done justice to the tale, well-known as it is in these Kintail hills."

"We've heard there is a stone of uncertain origin here, too," Gelis chimed, reaching to touch Aveline's knee. "At the Macpherson's family chapel."

Aveline shivered, thinking of the wet plaid.

And how she'd seen Neill's and Kendrick's bogles dancing in the churchyard—along with Hughie Mac.

He, however, was sitting quite contentedly on his stool beside the little charcoal brazier, munching his meat pastie and saying nothing.

Even though, for a moment, she would have sworn he'd looked about say a great deal. Something he'd apparently decided to keep to himself, for his lined face now wore a decidedly shuttered, wary expression.

Aveline frowned and drew her arisaid closer around her shoulders, suddenly feeling chilled. Icy cold and almost certain that someone, or *something,* was watching her from the shadows.

She could feel the stare boring holes into her. An unfriendly stare, almost malignant.

"Is there such a stone?" Gelis pressed, her eager voice breaking the spell.

Aveline blinked, resisting the urge to shudder. "You mean the Na Clachan Breugach monolith," she said at last, speaking to Gelis, but watching Hughie from beneath her lashes.

Whoe'er or whate'er had been glaring at her, she was certain he'd also sensed the malice.

"The Na Clachan Breugach?" Gelis nudged her again.

Aveline nodded. "It stands in the clan burial ground and guards the entrance to St. Maelrhuba's chapel."

" 'Tis but a few paces from my cottage," Hughie spoke up, looking over at them. "The churchyard is a hoary old place, with the chapel half in ruin."

Aveline looked at him openly now, but his blue eyes were twinkling again and he continued to eat his pastie with relish, sharing bits of the meat filling with Cuillin and his castle dog friends, seemingly unaware of any reason he should feel uncomfortable at the mention of the stone. Or the little churchyard with its sad row of nine burial cairns, Celtic crosses, and mist.

Far from it, the look he sent her way was anything but sad.

Not that she had time to think about it, because Lady Juliana was bearing down on the window embrasure, the look in her eye brooking no refusal.

She meant to see the MacKenzie sisters to their beds.

Proving it, she drew up in front of Gelis. "You are a sly one," she said, planting her hands on her hips. "You know all about the Macpherson's Na Clachan Breugach stone. We discussed it some nights ago when Morag recounted the stone's deeper past. How it is said to be the last remaining stone of a sacred Pictish scrying circle once known as the Stones of Wisdom. And, too, how it might just be the Lying Stone as later Christians dubbed it."

Juliana folded her arms. "You've no need to hear the tales again. You do need come abovestairs and get some sleep."

Gelis frowned. "It is still early and—"

"It is late for you." Juliana jerked her head toward the nearby stair tower. "Say your good nights and come along."

Arabella rose dutifully to her feet.

Gelis stood as well, but not without casting a longing look at the comfortable embrasure bench with its maze of soft, embroidered cushions and the deep-set window arch, gilded silver with moon glow and rain.

"Aveline saw the ghosts of two of Jamie's brothers near the Na Clachan Breugach stone," she said, gathering her forgotten stitching patterns.

"Many Highlanders see a bogle or two in their lifetime," Juliana minded her, guiding her by the elbow away from the window embrasure.

"He's seen them, too," Gelis blurted, dragging her feet as they passed Hughie's stool. "Aveline said so."

"She spoke true." Hughie looked up from his second meat pastie. "I have seen the lads a time or two. Often enough to ken they are well and content where they are."

Aveline doubted Gelis heard him for Juliana was herding the girls at a fast clip toward the stair foot. But she'd heard him and it took her several moments to notice what was wrong when she glanced over at him.

Cuillin was gone.

Even though Hughie Mac still clutched a goodly portion of his meat pastie in his hand.

E'er ready for a handout, Cuillin would only have left the old man's side for one reason.

Jamie had returned.

Aveline spotted him at once, even clear across the hall. He stood before the wall laver in the hall's shadowy entry arch and was washing his hands. Cuillin, apparently of far keener senses than her own, was pressing himself against his master's legs, his plumy tail wagging.

But even if she'd spotted him second, her pleasure in seeing him was no less exuberant. Not even Munro's scowling face and demonstrative departure dampened her excitement. Already her heart was pounding and the desire to be pulled into his arms and kissed again proved almost overwhelming.

He spotted her then, too, and grinned, lifting his hand in greeting. But the instant she started forward, a vivid image rose up before her, blocking the way.

Transparent, shimmering, and vibrant, the vision-woman hovered in the aisle between the trestle tables.

Aveline blinked, but the image didn't fade.

Instead, she glowed all the brighter. A tall voluptuous woman with a luxurious spill of long glossy black hair. Her heady, musk-like perfume wafted around her like a dark, sensual cloud.

Even worse, she was naked.

Quite happily naked, judging by the seductive curve of her full red lips.

The smoldering heat in her midnight eyes.

Aveline stopped where she was, the hall and everyone in it spinning wildly around her. The floor even seemed to pitch and sway, but when the wheeling and dipping finally stopped, the frightful image was blessedly gone.

Better yet, she found herself where she'd yearned to be.

Jamie must've flown across the hall, because he stood holding her, his chin resting on top of her head.

"Saints, lass, I thought you were going to swoon," he said, tightening his arms around her. "You went chalk white and swayed. You would've hit the rushes if I hadn't run to catch you."

Aveline drew a shaky breath and pulled back just enough to look up at him. "You do that well—as you've already shown me. In the chapel, if you've forgotten."

"I've forgotten naught," he said, capturing her hand and lifting it to his lips for a kiss. "And there is a matter of importance that I would speak with you about if you can give me your trust?"

At once, the sultry-eyed beauty flashed across

Aveline's mind again, but she steeled herself against the woman's persistence and summoned her boldest smile.

"I will always trust you," she said, the words coming from somewhere deep inside her.

She just hoped he would trust her.

That he'd listen when she urged him to treat his father with greater kindness.

But for the moment she let him grab her hand and pull her with him across the hall. Through the throng and past the high table with Munro's empty laird's chair, taking her, she knew, to his brother Kendrick's bedchamber.

Once there, she'd discover whate'er he wished to discuss with her. Just as she meant to voice some of her own cares. Determined to do just that, she straightened her back and let him lead her up the stairs.

If she could summon her daring, she'd also learn just how close he'd been to a certain Glenelg joy woman.

After all, knowing one's enemy was half the battle.

And Aveline wanted victory.

The fullest, most round triumph possible.

Chapter Ten

❦

Jamie stood in the middle of his brother Kendrick's well-appointed bedchamber and tried not to frown beneath Aveline's penetrating stare. He also wondered if his ears were playing tricks on him. Truth be told, he wished they were because he wasn't sure what to do if they weren't.

He did fold his arms over his chest and attempt to feign a look of manly innocence.

There were some things womenfolk were just not supposed to know about and, with luck, pretending ignorance would make the whole matter go away.

But the look in his lovely's eyes and the way her back seemed to be getting straighter by the minute told him this matter wasn't going anywhere until it was aired.

Jamie sighed.

An audible sigh and coupled with an expression that told Aveline exactly what she wanted to know.

Or better said, what she didn't want to know.

Folding her arms, she considered her options. Clearly, James Macpherson was well acquainted with the Glenelg joy woman. Even more obviously, he wasn't keen on discussing her.

Unfortunately for him, she was.

Not that she expected anything good to come of gaining such knowledge. Indeed, thrusting her hand into a wasp's nest might prove less painful. But the sultry beauty's image wouldn't let her go and neither would her own growing awareness of her smallness.

Aveline turned to a well-laiden table near the hearth and poured herself a generous portion of heather ale. An indulgence she regretted almost immediately because the table's silver candelabrum cast its telltale illumination onto her hands, highlighting their daintiness.

A fault nowise near as galling as her tiny breasts.

And much to her irritation, the vexatious candelabrum spilled light across her bodice, too. A lovely bodice, to be sure, crafted of finest linen and decorated with a delicate band of stitchery.

Stitchery designed by her own wee hand for the sole purpose of attracting the eye away from the lack of the great swelling orbs most Highland maids flaunted with understandable pride.

Aveline frowned and set down her ale cup untouched.

The frothy brew wouldn't help her grow a lush bosom. Nor would it solve a jot of her distress.

Sooner or later, Jamie would have to answer her questions about the woman—his paramour from the sound of it.

Resisting the urge to start tapping her foot, Aveline

simply pinned the man with a *look*. As her father often said, what she lacked in physical size, she made up for in patience and calm. Her ability to persuade without words.

But instead of telling her about the bawdy widow, Jamie appeared content to stand before her with a closed expression, his jaw set and his mouth clamped tight.

He did run a hand over his face and wish himself anywhere beside where he was presently standing. Somewhere, where the devil wasn't on the loose and out to get him.

Saints, even Cuillin was fixing him with a baleful, unblinking stare. An accusatory stare if e'er there was one. And coming from a male dog who'd ne'er denied himself his own pleasures, his disapproval stung.

All men visited willing-armed and succoring joy women, and he had a greater reason than most to do so. Ignoring that reason, he crossed the room to where Aveline stood near the hearth fire.

"Who told you of her?" he asked, putting his hands on her shoulders. "Gelis, I'll wager?"

Aveline's chin lifted a notch. "Then you admit there is a Gunna of the Glen?"

Jamie inhaled deeply and glanced at the ceiling. "Of course, there is a Gunna of Glen," he said, releasing the breath and looking back at her.

"See here, lass," he began, "there have always been such women and ever shall be. So long as men have a need, there will be such women as the fair widow of Glenelg."

He winced, realizing his mistake as soon as the words left his tongue.

His wee Aveline was jealous.

Proving it, she pulled free of his grasp and went to the window. She whisked open the shutters and peered out into the streaming night.

"So she is as beautiful as Gelis claimed?" she asked, her back even more rigid than before.

Jamie bit back a curse and followed her. "Most joy women are comely," he said, stopping a handsbreadth behind her but not touching her. "Though I vow some of the older ones are not so savory."

"Older ones?" Aveline whirled around. "Just how many such women do you know?"

"Just one," Jamie told her true. "I only e'er went to see the Glenelg widow. She is the only such woman I have e'er known."

Two spots of color appeared on his bride's cheeks and she looked down, fussing at her skirts.

She said nothing.

Not that she needed to for waves of distress rolled off her, each one lancing Jamie more than the last.

He wanted to soothe and reassure her, not make things worse.

Scowling openly now, he shoved a hand through his hair. He was sorely tempted to forget his chivalry and do bodily harm to the fiery-haired bit of MacKenzie baggage who'd told her of the lusty widow.

Jamie swallowed, misery weighing on him. Even the neck opening of his tunic was growing tighter by the moment. Worse, he was also finding it increasingly difficult to breathe.

Duncan MacKenzie had once warned him that facing

a woman's jealousy was more daunting than crossing swords with any manly foe. And Jamie now saw the wisdom of the Black Stag's words.

Feeling more discomfited by the moment, he glanced around the bedchamber, looking for inspiration. Anything he might seize upon to wend the night in a different direction.

One that didn't feel like a white-hot vise clamping around his chest.

Blessedly, his gaze lit upon a small hole in the deep-set arch of the window. Just a minor fault in the masonry, a place where a bit of stone had fallen or been worn away by weather or years.

But perhaps it was his salvation.

Hoping it so, he put back his shoulders and cleared his throat. "Would you not rather speak of the MacKenzies' marriage stone?" he asked, stepping forward to smooth a strand of hair off his lady's brow. "I have seen it many times and can tell you a few tales of the stone and the good clan's feasting revelries."

Aveline's head snapped up, but her expression hadn't improved at all.

"How long were you in the hall?" She looked at him. "'Tis obvious you know Hughie Mac regaled us with the legend of the MacKenzies' stone."

Jamie frowned, torn between admiring her persistence and wanting to throttle her for being so difficult.

"I heard every word of Hughie's tale," he admitted, not surprised by her arcing brows. "I stood in the shadows, not wanting to spoil the moment, then joined a few kinsmen for some hot roasted ribs and honey bannocks. You caught my eye just as I was washing my hands after our repast."

Her brows lowered at once, drawing together in a frown that surely bode ill. "Since you spent so many years squiring at Eilean Creag, you will know their traditions well," she said, something about her tone letting him know he could expect even more trouble.

"As it happens, I heard enough of their stories tonight to occupy me for months." She glanced down, flicking an invisible fleck off her sleeve. "'Tis the Glenelg woman who interests me," she said, looking up. "Your tales of *her* that I wish to hear."

Jamie blew out a breath and rubbed the back of his neck. Now he knew the devil was somewhere underfoot, and far too close for comfort.

Certain of it, he considered taking his bride into his arms and kissing her until such fool notions fled her mind.

A possibility he quickly dismissed.

In her present agitated state, she just might reward any such peacemaking attempt by biting off his tongue.

He frowned again.

Truth be told, she was being unreasonable.

After all, he'd not done anything wrong. So far as he knew, all men paid an occasional visit to a joy woman and in most instances to more than one.

Many loftier knights and lairds of his acquaintance kept a veritable string of mistresses, some even favoring their concubines and their offspring above their legally wed consorts.

Something Jamie would never consider; not with such a pleasing bride.

Saints, he was besotted with her.

"You're not being fair," he said, stepping closer to her again. "Surely you know that men have certain needs? Urges they sometimes tend by visiting such women as Gunna of the Glen?"

His bride said nothing.

Instead, she slipped past him and went to stand in front of the fire, staring down into the flames.

"I know of the heat of passion that blazes between a man and a woman—and what they do about it!" she said, not looking at him. "I am not ignorant."

She spun around then, her sapphire eyes snapping. "I *am* innocent. Should you wonder."

Jamie sighed. "Ach, sweetness, the thought ne'er crossed my mind," he said, leaving off how often he had thought about her innocence, but not for the reason she suspected.

Nay, he worried that her purity might remain a permanent state.

He looked down, then immediately wished he hadn't when his gaze fell on his hands. Saints, big as he was and tiny as she was, just holding her might crack one of her ribs if e'er he forgot himself and clutched her over-tight.

Jamie's mood darkened, the mere notion of causing her pain making his head throb. He'd sooner not touch her at all than risk hurting her.

"See here," he started to explain, "my concern is—"

"You said this woman, this Gunna of the Glen, is the only such female you've visited," she persisted, her gaze back on the hearth fire. "Have you then only lain with her? Have there been no others?"

Jamie rammed a hand through his hair.

"Of course, there have been others," he admitted, now feeling the devil's eyes on him.

"And who were they?"

"Kitchen bawds and laundresses. Big-boned, broad-bottomed lasses, light-skirted wenches free with their charms," he explained, his head now pounding in earnest. "I dinna remember the names of any of them. And from the time I went to serve my liege, Sir Kenneth Mac-Kenzie, the Keeper of Cuidrach, I only took my ease with the widow."

"No one else?"

Jamie shook his head. "No one."

"Then you must've been mightily fond of her?"

"I was, and am," Jamie said, smoothing a hand over his chin. "She is a good woman with a big heart. She misses her late husband and the bed sport they shared. That is the reason she welcomes such attention."

"That was baldly put." Aveline slanted a glance at him. "So she is a well-lusted woman?"

Jamie nodded, silently damning whate'er fool saint saw fit to bless him with such an unflagging penchant for honesty. "She is lusty, aye."

And so well-ridden even I can slide in and out of her with astonishing ease.

Something he needed to explain, however awkward. He could already see a slew of other interpretations slipping across his lady's face.

False notions that couldn't be farther from the truth.

So he inhaled deeply and crossed the room. Before she could move away, he seized her chin, forcing her to look at him. "What you are thinking is not how it was," he said, willing her to understand. "I did not seek out the widow because I had heart feelings for her. She suited me well for one reason and one reason only."

Aveline blinked, letting silence stretch between them.

Jamie swallowed. At least she hadn't looked away or tried to break free of his grasp.

It was a start.

Something to build on.

"So you did not love her?" she finally asked, her cheeks turning pink on the question.

"Love her?" Jamie's brows shot upwards. "I am fond of Gunna of the Glen," he spoke true again. "But she is a friend, naught else."

"An intimate friend."

"Aye, that indeed. As intimate as a man and woman can be." Jamie looked hard at her. "I will ne'er lie to you, lass. Dinna ask me questions if the answer will displease you."

Her chin rose. "Will you see her again?"

"Nay, I will not." Jamie shook his head. "That I swear to you. Leastways not for the reason I visited her in the past."

She looked doubtful. "Will you tell me what that reason was?"

"Och, aye." Jamie curled his hands around his sword belt, holding tight. "Truth be told, I must tell you."

Her eyes widened. "You must?"

Jamie nodded again. Then he let go of his belt and

reached for her, sliding his hands down her back and over the curve of her buttocks. He cupped them lightly and drew her to him, holding her just close enough so that she couldn't help but feel the thick bulge of his sex.

A *problem* blessedly at ease for the moment.

Hoping her soft feminine warmth and delicate violet perfume wouldn't alter that state too quickly, he glanced up at the ceiling again and sought the best words.

"Back in the hall, you said you wished to speak to me about something important," she said then, peering up at him, her eyes luminous in the candlelight. "Did it have aught to do with this woman? Or the MacKenzie marriage stone? I ask because Hughie Mac was telling the tale when you returned."

Jamie tightened his arms around her, squeezing her ever so lightly. "It has naught to do with those things and yet everything to do with them," he said, sweeping her up into his arms and carrying her across the room to lower her onto the edge of Kendrick's great four-poster bed.

"The only thing this has to do with the MacKenzie stone is that I needn't clasp your hand through a holed stone to know that our union will be mightily blessed," he said, hooking his hands beneath his sword belt again and pacing before the bed. "All I need is the assurance that I won't hurt you. That, and naught else is troubling me."

Aveline's jaw slipped. "Hurt me?"

She stared at him, confusion spilling through her.

This was the last thing she'd expected him to say. "I do not understand."

He shot a glance at her. "You ken we are now as good as legally wed?" he asked, pausing beside the foot of the bed. "You are aware that we can lie together now, this moment, and no one would raise a brow?"

Aveline nodded. His words caused a flurry of warm, fluttery tingles low in her belly.

She *wanted* to lie with him.

And she wanted more of his kisses.

Mayhap even the all-over kind of kisses one of her sisters had secretly told her about one night after she'd imbibed too much spiced wine, claiming her husband loved nothing better than to lie between her legs and lick her.

Aveline shivered.

The notion had excited her when Maili had shared it. Now, after being held and touched and kissed by Jamie these last weeks, the thought of him doing such an intimate thing to her—actually getting *down there* and touching his tongue to her—shattered her.

Truth be told, the notion filled her with such thrilling heat she had to clamp her thighs together.

"Did you hear me?" he prodded then, watching her. "We are bound now. Before God, man, and all these great hills surrounding us. Naught between us is a sin, even though we will not wed till spring. Our betrothal ceremony sealed our vows. We are as good as man and wife."

"Aye, I know this," she said, the tingles in her belly beginning to spread even lower.

He came closer again, stopping just in front of her. "Then you will not object if we speak freely about certain things?"

" 'Things'?"

Aveline's heart began to pound.

She shifted on the bed, her mouth going dry. Saints

preserve her if he'd read her thoughts. Half-afraid he had, she moistened her lips, sharply aware of his nearness, his clean masculine scent.

She blinked, his braw good looks and his scent distracting her. "What things?"

He stepped closer, so near his knees rested lightly against hers. "Man and woman things," he said, looking down at her. "You have said you know about them?"

She nodded. "My sisters have told me what happens at beddings and I have seen my father's men coupling with the laundresses in the shadowy corners of the hall and sometimes in the stables."

"And you have seen unclothed men?" he asked, watching her.

Aveline bit her lip. Scorching heat shot up her neck. Worse, wicked as it was, talking so openly about such things seemed to increase the hot prickly-tingly feeling between her legs.

And she was finding she liked the sensation.

She drew a slow breath, forcing herself to speak evenly. "Aye, I have seen my father's men undressed. Mostly of an e'en and in the hall as they readied themselves for sleeping."

Looking down, she smoothed a fold in the bed coverlet. "I've also bathed a goodly number of my father's loftier guests."

"But such guests would not have been aroused." Jamie held her gaze, his knees still pressing against hers. "Have you e'er seen a man thus stirred?"

"Only one," Aveline blurted before she lost the nerve. "He was standing behind a tree near St. Bride's Well when my sisters and I once bathed there. He was swollen, aye, and touching himself."

"Men do that sometimes, lass," Jamie said, his tone tight. "It relieves their need. But committing such an act while spying on you and your sisters was inexcusable and I hope he was severely punished."

Aveline curled her fingers into the bedcovers and glanced aside.

"He ran away before we could see his face," she lied, unable to tell him that two of her sisters had flaunted themselves, deliberately lying half-naked in a patch of sunshine beside the sacred well.

Jamie nodded, his fingers itching to curl around the neck of the dastard who'd taken such a cowardly means to find his ease. But he was also relieved his bride was familiar with a man's body.

Not taking his gaze off her, he unfastened his hip flask from his belt and tossed down a hefty swallow of fine and fiery *uisge beatha*. Highland water of life, a potent spirit well known for curing any and everything thought to ail man, including over-tight tongues.

He offered her some, then frowned because he hadn't thought to first fetch a cup for her, but she surprised him by accepting the flask and placing it immediately to her lips.

"So you see," she said after taking a sip and handing the flask back to him, "I know what to expect when we bed and I am not afraid. I also know you will not hurt me—that you'd never treat me as roughly as I've seen some of my father's men use the laundresses and kitchen lasses."

Jamie cleared his throat. "That is not the kind of hurting I meant," he said, not surprised by the flash of confusion in her eyes. "To be sure, I would ne'er treat you roughly. 'Tis my size that concerns me, see you? I fear hurting you because my man parts are overlarge."

To his surprise, rather than widened eyes or a scandalized jaw drop, her lips tightened and she avoided his eye, turning her head away to stare into the fire again.

"Is that why you were so fond of the widow?" she asked, her tone warning him that she was irritated again. "Because she relished your great size?"

Jamie sat down beside her on the bed. "I have told you why I call the woman a friend. She has a good and generous heart," he said, knowing it to be true. "The reason I went to her was not because she was fond of me, but because I needn't worry about causing her discomfort."

"I see." Aveline plucked at the bedcovers.

"I would that you do. My size has brought pain to more than one lass," he explained. "This caused me so much distress that I stopped lying with women and saw to my needs myself in the way you saw the man in the woods touch himself. Though I ne'er did such a thing save when I was certain I was fully alone."

Needing to make her understand, he reached for her chin again, turning her face so she had to meet his eye. "When I was urged to visit Gunna of the Glen, I was relieved to find a woman who could sheathe me with ease, fully without pain, and, aye, even take her own pleasure in the act."

Aveline's eyes rounded. "You are saying you went to

her because you could slide easily into her?" she asked, speaking more bluntly than she would have wished.

"Aye, that was the way of it," Jamie admitted. "There was no other reason. No heart feelings whatsoever, as I told you. I was pleased to have a woman I could lie with and not hurt."

"As you worry about hurting me?"

Jamie nodded. "Ach, lass, you are so wee that I canna imagine truly touching you without breaking you," he said, speaking as plainly as he could. "Even if resisting the temptation of you costs me my last breath, I willna cause you pain. There are other ways we can be intimate together. Other things—"

" 'Resisting the temptation'?" She opened her mouth to say more, but to Jamie's horror, her eyes suddenly started to glisten and she pressed a fist to her lips, blinking rapidly as she stared at him as if he'd suddenly sprouted two heads.

Or, judging by the tremulous smile curving her lips when she finally lowered her hand, looking as if he'd just handed her the sun, moon, and stars on a silver-gilt platter.

"You make it sound as if you desire me," she said, dashing the dampness from her cheeks, then frowning a bit when the tears kept leaking from beneath her lashes no matter how furiously she swiped at them.

"By the Rood!" Jamie gathered her into his arms, holding her as tightly as he dared. "Have I no' kissed you with enough passion for you to know how much I want you? How much you delight me?"

He began stroking her back, soothingly he hoped.

"Have you forgotten how much I enjoyed that one sweet glimpse of your breast?" he reminded her, his voice deep, growing husky with need. "Surely you know I'd love to see such beauty again."

"You want to see my breast again?" The words came so faint Jamie wasn't sure he heard her.

He pulled back a bit to look at her. "Perhaps with both nipples visible this time?"

She stiffened at that, so he slipped a hand between them, allowing himself the pleasure of cupping her breast and rubbing a single finger gently to and fro across her delicate swells. Touching her exactly as he had in her father's solar, only this time through the cloth of her gown.

"M'mmm . . . ," she sighed, melting against him. But she caught herself almost as quickly and reached circling fingers around his wrist, lowering his hand with astonishing strength.

"My breasts are small," she said, her eyes glittering suspiciously again. "That is the reason I fretted so much about the Glenelg joy woman. Gelis described her in great detail and I saw her in my mind, imagining her lush welling curves and huge ripe breasts."

Pulling away from him, she looked down, bunched her hands in her lap. "Nipples the size of my fists—"

"Hah! And so they are!" Jamie threw back his head and laughed, a quick image of the widow's large dark-hued nipples flashing across his mind.

Ah, the hours he'd spent licking and sucking them. Or simply plucking and pulling on them, rubbing and toying, circling a fingertip endlessly around the wonderfully crinkled flesh of her large aureoles.

Memories and images that stirred him not a whit.

His man parts, usually so responsive when thinking of the joy woman's bountiful charms, didn't even twitch.

Aveline touched his thigh. "So her breasts really are large and ripe."

"And yours are straight from heaven," Jamie owned, meaning it. "Do you know, sweetness, that since seeing you in the wood, a thousand full-breasted, well-curved females could come flouncing their wares into this room and I would still see only you?"

She looked aside, the color in her cheeks giving away her doubt.

"'Tis true." He leaned close to brush a feather-light kiss across her temple. "I am quite besotted."

Reaching for her braid, he began undoing it, letting the shimmering flaxen strands spill through his fingers until the whole gleaming mass cascaded about her shoulders, a riot of moon-spun silver tumbling down past her hips.

Looking at her sitting on Kendrick's bed, her unbound hair making such a bold statement of accepted intimacy, Jamie's heart began a slow, hard thumping and his loins tightened.

Not that he intended to touch her.

Not in *that* way.

He still had serious reservations about the like. But he could give her a soft, lingering kiss.

"You are a prize beyond measure," he vowed, finally releasing her.

Holding her gaze, he scooped up a thick handful of her hair, looping the luxuriant strands around his wrist and then bringing his hand to his lips, burying his face in the glossy, fragrant skeins.

"You take my breath," he vowed, kissing her hair, rubbing his cheek against its silkiness.

"And you please me." She traced a finger along his jaw, the wonder in her eyes stopping Jamie's heart.

She was watching him kiss and nuzzle her hair, her lower lip caught between her teeth as he let his fingers glide over the laces of her gown.

"You are lovely," he told her, his hands aching to undo her bodice. "I have ne'er seen a more beautiful maid and will ne'er tire of looking on you."

Smiling now, she brought her own hands to her bodice, her slender fingers deftly working the ties. "If I please you, you can look upon me all you wish," she said, the color in her cheeks deepening even though her words rang bold.

"But I would see you, too," she added, glancing downward.

"Me?" Jamie drew a tight breath, more aware of her than was good for him.

Aware of how much he wanted her.

How easily she could make him lose control.

Especially with the not-so-discreet direction of her gaze letting him know exactly what part of him appeared to interest her.

Proving it, she reached out to touch him. Not *there*, only on his chest. But her fingers warmed him clear through his plaid, the pleasure of her touch stirring him even if her hand hovered well above his sword belt.

"You tell me you're worried you'll hurt me," she said,

challenge thrumming behind every word. "Why not let me decide if I am afeared of your touch or nay?"

Jamie frowned.

"You do not know what you are saying," he argued.

She only smiled and reached again for her bodice laces, untying them until the top of her gown gaped wide and her naked breasts winked in the firelight, all creamy white, her rosy nipples already puckering.

"Well?" She looked at him, waiting.

"Well, indeed." Jamie could only stare at her.

Truth be told, he couldn't even move.

Ne'er had he seen a vision more lovely.

And ne'er had he run hard so swiftly.

So granite-hard, he was certain the slightest touch or movement would cause his shaft to snap in two. But then, he had hoped to begin acquainting her with his body tonight. He'd just envisioned an entirely different situation, had thought they'd progress slowly.

He'd certainly thought to remain fully at ease and then perhaps brush casually against her, letting her feel for herself why such worries plagued him.

Perhaps, too, he might have simply flipped aside his plaid, easing down his hose and braies just enough for her to have a wee peek. Then later, if the sight of him didn't frighten her, he'd hoped to encourage her to touch and explore him—if she'd shown herself so inclined.

Having her sit before him on a bed with her naked breasts all agleam and then expecting him to show himself to her, that was an entirely different kettle of fish.

An unexpected turn of events that set him to reeling

and made him want to clutch her to him so fiercely he feared he really would break her.

"I am not fragile. Nor am I afraid of things that are natural," she declared, moistening her lips in a way that only increased his discomfort. "If you find pleasure in looking at me," she added with a quick glance at her breasts, "then why would I not enjoy seeing you?"

Jamie pressed his lips together and took a deep breath.

She turned a look on him filled with more self-possession than he would have e'er dreamed in such a teeny lassie. But he could see it all over her, and she wore it well. So beautifully that just watching her proved a temptation he'd not be able to resist much longer.

"I will touch you if you wish," she said, as if she knew. "Anywhere it pleases you."

That did it.

Like a man possessed, Jamie sprang from the bed and unlatched his sword belt, tossing it aside to clunk to the rushes somewhere behind him.

His heart thundering, he kept his gaze fastened to the sweetness of her creamy, perfectly formed breasts and undid the great plaid brooch at his shoulder, swiftly sending it and his plaid sailing after his blade.

Grinning now, he reached for the bottom of his tunic and began pulling it over his head. But before he could wrest it fully off, or even think about shoving down his hose, a rude hammering sounded on the door.

"Hellfire and damnation!" He yanked down his tunic and glared across the room. "We need naught," he roared, his brows snapping together when the pounding only increased. "Come back in the morn!"

" 'Tis your da," Morag called anyway, her voice loud and unrelenting. "You'd best come. Now!"

Jamie froze, the old woman's tone icing his blood.

"Go!" Aveline gave him a shove toward the door, began hastily redoing her bodice. "Morag would not be calling for you if aught wasn't seriously amiss."

"That I ken," Jamie swore, already striding across the room to unbolt the door and fling it wide.

"Merciful saints!" he demanded of Morag, glaring down at her. The old woman's eyes blazed and her hair looked wild, its straggly ends poking up in all different directions as if she'd been standing in a fierce winter gale.

Jamie shot a look at Aveline, then turned back to Morag. "Lucifer's knees," he swore, "what has happened?"

"Aye, the Horned One will have had his hand in this!" Morag grabbed Jamie's arm, her gnarled fingers closing on him like talons. "Make haste! And bring your sword and ax," she urged, glancing at his discarded sword belt and blade, the Norseman's ax propped against the far wall. "We're under attack."

Jamie eyes flew wide. "Under attack?"

Morag nodded. "So everyone thinks," she said, turning to hasten back down the dimly lit passage, making for the stair tower as fast as her spindly legs would carry her.

Jamie and Aveline exchanged glances.

"God's bones," Jamie swore again, running back across the room to fetch his brand and the ax.

"Morag—hold you!" he yelled, grabbing Aveline's hand and pulling her with him from the room. "Wait!" he called again, amazed the old woman could move so quickly. "You said it was my da? What of him? Has he been hurt?"

But Morag was already far ahead of them, her tiny form swallowed by the shadows of the turnpike stair, the bobbing, wildly flickering flame of her rush light the only sign they'd even seen her at all.

Until her voice floated back up to them, her words echoing in the stair tower.

"I dinna ken how he is. Only that he's been shot by a crossbow."

Chapter Eleven

✤

O-o-oh, nay!"

"I dinna care how many wounds you've stitched, lassie, you willna be a-sticking that needle in my arm!"

Munro's protests echoed off the walls of the great hall, his bellowing rising above the din and catching Jamie's ear even before he and Aveline reached the bottom of the stair tower and burst into the crowded hall's chaos and turmoil.

A quick glance showed that the entirety of the MacKenzie guardsmen and at least half of Jamie's father's men appeared to have vanished, though he strongly suspected they'd hastened away to man the wall walks.

Those remaining dashed about shouting orders and cursing, some stoking the already blazing fires and heating great cauldrons of water, useful on the walls, Jamie knew.

"Dear saints, Morag spoke true. They're readying for a siege," Aveline gasped beside him, her gaze on a group of garrison men who stood nearby strapping on sword belts and other war gear.

Jamie frowned. "If so, I doubt our attackers hail from the Otherworld," he observed, certain of it.

Everywhere men rushed about snatching up more assorted, wicked-looking weapons than he'd realized his da's men possessed. Some had already taken defensive positions at the windows and doors, and still more were running for the stair towers, their clattering footfalls loud and echoing as they hurried to the battlements.

Aveline glanced at him. "I know you don't believe Neill and Kendrick—"

Jamie snorted. "Ghosts dinna shoot crossbows—or wear wet plaids," he said, tightening his grip on her hand as they pushed through the chaos, heading for the hall's crowded dais end.

Nor did they mix fish bones into harmless porridge he added in silence, not about to frighten her by revealing that particular incident.

A threat that had come to naught but just the kind of nonsense he was determined not to let happen again.

As for shooting old men with crossbows . . .

Jamie set his jaw, his blood heating as they neared the raised dais.

"Wench, be gone with you—you, and your devil's needle!" his da roared again, and Jamie spotted him at once.

He stood behind the high table, his left arm bright with fresh, streaming red blood, his hands in a white-knuckled grip on the back of his laird's chair.

Wild-eyed and furious, he was glowering at anyone who attempted to approach him.

At present, that seemed to be Lady Juliana.

"'Tis only a scrape, I tell you!" Munro insisted, glaring at her. "I'll heal just fine—without you jabbing new holes into me!"

Ignoring his wrath, Lady Juliana took two steps closer to the dais. "This is only a very thin bone needle," she said, holding it up for him to see.

White-faced, Gelis and Arabella trailed after her, both girls in their bed robes, a pile of clean-looking linens clutched in Arabella's arms, while Gelis carried a bucket of steaming water.

Munro raked them with an equally black-browed stare. "Go back to your bed, lassies!" he yelled at them. "I've no need o' your nursing."

"Or yours." He rounded on Jamie and Aveline, agitation rolling off him. "I like you fine," he said, his gaze latching on to Aveline, "so dinna tempt me to change my opinion. Just stay where you are and leave me be."

"But, sir, your arm must be treated." Aveline started forward. "Like Lady Juliana, I, too, can—"

"You can stop right there and no' be a-joining up with this devil's besom and her needle," Munro exploded, glowering.

"Come you, Sir Munro," Lady Juliana tried to soothe him, her voice calm and low. "My stitches are so fine and quick, you'll ne'er know I've even touched you."

"So spoke the wolf before he ate the lamb!" Munro pulled his dirk from beneath his belt, brandishing it in her direction. "I'll poke any one o' you who sets foot on this dais. Including women!"

He threw an especial glare at Morag. "And no quarter given for age!"

Undaunted, she frowned back at him, her hands planted firmly on her scrawny hips. "I'm thinking that *scrape* will be needing more than stitching," she said, sliding a glance to the hall's massive central hearth where a stable youth held a broad-bladed dagger to the flames.

"Lady Juliana means well, but the wound is too deep and jagged, the blood spilling too swiftly for her dainty stitches to do much good," she added. "More the pity as sealing the wound with a hot blade will hurt far worse than being sewn up!"

Munro thrust his dirk back beneath his belt and whipped out his sword. "God's living eyes, any one of you goons try and bring a fired blade anywhere near me and I'll skewer you through! Be warned!"

He frowned darkly but when he made to shake his sword at the small group of friends and kin gathered before the dais steps, he swayed on his feet and the great brand slipped from his bloodied fingers, clattering to the floor.

Munro grabbed at his chair again, this time leaning heavily against its carved oaken back. "I meant what I said," he vowed, his eyes snapping defiance. "Dinna any one o' you dare come near me."

And then he ran chalk-white and slumped to his knees.

"Damnation!" Jamie vaulted over a trestle bench and leapt onto the dais, Aveline running after him.

"Clear the table," he called to her as he scooped his father into his arms.

"Someone bring *uisge beatha*! We'll need lots—a

good measure for Da to drink and even more to pour o'er his wound. And you"—he looked to the MacKenzie women—"help Morag fetch her salves, bandaging, and whate'er else she'll need. She knows better than any what must be done."

Pausing for breath, Jamie scanned the hall for Hughie Mac. He glanced at Morag when he didn't see him. "Where's Hughie? He'll know what to do, too. He's nigh as good as you at healing."

Morag sniffed. "That one left some hours ago," she told him, taking the steaming water bucket from Gelis. "He hasn't spread a pallet here in a while, fussing that his legs pain him of a night and that he only finds comfort in his own wee cottage."

"Hughie fussing?" Jamie lifted a brow.

He'd ne'er heard the erstwhile herd boy complain about anything. Like any true Highlander, Hughie Mac possessed an inborn imperturbability as solid and unshakeable as the hills he called home.

Jamie looked at his old nurse. "Nay, I canna believe it," he puzzled. "Hughie would ne'er fash about aught."

Morag only shrugged. "Hughie Mac's turned queer of late if you're asking me," she said. "But ne'er you worry. I know well enough what we need to do."

"Ye gods! There isn't aught *to* do." Munro's voice rose to a shout as Jamie held him while Aveline and Lady Juliana spread a clean linen cloth over the emptied high table.

He glared at everyone, his scowl darkening even more when Jamie lowered him onto the tabletop.

"Tell those fools to stop running around like twittering

women," he raged, twisting his head toward the bustle in the hall. "There's no need. Baldreagan isn't under siege. 'Twas Neill's bogle who shot me and no other—as I've already told the lackwits!"

Morag huffed. "I'd sooner believe it was God Almighty. You've e'er given Him ample reason to be vexed with you!"

"'Twas Neill's bogle so sure as I'm looking at you!" Munro narrowed his eyes on her.

Jamie and Aveline exchanged glances.

"Bogles dinna use crossbows," Jamie said, beginning to ease back the edge his father's blood-drenched plaid. "And lest you've forgotten, so far as I recall, Neill was a master with a blade but he ne'er fired a crossbow in his life."

He slid another glance at Aveline. "If you didn't know," he told her, "most knights frown on crossbows. Neill held them in particular scorn."

Munro sniffed. "How would you ken what he can or canna do now, in his *after*life? Him, being a bogle and all?"

"My brothers may be dead, but I've yet to see proof that any of them are returning here as ghosts. Despite all the reports to the contrary." Jamie bit back his temper and kept working at getting the bloody plaid off his father without causing him more discomfort than necessary.

The man's failing wits were suffering enough. If he had them in better order, he'd recall his eldest son's vaunting pride.

Truth was, Neill had despised crossbows, calling them

a coward's weapon, good only for the lowliest paid mercenaries and brigands.

Neill had loved their father, too. Ne'er would he attempt to harm him. Not in a thousand lifetimes—whether Munro had neglected to repair the old footbridge or no.

Jamie pressed a hand to his brow. His temples were beginning to throb again.

"You don't think it was one of my father's Pabay men?" Aveline stepped close, pitching the question for his ears alone.

He looked at her. The notion had flashed across his mind, but he dismissed it now.

"Nay, lass, with surety not," he said, speaking equally low. "One of your father's reformed brigands would ne'er have missed their target. My da lives because the shot was clumsy. A true crossbowman would've had the skill to send his bolt through my father's heart and not his arm."

She bit her lip, looking unconvinced.

Jamie shook his head, seeking to reassure her. "I'd wager my last breath that none of Fairmaiden's Pabay men did this. Dinna you worry. I only meant to say it wasn't Neill's ghost, either."

Proud as he'd been, he wouldn't have touched a crossbow, insisting that doing so would've been beneath his dignity as a noble and belted knight.

If Neill, Kendrick, or any Macpherson stood on the wrong foot with a man, they'd challenge their foe outright. It wasn't their clan's way to hide in the shadows, using darkness to cloak their blows.

Truth be told, such wasn't the way of *any* Highlander.

Jamie turned back to his father, that knowledge making his head hurt all the more.

"Tell me, Da, was *Neill* wearing his wet plaid again when he shot you?" he prodded, certain that whoe'er was masquerading as his brother's ghost had also fired the crossbow. "Did you see him?"

"Of course, I saw him." Munro's eyes blazed, but his voice sounded wheezy, hoarse and growing fainter. "Do you think I'd say it was him if I hadn't seen him?"

Pushing up on his elbows, he pinned Jamie with a fierce stare. "I'm no' the only soul hereabouts who's seen Neill lurking about and Kendrick, too. So dinna go a-telling me I'm daft."

Ignoring his da's outburst, Jamie only cocked a brow. "And the plaid?"

Munro clamped his lips together, wincing when Jamie eased away another blood-sodden bit of cloth from the wound. "Nay, he wasn't in his plaid," he finally admitted, pushing the words past gritted teeth. "He— *eeeeeei-ioooow!*"

The scream speared Jamie's heart, hurting him, he was sure, a thousand times more than the old man writhing on the high table.

"I am sorry," he said, hating the tears filling the older man's eyes. "The last bit of plaid and your tunic had to be ripped away."

He didn't mention that still more of the cloth would have to be picked and dug from his flesh. Deep in his flesh, for the iron-headed crossbow quarrel had gone clear through Munro's arm.

Morag, Lady Juliana, or even Aveline would perform

the task with great care, seeing to it as soon as the wound was washed and rinsed, though Jamie doubted his father would appreciate their gentleness.

"I willna have the wound seared." Munro grabbed Jamie's wrist then, staring up at him with glittering, fear-glazed eyes. "Tell them. No hot blade on my flesh."

Looking down at him, something inside Jamie snapped and broke. Hot and jagged, it spun free to whirl ever upward, lodging in his throat, making it thicken and swell, burning his eyes.

He blinked, needing to clear his vision.

When he did, he recognized it was the panic in his father's eyes that twisted his heart. And made him angry. Munro Macpherson had never been afraid of anything.

Saints, Jamie wouldn't have been surprised to hear his da challenge the Horned One himself. A fight to the death and with the devil's own weapons of choosing!

Yet now the old man's every indrawn breath was tinged with fear.

A grievous state he'd lived with e'er since a certain faceless coward began using the tragic deaths of his sons to haunt and break him. A miserable gutter-sweep Jamie strongly suspected might even have caused those deaths.

And whoe'er he was, Jamie would find him. Even if doing so meant overturning every stone and clump of heather in all broad Scotland.

"Mother o' the living God!" Munro bellowed then, flailing with his good arm. "You're both right pests," he added, trying in vain to knock Morag and Lady Juliana away from him.

But with the fortitude born of women, they ignored his

curses and thrashings, only nodding calmly when four braw clansmen appeared to help Jamie hold his father in place as they washed and tended the wound.

"Come, sir, one sip—for me."

Jamie heard his bride's voice in the midst of the chaos, soft, sweet, and soothing as a gentle spring rain. Glancing at her, he looked on as she tried to coax Munro to drink the *uisge beatha*.

A cure he needed as surely as having his wound cleaned because the moment the women finished, the dread sealing would follow.

Whether it pleased Munro or nay.

He'd die otherwise for nothing else would staunch the bleeding.

Jamie shuddered. Having once had a sword cut on his thigh sealed by such hot branding, it was a pain he'd prefer to spare his da, so he nodded to the four kinsmen holding Munro and went to the head of the table, taking the flask of fiery Highland spirits from Aveline's hand.

"Drink," he said, clamping his fingers on to his father's jaw and tipping back his head. He held the flask to the old man's tight-pressed lips, nudging. "As much as you can."

Munro glared at him, tightening his lips even more.

Jamie glared right back at him. "You know I will pry open your lips and pour the whole flask down your throat if you dinna take a swallow—or two."

Apparently believing him, Munro shut his eyes and opened his mouth. Not much, but enough to allow Jamie to send a healthy measure of the healing water of life flowing down his father's throat.

Before he could get him to accept a second gulp, a commotion in the hall drew all eyes.

Beardie came pounding up onto the dais, red-faced and panting, but resplendent in his great-great-grandsire's rusted Viking helmet and his huge and shining Viking battle-ax clutched tight in his hand.

"The siege is ended!" he announced, coming to a skidding, graceless halt. "And without a single scaling ladder being thrown against our walls. No' one enemy fire arrow sent whistling through the air!"

Beaming, he swiped a hand across his glistening brow. "My Viking helmet must've scared them! One glimpse of a true-blooded Norseman hanging o'er the parapet and waving a battle-ax, and the spineless bastards tucked their tails between their legs and ran."

Jamie stared at his cousin. He couldn't believe there really had been attackers.

"You saw them?" he asked, his mind whirling with the consequences if Beardie spoke true.

"Well . . ." Beardie looked down, taking a moment to hitch and adjust his belt. "We had to have frightened them off because there was nary a sign o' them anywhere," he admitted, removing his Viking helmet and scratching his head. "Nary a glint o' steel, no whinnying horses or clink o' armor. Not one insult hurled at us as we looked for 'em."

He jammed his rusty helmet back on, looking puzzled. "Truth is, the castle dogs didn't even bark."

"I told you it was the bogles," Munro said from the table, his eyes popping open. "Neill's bogle. I saw him take aim. He was wearing his burial shroud and he was *in* the bailey. Only a ghost could've slipped past the gate-house."

A ghost or someone who comes and goes as he pleases.

And has a right to do so.

Jamie's blood chilled.

He should've asked where the attack had occurred.

Now he knew.

And the answer was more disturbing than if a whole band of hostile clans had arrived to storm Baldreagan's walls; such foes can be fought. Unseen enemies in one's own midst were far more difficult to besiege.

"But I don't understand . . ." Aveline touched Jamie's arm.

He turned to her. "Dinna understand what?"

She edged closer, her brow knitting. "The bailey," she said, sliding a glance at Munro. "He swore he'd not set foot outside the keep, yet he was attacked in the bailey."

Munro tried to push up on his good arm. "Of course, I was in the bailey," he wheezed. "Neill told me to go there."

"He spoke to you?" Aveline hurried back to the head of the table, smoothed the damp hair back from the old man's brow. "When was this? Why didn't you tell us?"

"He came to me in *his* bedchamber," Munro managed, his gaze sliding to Jamie. "He told me if I took all the candles I can carry to St. Maelruhba's chapel and lit them in penance, he'd ne'er visit me again."

" 'Candles'?" Aveline glanced at Jamie.

Jamie shrugged.

Morag stopped dabbing at Munro's wound long

enough to jerk her head toward a dark corner of the dais. A familiar-looking wicker basket stood there, heaped high with fine wax tapers.

Fine wax tapers splattered with red, as was the basket itself.

"The candles the Lady Aveline brought for him from Fairmaiden," Morag explained, taking the fresh wet cloth Gelis handed her and dropping the bloodied one into a pail.

She pressed the new cloth against Munro's torn flesh, then looked their way again. "We found the crossbow bolt in the basket of candles. He was carrying it when he was hit."

Aveline gasped, clapping a hand to her breast.

Jamie frowned.

He could well imagine why Neill's *bogle* wanted Munro's hands full once he'd lured him outside the keep.

Even old and addle-headed, Munro Macpherson was a hard man to beat with blade in his hand.

And everyone in these parts knew it.

But before Jamie could think on it further, a cleared throat and a hesitant touch to his elbow startled him. Turning, he came face-to-face with the stable lad who'd been holding a dirk in the flames of the hearth fire.

The lad indicated that dirk now. He'd wound several layers of thick leather and cloth around the hilt and was holding the thing as far from his body as he could.

Jamie understood why.

The dagger's broad, two-edged blade glowed redder than the gates o' Hades.

"Holy saints," Jamie swore, his stomach clenching. He nodded to the stable lad, all else forgotten.

He didn't dare look at his father.

But he had to.

Yet when he did, Munro was staring past him, an awed-looking smile hovering on his lips. "Iona," he breathed, his gaze fixed on the empty shadows of a corner.

Chills swept down Jamie's spine and the fine hairs on the back of his neck lifted. Iona was his mother's name. And with surety, she wasn't standing across the dais looking at Munro.

She'd been dead since Jamie's birth. A tragedy his father had ne'er let him forget.

"My Iona," Munro said again, and a tear trickled down his cheek. "Nay, I am not afeared," he added, his strained voice sounding just a shade stronger.

Then his eyes cleared and he looked straight at Jamie. "The searing," he said, unblinking. "Do it now, son, and be done with it."

"So be it." Jamie took the red-hot dagger from the wide-eyed stable lad. He jerked the instant his fingers closed on the well-padded hilt, the throbbing heat from the blade nigh scalding his hand. And he was only grasping layers of cloth and leather! Unthinkable what the fired blade would do to his da's naked flesh.

Wincing, he slid a warning glance to the four men holding his father. At once, Morag nodded and pressed the gaping flesh together. Then, before Jamie lost his nerve, he stepped closer and lowered the blade to the wound.

"Awwwwwwwwggghhh!"

Munro's cry and the loud *zish* of burning flesh pierced the silence. Blessedly, his eyes also rolled back into his head and his body went still, leaving the echo of his pain and the horrible smell of singed flesh to his kin and those others who cared for him.

The deed finished, Jamie stepped back, glad to drop the searing dirk into the pail of water someone thrust at him. Then he wheeled away from the table and stood silent, waiting for the bile to leave his throat.

From the corner of his eye, he could tell that Morag and the MacKenzie women had taken over. His old nurse and Lady Juliana were already spreading a healing salve onto the newly-branded flesh and Gelis and Arabella stood close by, strips of clean bandaging in their hands.

"Come, you, let us be away abovestairs."

Jamie turned and found Aveline peering up at him, an indefinable promise in her sapphire eyes, a pleasing curve to the sweetness of her lips.

She reached for his hand, lacing her fingers with his bloodstained ones. Her gaze went to Munro then back to Jamie. "You can do no more for him. Not this night," she said, leaning into him, her words for him alone. "I would see to *your* needs. If you will come with me."

"My needs?" Jamie cocked a brow, wishing he hadn't let show how deeply branding his father's flesh had affected him. "It had to be done, lass. Sorry though I am to have hurt—"

"You misheard me. That is not what I meant, though I know the searing cost you," she said, her gaze dipping just enough to let a heat of a very different sort begin flickering across a certain sensitive part of him. "I am thinking you might favor a bath?"

The flickering heat became an insistent throbbing. Jamie cut a glance at the hall's large double-arched hearth fires, the heavy iron cauldrons of steaming water suspended above the crackling flames.

Water heated in vain for a siege that wasn't.

He looked back at his bride, his pulse quickening even when his conscience balked at leaving his father.

"He will not waken until the morrow," Aveline said, making him think she'd peered into his mind. When her gaze then slid to the steaming cauldrons, he was sure of it.

"The water is already heated," she added, the soft huskiness of her voice convincing him. "There is surely enough for a long, leisurely bath."

Jamie nodded. He agreed entirely.

His lady smiled and Jamie was well pleased to let her lead him toward the stair tower. He could use a bath. The morrow would be soon enough to renew his efforts to root out the mysterious *bogle*.

Neill's bogle. And a few other things weighing heavily on his mind.

But one of those things resolved itself halfway up the winding turnpike stair, the answer hitting him in the gut with all the punch of a well-aimed fist.

As if someone had reached out and ripped blinders from his eyes, he knew why he'd felt such a wrench when he'd seen the fear in his father's eyes.

That fiery squeezing sensation had been more than mere sympathy.

His heart had heard what he hadn't.

Tell me, Da, was Neill wearing his wet plaid . . .

His own words came back to him and he paused to press a hand against the cold stone of the stair tower wall lest his knees buckle beneath him.

A crossbow bolt and a red-hot searing knife were not exactly the means he would have chosen to come to such a stunning pass. The result was earth-shattering all the same.

And so utterly amazing he was tempted to whoop for joy.

Under any other circumstances, he would have.

As it was, he simply gave himself a much-needed shake before grabbing his bride's hand again so they could resume their spiral ascent to Kendrick's bedchamber.

He didn't need whoops and chest-thumpings to celebrate. Nor even a night of revelry and free-flowing ale. What he'd learned was more than enough.

In truth, more than he'd e'er expected.

For the first time since he could remember, he'd called his father *Da*.

And even more astounding, his father had called him son.

Chapter Twelve

✦

That same night, Baldreagan's kitchen lads filled buckets of hot water from great iron cauldrons and lugged their sloshing burdens abovestairs to the linen-lined bathing tub in Kendrick's bedchamber. And as they went about their task, another very different cauldron simmered and bubbled elsewhere. Across darkening peaks and silent glens, dubiously scented steam rose from this second cauldron. A fine, black-sided cauldron, this kettle's murky waters weren't intended for any lairdly son's leisurely bathing pleasure.

Nor were the nameless objects floating on the water's surface meant to fill anyone's hungry stomach.

A *scrying* cauldron, the kettle served one purpose and one indomitable soul.

And its keeper, Devorgilla of Doon, the most far-famed cailleach in the Highlands, had already made use of its powers earlier that night.

Just as she had every e'en for some while, hoping to

catch a glimpse of a certain faithful friend. A valiant, true-hearted friend who'd been away on a special mission, and was overdue to return.

She'd tried to scry his whereabouts in the soft hour of the gloaming, when the veil between all things of legend and wonder tended to be at its thinnest. But this e'en as on the other nights, she'd failed.

Even the especially powerful charms she'd tossed into her cauldron in the hopes of enhancing her success only turned the usual pungently scented steam into rankly foul smoke. She addressed this nuisance by opening her window shutters and seeking her pallet for an early night of *dream*-scrying. A method nowise as reliable as her cauldron's *seeing* steam, but the best she could hope for if the steam refused to cooperate.

Annoyingly, her dreams denied her as well and rather than the return of her brave and adventurous friend, she only saw Baldreagan's distant walls. Her dreams showed her through those walls and into one of the keep's darkest and oldest stair towers, her sleep filled with images of trudging feet and well-filled pails of heated water.

Churning, racing water, too.

White and deadly.

Blessedly, the tiredness of her bones let her slip into a deeper, dreamless sleep. One not plagued by such devil's waters, though her ears, e'er sharp and keen, still rang with endless, trudging footfalls.

Even though she made her pallet a good distance from Kintail and the deep pine hills of Baldreagan.

Truth be told, anyone seeking her wisdom would have to journey for days over rough and treacherous land, then sail across miles of shining, moon-silvered water to reach the great sea cliffs of Doon. Proud and forbidding, they rose darkly from the Hebridean Sea, their precipitous heights privy to many ancient secrets.

Now, as Devorgilla slept, heavy sea mist clung to those cliffs and the night wind fell light. Especially along the crone's own stretch of the jagged, rock-bound coast. There where the Old Powers still lived and breathed, and only Devorgilla's wee cottage broke the loneliness of the shore.

Few dared follow the narrow stony path to her dwelling's misty hiding, tucked as it was in deep heather and dark, sheltering rock, but of those souls brave enough, most were made welcome.

All were received hospitably.

Even those of darker hearts and ill luck, for such was the Highland way.

Some visitors, of course, were eagerly seen and even greeted effusively.

One such soul arrived now, slipping quietly out of the inky black shadows and into the little clearing in front of the low, thick-walled cottage. Sure of his welcome, the visitor sought the center of the moon-gilded clearing, knowing well that he'd soon be noticed.

He was expected, after all.

And the cailleach had been getting impatient.

He knew that because the thin blue line of peat smoke rising from the cottage's thatched roof carried a tinge of the crone's more powerful spelling goods.

Pleased by such tangible evidence of the crone's

regard, the visitor stretched and yawned, then sat on the night-dampened grass and waited.

Soon he'd be praised for a job well done.

And the crone's eagerness to see him might mean he'd receive a more generous reward than usual—especially when she learned how successful he'd been.

Not that anyone named after the great Somerled, King of the Isles, would be anything outside of victorious.

He was hungry, though. And thirsty. He'd journeyed far and his task hadn't been easy. *O-o-oh, aye,* he decided, watching the moon slide out of the clouds, he could use a bit of the pampering the crone showered on him when he pleased her.

And tonight, she'd be very, very pleased.

So he looked round to make certain none of his friends or kin were about and might see him. Then, once assured that he was alone, he allowed himself a small and seldom-used breach of his usual dignity.

He barked.

Devorgilla's eyes snapped open.

Somerled. He'd returned.

Relief sluicing through her, the crone pushed up on her elbows and peered about, looking for her little friend. Then full wakefulness came and she realized he'd be out in the moonlight.

Somerled favored silvery, moonlit nights, claiming they were as conductive to his magic as Devorgilla's own favorite soft hour when night fell and the mists gathered.

He barked again and Devorgilla cackled with glee, her pleasure helping her to her feet.

"He is hungry," she said, glancing at her other four-legged companion, her tricolored cat, Mab. A creature nigh as old as Devorgilla herself but a deal more crotchety.

Leastways in Devorgilla's view.

Curled at the most comfortable end of the pallet, Mab pointedly ignored her rival's return.

She simply opened one eye, her look of disdain assuring Devorgilla that her feline sleep concerned her far more than a certain adventure-seeking red fox was troubled by an empty belly.

"You, *mo ghaoil*, ate your fill of herrings this e'en," Devorgilla reminded her as she pulled on her boots. "So, my dear one, surely you will not begrudge Somerled a wee bowl of gannet stew?"

Another of Mab's superior stares said that she did. The seabird stew was one of Mab's favorite dishes. And definitely tasty enough to please Somerled.

Even so, Devorgilla hobbled to the door and opened it wide. Her little friend sat silhouetted in moonglow in the middle of her charmed glade, the grassy clearing that shielded her from unwanted, prying eyes.

Somerled's eyes watched her now.

The little red fox had magical eyes.

Beautiful, expressive, and wise, his eyes could tell whole tales with one carefully aimed stare and as he stretched to his feet and came forward, Devorgilla knew that his mission had been a success.

A tremendous success.

"Ah, my precious," she crooned, stepping aside to allow him into the cottage, "I see everything went as planned."

Somerled strolled around the cottage, then chose to sit

in the warmth cast by Devorgilla's charcoal brazier, his expression assuring her that he'd succeeded indeed.

But his task hadn't been without difficulty and as she filled a wooden bowl with the fine-smelling gannet stew, he let her know that he suspected she'd soon have reason to send him back to Baldreagan.

Truth tell, he was so sure of it, he would have stayed and not yet bothered himself with the long journey to Doon did he not know the crone would be fretting about him.

That, of course, he would keep to himself.

Devorgilla had her pride, he knew.

And while she also had a surprisingly tender and sentimental heart, he knew she secretly enjoyed knowing how fearsome some folk considered her.

"We shall not think about that this night," she said, setting down the stew and a small platter of bannocks smeared with honey and bramble jam. "If there is a need for you to return, the Old Ones will let us know."

A large bowl of fresh spring water followed, and a smaller bowl filled to the brim with her very own specially brewed heather ale.

But Somerled deserved a special treat, so she waited until he began eating the gannet stew, then she shuffled to a hanging partition of woven straw that hid a small larder off the cottage's main room.

Shoving aside the straw mat, she stepped into the cool dimness of the larder, quickly gathering choice portions of her best cheeses and dried meats, a generous handful of sugared sweetmeats.

These treats she arrayed on not one but two good-sized

platters, carrying them over to the handsome little fox with all the glory-making ado a woman of her years could muster.

"So-o-o, my fine wee warrior," she crooned, her face wreathing in a smile, "in honor of your triumph, *two* platters of delicacies for you."

Raising his paw in acknowledgment, Somerled thanked her, then made haste to avail himself of his reward.

His just reward, if he did say so himself.

Much pleased, he deigned to ignore Mab's hostile stare and finished off the gannet stew. He'd enjoy his remaining victory victuals—both platters of them—at a slower, more leisurely pace.

As befitted a great hero.

And he had no doubt that he was one.

Indeed, if he had two long legs rather than four short ones, he was quite sure someone would've knighted him for his most recent knight-like accomplishment.

Sir Somerled.

He could almost hear the accolades. The trumpet blasts and horn blowing, the cheers from maidens fair.

Instead, he realized with a start, his horn tooting was only old Devorgilla's fluting snores.

Poor soul, she'd fallen asleep on her three-legged stool beside her cook fire. Not wanting her to waken any more stiff than could be avoided, Somerled fixed his golden stare on her, working his magic until she stirred herself and, still sleeping soundly, returned to her plaid-covered pallet.

A penetrating look at her thin-soled black boots saw

them slide easily from her feet. And one last stare tucked the plaid gently around her, draping her clear to the tip of her grizzled chin.

Satisfied, he decided he really should begin to think of himself as Sir Somerled.

He was, after all, the wisest, boldest, and most magical fox in all the Highlands.

He was the most successful, too.

A true champion, as his two platters of reward delicacies proved.

He just hoped he'd be as triumphant the next time.

Back at Baldreagan, darkest night curled around a certain stout-walled tower and a biting chill slipped through the wooden slats of the bedchamber's brightly painted window shutters. Freezing autumn rain pelted those shutters, but the brilliant, jewel-toned colors shone fetchingly in the candle-and-torch-lit room, their romantic whimsy bearing yet another reminder that the chamber had belonged to Kendrick.

His private lair and love nest.

The scene, Aveline was certain, of many heated embraces and other lascivious delights. Kendrick's bed-sporting exploits were legion, though a thoughtful soul might credit some of the wilder tales to hopeful female hearts.

Boastful female hearts, she suspected.

In truth, Kendrick could ne'er possibly have bedded all the lasses who claimed they'd enjoyed his favor. And ne'er had she actually encountered one of the countless bastards he'd supposedly sired throughout the neighboring hills and glens.

A great red-haired giant, though not quite as big as Jamie, Kendrick's twinkling blue eyes and his quick-flashing smile could bedazzle at a glance. And if his high good looks weren't enough, he'd possessed a merry tongue and a soft Highland voice almost too beautiful for a man this side of heaven.

Aveline shivered, the image of Jamie's roguish brother having his way with angels almost making her smile, had it not been so sad.

He ought to be here still, wooing and winning *living* hearts.

Ravishing byre maids and knights' daughters alike, whisking them away to his high-towered love lair and filling hours with naught but laughter, song, and uninhibited carnal bliss.

The deliciously decadent kind as hinted by the naked images painted into the innocent-seeming pastoral scene gracing Kendrick's window shutters.

At first glance, it seemed a tranquil woodland landscape filled with mythical creatures and a fanciful distant castle. A closer inspection showed unclothed wood and water nymphs in a variety of suggestive poses, some even attended by handsome knights in equal states of dishabille.

Aveline shivered again, seeing the painted images as clearly as if she were standing in front of the shutters and examining them. An undertaking she'd already allowed herself, carefully inspecting each and every depicted pair until the possibilities were emblazoned across her mind.

Erotic possibilities.

Images of lust and bared flesh, limbs entwined and handsome faces awash with rapture. She just hoped her joinings with Jamie would be as joyous.

Willing it so, she pressed a hand to her breast, trying to steady her breathing, the thrilling sensations that spun through her each time she imagined herself and Jamie as one of the mythic pairs depicted on the shutters.

Ach, to be sure, Kendrick's bedchamber revealed a man who'd savored his sensual pleasures. And this night, she hoped, he wouldn't mind if she borrowed his love nest for her own.

A step she'd already taken in ordering a bath for Jamie, then setting out and lighting her finest beeswax candles. Aveline smiled and smoothed her hair. Faith, she'd even tossed a handful of pleasantly aromatic herbs onto the hearth fire. Preparations she'd finalized when she'd bolted the door behind the retreating army of kitchen lads who'd carried up a seemingly endless supply of steaming water pails.

She looked again at the heavy oaken door and the sturdy drawbar now slid so soundly into its socket inside the wall. The bolted door was more than just a shielding barrier for their privacy: it was a tangible sign of her new life. The happy and fulfilling existence she meant to seize for herself as James Macpherson's bride.

His soon-to-be wife.

And in every conceivable way.

Aveline drew a deep breath. His notions about hurting her were absurd. Even innocent, she knew that nary a child would be born if a woman weren't capable of stretching enough to let the babe slide out of her.

No matter James of the Heather's great size, she doubted his manhood was larger than any smiling, gurgling bairn she'd e'er bounced on her knee. And with so many married sisters, she'd seen her share of newborn babes.

She just needed to convince Jamie that if bairns can come out of a woman, a man's privy part will surely always fit in.

To that end, she completed the reason she'd kept her back to him so long, pretending she was waiting until the last of the kitchen lads' loud, pail-clattering descent faded from the stair tower.

In truth, she used the time to undo her stays and laces. Taking her lower lip between her teeth, she mustered her courage and then let her gown slip to the floor.

Jamie's sharp indrawn breath from somewhere behind her, marked her victory.

Her next triumph would come when she turned around and he glimpsed her standing before him wearing nothing but her near-transparent undershift.

And, she hoped, a seductive smile.

A look bold enough to rouse and excite him, tempting him into forgetting the night's horrors and thinking only of the pleasure she wished to give him.

But if his eyes narrowed or clouded with disappointment, she'd retrieve her gown and re-don it. Then she'd bathe him as chastely as she'd tended the worthies who'd visited Fairmaiden Castle.

"They are gone," she said, referring to the kitchen lads and their racket. "And you, my lord, shall now be treated to a bath like no other," she added, turning at last.

Her pulse quickening at her daring, she eased down the straps of her shift, gently lowering the top piece until her breasts were fully uncovered.

Jamie's brows shot upward and his breath snagged in his throat. His reaction seemed to please her for she made no move to cover herself. She simply stood where she was, her shift falling loosely around her hips and her breasts delightfully bared.

And, he saw at once, not just her sweet, rose-tipped breasts. Through the thin cloth of her camise, he could also make out the silky curls of her woman's mound, a tempting triangular shadow just topping her thighs.

"Holy saints." He knew he was staring, but couldn't stop. "Sweet lass, do you ken I can see all of you?"

"To be sure, I know." She looked at him, her chin lifting. "Would I have undressed for your bath if I meant to keep myself covered?"

Jamie hesitated, an unpleasant thought stealing into his mind.

Saints, now *he* was the jealous one.

"Did you bathe your father's friends thusly?" he asked, damning the question, but needing to know.

She shook her head. "Nay, I was e'er fully clothed when seeing to the comforts of Fairmaiden guests."

"I am glad," Jamie admitted, his relief almost a living thing.

Humbling, too, for its portent. Truth was, he'd often lain with Gunna of the Glen on a pallet still warmed by another man's rutting. Yet all he'd cared about was taking his ease.

Aveline was different.

He wanted her body, aye. But more than that he wanted her companionship and caring, her wit and intelligence. The way she could make him laugh. Her appreciation for the beauty of the great hills and moors they called their own. The respect she'd displayed for the Old Ones and the ancient ways by bathing naked at a sacred well, garbed in naught but her unbound hair and the silver of the moon.

Her kindness to his father and Hughie Mac touched him, too. As did the softness that came into her eyes when she knew he was missing his brothers.

And though he'd ne'er admit it, he loved the way she passed the best tidbits from her supper trencher to Cuillin or whate'er other castle dogs might come nosing up to her for a handout.

Jamie drew a deep breath, astounded by the clutch she already had on him.

As if she guessed his thoughts, she glanced at her naked breasts and then back at him, suddenly looking shy. But she recovered as quickly, sending him a bright, dimpling smile.

Stepping closer to the bathing tub, she swirled a finger in the steaming water, then turned away to fill a small earthenware bowl with violet-scented oil, carefully placing the bowl near the hissing, red-glowing charcoal brazier.

"Hot scented oil for after I've bathed you," she told him, moving to the tub again. "That, and more."

"More?"

"You will see." She drew up a low three-legged stool and placed a small jar of soap and washing cloths onto its seat. "But first, I must see you. Out of your clothes and into the water."

Jamie nodded, but he still wasn't certain he wanted her to see him at all. It was one thing for her to be daring so long as his clothes hid the dangers, and quite something else for her to actually see that *danger* hanging heavy between his thighs, long, thick, and swaying.

Blessedly, he was still relaxed, but staying that way was proving a ferocious struggle.

Jamie frowned.

Aveline dipped her fingers into the bathwater again, watching him. "You were about to show yourself to me when Morag came abovestairs," she reminded him.

"Sweet lass, this has naught to do with removing my clothes." He raked a hand through his hair. "I am trying not to run hard, is what I'm doing. Think you I can get naked and into that tub, have you touching me intimately, and not wish to touch you in a like manner?"

She smiled. "Then do."

"I can hardly breathe for wanting you and—" He looked at her, his jaw slipping. "What did you say?"

She studied him, her lovely face turning serious. "You did say we are so good as legally wed, did you not? That because of our plight troth anything we do isn't a sin?"

Jamie nodded, unable to deny his own words, or the truth of them. Leastways to his way of looking at things.

Such as his conviction that she was his the instant he'd seen her gliding through that moonlit glade near Hughie Mac's cottage.

Or that he'd been hers since that moment.

And anyway, come the spring, they would be man and

wife in truth. Their union blessed and sanctioned by man, Church, and God. Until then, he'd personally slay anyone who dared try to come between them.

Be it man, dragon, or bogle.

Especially bogles. Wing-backed and haloed, ring-tailed or horned. He'd have done with whate'er variation of the beasties cared to come at him.

She tapped his chest, looking pleased. "Then," she said, a dimple flashing in her cheek, "if you agree that we are as good as wed, get in yon tub and let us see what happens!"

Jamie groaned. She was the one who needed to be worrying about what would happen. He could already feel what was happening.

Or rather, what was stirring.

But it couldn't be helped. Not with her rosy nipples so tight and thrusting, and her perfect little breasts jiggling so delightfully each time she swirled her fingers through his bathing water.

So he made short work of sword belt and clothes, tossing off every last stitch with a speed that would serve him wonders if he could duplicate it on a field of battle.

Full naked, he fair leapt into the tub. But not so quickly that he hadn't seen her eyes widen in shock, the look of horror that flashed across her beautiful face.

Jamie's heart sank.

She clapped her hands to her cheeks and stared down at him.

"Dear saints in heaven," she gasped, shaking her head. "You—"

"I tried to warn you," Jamie said, his world tipping,

narrowing to her stunned face and the tears suddenly glinting on her fine, gold-tipped lashes.

He sank down into the heated water, damning his uncommon height, his over-long legs that made it impossible to scrunch himself deep enough into the wooden tub to hide what he'd known would shock and scare her.

And it had.

Horror stood all o'er her and he wouldn't blame her if she fainted away in a swoon. Or crossed herself and ran screaming from the room.

Frowning, he grabbed a washing cloth and used it to cover himself. "Sweet lass, please dinna fret," he said, searching for the right words. "I've told you, I will ne'er hurt you. There are ways—"

"Och, Jamie!" She dropped to her knees beside the tub and flung her arms around his neck, kissing him everywhere. His lips, his temples and brow, his eyelids and ears, even his nose. "Jamie, Jamie, 'tis not your size that shocked me," she said, grabbing his face between her hands, her tears spilling freely now. "I knew to expect *that,* and am thrilled and excited to explore you most thoroughly!"

Jamie blinked.

His heart split wide and blinding heat slammed into the backs of his eyes. "By the Rood," he managed, pushing the words past the thickness in his throat, "then whate'er made you go so pale?"

"This." She thrust her arm into the tub and ran her fingers down his hip and farther until she reached the long puckered scar marring the outside of his left thigh. "You ne'er told me you've had a wound seared. It grieved me to see the scar after what happened tonight."

"Ach, lass." Jamie leaned back against the linen-padded rim of the tub. "The scar is one I brought back from Crossgate Moor," he said, blowing out a breath, wishing one great gusty sigh could banish the images of Neville's Cross and its arrow storm of English longbows.

The shattering defeat and the incredible blow of Scotland's young King David being captured and taken prisoner from right beneath the noses of the realm's greatest nobility. And none of them able to do aught but look on in appalled horror as the English routed and slaughtered them, then plucked their hiding king from beneath the span of a bridge.

Shuddering at the memory, Jamie reached for his bride's hand, kissing her fingers one by one, the soft, silky warmth of her inner wrist.

And as he'd hoped, the sweetness of her smooth, white skin helped chase away the shadow images of angry and torn flesh, bright red and streaming. Or cold and gray, once death claimed the countless poor souls who'd left their lives on that devil-damned Sassunach bog.

"I'd forgotten you were with the king at Neville's Cross," she said, her expression pensive.

Jamie shrugged. "Compared to most, I came away unscathed," he said, truly believing it. "What saved me was the good fortune of riding with Robert, the High Steward. He commanded the left of the field and we fared better than most, having the luck of more stable terrain to fight on. Even so, we were still unable to stop King David's capture."

He looked down at his scar, then back at her. "After the carnage I saw that day, I can ne'er think of myself as having even been wounded in the fray. Truth be told, I canna even recall the moment it happened."

"I am glad." She slid her arms around his neck and kissed him, and this time her kiss was leisurely, soft and sweet, and full on the lips.

When at last she eased back, she smoothed her hand down his cheek. "It is best not to dwell on painful things we cannot undo or change. God was kind in letting you forget."

"Ah, but I do remember the searing," Jamie admitted, her caress already taking his mind elsewhere. "'Tis why it grieved me to brand my own da. I knew the pain I'd be giving him."

"You also gave him life, did you not?" Aveline stood. "I vow he will be right pleased about that when he comes to his senses again."

To her surprise, Jamie laughed. "Not pleased enough to apologize to Lady Juliana and Morag for threatening them with his sword, I'll wager!"

Smiling back at him, Aveline leaned forward and kissed his cheek. "Then I shall apologize to you for looking so shocked upon seeing your scar and making you think the reason was otherwise."

He cocked a brow. "You truly are not frightened by that particular 'otherwise'?"

"Frightened?" Aveline dipped one of the washing cloths into the little jar of soap and began to scrub his shoulders. "My only fear is that you might withhold yourself from me and"—her gaze slid to Kendrick's painted window shutters—"I find myself eager to share pleasure with you."

"Eager enough to remove your shift and join me in this tub?" He arched a brow at her again, the simmering heat in his eyes and the way his voice deepened sending delicious thrills all through her.

Making it impossible to say no.

"O-o-oh, aye," she agreed, already reaching to shove down the camise.

But he shot out a hand, strong fingers encircling her wrist. "After you've finished bathing me," he said, flashing a wolfish grin.

"Of course," Aveline agreed, slipping away to fetch a flagon of sweet, spiced wine.

Returning to the tub, she handed him a filled chalice, watching as he sipped. Two heavy wax candles burned on a nearby table and the bright flames illuminated his naked body, casting an alluring pattern of flickering light and shadow across his broad shoulders and back.

Rivulets of water trickled down his chest and she followed their path, admiring the fine glint of his chest hair and how some of the droplets caught there, clinging to the smattering of wiry red-gold hairs and hovering like glittery little diamonds before breaking free and rolling lower.

Her gaze drifted lower, too, but this time he smiled and made no attempt to hide himself. Or his pleasure. The steadily increasing beat of the pulse in his throat bespoke his excitement, as did the rise of his maleness.

An answering pulse quickened inside her. Her heart thumping, she dipped her hand deeper beneath the water, letting her fingers glide across and then tangle in the thick coppery curls springing at his loins.

Her own loins went molten at the intimacy, especially when the backs of her fingers brushed against the smooth, silky skin of his thick, swollen shaft.

Aveline's breath caught and her hand froze, her fingers curling deeper into his nether curls as his manhood twitched and jerked against her. And though she could scarce believe it, swelled and lengthened even more.

"Dear saints," she whispered, looking down at the large, plum-sized head. Jutting well above the still-steaming water, a tiny glistening droplet of moisture appeared on its tip. Dewing moisture she knew had naught to do with the water droplets trickling down his chest.

She swallowed and wet her lips, fascinated. Aching to stroke and fondle him, yet too awed to touch such magnificent male perfection.

He must've sensed her hesitation, for he shifted in the tub, opening his thighs a bit more to give her a better view. Or greater access. Tingly heat swept her at either notion. Nay, he was definitely not hiding himself now.

Not that he should.

She was quite sure he was the most beautifully made man she'd ever seen.

Watching her, he reached to capture a loose tendril of her hair, curling it slowly around his finger. "Touch me," he said, firelight reflecting off his own vibrant, auburn hair. "I'd meant to wait, would've abstained totally—or tried! But it is too late, sweetness."

His gaze went to her little bowl of warming oil, its

heady violet scent already rising. The drifting fumes perfumed the air, intoxicating his senses.

"'Tis too late for warmed oil massages, too," he added, his voice turning husky. "Too late as well for the removal of your shift."

He flashed her a smile, one that quickly spread into a roguish grin when her sapphire eyes deepened with her own desire and she stood to retrieve the bowl of oil anyway.

"There is another use for the oil," she said, placing one foot on the stool and easing up her shift's dampened skirt, her position leaving her fragrant woman's curls but a handsbreath from his face.

"Sweet Jesu!" The two words escaped between Jamie's teeth as he realized her intent. "Where'er did you learn such a wanton's trick?"

"From my sister, Maili," she explained, already dipping her fingers into the bowl. "Her husband is also quite well-proportioned, though I canna believe he is so large as you. Maili told me if e'er I were to wed such a well-favored man, I might rub myself with warmed oil before the first few couplings and thus ease the joinings."

Jamie swallowed.

She touched glistening fingers to her sex. Holding his gaze, she began gently rubbing the oil between her legs, even applying some to the tender flesh of her smooth inner thighs.

It took Jamie all of a heartbeat to know what he wanted to do.

"Nay, lass, let me," he said, thrusting his fingers into the bowl of heated oil. "I will rub you."

And in ways that would make her far more ready for him than any scented oil, heated or otherwise.

"Come closer," he urged her, "and part your legs for me. Just enough so that I can see and touch you."

And she did, stepping so near that her sweetness hovered just above him. The rich musk of her arousal flooded his senses, making him drunk with desire.

He touched his fingers to her then and a startled gasp broke from her lips. Pleased by the sound and the flare of desire in her eyes, he rubbed her, carefully massaging the oil onto her most tender, sweetest flesh.

She trembled beneath his caress, her own fingers digging into the folds of her shift as she held the bunched material well above her thighs.

"Holy saints," she breathed, a great rippling shudder streaking through her when he ceased his feather light strokings and began sliding a slow, probing finger up and down the very center of her.

"Ach, lass, you are just beginning to explore pleasure." At last, Jamie flicked lightly at her most sensitive spot. "This will melt you as naught else," he told her, circling his finger over her quivering flesh.

Slow, deliberate circlings he kept up until she closed her eyes and began to rock her hips. She arched her heat against his hand, her hitching breath and the slick moisture damping his fingers letting him know it was time.

"I can wait no longer," he vowed, seizing her by the waist and lifting her into the tub. "I am sorry, lass, I would that it could've been otherwise."

"It is perfect," she cried, looking down to where he

held her poised above him. "You are perfect. Fully magnificent, and I would have no other."

She wriggled against him, her slick female heat slipping across the swollen tip of his shaft, a sensation almost blinding in its exquisiteness. Jamie threw back his head and clenched his teeth, unable to keep his hips from lifting in response, the tip of his iron-hard shaft sliding right into her.

Not the long fluid thrustings he burned to give her, sure, deep, and smooth. This was only a first tentative sheathing, her slick and tight wetness taking only a few throbbing inches.

Or so he thought until she flung her arms around his neck and, kissing him, slid the rest of her sweet, clinging tightness right down over him.

"*Mother of God!*" he cried, his seed shooting into her even as he tore through her innocence. Her own precious little body jerked and tightened against him, the glory of her pleasure cries shattering him even more than the power of his release.

A wonder he would ne'er have believed possible.

Even if, in truth, she'd only taken half of him.

There would be time later to accustom her to more. And he knew now that she'd welcome each joining with him, for there could be no mistaking that her passion had burned as hotly.

But his wonder was the greatest, he decided, reveling in the feel of her, all soft and silky warm in his arms. His heart clenched, and he was certain he'd ne'er be able to have enough of her.

Never be able to hold her closely enough or slide

deeply enough inside her, kiss her long enough or explore every sweet inch of her with his hands and lips and tongue. Live enough days to love her as endlessly as he wished to do.

And, in time, he hoped, make her love him.

She consumed him and ne'er had he felt such a burning need to make a woman his.

She was also still straddling him. Her sweet rose-puckered nipples pressed into his chest and her sleek female wetness proved an irresistible delight. He'd thought to wash and tend her, making certain he hadn't hurt her. But already he was swelling again, each hot slick glide of her softness over his shaft, causing him to pulse and throb anew.

"You dinna ken what you're doing, sweetness," he warned, pushing to his feet and sweeping her up with him. "I can no longer be responsible for what happens between us behind closed and barred doors."

"And beyond those doors?" She stepped out of her dripping camise and kicked it aside.

"Beyond them?"

She stepped closer, trailing her fingers through his glistening chest hair. "I know a fine woodland glade," she began, letting her hand glide lower as her gaze slid to Kendrick's erotic window shutters.

She looked back at him. "You did say there are many ways for us to be intimate?"

Jamie nodded, his throat too thick for words.

He'd followed her glance and knew full well what stood painted on Kendrick's shutters.

The notion of enjoying even one of the shutters' sensual pleasures with her almost robbed his breath.

"There are many ways for a loving couple to enjoy each other," he said when he could speak. He watched her carefully, waiting to see if she'd respond to his unspoken question.

And she did, the comprehending light in her eyes nearly bringing him to his knees.

Her gaze flew once more to the shutters. "I hope you will show me all of those ways."

"As you wish it," he agreed, silently thanking Kendrick for acquiring the shutters.

She need never know how much he and his other brothers had ribbed Kendrick about his choice.

"Aye, lass, so it shall be," he said again, just because it pleased him. "There is naught I would deny you."

Chapter Thirteen

❖

Y ou did say there was naught you'd deny me."

Jamie's words came back to haunt him just a few days later. In fine Highland tradition, he put back his shoulders and folded his arms, determined to maintain his dignity. Even so, he couldn't quite keep his lips from twitching and only the solemnity of the day kept him from laughing out loud.

That, and the great press of kinsmen and friends crowding Baldreagan's bailey.

"Naught, you said," his lady reminded him.

Jamie gave a noncommittal *humph.*

He should have known better than to trust a woman with such a broad and all-encompassing statement.

Aveline Matheson included.

Nay, her in especial.

Blessedly, she'd leaned close, pitching her voice soft and low so that only he could hear her. Still, knowing what sharp ears the MacKenzie lasses possessed, he was quite sure they'd heard her, too.

Likewise their puissant father's hovering, ever-present guardsmen, however busy they were dashing about with travel coffers and all the other goods the Black Stag's cosseted daughters deemed essential to their well-being. Jamie's own da had surely heard as well, along with Morag and anyone else who'd gathered to bid farewell and good journeying to Baldreagan's departing guests.

"It would be so nice to see them again," Aveline persisted, watching the bustle.

Jamie slid a glance at her, bracing himself for more carefully crafted persuasion. They were standing in the shadow of the keep's forebuilding and he stepped closer now and hooked his fingers under her chin, lifting her face so she had to look at him.

"The MacKenzies have already promised to come here for our wedding revelries in the spring," he told her, lowering his own voice.

Not because he cared if Gelis Long-nose and the MacKenzies heard what he had to say, but because he did not relish his father hearing him.

Even though the thrawn old goat stood a good distance away. Looking more stubborn than usual, he leaned heavily on Morag's arm, having stoutly refused to use a crummock for support. But walking stick or no, Jamie knew there was nothing wrong with Munro's hearing.

Truth be told, he'd often suspected the man could listen through walls.

Indeed, for all Jamie knew, such a feat might well be how he always managed to get the better of his fellow

Highland cattle lairds, e'er seeming to know what the men said behind his back or when they believed Munro out of earshot.

"I have ne'er sailed the Hebrides," Aveline pressed him then, hooking her hand through his arm and squeezing. "Lady Gelis says her father or his friend, Sir Marmaduke, would surely take us on a grand sailing adventure. Perhaps even as far south to the Isle of Doon? We could visit Devorgilla—"

Jamie laughed despite himself. "The wise woman of Doon? For truth, lass, that one ne'er misses a wedding feast anywhere in the Highlands and the Isles," he said, secretly certain the indomitable cailleach could even appear at two celebrations at the same time if she wished it. "You will surely see her in the spring as well. Without—"

"But—"

"Without us having to make the long journey to Eilean Creag and even farther to Devorgilla's fair isle," he finished for her, looking pleased with his logic.

Aveline cast a wistful glance at the MacKenzie pannier ponies. Well-burdened and restless, they appeared eager to be on their way. Excitement began to beat through her. Lifting her chin, she gave Jamie her most hopeful smile.

"Visiting the MacKenzies would be an adventure," she said, certain of it.

But Jamie only shook his head.

"Nay, lass," he disagreed, speaking close to her ear, "it would be a strenuous excursion that would push my da past his limits."

"Oh." Aveline's face fell. "You are right, of course. And he would ne'er stay behind."

"There you have the way of it."

Jamie sighed, sliding a quick glance at his father. Although he kept his bearded chin proudly lifted and was even making an effort to be halfway gallant and charming to the three MacKenzie women, Jamie was certain he was leaning even more heavily on Morag's arm than he had been moments ago.

Most troubling of all, the sparkling glint in the old man's eyes that Jamie knew most would mistake for a host's laughing good cheer, wasn't the like at all.

Munro's eyes were misting with emotion.

He was sorry to see the girls depart and Jamie worried that without their light and laughter, their lively and spirited chatter filling the hall of an e'en, his da's spirits would grow even bleaker.

To be sure, he cherished Aveline. As, it would seem, did everyone at Baldreagan. They'd heartily welcomed her into their midst. But she'd become family; the MacKenzies had provided a distraction.

A most welcome distraction. And a needed one, especially for Munro.

Jamie ran a hand through his hair and pressed his lips together, trying not to frown. His father wasn't healing as fast as he should either and much as Jamie wished otherwise, a long journey by land and sea, now, or even in the spring, would surely be too much for him.

"Sorry, lass." Jamie turned back to his bride. "A spring journey to Eilean Creag is one pleasure I canna give you."

He smoothed his knuckles down her cheek. "Leastways no' this year."

"But you will keep your word and take me to St.

Maelrubha's this afternoon?" She kept her sapphire gaze fixed on him. "I thought we'd take some heather to your mother."

Jamie frowned after all.

And promptly recalled another bit of masterful manly wisdom the great Black Stag of Kintail had once shared. Namely that females have an astonishing ability to take the slightest slip-of-tongue and embroider it to suit them. Most often to an unsuspecting male's distinct disadvantage.

Jamie blew out a breath and shoved back his hair. Truth was, he'd said a very vague something about wishing to pay a call on old Hughie Mac. Close as Hughie's cottage was to the Garbh Uisge, Jamie thought to question him.

After all, Hughie, too, claimed to have seen the ghosts of Jamie's brothers.

That alone made a visit worthwhile.

But a return to the Macpherson kirkyard and the dark and dank-smelling little chapel had not been mentioned. Nor was going there how Jamie preferred to spend the day with his lady.

Especially if such a visit involved taking a clutch of heather to his mother's tomb. Jamie stiffened. That kind of folly was something he hadn't allowed himself since he was a wee lad. Munro had caught him, chasing him from the chapel in fury, ranting that he'd had no right to lay blooms on the grave of a mother he'd killed.

But before he could tell Aveline he had no desire to go there, Gelis ran over to them, all ringing laughter, glowing cheeks, and bright, wind-tangled hair.

"I' faith! Have you e'er seen such frowners?" she cried, tossing a glance at her father's guardsmen, nary a scowling man amongst them. "They are complaining that I've brought too much baggage! But"—she flung an arm around Aveline and smiled— "Arabella and I were fore-warned. 'Tis said that the farther north one travels, the less likely it is to expect even a lumpy pallet to sleep on, much less a palatable meal!"

"No one told us any such thing," Arabella amended, joining them.

She reached to smooth Gelis's hair, her own braid sleek and black as a raven's wing and nary a strand out of place. "You know we are going to visit Lady Mariota's father in Assynt. Archibald Macnicol is as proud a chief-tain as our own da. His holding, Dunach Castle, will surely have no less comforts than Eilean Creag."

Gelis swatted at her sister's hand. "Loch Assynt is also known for its dread water horse—lest you've forgotten!" she exclaimed, pulling a face. "And if we do venture on to Lady Juliana's Mackay kin in Strathnaver, 'tis said the land thereabouts is riddled with the faery mounds of the *Sithe* and that the ghosts of fearless and bloodthirsty Norsemen sleep in the high dunes of every strand!"

Arabella sniffed. "Sleeping Norsemen you'd no doubt waken with all your twitter and babbling."

Jamie choked and hid a smile behind his hand.

"Go ahead and laugh," Arabella said, looking at him. "You know it's the truth."

Unfazed, Gelis fluffed her skirts. "Vikings were braw men. Tall blond giants with hot blue eyes and huge, wicked swords they gave names like Wolf Tooth or Leg Biter. They—"

"They were heathen sea-raiders," Arabella corrected.

Flipping her neat black braid over her shoulder, she sent a meaningful glance across the bailey to where Beardie was helping the MacKenzie guardsmen load the long line of pannier horses. As always, he wore his huge Norseman's ax thrust proudly beneath his belt, though he'd forgone his rusty winged helmet. Catching the girls' stares, he lifted a hand in greeting but his most-times good-natured smile appeared a tiny bit forced.

Looking back at her sister, Arabella shook her head. "I daresay you've already broken one *Viking* heart and you can be certain Lady Juliana and I will be watching you closely when we get to Dunach."

Gelis rolled her eyes. "I truly do fear we'll get naught to eat in the far north but dry oatcakes and salt fish," she fussed, hot-eyed Vikings and their swords apparently forgotten. "For truth, I'd rather stay here."

She paused to look at Jamie. "Mother sent us here for a reason. And—"

"We've seen her concerns addressed," Lady Juliana finished for her, "and your father's men are waiting on us. They are ready to ride."

She placed a hand on both girls' shoulders, offering an apologetic look to Jamie and Aveline. "You will have a care?" she asked, speaking to them both though her words were clearly meant for Jamie.

He nodded, wishing the sun hadn't chosen that moment to slip behind a cloud, its abrupt disappearance casting the bailey in shadow and drawing attention to the chill, knifing wind.

"All will be well." Aveline gave the older woman a quick, impulsive hug. "God go with you, and let us know when you've safely returned to Kintail."

When she stepped back, Jamie took Lady Juliana's hand, bringing it to his lips for a farewell kiss. "We shall look forward to seeing you in the spring, my lady. Here at Baldreagan, God willing."

I shall ask the Old Ones to watch o'er you, Jamie thought he heard her say as he released her hand. But already she'd turned and was striding briskly toward the waiting MacKenzie guardsmen and, he saw, his father's own men who were scrambling to open the gates.

"Till the spring!" Gelis cried, throwing her arms around both Jamie and Aveline, hugging them tight. "I shall dance the whole night of your wedding!"

"If you do not run off with a hot-eyed Viking before we return home!" Arabella quipped, waiting for her own chance to embrace her hosts.

When it came, she blinked furiously and dashed at the tears suddenly wetting her cheeks. "Do not do anything foolhardy, James Macpherson," she warned. "My da has a formidable temper as you well know—you willna want him grieved with you for not heeding Mother's message."

Then she whirled on her heels and was gone, Gelis flying after her. A flurry of skirts, a few frantic hand waves and cries, and the whole loud, racket-making party of MacKenzies were through the gates and vanished.

Gone, from one instant to the next, the creeping

autumn mists closing around them, muffling the sounds of their departure and blocking them from view.

At once, deep silence settled over Baldreagan's bailey . . . until Munro noisily blew his nose.

Jamie glanced him, even started toward him, but Munro scowled and waved him away. "Do you not have anything better to do than gawk at an auld done man?" he snapped, his voice at least two shades thicker than it should have been.

His jaw thrusting forward, he fixed Jamie with his fiercest glare. "Patrolling the battlements mayhap? Or sharpening your sword?"

"Lucifer's knees," Jamie swore beneath his breath. "He'd try the patience of St. Columba. Does he not ken that I—"

"Leave be," Aveline urged, placing a hand on Jamie's arm and squeezing. "He is only sad to see the MacKenzies leave. Come nightfall, he will be in better fettle."

"Ach, to be sure," Jamie agreed, watching Morag help his da back inside the hall. "So soon as he is hungry and kens no one will serve him so much as a dried bannock unless he wipes the frown off his face."

Not that Munro was alone in his grimness.

If truth be told, everyone still lurking about the bailey was frowning.

Or at least looking dispirited.

Glum.

Even the sun's feeble autumn warmth had fled and the afternoon's chill was increasing with the lengthening shadows, a faint smirr of cold thin rain even beginning to splatter the cobbles. The wind was picking up, too, its random gusts sending wispy curtains of damp, gray mist scuttling over the walls and across the bailey. But no one complained, even if something somewhere had set the castle dogs barking and snarling.

The gloom matched the moods of those slowly returning to the keep, the usual goings-on of the castle's daily business.

Only one soul smiled.

A tall and hooded figure standing unnoticed in the deep shadows of one of the wooden byres stretching along the curtain wall.

The departure of the MacKenzie she-bitches and their pack of swell-headed, muscle-packed watchdogs would prove the turning of the tide for Clan Macpherson.

It'd been tedious to move in and out of the keep with so many souls in residence.

So many sets of curious, probing eyes and too many extra sword arms.

The nuisance of unexpected interference.

The figure allowed one slight tightening of the lips. Had it not been for the ill-timed appearance of a drink-taken MacKenzie guardsman careening out of the shadows near the postern gate, a half-clothed kitchen wench still clinging to him, all giggly and smitten, a certain crossbow shot would have fired true.

Blessedly, they'd both been too ale-headed to notice anything amiss.

Indeed, the MacKenzies' visit had been an annoyance, but they'd left now.

The figure's smile returned.

Any other difficulties and disturbances could be easily dealt with. Proving it, the figure wagged a finger at the handful of bristly-backed, snarling castle dogs, then began scrounging inside a worn leather pouch kept for just such purposes.

A fine and large meat bone soon appeared and sailed through the air, landing on the rain-dampened cobbles with a satisfying *kerplunk*.

As was to be anticipated, the offensive yapping and growling ceased at once. The figure forgotten, the mangy curs pounced on the bone, their greedy hunger outweighing the danger of a mere two-legged trespasser.

The figure watched them with pleasure, sure in the knowledge that it mattered not a whit how many dogs prowled Baldreagan's bailey or how often the addle-witted laird changed his sleeping quarters.

Nor would it avail any of them that one son yet lived.

For the nonce.

A grievous betrayal would soon be righted, fullest vengeance achieved at last.

And this time nothing would go wrong.

Do not do anything foolhardy.

Arabella MacKenzie's warning rang louder in Jamie's ears the longer he stood in the cold, dank shadows at the back of St. Maelrubha's chapel, an armful of late-blooming heather clutched against his chest and his feet seemingly frozen to the stone-flagged floor. Damnable feet, for each one refused to move, stubbornly ignoring his best efforts and not letting him take the last few steps toward his mother's tomb.

His bride, bless her, showed no such infirmity.

Looking wholly at ease, she moved about the nave placing new candles on wrought-iron prickets, her shining pale-haired presence and fresh violet scent a breath of welcome life in the damp and musty little chapel.

Scores of tiny votive lights were already lit and burning when they'd entered and to Jamie's mind, the pinpoints of twinkling light only strengthened the image of her as a *Sithe* princess in a gold-lit, enchanted glade.

He frowned.

In truth, it was a dark rain-chilled eve with thick mist shrouding the churchyard. Eerie, drifting swaths of gloom, each swirling curtain of gray demonstrated how easily a gullible soul might mistake the like for a bogle gliding across the burial ground.

Jamie put back his shoulders, willing his heart to stop knocking so crazily.

He was anything but gullible.

But if coming here wasn't foolhardy, he didn't know what was.

He swallowed, then immediately wished he hadn't. Doing so only let him know how dry his throat had gone. How discomfited he was. At least this time none of his knightly ancestors were draped in wet plaid, though someone had replenished the rowan clusters.

New sprigs of the bright, red-ribboned charms were tucked in niches throughout the chapel and the Na Clachan Breugach stone just outside the door arch also appeared to have been redressed with a fresh rowan garland.

Red ribbon and all.

Whoe'er had seen to the rowan, and Jamie suspected that someone was Hughie Mac, was looking after the chapel as well, for a trace of recently burned incense overlaid the smell of old smoke and damp stone, and a fine, clean-looking cloth graced the altar.

Even so, the air of oppression almost choked him. He looked about, seeking escape yet knowing he'd ne'er take it.

Not with Aveline already standing at his mother's tomb, her head reverently bowed. She'd clasped her hands solemnly before her and her softly spoken prayers proved a heart-gripping contrast to the chapel's cold stone vaulting, its wicked bone-biting chill.

Glancing aside, Jamie noticed that the door of the aumbry in the chapel's east wall stood cracked, the little cupboard appearing filled with candles. Going there now, he set down his clutch of heather long enough to use his steel and flint to light a taper, then touched its flame to several others, hoping the additional light would help dispel a bit more of the chapel's gloom.

And once lit, the long wax candles did throw warm golden light onto the weathered stone walls. Unfortunately, the light also fell across the carved and silent faces of Jamie's slumbering forebears.

A shudder slid down his spine. He breathed deep, trying not to see the rows of knightly effigies. He also did his best not to imagine the nine new ones that would soon join them.

Above all, he sought to ignore the finest tomb of all, the lovely marble one looming just ahead of him, behind the high altar and the dark oaken rood screen.

There, where his feet refused to go.

Determined to have done with the visit and be gone, he tried to move forward again, and couldn't.

He started then, for the air suddenly felt different. A slight shifting perhaps, almost as if the ancient stone walls had begun to breathe. Shivering openly now, he rubbed his arms and looked around.

The wind must've blown away some of the night's lowering clouds for moonlight was beginning to stream in through the arched doorway and the thin slit windows, each bright and slanting moonbeam an illumination he could have done without.

Jamie, come close . . . I would see you.

He froze, his heart slamming against his ribs.

A beautiful woman, tall and well made, stood beside his mother's tomb, her lush curves limned silver by the moon, the streaming mass of her tumbled, unbound hair the same burnished copper as his own.

She smiled at him and reached a milky white hand in his direction, the peace and love pouring off her making it impossible not to go to her.

But as soon as he took the first step, the moonlight shifted and the illusion faded. The woman standing before him was still beautiful, but her hair was shimmering flaxen, not the gleaming fire of a thousand Highland sunsets.

And though sweet and dear and perfect as he'd e'er wish, her womanly curves were lithe and delicate, not bold, lush and welling.

Nor was she tall.

"Jamie, come close," she said, smiling at him, offering him her hand. "I want you to see how beautiful she is."

But Jamie already knew.

Just as he'd heard his bride's words a moment before she'd spoken them.

If indeed they'd been her words.

He *did* know that now, finally, he'd be welcomed when, after so many years, he looked again on his mother's ornamental grave slab. The hauntingly exquisite effigy so lovely he'd blocked the image from his boyhood mind, unable to bear the guilt of being responsible for her death.

"Jamie, the heather." Aveline touched his arm, giving him a slight shake. "You've dropped it."

And he had, without even realizing.

The whole great bundle of tiny purple and white blooms lay strewn across the floor.

Kneeling, he began to gather them, his annoyance at having dropped the heather turning to dismay when he saw the poor state of the chapel floor beneath his mother's tomb.

Cracked and uneven, the stone flagging looked in dire need of repair. Some of the stones were even broken away, leaving dark holes in the floor's surface.

A dangerous and unacceptable circumstance, especially when he recalled how Aveline had slipped on the slick chapel flooring during their previous visit.

"Nay, stay there." He waved her away when she made to drop down beside him. "I have the blooms," he added, snatching up the last bit of the fallen heather and getting to his feet. "We'll lay them and be gone."

He narrowed his eyes on her, his voice brooking no refusal. "And I'll not have you returning here until the floor is renewed."

"Then come," she acquiesced, reaching for his hand again and pulling him to the tomb. "She is beautiful, is she not?"

"Aye, she is," Jamie agreed, looking down at his mother's serene marble face but seeing the woman he'd glimpsed in the moonlight.

Remembering her smile.

And knowing it would always warm him.

"You are beautiful, too." He glanced at his bride as he placed the heather atop his mother's folded hands. "And I am certain my mother would bless our union," he added, half-believing that she just had.

Aveline looked so fetching in the flickering golden light that other, bolder thoughts flashed through his mind. Especially when her lips curved in a slow smile and she lowered her lashes, glancing through them at the chapel's narrow, deep-set windows.

"The moon rises ever higher," she said, her word choice giving a certain part of him a most inappropriate twitch. "And the rain looks to have stopped as well. Perhaps if we leave now, there will still be time to refresh ourselves at St. Bride's Well before we return?"

Jamie drew a swift breath, the thought of her bathing naked in the moonlight beside that very well sending pulsing, molten heat pouring into his loins.

He stepped closer to her, reaching to touch her cheek. "A quick stop at Hughie Mac's and then, I promise you, we shall visit the well," he said, sliding his thumb over the fullness of her lower lip.

But he let his hand fall away almost at once, the temptation to seize her against him and kiss her almost too powerful to resist, yet too unseemly to indulge with his mother and all his reposing ancestors looking on.

"Aye, we will stop at Bride's Well," he said again, grabbing her hand and leading her from the chapel. "But be warned," he added as they stepped out into the cold moonlit night, "the Old Ones who held such ground sacred were not as pious as Maelrubha and his fellow saints. It may be that visiting the well might inspire me."

"That is my wish," Aveline owned, smiling as he lifted her into her saddle.

But her smile and his own faltered, turning to bewilderment, when a short while later they drew up before Hughie Mac's door. The rain had stopped indeed and a handful of glittering stars could be seen through thin, wispy clouds. But mist still curled across the grass and bracken; along the dark edge of the pine wood crowding Hughie's cottage.

A small white-washed cottage, thick-walled and neatly thatched, Hughie's humble dwelling should have welcomed with its usual air of homely pleasantness. Instead, it appeared surprisingly deserted.

Even though a thin blue drift of peat smoke rose from the chimney and, Jamie would have sworn, they'd both seen the beckoning flicker of soft yellow light winking through trees as they'd ridden near.

Candlelight hastily extinguished—or purposely hidden behind quickly latched shutters.

The back of Jamie's neck began to prickle as he swung down onto the damp grass. He was certain he'd seen lights in Hughie's windows and a sidelong glance at his bride assured him she'd seen them, too.

"Could it be he doesn't want visitors?" she asked, proving it.

"Hughie?" Jamie cocked a brow, motioning for her to stay where she was. "That one's door e'er stands open," he said, puzzled, glancing around at the dripping trees and shadows, ill ease licking up and down his spine.

Something was sorely amiss.

Hughie Mac would ne'er turn away a guest. Such just wasn't the Highland way and Hughie was more Highland than most. The old man *wore* these hills, swearing he lived and breathed for love of his home glen. The wee bit of rock and heather he hadn't left since his birth and ne'er cared to.

Jamie frowned. Something was indeed badly wrong.

His pulse quickening, he stared at the darkened cottage, well aware that the erstwhile herd boy even kept the shutters of his windows flung wide just so he'd note a visitor's approach. Hughie liked to know when to toss another peat brick onto his fire and set out his special self-made oatcakes and cheese, a fresh ewer of ale. And, the old man's great pride, his somewhat battered pewter drinking cup, a treasure he saved for guests.

Yet now the shutters were tightly closed.

And Jamie knew without trying that he'd find the cottage door soundly barred.

But he meant to test it all the same.

"Hughie!" he called, hammering his fist on the bolted door. "'Tis Jamie, come to see to you!"

Only silence answered him.

Yawning emptiness, the sighing of the night wind, and from somewhere behind the cottage, the disgruntled bleating of Hughie's sheep.

Jamie's skin began to crawl. He would've sworn he felt eyes watching him. *Hidden eyes.* And with surety, not Hughie Mac's.

Nor any sheep's.

His heart racing, he stared at the cottage, indecision sweeping him. He considered drawing back his foot and kicking in the door, a difficult feat to be sure, but not impossible.

Not for a man of his size and strength.

But Hughie Mac was anything but a fool and if he didn't wish to be disturbed this e'en, he'd have his reasons.

Even so, Jamie couldn't help from lifting his foot and swinging it backward—until his bride's voice stayed him, her small hand lighting on his arm.

"He could be entertaining a woman."

Jamie's eyes rounded and he lowered his foot at once. He wheeled about, turning so quickly, he near tripped over a tree root.

Aveline stood calmly in the moonlight, her placid expression assuring him that she'd meant what she'd said.

"Hughie is older than my da," Jamie blurted, staring back at her. "He—"

"He has e'er kept his dalliances," she informed him, glancing past him to the cottage. "Even in recent years.

Such things canna be kept secret. Not in these hills and glens where ears are e'er peeled and interesting tidings spread like birch seed on the wind."

Still, Jamie couldn't believe it.

He rubbed a hand over his jaw, frowning at the dark night closing in on them. He could feel his brow furrowing despite Aveline's certainty.

"I have heard skirling female laughter coming from those very shuttered windows," she insisted, her smile dimpling. "And I know of two laundresses from Fairmaiden and an unmarried lass in the next glen who openly admit to having succumbed to Hughie's charm."

She came closer, leaning up on her toes to kiss him. "More than once, I was told, and gladly."

"Ah, well . . ." Jamie let his voice trail away, trying to believe her.

"Come," she teased then, sliding a quick hand over a place she knew would stir him, "you can check on Hughie on the morrow if you are still worried. Let us be away to Bride's Well before the night grows colder."

The invitation made, she whirled and strode back to their horses, the pert swaying of her hips leaving no doubt about just why she wished to stop at the sacred pagan well.

But when Jamie started after her, he tripped over the tree root again, his arms flailing as he righted himself before flying facedown into the night-blackened grass.

Slick, wet deer grass, knee-high and tussocky where not clipped short by Hughie's grazing sheep. Scattered patches of autumn-red bracken, dead, soaking, and slippery.

Looking round, he realized the impossibility of his stumbling, leastways over a tree root.

The nearest trees were the tall Caledonian pines edging the steeply sloping braeside to the left of Hughie's cottage and the little birch and alder wood rimming a burn channel a good ways to the right.

There were no other trees in sight.

His ill ease rushing back, Jamie peered down at the *root* he'd tripped over, the mystery quickly solved when he recognized Hughie's walking stick laying half-buried in the grass.

But that posed a question, too, for the old man could scarce move about without the aid of his crummock.

Frowning yet again, Jamie reached down to retrieve the thing, his relief great upon seeing the crummock wasn't the one Hughie favored, but newly whittled.

A fine hazel walking stick, clearly carved by Hughie's hand and, it would seem, dropped unnoticed as the old man shuffled about.

Not quite certain that would have been the way of it, but not knowing what else to think, Jamie carried the crummock back to the cottage and leaned it against the door.

And it wasn't until a short while later when he and Aveline rode into Bride's moonlit glade that he realized why the crummock had bothered him.

It wasn't the crummock at all.

Not truly.

The thing had been a fine walking stick, perfectly made and smooth and pleasing beneath the fingers.

And everyone knew Hughie carved himself a new one

whene'er the need arose. But this crummock could not have been made for Hughie.

Not bent and gnarled as he was, his slight frame barely coming to Jamie's shoulder.

The fine hazel walking stick Jamie had propped against the cottage door had been carved for a much larger man.

One nigh as tall as Jamie.

Chapter Fourteen

❧

Jamie forgot all about Hughie's newly whittled crummock as soon as he and Aveline rode out of the sheltering wood and emerged into the secluded, moonlit clearing of St. Bride's holy well.

They dismounted a few paces from the venerable Celtic site, an innocent-seeming tumble of smooth, lichen-flecked boulders and an ancient altar slab, cracked now but delicately incised with serpent-like creatures and intricate scrollwork. These framed a small stone basin into which the spring's clear, gurgling waters flowed and gathered before disappearing again into the hidden depths of the glade's sacred earth.

Dark, pungent earth filled with long forgotten memories.

Distant hurts that rushed Jamie, called forth just from breathing in the mysterious scent of the holy place. A wild place, it stirred the soul with its blend of wet stone, rich black peat, clean water, and lush, rain-spangled grass.

Inhaling deeply, he could almost feel the years spiraling backward, making him young again.

A wide-eyed and vulnerable lad, ready to believe anything.

But he was a man grown now, so he stood tall and adjusted his plaid against the chill night wind. Not that such measures did much good. Certain powers couldn't be denied. Especially those older than time. Besides, the well's endless array of votive offerings had already caught his eye, beckoning.

The objects, mostly metal, glinted in the moonlight, each one bespeaking some hopeful soul's deepest wish or need. A mad jumble of pins, elaborately carved wire, coins, and even colorful threads and small polished stones, the offerings winked from every imaginable crevice or narrow ledge of the outcropping.

Other votos, coins especially, had been thrust into the living trunk of a nearby holly tree.

Including an ancient Roman coin he'd put there himself.

Jamie ran a hand through his hair, remembering the day as if it were but an hour ago. One of his father's friends had given him the coin when he'd been a lad. The very next morning he'd slipped away from Morag's watchful eye and run all the way to the clearing to kneel at the well and ask St. Bride for his da's favor.

Then he'd pressed the precious coin deep into the wild holly tree that grew up out of the boulders, certain his father would look on him with affection from that moment forward.

But, of course, he hadn't.

Not long thereafter, Munro had turned him out, claiming he should return to the heather that had given him his name.

And so Jamie had gone.

Leaving kith, kin, and the only hearth he'd ever known, he'd set out, making his way south and eventually calling at Eilean Creag Castle where, thankfully, he soon found himself squire to Duncan MacKenzie, the Black Stag of Kintail.

He blew out a breath and frowned, the venerableness of the place clearly getting to him.

"I have not been here for years," he finally said, the winking votives and old memories vanishing when his bride began unbraiding her hair.

An auspicious sign and enough to make his blood quicken with desire.

He took a step closer, his fingers itching to help her. But watching her pleased him, too. Especially when she finished and the pale shimmering strands spilled down past her hips, silky and gleaming.

"You know when I was last here." She looked at him through her lashes, her dimple flashing—"I saw you there, through the trees," she added, gesturing across the clearing to where he'd sat his garron, staring at her.

Slack-jawed and smitten, quite convinced he was seeing a Sithe princess riding moonbeams through the glade.

She angled her head, her sapphire gaze flicking over

him. "I thought I'd ne'er seen a more splendid-looking man."

"And now?"

"Now I know you are."

"Splendid?" Jamie didn't think so at all, but the thought warmed him.

"More than splendid." Her lovely gold-tipped lashes dipped again and she settled her gaze just there where it caused the most havoc. "You are magnificent," she said, the look coming into her eyes heating him.

Stealing his ability to form a single coherent word.

She tilted her head, her bright hair reflecting the moonlight, rippling and tempting him. "Aye, full magnificent—everywhere."

Jamie's breath stopped, his *everywhere* suddenly rock-hard and aching.

Hot all over, despite the cold wind and the night's misty damp.

Even the wet grass beneath the soles of his booted feet felt warm.

Almost alive.

Pulsating with the same hot thrumming warmth coursing all through him.

He closed his eyes and drew a deep breath, almost dizzy from the sweeping force of his need. The fierceness of his passion and the odd sensation that the earth and air around them was altering, that the very ground, grass and trees, even the stars, were beginning to vibrate in rhythm with the wild rushing of his blood.

His mounting desire for Aveline.

He opened his mouth to tell her that he was on fire for

her. That he burned to strip the clothes from her and from himself and then, full-bared and mother-naked, love her until the world stopped spinning or the stars went out, whiche'er came first.

Or perhaps something more romantic like his brother Hamish might have said. That she was the light of his life, his heart's desire, or maybe that he'd love her all their days, even use his last breath to call out her name.

But the words froze on his tongue, held fast by the strange way the air crackled and shimmered. The low, muted humming he'd swear pulsed somewhere deep beneath the glade.

She didn't seem to notice.

Or perhaps she did and just didn't care because she only smiled, then flipped her hair over her shoulder as she turned aside, rummaging in her saddlebags until she withdrew a folded plaid.

"Aye, you are a bonnie man," she declared, flicking out the plaid. "But bonnie or no, you've scarce eaten all day. I heard your stomach growling in the chapel and at Hughie Mac's."

Making for a particularly lovely patch of moon-washed grass not far from the well, she sent him a decidedly bold glance. Cheeky and flirtatious. "'Tis time we do something about your hunger."

Jamie almost choked.

She certainly had the rights of it. He hadn't yet eaten, but it wasn't bread and ale he craved.

O-o-oh, nay.

He ached to pull her against him, lowering his head to nip at the tender flesh beneath her ear, then nibble his way down the smooth arch of her neck, his teeth just grazing her lightly, his tongue lingering.

Lingering and tasting. Savoring and relishing every sweet inch of her, then moving ever lower to explore and claim each dip and curve, worshiping her gleaming moon-silvered flesh until he lost himself in her darker, shadowy places.

Aye, he was especially interested in those dark and shadowy places. Biting back a groan, he reached down to adjust the fall of his plaid.

Seemingly unaware of his discomfort, she was beaming at him again, her eyes alight with promising mischief.

"See, I've brought refreshment," she announced, spreading the plaid on the ground with a flourish. "A feast to strengthen and sustain you for the long hard ride back to Baldreagan."

Jamie's brows shot upward, another rush of hot need tearing through him. He clenched his hands at his sides, wondering at the sudden savageness of his lust. Saints, he could scarce breathe for the near overpowering urge to grab her, lift her high into the air, her skirts flying, then lower her to his mouth, devouring those *shadowy parts* until he was so sated he collapsed to his knees, trembling, his great hunger for her assuaged.

He looked at her, his entire body so hot and tight, he didn't trust himself to move. Her words were making him crazy.

A long hard ride, indeed.

He narrowed his eyes on her, already tasting her, imagining her hot, wet sleekness on his tongue. How her musky female scent would drench his senses until his every indrawn breath delighted and intoxicated him.

The thought nearly made him spill.

Steeling himself lest he join the ranks of those lesser men unable to control their urges, he studied her in the moonlight, admiring its silvery gleam on her hair, his blood heating to think what such soft, luminous light would do to her naked body, all warm, and pliant beneath him.

Or on top of him.

He smiled.

A wolfish smile, he knew, but he didn't care. Ever since swinging down off his garron, he *felt* wolfish. Consumed with a hot, blazing passion he wasn't sure he'd e'er be able to quench. And maybe he didn't even want to.

He only knew that he had to have her, and badly. Here in the glade, beside St. Bride's Well and beneath the streaming moon.

And back at Baldreagan, in Kendrick's large, fur-covered bed. Truth be told, if the mood so took him, he might even ravish her in the stair tower on the way up to Kendrick's room. Not even on a landing, but right on the tight, winding stairs with a brisk chill wind blowing in through the slit windows to cool their heated bodies, their only witness a hissing, smoking wall torch.

Och, aye, he needed her.

Just now, though, she'd gone back to the horses and was busying herself unfastening the wicker basket she'd secured to the back of her saddle.

A basket he'd thought only contained the extra candles and flint she'd taken to St. Maelrubha's.

"Our feast," she declared, coming back to kneel on the plaid. Smiling at him, she opened the basket's lid, revealing the treasures inside.

Wondering if he guessed that, to her, *he* was the greatest treasure.

A prize she'd ne'er dreamed would be hers.

"A flagon of your da's finest Gascon wine," she informed him, hoping to please. "To toast our first meeting," she added, her gaze going again to the other side of the little glade.

There, where he claimed he'd lost his heart.

Aveline swallowed, the notion melting her.

"I shall ne'er be able to pass that spot or this clearing again without remembering," she went on, pulling savories from the basket. A round of cheese, two cold meat pasties, a spiced capon, several freshly baked bannocks, a small jar of butter and another of bilberry jam, sugared almonds, and honey cakes.

After arranging them on the plaid, she looked at him, certain her deepest feelings must be writ all over her.

She gestured to the victuals. "A feast—did I not tell you?"

"O-o-oh, aye, and fit for a king's palate," he agreed, dropping down beside her, then reaching to place one treat after another back into the wicker basket.

Aveline blinked, not missing how his smile turned more wicked, nay, more *devilish*, with every item of food he cleared from the plaid.

So devilish he almost looked capable of teaching Kendrick a thing or two about rogueing.

"What are you doing?" she asked, but a suspicion was already beginning to curl through her.

A deliciously stirring one.

He had to be famished. And she'd taken care to wheedle all his best-loved foods from Baldreagan's cook.

She looked at him, her suspicion strengthening when he returned the honey cakes without even a flicker of an eyelash.

The cook had sworn he loved honey cakes above all else.

The sugared almonds disappeared as quickly and then he sprang to his feet. He began jerking on his sword belt, the look in his eyes warming her and making the special place between her legs tingle.

Not that she minded the tingles.

Or even the long liquid pulls working such wondrous magic deep in her belly. A beautiful, fiery heat pooling low by her thighs and so exquisite her breath was already hitching with fine kindling passion.

Och, nay, she didn't mind.

Seducing him in the glade was her plan, after all.

The whole reason she'd bedeviled him into stopping at the well.

But she'd envisioned a slow and leisurely seduction. A candlelit supper on a plaid beneath the moon, the exchange of long hot-burning gazes and love words as they sipped wine and served each other bits of honey cake.

A tender wooing.

She knew, after all, that he had skilled and tender hands.

Gentle hands.

But there was nothing gentle in the way those hands were now tugging at the latch of his sword belt.

"Are you not hungry?" She glanced at the wicker basket. "Do you not want to eat?"

He whipped off his belt and tossed it aside. "Och, aye, I am fair starving," he said, his boots following the belt and sword. "And you can be sure I intend to dine."

Aveline moistened her lips, everything her sister Maili had e'er told her about her husband ravishing her, flashing in bold and bawdy detail through her mind.

Bold and exciting detail.

But she still had difficulty imagining such a thing. Even though she'd seen the act painted quite unmistakably on Kendrick's window shutters.

Her heart began to thump. The very idea thrilled her. Already her breasts were tightening in anticipation and it was all she could do not to lift her arms and pull him down to her, beg him to fulfill the erotic wish that had been burning inside her ever since he'd first kissed her and she'd wondered what it would be like to have his lips touch her *there*.

And if Maili had spoken true, maybe even his tongue.

She shivered at the deliciousness of that possibility, but before she could encourage him, he stopped flashing his wicked-eyed smile and frowned.

"You are cold," he said, clearly misinterpreting her shiver.

"Nay, I am fine." She lifted her chin, trying to appear as *un*-cold as possible.

Looking unconvinced, he dropped down beside her and slid an arm around her, drawing her close against him. "I won't have you uncomfortable," he said, stroking her hair. "We can ride on to Baldreagan now, going straight to Kendrick's chamber when we return. Though . . ."

He let the words tail off and glanced over at the well and its tumbled outcropping, the stones gleaming white against the black pine wood rising so darkly behind them.

Even the ancient pagan altar stone, cracked, slanting, and half-covered with moss, shimmered bright in the moon glow.

"Though?" She followed his gaze, for one fleeting moment looking as if she, too, were not seeing just the stones and the well, but peering into a distant past.

A long ago time when the old Celtic gods would have called this glade their own.

At the thought, gooseflesh rose on Jamie's arms and the tiny hairs on his nape lifted. His senses alert, he raised a hand to rub the back of his neck, his gaze scanning the dark edge of the encircling trees.

Trees he could well imagine dressed in Druid mist—or bearing silent witness to the mysterious rites of the ancients.

Truth was, he almost believed they still held sway here.

That they'd only slipped away for a few hours and would soon return, their fair voices in the music of the wind, their cautious, watching presence hidden in the soft blue haze that e'er cloaked the hills.

"Though you would rather stay here?" Aveline persisted, watching him closely, almost as if she felt it, too.

"To be sure, I meant to stay here . . . a while," Jamie

admitted, reaching to touch her hair again. "But I'll no' risk you catching a chill. See you, I—" He broke off again, shaking his head to clear it of nonsense.

But even after a few good head shakes and manly denial, the damp grass beneath the plaid still felt warmer than it possibly could and he'd wager all his meals for a year if he honestly couldn't detect a distinct humming deep in the ground beneath them.

He frowned.

His faery was smiling.

"Ach, lass," he blurted, rushing the words, "there is something strange here. A warmth and shimmering in the ground that canna be, but is. I'd hope whate'er it is would warm you as well, that it would keep us from noticing the night's cold if we—" He paused and blew out a frustrated breath. "But I saw you shiver—"

"I shivered because I want those things, too," she said, leaning into him, lighting kisses along his jaw, down his neck. "And I do feel the warmth. As a Highlander, 'tis only natural that you noticed it, too."

She pulled back then, looking over at the well. "'Tis Bride's blessing, see you. Hers and the sun's."

"The sun's?" Jamie's brows arched.

She nodded and a vague memory stirred. Some fireside tale he'd heard as a lad, sung by Hughie Mac or maybe even Morag, he couldn't recall.

"You've heard the tradition but have forgotten," she said, glancing at him. "Shall I retell it for you?"

Jamie shrugged, interested indeed but not wishing to appear overeager to hear what he was sure could only be blether and nonsense.

Clearly thinking otherwise, she nodded solemnly and began. "Far back in time, some might even say farther back than forever, the Old Ones believed the sun disappeared beneath the waters of a night," she said, her voice softening as she settled against him. "They thought the sun needed its rest, you see. But while the sun slept, the waters absorbed the sun's healing power and strength, its warmth and beneficence."

Jamie angled his head and narrowed one eye at her, skeptical. "Are you saying the sun slipped down into St. Bride's well this e'en and is sleeping in its waters? Even now as we sit here?"

She smiled and kissed his nose. "I am saying that the ancient ones believed it, aye. Were they here, they would tell you that it is the underground sun's power throbbing in the earth beneath us, its warmth taking the chill out of the ground we are sitting upon."

"Because we are sitting so near to the well? The well where the sun is now sleeping?"

She nodded again.

Jamie did his best not to snort.

"And you think we feel this warmth and *earth-shimmying* because Bride is blessing us?"

"To be sure," she said, her eyes lighting with a warmth even a thousand suns couldn't match.

Sleeping or otherwise.

"Bride is pleased by our union and showing us."

Jamie *humphed*. "'Tis you I'd wished to please this night."

She smoothed her hand down his arm, then laced her

fingers with his, squeezing lightly. "Are you still hungry?"

Jamie hardened at once, his entire body tightening.

"Och, aye, I have a ravenous hunger," he admitted, putting Bride and her sleeping sun from his mind. "And I think you know what it is I'm craving."

Her lashes fluttered and a quick flush swept into her cheeks, telling him she knew indeed. The sudden catching of her breath and the flash of excitement in her eyes giving him the permission he needed to indulge.

"Aye, I know—I think," she said, banishing any lingering doubt.

Jamie grinned.

"Sweet lass, you willna be sorry." He grabbed her face between his hands and kissed her deeply, a hard and hot tongue-tangling kiss, slaking and furious, sizzling in its intensity.

She returned the kiss with equal fervor, winding her arms around his neck and pressing close, so close he could feel her tightened nipples rubbing against his chest, a sweet torment that only increased his hunger for her.

Breaking the kiss at last, he pulled back to look at her, his breath coming hard and fast. He was fairly certain the whole of his heart must be standing in his eyes, staring right at her.

Trumpeting how much he wanted and adored her.

How deeply he'd fallen in love with her.

And he had.

Truth was, he'd barter his soul to know her safe, make

her happy and see her rise each morn wearing naught but a smile and ne'er even a single care.

He drew a deep breath, certain *cares* of his own throbbing too insistently for him to wax romantic. That could come later, after he'd slaked his need to taste and savor her woman's wetness. And after he'd done so often enough to leave her sleeping the whole morn through. Just the time he figured he needed to return to Hughie's and also take a good look at the Garbh Uisge.

But first he'd look his fill on her.

"This, sapphire eyes, is what I meant by other ways for us to pleasure each other," he said, doing just that as he pushed up her skirt. He slid his hands behind her knees, caressing the tender flesh there, then exploring higher, his breath catching when his fingers skimmed across dampness on the smooth, hot skin of her inner thighs.

"O-o-oh, that is sweet," she breathed, lying back and arching her body for him. She even parted her legs, instinctively giving him greater access. "Don't stop touching me."

"Och, lass, I haven't begun to touch you yet—no' the way I mean to." He looked down at her, deliberately letting a fold of her skirt dip down to shield her nakedness.

And she *was* naked beneath the modesty of that one wee skirt fold.

Her rich musky arousal drifted up between them and he could feel the melting heat of her. Even just kneeling on the plaid, gazing at her.

Och, aye, without doubt Aveline Matheson wore nothing but her own tender flesh and woman's curls beneath her gown and he wasn't quite ready to look fully on such sweetness.

He'd spill when he did. Leastways he suspected he would. Especially when he touched his mouth to her. So he kept her covered for the now and simply savored the sleek, smooth feel of her naked thighs, relishing how each time he slid his hands up and down them, they fell open just a wee bit more.

He wanted her opened as wide as possible when he settled himself between her legs and licked and nibbled his way from her knees up to the soft, fragrant center of her.

A center suddenly freed completely to his view when a particularly soft and warm-feeling wind swept across the glade. Sweet and fragrant as spring sunshine, but brisk enough to lift a certain skirt fold until the moon shone fully on the silky-curled triangle between her legs.

"O-o-oh, lass." Jamie stared at her, incredible heat surging into his loins. "You leave me breathless!"

Not taking his gaze off of her, he reached to touch her, tracing a wondering finger down the very center of her, finding her sleek, slippery, and moist as sun-warmed honey.

Certain she'd taste as delectable, he urged her to lie back on the plaid, then bent her knees, spreading them until she was even more fully exposed to him. The whole of her female sweetness completely open, hot, wet, and glistening.

Her beauty stilled his heart and for several long-seeming moments, he could only sit and look at her. Everything else in the night lost importance. Nothing ex-

isted but the lure of her silver-shimmering female curls
and the strange warm wind swirling over and around
them. A fey wind, it riffled their hair and tugged at their
clothes until, somehow, they were both quite naked and
the gently swaying grass and the dark ring of trees sheltering the glade sighed in approval.

"Keep touching me," she pleaded then, arching against
him when he withdrew his hand, thinking only to cup and
knead her breasts for a moment, perhaps tease a bit at her
nipples.

She looked at him, her eyes passion-glazed. *Needy*.
"Keep touching me there, where you have been," she
urged again. "I can't bear it if you do not."

And so he did, returning his hand to her sweetest heat,
stroking, probing, and swirling his fingers, teasing ca-
resses across her wet and eager flesh, rubbing and circling until even his most skilled touches weren't enough
and she lifted her hips off the plaid, her body begging in
a silent, urgent cry as elemental as the sacred ground beneath them.

But when her writhing and gasps of pleasure began
growing frantic, he did lift away his hand, quickly posi-
tioning himself there where he'd burned to be all night.

"Ach, dia!" she cried when he opened his mouth over
her, sucking gently. Then his large hands slipped beneath
her, his fingers splaying across her bottom, cupping and
lifting her, drawing her even deeper into his seeking
mouth.

White-hot pleasure shot through her, the intensity of it
almost too glorious to bear.

Especially when he looked up, locking gazes with her as he began doing just what she'd hoped he'd do.

And so wondrously, his eyes never leaving hers as he dragged his tongue over her, again and again, each sweet, slow lick enflaming her, making her twist and wind on the plaid, certain she would soon splinter into so many bright-sparkling pieces she'd ne'er be able to gather them.

His tongue plunged into her then, and the shattering began. A slow, free-falling glide into blinding bliss as his tongue dipped in and out, mirroring the most intimate of acts, then withdrawing to swirl over her again, each luxurious, sweeping glide of his tongue making the earth beneath her tremble and sigh, the very hills around them quivering, crying out with the darkness of her need.

Until his laving tongue found *that place* and she realized the tremors and cries were her own, each hot, fluttery flick and swirl of his tongue on her most pulsing, sensitive spot, hurtling her deeper into the glittering madness, the silent little glade and the whole of the cold, moon-washed night spinning wildly around her.

And still he ravished her. Now grazing his teeth ever so lightly on that tiny, hot-throbbing place, nipping gently. Then drawing back to blow softly on her trembling flesh, cooling her before he lowered his head again, burying his face deeper into her sweetness, losing himself in the heady, saturating taste of her.

He feasted on her, some lone, still-thinking corner of his mind certain he'd ne'er get enough of her. That she was a *Sithe* maid indeed and had ensorcelled him, making him crave her scent and taste. The intoxication of her hot, wet, and slippery femaleness.

"Lass, I canna stop," he groaned, licking her harder, his hunger for her only intensifying.

He looked up at her again and saw answering passion heating her eyes. Her hair spilled all around her, her rosebud nipples were thrusting at him through the silvery blond strands. She looked so beautiful that his edge raced closer, a wild, tumultuous release almost breaking when she reached for him, pulling him up on top of her.

Crying out, she arched her hips and clamped her legs around him, rubbing against him in a way he couldn't refuse. Already her body trembled, shuddering and tensing, her pleasure seizing her, sweeping over him, too, as he plunged inside her, sliding deep.

So deep into her sleek, drenching heat, it was as if the earth split beneath him, revealing the sleeping sun and he'd slid right into its fire, the licking flames consuming him, the glory of her almost bursting his heart.

His passion *did* burst, the hot seed streaming into her even as the first spasms of her own release rocked through her and she clung to him, thrusting her fingers into his hair and pulling him close for a deep, open-mouthed kiss.

A rough and savage kiss so wild and uninhibited, he jerked inside her, the endless-seeming flood of his release still pouring into her. The hot-blazing sunfire licked at them, its heat turning the cold, silent glade into brightest summer.

And only later, when he collapsed against her, full-sated and his breath ragged, did Jamie begin to notice the night's chill. They hadn't been transported to some long-past pagan fire festival, Beltane, or the even greater Midsummer revels, but still lay hotly entwined on their plaid, St. Bride's enchanted glade quiet now. The earth no longer warm and humming, but cold and damp with the wetness of the grass beginning to seep through the plaid's wool.

The prickles at the back of Jamie's nape returned as well. The unnerving sense that they weren't alone, and that whoe'er or whate'er lurked near, their purpose was not to wish them well.

The glade seemed smaller now. Dark and more shadow-filled. Even the well and its outcropping had slipped from sight, the stones and the hoary altar hidden by the night's encroaching mist.

A Druid's mist some might say.

Deep, gray and impenetrable, its shimmering silence surrounded them as they dressed for the ride back to Baldreagan. A silent ride through thick, swirling mist that blotted the hills and slipped through the trees, its luminous, rippling curtains shielding them as they rode. Guarding them, too, from a certain hooded figure's prying, malevolent eyes.

Eyes that had seen far too much.

Not that the galling images couldn't be wiped from memory.

They soon would be.

Banished and forever erased, the cries and writhings forgotten as if they'd never been when shock and recognition replaced blazing passion and cold, deserved death claimed its own.

And all the saints, holy wells, pagan glades, or Highland mist wouldn't save them.

This insult had been too great.

It was time, the figure decided, for the last of the Macphersons to meet their fate.

Chapter Fifteen

✦

Early the next morning, it scarce mattered whether the sun slept in St. Bride's Well or elsewhere. It certainly hadn't yet bestirred itself when Jamie slipped from Aveline's arms. Kendrick's painted shutters were still tightly fastened against the cold and the thin smirr of rain that had started sometime in the small hours of the night, and the bedchamber was yet in deep shadow. Scant illumination came from the hearth fire for it had burned low, its one-time warmth and bright reddish glow, little more than a memory.

Even the thick night candle had guttered out, but a single wall sconce yet flickered, its feeble light slanting through the parted bed curtains and across his bride's nakedness.

Her slumbering nakedness.

Jamie stood looking at her, branding her beauty on his heart, the sweetness of her in his mind.

The image of her sleeping, her vulnerability, would

strengthen his purpose. Not that he wasn't already more than determined and able to put an end to bogles-that-weren't and other mysterious doings.

Perhaps then he could turn more of his attention to winning a certain *cantankerous* heart. Or at the very least, see the fear leave his father's eyes.

That, too, would be a victory.

Naught would please him more than if the clan's famed Horn of Days remained in its place on the wall above the high table for a good many years to come, Munro once again lairding it in high style. Mayhap with a bouncing grandbairn or two on his knee.

Jamie's heart filled at the image and he reached for his bride, pulling back just before he stroked her lovely hair. This morn, simple looking would have to do.

And she did make a fetching sight, sprawled so wantonly across the great four-poster bed, her sweet thighs opened just enough to make it nigh impossible to leave her. The tumbled masses of her luxuriant hair spilled across the pillows, each gleaming strand looking bright and silky even in the half-dark of this early hour.

A devil-damned hour, good only for mewling bairns, graybeards, and those sorry souls unable to appreciate the benefits of deep and restorative sleep.

He certainly did.

Little good that it did him this particular morn.

Other, more pressing matters took precedence, so he stretched and looked round, searching for his strewn clothes. It wouldn't do to stumble and cause a ruckus.

Or worse, step on poor Cuillin's tail. A distinct possibility given the room's darkness and the old dog's penchant for plopping down in the most inconvenient places.

Jamie scratched his elbow and frowned.

Saints, but he loathed rising before cockcrow.

Even if the strictures of his world often required it. At the thought, he almost snorted and would have, did he wish not to disturb his sleeping bride.

Truth was, he crawled from bed so early almost every morn.

But rising before the unholy hour of prime when he hadn't slept a wink was an unnatural evil.

A very great evil.

Though the reason for his lack of a good night's rest had surely been worth it.

Grinning, he slid another look at the bed.

A lingering look, and focusing immediately on the sweet triangular tangle of curls he'd spent so much of the night enjoying. Still damp and fragrant from hours of vigorous love play, those silky-soft curls beckoned irresistibly.

But he'd drained himself at least eight times in the long endless night and the saints only knew how often she'd found her like satisfaction, minxie and insatiable as she was proving herself as a bedmate, much to Jamie's delight.

But he'd pushed himself for another reason as well, needing to get away before she rose and attempted to accompany him about his morning's business.

Manly business.

Doings he hoped to shield from her.

He also didn't want Cuillin trailing after him. The

dog's heart and spirit far exceeded his strength and abilities, so he, too, had been treated to extra care the previous e'en, receiving a generous and rich meal. As well, an especially well-fleshed meat bone waited near the hearth. A precautionary measure to content and distract the dog if he stirred before Jamie had a chance to exit the room.

Blessedly, that didn't seem likely; both bride and dog slept deeply.

And if the saints were merciful, he'd have time to see everything tended and be back at Baldreagan, breaking his fast with his da in the great hall before Aveline or Cuillin even opened their eyes to the morning.

Willing it so, he finished dressing and latched on his sword belt, tucking his trusty Norseman's ax into place as well, just for good measure.

If aught was truly amiss at Hughie Mac's, he'd be prepared.

Though he hoped Aveline had the rights of it and the old rogue had only been enjoying a tryst with one of his female admirers last night.

Aye, he'd much prefer to arrive at the cottage and find Hughie fit and hale, perhaps seeing to his sheep or tossing seed to the broody hens e'er running in his wake.

However he found him, Jamie would insist on an explanation for the discarded crummock he'd tripped over in the grass in front of Hughie's cottage. The size of the thing nagged at him as did something else . . . something he'd thought about his da recently but couldn't recall just now. Jamie pressed his lips together and scratched his elbow again.

That was another reason he so disliked early morn-
ings; they befuddled his wits.

Wits that came spiraling back a short while later as he
rode through the empty woodlands toward Hughie's cottage and, by necessity, passed near the great out-thrusting
shoulders of the steep, rock-strewn slopes that formed the
deep gorge of the Garbh Uisge.

Jamie shuddered. The roar of the rushing water filled
his ears, even a safe distance from that dread, lonely
place.

But louder than the boiling white waters of the
cataracts, his own words slammed into him—words he'd
thought when he'd made farewell courtesies to the
MacKenzie lasses.

Then when he'd not wanted his da to hear his reason
for denying Aveline a springtime visit to Eilean Creag,
fearing the travails of the journey and, especially, the rig-
ors of the anticipated sailing adventure on one of the
Black Stag's galleys, would prove too strenuous for
Munro.

Och, nay he hadn't wanted his da to hear such concerns. Yet, he'd suspected he might.

Again, Jamie's own words flashed through his mind,
just as he'd thought them in Baldreagan's bailey.

*Truth be told, he'd often suspected the man could lis-
ten through walls.*

*. . . such a feat might be how he always managed to get
the better of his fellow Highland cattle lairds, e'er seeming to know what the men said behind his back or when
they believed Munro out of earshot.*

Jamie's blood ran cold.

He jerked on the reins, pulling up at once. "Well, then!" he swore, wrenching around his garron and digging in his spurs to thunder down a sloping braeside choked with gorse and broom, making for an innocuous-looking outcrop not unlike the stones that sheltered St. Bride's Well.

Only these boulders hid something far more treacherous.

Something he should've recalled long ago.

The latest when he'd mused about his da's seeming ability to hear through walls.

By all the saints, there'd been a time when Munro Macpherson *had* listened through walls.

Baldreagan was riddled with hidden passageways, squints, and subterranean corridors. In the glory days of his cattle dealing, Jamie's father had used them with glee, taking advantage of being able to leave the dais on some cock-and-bull errand while, in truth, sneaking into a secret passage cut through the walls, circling back, and spying on his guests. Listening raptly, then using his gleaned knowledge against them.

Until Jamie's brother Hamish had one day wandered into the maze of passages and gotten lost.

For three days and nights the entire clan had searched for the lad, finally finding him cowering and half-frozen on the morning of the fourth day, huddled in one of the underground passages that led farthest from the keep.

The very one that exited into the outcrop looming up out of the whin and bracken at the bottom of this braeside.

Another, similar passage opened closer to the Garbh Uisge and he'd investigate that one, too.

If he could find the old opening.

Not an easy task, as his da had ordered every last passage filled and sealed after Hamish's disappearance.

Even his favorite squint in the great hall, a craftily placed laird's lug with a fine view onto the dais, had not been spared.

And, Jamie saw, pulling up in front of the outcrop and swinging down to take a better look, whate'er hidden entry to a subterranean passage may once have been concealed in the tumbled rocks, with surety, was no more.

His father's men had been thorough.

All that remained here were boyhood memories of playing with his brothers near the outcrop, each brother daring the others to venture deeper inside the passage's dank and inky darkness.

Jamie shuddered again and pulled a hand down over his chin.

Such a passage, if a passable one yet existed, might be the answer to his da's *bogle* visits.

"By the Almighty God," he swore, certain of it.

His mood darkening, he remounted, his gaze falling on the plump little sack of honey cakes hanging from the saddle bow and meant for Hughie Mac, should the old man need persuasion to discuss his odd behavior last night—and the newly whittled hazel walking stick. But the honey cakes and his questions for Hughie would have to wait.

Whether it would displease his bride and certain long-nosed, clack-tongued MacKenzie females, he needed to spend some time looking around at the Rough Waters. Even so, he couldn't suppress the chill that swept through him. After years squiring at Eilean Creag, he knew better than most how accurate were Lady Linnet's visitations.

Her warnings of doom—when she felt compelled to make one.

But if he ignored his suspicions and further grief came to those he loved, he'd be dooming himself. He *had* to put an end to the misery someone was so determined to inflict on his family.

No matter the cost to himself.

Thus decided, Jamie dug in his spurs yet again and raced onward, sending his garron plunging back up the steep braeside. But at the hill's crest, he turned away from the tall Caledonian pines sheltering Hughie Mac's cottage and headed elsewhere.

Straight for the Garbh Uisge.

The roar of the falls and crashing, racing water soon became deafening, the sound blotting all else as he neared the soaring birch-clad shoulders of the dread defile. The temperature plummeted, too, and the air grew colder, chilled by the icy, foaming cataracts and because the sun had scuttled behind the dark, low-lying clouds.

Jamie's mount balked. Hill-bred and sure-footed, the shaggy-coated garron tossed its head and sidled when a great plume of frothy spray shot up over the edge of the ravine and the beast's hooves slithered on the slick, slippery ground.

"Dinna fret, my friend," Jamie soothed him, "you needn't go any closer to yon gloomy precipice."

Swinging down, he gave the beast an encouraging

open-palmed *thwack* on his broad rump, then watched as he plunged away into the bracken and whins, seeking the safety of a nearby rocky knowe, his scrabbling, clambering hooves sending a glissade of pebbles over the lip of the gorge and into the swirling, splashing water.

Water Jamie meant to ignore, concentrating only on a nearby birch-clad slope and the mossy, broken-down wall of a long-disused cot house, its ancient stones disguising another entrance to one of Baldreagan's subterranean tunnels.

The only other underground passage that stretched for such a goodly distance, all others ending not far from Baldreagan's stout curtain walls.

His heart pounding, Jamie followed the narrow, twisting deer path that ran along the edge of the gorge, the thick, silver-shadowed birchwood pressing close on one side, the steep drop to the ravine and its cataracts on the other.

Twice, his feet slid on the loose stone and the slick carpet of wet, brown leaves. And once, when throwing out an arm to catch his balance, he plunged his hand right into a patch of stinging nettles growing on a pile of tumbled boulders.

"Damnation!" He scowled, rubbing his palm furiously against his plaid.

This was not promising.

His hand burned worse than if a thousand fire-eaters had spewed flames on him and the dismal, pallid light of the birch wood was seeming to dim the farther along the path he went. Equally disturbing, the back of his neck was beginning to tingle.

Someone was watching him.

He was sure of it.

Especially when a twig cracked somewhere behind him and, with a quick rustling of brittle leaves, another scatter of pebbles went sliding into the leaping, swirling waters of the abyss.

"Hold!" he cried, whirling around, his hand reaching for his sword. But nothing more sinister moved in the birch-clogged, rocky-sided gorge save a family of red foxes.

Jamie blew out a breath and shoved back his hair. The foxes, a fine-looking pair and three older pups sure to soon be on their own, ignored him and continued on their way through the bracken. No doubt heading for a cozy den hidden deep in one of the mist-filled corries gouged into the sides of the gorge.

Only the male fox looked back to stare at him. Oddly familiar though Jamie couldn't say why, the creature's queer golden eyes bored into him in such a disconcerting, penetrating manner that the prickles erupted again on his nape. This time they even spilled down his spine.

The little red fox had strange eyes.

But before Jamie could ponder what else about the creature disturbed him, the fox was gone.

And only then did he realize he'd reached his destination: the tumbledown dry stone wall and the ruined cot house, relics of a long-ago time. And, Jamie saw, little more than a pathetic heap of moss-grown stone. Almost entirely covered by thigh-high bracken, the one-time entrance to the Macphersons' secret tunnel was as much a faded memory as the souls who once called this desolate little patch of earth home.

Jamie frowned.

He'd wasted time and effort. And the palm of his left hand still stung like Hades.

He'd been so sure.

But then, he'd also been certain he'd felt hostile eyes watching him. He would've sworn the rustlings and pebble-scatterings behind him had been of malevolent origin.

Truth was, he could still feel a presence.

And not the ethereal, wispy passing of *bogles* he didn't believe in.

Nor strangely gleaming golden fox eyes, odd as the wee creature had struck him.

Then something *did* strike him.

A great running shove from behind. Hard, breath-stealing, and full to the center of his back. So swift and unexpected he only caught a lightning-quick flash of Macpherson plaid as the tall, powerfully built *bogle* skidded to a lurching halt and Jamie, far from halting, went sailing over the cliff edge.

Horror whipped through him as he fell, the wild rush of the wind, icy flying spray, and the roar of the falls all he knew until the churning cauldron of white rushed ever closer and then, blessedly, went black.

There hadn't even been time to cry out.

Not that he'd have been able to with the wind knocked out of him.

Nor could he scream now with frigid, surging water swirling all around him, rushing into his ears, mouth and nose, choking and blinding him, tossing and rolling his body, hurtling him against the rocks, drenching and drowning him.

Just like his brothers had drowned.

Only Jamie didn't want to die.

Not now.

And not like this.

But he couldn't breathe. Each spluttering, gasping attempt only sent more freezing water shooting into his mouth and nose, filling his lungs until he was sure they'd burst.

And if the water was freezing, his body was on fire. His throat burned and his eyes stung and if the searing pain in his chest meant anything, he'd surely cracked his ribs.

But at least he was alive to realize it!

Determined to stay that way, he thrashed about, trying to keep his head above the rapids and using his arms and legs as best he could to avoid crashing into the worst of the jagged, black-glistening rocks.

A battle he was losing, no matter how fiercely he wished otherwise. Desperately, he grabbed at every crack and fingerhold of each rock he shot past, but the rocks proved too slippery, his fingers too numbed by the cold, his split-second chance at each rock too fleeting.

His teeth were chattering now, too, and the weight of his clothes dragged him down, pulling him under the icy, churning water.

There was nothing he could do.

And what he could have done—namely heed Linnet MacKenzie's warning—he'd ignored.

Then, just when he was certain his lungs truly were on fire and his end must be imminent, he saw the fox again.

That it was the same fox, he was sure. The creature had the same startling eyes.

Alone now, he kept pace with Jamie, running along the rock-strewn edge of the rapids, his golden gaze fixed on Jamie even as he seemed to be looking about for something.

Something he apparently spied, for he suddenly shot ahead, vanishing like a flash of red-gold lightning only to reappear where a fallen tree cluttered the riverbank.

A fallen tree that had split into several pieces, one of which was a fat, good-sized log.

Jamie coughed and spluttered, blinking hard.

He couldn't see well at all.

Not tossing about in the rapids as he was. But he *did* see the little fox stop beside the log and the giddiest sense of hope swept him when the creature began nudging the log forward, rolling it ever closer to the water's edge.

"By the saints," Jamie gasped, not caring that the vow cost him another mouthful of choking, freezing water.

By the holy saints! He cried the words in silence the second time, his throat too tight to voice them when the fox gave the log one last push and it fell into the water.

Just there and then when Jamie hurtled past.

His spirits surging, he lunged for the log, his arms closing around its life-saving girth in the very moment he was sure the last of his strength left him.

Clinging tight, he tossed his head, trying to shake the water from his eyes. But the splashing rapids and cold, tossing spray made it impossible. Renewed hope *did* give him a resurgence of strength, though, and he thrashed his legs with greater fervor, summoning all his will and might to reach the water's rock-torn edge.

Then suddenly the log slammed into solid, pebbly ground and Jamie felt the stony riverbank beneath his weakened, quivering knees.

"Saints o' mercy," he gasped, hot tears blinding him this time.

Too weary to do aught but drop his head onto the log and lay sprawled where he was, he dragged in great gasping gulps of air, too grateful to be alive to care that the icy water still swirled over his lower legs.

His heart thundering, he looked around for the strange-eyed little fox, but the creature was gone, the riverbank empty and quiet.

Silent save for the ever-present din of the Rough Waters and, saints preserve him, the rustling *crash* of someone hurrying toward him through the underbrush.

A large someone, tall and powerfully built judging by their pounding footsteps. They were running now, wild-eyed and shouting, their expression murderous.

And they were wearing a Macpherson plaid, its telltale folds flapping in the cold wind as the figure raced near, leaping and vaulting over broken stone and debris in their haste to reach him.

A figure Jamie knew, the shock of recognition stilling his heart. The man's tall frame and awkward, somewhat clumsy gait gave him away.

As did the huge wicked-looking Viking ax clanking at his side.

It was Beardie.

*   *   *

Aveline knew something was wrong the instant she came awake.

Dread sluiced over her like icy water and she didn't need to fling out an arm and feel the cold emptiness on Jamie's side of the great four-poster bed to know he was gone.

Or that something dire was the reason for his absence.

Cuillin knew it, too.

The old dog paced in front of the closed bedchamber door, pausing now and again to paw, sniff, and scratch at the door's heavy oaken planks. Or just sit and whimper.

It was his whimpering that had wakened her.

Dogs didn't fret and whine at doors without good reason. Nor did they ignore large and well-fleshed meat bones.

Just such a bone lay temptingly near the hearth fire, Cuillin's favorite sleeping spot, and that could only mean one thing.

Jamie had sought to keep the dog quiet so he could slip away unnoticed. And the wish to do so bode ill. It meant he was off on some nefarious scheme.

Something dangerous.

And without doubt foolhardy, though it was the *danger* part that had Aveline dashing about the room snatching up her clothes and dressing as quickly as possible.

There were only two places he would have gone.

To Hughie Mac's; she'd seen last night that he hadn't accepted her notion that the old man had been entertaining a lady love.

Or he'd gone to the Garbh Uisge.

Indeed, as soon as the dread name crossed her mind, she knew that was where he'd headed. The certainty of it made the floor dip and weave beneath her and she grabbed the bedpost, holding fast as a great, icy shudder ripped through her.

Her stomach churned and her mouth went dry. Every warning that had passed the MacKenzie women's lips flew back at her, each word taking stabs at her, freezing her heart with such ice-cold fear she couldn't breathe.

"I won't let anything happen to him," she vowed, clutching the bedpost, certain that if she let go the floor would split wide and swallow her, plunging her into a deep dark void so cold and unending she'd never see another glimmer of light for all the rest of her days.

A horror she had no intention of allowing.

She lifted her chin and set her jaw, determining to be strong. But even then, her fingers slid over the smooth cool wood of the bedpost and she remembered caressing Jamie's face just the night before.

Anything but cool and unresponsive, he'd turned his cheek into her palm, pressing against her hand until his warmth flowed sweetly through her fingertips, reaching clear to her heart.

A heart that now squeezed with dread.

Her chest tightening, Aveline jerked away from the bedpost, her pulse leaping. She looked at her hands, half certain the bed frame's satiny, impersonal wood had grown viper heads and bit her. She wanted the warmth and solidness of *Jamie*.

She blinked hard, cursing the sleep that had claimed

her so fully. The dark night and its stillness, the quiet cloak of morning he'd used to slip away.

Away on some knightly hero's mission, she was sure.

Saints preserve her if aught should happen to him.

She wasn't sure when or how it had happened, but she'd fallen crazily in love with him and couldn't imagine her life without his sunny-natured smiles and grins. The way he treated her as if she were infinitely precious, worth everything to him. And not despite her smallness, but because he prized her just as she was.

She began to pace, trying to think what to do.

But most of all, she just wanted him safe, and in her arms.

Och, aye, she loved him.

Desperately.

And for many more reasons than his high looks and gallantry.

It was the warmth that welled inside her each time he looked at her or she even just thought his name. The sense of feeling whole only when he was near, and empty and bereft when he wasn't.

She loved him to the roots of her soul. A truth borne home by the lancing pain inside her now, her surety that something horrible had happened to him.

She *knew* it.

And the knowledge gutted her.

Closing her eyes, she sank down onto the bed and bit her lip. She would not cry. If she did the pain already ripping her would tear her into jagged little pieces.

Clearly sharing her dread, Cuillin trotted over to her,

first nosing under her elbow, then nudging her knee, his troubled gaze alternating between her and the door.

But when he leaned into her, dropping his head on her lap with a groan, her resolve almost broke.

"Nay, nay, nay, Cuillin," she said, pushing the words past the tightness in her throat. "Mooning about will serve naught—I only needed to catch myself and now I have."

She pushed to her feet, reaching down to stroke the old dog's head. "Truth is, he may only have gone down to the hall to break his fast earlier than usual."

A lie if ever one passed her lips.

Hearts didn't lie and she felt in the depths of hers that he was in mortal danger.

Her heart also told her who had to be informed first— even if she knew waking his da with such news would only distress him.

It couldn't be helped.

But as soon as she opened the door and stepped into the dimly lit passage a low, keening wail reached her ears.

Munro's wail.

And coming from the stair tower.

Hitching up her skirts, Aveline ran down the corridor, Cuillin trotting at her heels. She nearly collided with Munro in the gloom for he stood teetering in the shadows at the top of the turnpike stair, one hand pressed to his heart, his stricken gaze on a tall, plaid-draped figure slowly mounting the stairs toward him.

A figure Aveline recognized at once, her shock so great she could only stare in horror.

Cuillin growled.

The figure smiled.

Then she nodded at Aveline, looking so pleased Aveline knew before her sister opened her mouth what she'd have to say.

"Jamie is dead," Sorcha told her, confirming it. "I pushed him into the Garbh Uisge—just as I had done with his nine vainglorious brothers."

Chapter Sixteen

✠

"Sorcha!" Aveline stared at her sister, disbelief clamping ice-cold talons around her heart. "What have you done?" she cried, the stairwell tilting crazily, the whole world seeming to spin around her. "You've run mad!"

"O-o-oh, with surety," Sorcha agreed, smiling. "Full mad and with the best of reasons!"

Aveline shook her head, shock laming her.

Her sister *was* mad.

The best of reasons?

Chills swept down Aveline's spine. There could be no reason for what Sorcha claimed she'd done.

Nor for her appearance in the stair tower. Her blood-curdling appearance, dressed as she was in her long-flowing hooded cloak, with a Macpherson great plaid slung around her shoulders.

She stood a little more than halfway up the spiraling, corkscrew steps, not far from a well-burning wall torch. The smoking, hissing flames threw a wash of light across her from above, casting her face in dark and eerie shadow while showing the wild, unnatural glint in her eyes.

Looking at her, Aveline shivered, denial pounding through her. Her heart was splitting, such tight, blinding terror winding around her that she couldn't breathe.

Jamie couldn't be dead, he just couldn't.

And her e'er quiet and unassuming sister couldn't possibly be the crazed woman standing before her, with such scorn and hatred blazing in her eyes, her lips twisted with malice.

But the figure was her sister and what she'd said ripped Aveline's soul, rending to shreds every precious, tenuous bit of joy she'd found and relished in Jamie's arms. A loss that slammed through her, spilling her heart's blood and condemning her to an existence in which every indrawn breath would pain her.

Each exhale reminded her of what could have been.

Yet could ne'er be, save in her dreams.

Her memories.

And all her hopes for a future filled with kith, kin, and happiness.

Aveline pressed a hand against her breast. Panic welled inside her, each sickening wave making her stomach clench and hot bile rise in her throat, its bitterness choking her.

She bit her lip, trying to concentrate, to think what to do, but a cold emptiness was spreading through her and an even colder dread pressed heavily on her shoulders. A weight so great she feared she'd soon crumple to her knees.

Shuddering, she reached for Munro's hand, holding

tight to his shaking fingers, fearing that he, too, might slump to his feet any moment.

Watching her, Sorcha laughed. "Hold on to him all you wish. You canna help that one," she sneered, her lip curling. "The *bogle* has already scared him into his grave. His wits are gone."

" 'Tis you who've lost your wits." Aveline's heart raced, her mind reeled. "Munro knew all along you weren't a ghost," she blurted, lying to save the old man's pride if nothing else could be salvaged.

She squeezed his hand, hoped he'd heed her warning.

"You ne'er frightened anyone," she continued, scrambling for words. "Munro only pretended to be afeared so you'd feel secure and expose yourself. And now you have!"

"Hah!" Sorcha snorted. "Pretended did he? Did he tell you he sent to Devorgilla of Doon, asking for powdered toadstone and other fool folderol? Charms against *bogles*?"

She laughed again, the sound echoing in the stair tower. "He wanted the spelling goods because his red-ribboned rowan couldn't keep me away."

"I sent for no such foolery!" Munro denied, his fingers tightening on Aveline's, the angry quiver in his voice letting her know he'd sent to the Hebridean wise woman indeed.

"Ahhh, but you did," Sorcha corrected him, looking amused.

She ascended a step or two as she spoke, coming steadily closer. "Your plea ne'er reached the great Devorgilla. See you, your courier called at Fairmaiden on his way and was e'er so pleased when I told him that one of my father's Pabay men had business on Doon and would deliver your missive with gladness."

Munro spluttered and took a step toward her, his hand going to his sword hilt—until he realized he was wearing naught but his bedrobe. "Murderess!" he roared all the same. "I've ne'er laid a hand to a woman, but . . . you! You—" he broke off, his face contorting and would surely have lunged at her if Aveline didn't seize him.

Livid or no, he was no match for Sorcha.

Not weakened and confused as he was these days. Aveline also caught the flash of steel at her sister's waist, knew how deftly she wielded a dagger. Their father's men of Pabay had taught her, as they'd instructed all the Fairmaiden lasses, claiming a woman ought know how to defend herself.

So Aveline kept a firm grip on Munro.

But she couldn't stop Cuillin.

Barking furiously, he plunged down the steps, making straight for Sorcha but brushing past her at the last moment, bounding down the stairs as fast as his stiff legs would carry him, clearly fleeing what he still viewed as a phantom.

"See?" Sorcha glanced after him, her mouth quirking. "Even he thinks I am a bogle," she mocked, lifting her arms and flapping them.

Tall and large-boned as she was, and costumed so oddly, she did look like a ghost.

Even so, Aveline would have recognized her anywhere.

That she hadn't noticed how disturbed her eldest sister

must be and that her oversight had cost Jamie his life was a horror that would haunt her beyond forever.

"You are mad, is what you are," she said again, tightening her fingers on Munro's uninjured arm and slipping around him, placing herself between him and her sister.

The old laird was standing taller now, and no longer trembling. Leastways not with anything that resembled fear. But he was still injured, his wounded arm not yet healed.

And Sorcha had proved herself dangerous. Ruthless and without conscience.

Worse, she was advancing on them again. Her eyes shone with an even wilder glint, her stare seemingly turning inward, unfocused and chillingly blank even as she looked right at them.

Pausing, she whipped out her dirk and flourished it, glancing down and smiling as she turned the blade to catch the light of a flickering wall torch.

Then her head snapped up with frightening speed and her eyes were perfectly clear again, her face flushed with fury. "I ne'er miss with a dagger," she said, pinning Munro with a hate-filled stare. "The fool MacKenzies distracted me when I fired the crossbow at you, but I'll gut you in one slash with my dirk, ridding the world of you just as easily as I had done with your sons."

"But you loved Neill," Aveline reminded her, trying to remain calm, to say something that would stall Sorcha's menacing approach.

Neither she nor Munro had a weapon. And crying out might cause Sorcha to hurl herself at them, her blade sinking home before the first alerted guardsman could reach them.

Aveline drew a breath, relying on her wits. "I know you loved Neill," she said again. "We could all see it, how you bloomed when you spoke of him."

"*How I bloomed!*" Sorcha scoffed, her voice dripping contempt. "Och, I loved him, aye. Neill the beautiful. Neill the betrayer. The breaker of promises."

She'd spat the words and now she stopped on the curving stairs, her eyes narrowing to furious slits.

"I loved him dearly, aye. And I would have followed him into the deepest pit of hell and back," she said, a tear suddenly trickling down her cheek.

Swiping at it, she raised the dagger again, stabbing the air to emphasize her every word. "I loved him right up to the hour he told me he was calling off our wedding. The day he vowed he didn't care how many of his da's alliances ran afoul, he'd rather pick winkels on the farthest Hebridean shore than turn his back on the woman he loved! Some light-skirted Ulster female he met on a journey to Ireland."

Jabbing the dagger in Munro's direction, she seethed, "*You* sent him there! To Lough Foyle where he said you'd hoped the Irish lords might prove eager cattle buyers. But instead of a taker for your stirks, he found his heart—or so he claimed!"

Aveline stared at her. "So you killed him?"

"All ten o' my sons?" Munro's rage filled the stair tower. "The fiend take you!" he shouted. "On my soul— you'll suffer for this!"

"I had no choice," Sorcha said, her eyes going queer

again. "The shame would've been unbearable with all my other sisters wed and her" —she gestured with the dirk at Aveline—"fair as she is. Anyone would have taken her and I'd be left to wither alone, looking on as Neill flaunted his Irish bride."

She raised her voice above the sudden clamor of barking dogs and cries rising up from the hall. "I ne'er meant to kill them all. Only Neill. 'Twas his wont to cross the footbridge more often than the others. And most times alone. I canna be faulted if they chose to join him that day."

Flicking at the Macpherson plaid she'd donned, she glanced over her shoulder, peering down into the gloom behind her, clearly annoyed by the noise.

"After the deed, I knew why they all went to the Garbh Uisge that morn. 'Twas clear I was meant to have done with all of you," she said, looking at Munro. "Neill for his perfidy, the others for their arrogance and pride, and you because you sent Neill to Lough Foyle! We'd be wed this night were it not for you and your meddling."

"Sorcha, how could you?" Aveline's heart twisted. "We all loved you," she said, throwing a glance at Munro. "Even Laird Macpherson oft spoke of you with affection. He—"

"He caused all this!" Sorcha exploded, her face purpling. "These hills will be better served without him. Once he's gone, our father as nearest neighbor and friend, can take over his lands and cattle. He'll thank me, finally seeing how much more useful I am than you. He—"

Munro hooted. "Your da only wants to sit before his hearth fire and have his men drink his health!" he bellowed, glaring at her. "He'd sooner cut off his arms than burden himself with a second holding! 'Tis mad you are, full mad."

"I am not the one who sees bogles," Sorcha quipped, brandishing her dirk.

She lunged forward then, the tip of her blade catching Munro's plaid—until her eyes flew wide and she flung up her arms, her terrified gaze fixed on something behind them, her dirk slipping from her hand and clattering down the stairs.

"Eeeeeeeee . . ." she cried, her eyes rounding even more as she swayed and staggered, tipping right off the steps into nothingness.

"God's mercy!" Munro crossed himself.

"Dear saints," Aveline gasped, clapping a hand to her cheek as her sister fell, Sorcha's flailing arms and a flash of her long white legs, the last Aveline saw of her, the horrible bumps and *thumpings* as she rolled down the stairs, echoing loudly in the stairwell.

Of a sudden, an eerily silent stairwell.

But not quite as dark as it'd been for the warm golden light of one of the wall torches farther up the steps suddenly flared bright, illuminating the now-empty stairs.

A golden light far too luminous for any smoking pitch-pine torch.

"Iona!" Munro cried, staring up at the landing above them, the wonder in his voice leaving no doubt that he saw his wife standing there.

Or, as Aveline was certain, that she'd come to avert further tragedy.

Munro blinked and pressed a trembling hand to his mouth. "By all the living saints!"

Aveline saw only the shimmering light.

Perhaps, if she squinted and looked hard, the vague outline of a tall, shapely woman. Very feminine and loving in spirit, her tumbling, unbound hair a bright and fiery red-gold and gleaming where the torchlight played upon it.

But then the image was gone.

And with its disappearance, the shadows returned and the stair tower was cold and dark once more. The silence vanished, too, shattered by the chaos in the hall. Crashing, banging, and the sound of running feet, great bursts of shouting and cries, the shrill barking of the castle dogs.

Morag spluttering curses and calling out orders, her sharp voice rising above the din, a sure sign that Sorcha's fall had been observed.

Her body discovered.

"Come!" Her emotions whirling, Aveline peered down into the mirk and saw nothing. She flashed a glance at Munro, then hitched up her skirts and raced down the steps to the hall.

Munro hurried after her, surprisingly quick on his heels for an auld done man with tangled, sleep-mused hair, a bandaged arm, and a furred bed robe flapping about his naked legs.

But when they burst out of the stair tower and into the tumult, it wasn't Sorcha's broken body that caught their eye.

Dead beyond doubt, someone had already tossed a

plaid over her and only her large booted feet and one out-thrust arm peeked from beneath it.

Aveline sucked in a breath, but glanced aside as quickly, scanning the throng for the true source of the ruckus if Sorcha's fall had caused so little a ripple.

Something surely had for the hall bustled with raucous, jostling clansmen and the cacophony was deafening.

Pitch-pine torches blazed everywhere, their sputtering, smoking light casting a flickering reddish glow over the whole of the great cavernous area, while the pleasing, homey smells of wood smoke, ale, and roasting meats gave the deceptive impression that this was a day like any other.

As well it would have been save for the sad plaid-draped form lying just inside the shadows of the stair foot.

A pathetic figure, all but ignored for it was Beardie's huge bear-like form that drew all eyes and attention.

Beardie, the aged, barking dog Cuillin running excited circles around him, and the plaid-hung, auburn-haired giant clutched so protectively in Beardie's arms.

Jamie.

Bruised, disheveled, and dripping, but gloriously, wondrously alive.

Aveline stared, her jaw slipping. Her heart split wide.

"Dear saints," she choked, tears burning her eyes. "He's not dead! God be praised!"

A great sob escaped her and she started running, relief surging through her, giving her the strength to plow her way through the crowded hall, chasing after Beardie as he carried Jamie toward the dais.

"By the Rood! My son lives!" Munro shot past her with remarkable speed, elbowing his way through his kinsmen to arrive at the high table even as Beardie lowered Jamie onto the scarred wood of its cleared surface.

"What did that she-bitch do to you?" Munro demanded, his gruff tone belied by the wetness on his cheeks. His tears flowing, he smoothed back Jamie's damp, tangled hair. "I'd pull her apart with my own hands had she no' fell down the stairs!"

"She pushed him o'er the ledge." Beardie stepped back from the table and shoved his own shock of red hair off his face now that he'd laid down his burden. "I saw it all," he revealed, his great bushy beard jiggling as he looked around, clearly eager to share his tale. "She ran right at him, her arms stretched out before her like a lance and hit him full in the back. He ne'er had a chance, just went flying o'er the edge."

Aveline's heart lurched as she listened, the words making her tremble with shock and anger.

"O-o-oh, Jamie," she cried, grabbing his face and raining kisses on his cheeks and brow, every inch of him that she could reach. "Oh, my heart. Why did you go there?" She blinked hard, dashed the tears from her eyes. "You were warned! Linnet MacKenzie sent word. You knew the danger—"

"I had to go." He opened pain-glazed eyes to peer up at her. "Hughie Mac's . . . the crummock," he added, his thoughts running together in a confused jumble.

But he saw her brow knit and knew he wasn't making

any sense, so he swallowed hard and tried again. "I was on my way to Hughie's and remembered Baldreagan's old underground passages. How some ended near the Garbh Uisge. I thought that might be how the *bogle* gained entry, so I went to have a look and—"

"If you'd just asked me, I'd have told you those passages were made unusable years ago!" Munro barked, folding his arms and looking very lairdly despite his bed robe and bare feet. "Sakes, son, I swear if you were still a wee laddie, I'd take a hazel stick to you!"

"And so would I!" Aveline put in, frowning through her tears and looking anything but ferocious.

Truth was, she was the most beautiful sight Jamie had e'er seen. Even with mussed hair, streaming eyes, and a bright red nose.

Nay, especially with those things.

Looking at her, his own eyes began to burn so he grabbed her quickly, pulling her close for a kiss.

A hard and fast kiss because Munro was glaring at him, his bushy brows snapping together. "Aye, 'tis a good lashing with a hazel stick you need," he vowed. "Giving us such a fright. If it weren't for Beardie, we might have lost you."

"Giving you a fright?" Jamie looked at him. "You mean the *bogle*?"

Munro snorted. "Nay, lad, I meant almost losing you. My only remaining son." His face darkened. "And dinna go asking me to explain myself. I've already said more than your flapping ears deserve to know!"

Jamie blinked, trying to make sense of his da's agitation. Not that he really needed to make the effort. The fierceness of the old man's grip on his shoulder and the tears shimmering in his rheumy blue eyes spoke louder than any explanations his father might have given him.

It meant enough to make Jamie's heart slam against his aching ribs.

The love shining in his bride's eyes as she smothered him with kisses meant even more. He caught her hand and pressed a kiss in her palm. "Have I told you how much I love you?"

She shook her head and a tear dropped onto his cheek. "Nay, you haven't—but I know." Leaning close, she whispered in his ear, "As soon as we're alone again I will show you exactly how much I love you, too."

"Ach, lass." Jamie kissed her fingertips. He would've grinned like a fool, but the words *hazel stick* kept circling back to taunt him, weaving in and out of his mind.

Bedeviling and irritating him.

But his head pounded too fiercely to concentrate on why. Even drawing breath was becoming an agony, each hard-won gasp sending new bursts of pain flashing across his ribs, new spurts of dread flitting across his memory.

Ghastly images he couldn't forget.

The dizzying blur of black cliffs and jagged rocks. Flying spray and the thunder of the falls, the roar of his own blood in his ears. The fiery numbing pain when he'd plunged into the icy surging water.

Water that might well have reclaimed him had Beardie not come along when he had, scooping him into his arms and then heaving him onto his horse. He led the beast all the way back to Baldreagan at a snail's pace—to keep from jarring Jamie's cracked ribs, the big lump had said.

And half the torturous journey, Jamie had expected to be dirked in the back.

Guilt squeezing him, he swiveled his head to look at his cousin, not surprised to see the loon had retrieved his rusty Viking helmet and jammed the fool thing on his head.

Something Beardie did whenever he felt . . . in need.

Jamie frowned and drew as deep a breath as his sore ribs would allow.

"What were you doing there?" he rasped, shamed at having suspected Beardie of being the figure. "Skulking about in the mist at such an ungodly hour?"

Beardie flushed and looked at the floor.

"Does it matter?" Aveline leaned down and kissed him, then reached for one of his hands, rubbing warmth into his still-freezing fingers. "You are here, and alive." She paused, sliding a sidelong glance at Munro. "Hearts have been found and mended. Naught else is of importance."

But she erred.

The hazel walking stick was of dire importance.

Jamie was certain of it.

Every inch of his heart and soul screamed it at him.

". . . a sweet lassie," Beardie was saying, his broad face glowing a brighter red than a harvest moon. "She's a tanner's daughter in the next glen and she even likes my bairns." He looked up again, his chest swelling with pleasure. "I've asked her to marry me and she's agreed."

He reached up to adjust his Viking helmet, using the pause to clear his throat. "The way to her glen runs past the Rough Waters and I was coming from her da's cottage when I saw what happened."

Jamie frowned, his cousin's words only reminding him of another cottage.

Namely Hughie's.

And his need to go there.

A need so urgent, he sat up, doing his best to ignore the fire blazing in his chest, the old and gnarled female hands trying to bind his ribs with a length of suffocatingly tight linen.

Or maybe it wasn't Morag at all, but his faery's arms squeezing him so tightly.

But no, she was leaning into him and smoothing his brow again, touching him as if there'd be no tomorrow and lighting so many soft, sweet kisses across his face that he couldn't well see *who* was crowding around him, stroking, prodding, kissing, and fussing.

Shedding tears and loudly blowing noses.

Crying out names he ne'er expected to hear again.

Jamie's heart froze and he cursed his light-headedness. The dizziness making it difficult to stand, to see as well as he would've wished. But he did see the gaping, open-mouthed stares some of his kinsmen were aiming toward the far side of the hall.

Jamie's pulse began to race.

He started grinning. Even if he was having a bit of trouble keeping on his feet, there was nothing wrong with his ears.

"Holy St. Columba!" his da cried, proving his ears were working as well.

His tears spilling freely now, the old man threw back his head and whooped.

Grabbing Jamie by the shoulders, he hugged him so

fiercely he almost crushed him. "A day o' wonders," he cried, whirling to Aveline and throwing his arms around her in a quick, joyous squeeze before he took off running.

Others ran, too, pounding in the same direction until a great swelling uproar filled the hall. The shouts and calls came from all around, the cries rising to the rafters, shaking the smoke-blackened walls.

The noise was deafening.

Everywhere, men fell over themselves to hasten to the hall's shadowed entry arch, the center of the ruckus.

Men were loosing their swords and waving them in the air, stamping feet and slapping backs. Shouting, jesting, and laughing with glee, wiping streaming tears from grinning, bearded faces.

And then, still making his way across the hall, Jamie saw why.

It was the hazel walking stick.

Hughie Mac's newly whittled *crummock*.

Only it was the tall, broad-shouldered man gripping the *crummock's* bone handle that stole Jamie's breath and sent his heart to thundering. A tall, auburn-haired man who could have been Jamie himself, save that he was a number of years older.

His brother Neill.

Looking as hale and fit as the day Jamie had last seen him, excepting a slight limp and the fine long hazel walking stick clutched tightly in his hand.

"'Tis Neill! I dinna believe it!" Jamie stared, tears choking him, blinding him.

He grabbed his faery, lifting her in the air and twirling her before dragging her tight against him, aching ribs or no. "'Tis Neill," he said again, kissing her soundly. "Neill, and he's no' ghost, sure as we're standing here!"

"And look! There's Kendrick!" She pointed as they ran, knocking into trestle tables and benches in their haste. "He's here, too! With Hughie!"

And he was.

There could be no mistaking him.

Just as Jamie knew him, his roguish, laughing-eyed brother stood in the very midst of the chaos, grinning broadly and looking more rakish than ever with a jaunty bandage wrapped around his head.

Hughie Mac was grinning, too.

He stood a bit apart, his arms folded. "'Tis a long tale," he said, his eyes twinkling when Jamie and Aveline drew up beside him. "Word spreads quickly in these parts and when we heard what happened at the Garbh Uisge, we knew it was time for Neill and Kendrick to come out o' hiding and return home."

Looking pleased with himself, he glanced around. "Truth is, so many folk hereabouts have seen the lads, we wouldn't have been able to keep them secret much longer."

"And just where have they been?" Munro's deep voice boomed beside them. "They were dead—I saw their bodies lowered into the ground. Saw the cairn stones piled on top of them with my own two eyes."

He folded his arms over his bedrobe, his narrow-eyed stare latching onto his two returned sons. "Dinna tell me you were sleeping under those stones all this time, for I know full well you aren't bogles! Ghosts don't wear bandages and walk with limps."

Kendrick and Neill looked at each other.

"Och, we slept beneath them long enough," Neill owned, leaning on the crummock. "Two nights, to be sure."

Kendrick moved to stand beside Hughie, sliding an arm around the little man's shoulders. "Hughie dug us out," he explained, flashing a grin at the old man. "Single-handedly, though he did have some wee assistance."

"*'Wee assistance'?*" Jamie lifted a hand to the back of his neck, rubbing—before the prickling could start. He glanced at Hughie. "What kind of assistance?"

Hughie lifted his chin. "You wouldn't believe me if I told you," he said, shaking his head. "Sometimes I wonder if I imagined it myself."

"I would believe you," Aveline spoke up, her soft voice encouraging. "I've always believed in Highland magic."

Munro grunted, but his gaze whipped to Jamie. "I'll no be denying it either," he said, his expression softening. "My own father swore there's wonder in these hills."

"That's what it must've been," Hughie agreed, nodding vigorously. "See you," he began, lowering his voice, "not three days after we'd laid the brothers to rest, I couldn't sleep because of a pesky scratching at my door. Yet whene'er I went to open it, no one was there."

"No one?" Jamie reached for Aveline, drawing her close.

Hughie looked down, nudging his boot into the floor rushes. "Och, no one save a wee red fox," he finally admitted, his cheeks coloring. "I ignored the creature, but he kept coming back, always scratching at my door and running away when I opened it. After a while I decided to follow him."

"The fox led Hughie to the cairns," Kendrick finished for him. "Neill and I wakened, finding ourselves beneath the stones, alive, but unable to work our way free. We did call out, but no one heard."

"Except the fox?" Aveline smiled.

A chill slipped down Jamie's spine.

Kendrick shrugged. "Who knows? We only know the creature alerted Hughie to our plight." He looked at his da, shaking his head. "A pity it took longer to rout Sorcha."

"Ahhh, but we knew foulness was afoot," Hughie said, taking his two charges by the arm and leading them deeper into the hall, toward their old places at the high table. "We just didn't know who it was or if there were any accomplices."

"That's why we stayed at Hughie's, watching and waiting," Kendrick explained, reaching down to rub Cuillin's ears when the dog nudged his arm. "For all we knew, there was a traitor within Baldreagan's walls and we didn't want to risk endangering the rest of you if word of our survival enraged the *bogle*."

"Nor did we want to attract attention to Hughie," Neill put in. "Not when we were staying beneath his roof to re-cover, and us too weak and injured to lift an eating dirk much less swing a brand had trouble come calling at Hughie's door."

"So that's why the place was locked and barred the other night?" Jamie asked, glancing at Aveline.

She blushed and looked aside.

Hughie nodded. "We weren't yet ready, lad," he said. "No one e'er meant to deceive or fash you. Too much was at stake to risk letting out our secret too soon."

But much later, after a restorative meal of beef and marrow fritters, stewed eel, and more honey cakes and spiced wine than was wise, Jamie still had questions.

Setting down his wine cup, he cleared his throat. "If Sorcha was behind all this—how did she get in and out of here so easily? And always unseen?" He slid a glance at his da. "You said the secret passages were made unusable."

"And so they were," Munro insisted. "Unless someone reopened one."

At that, Kendrick stood. "I'll just be visiting the priv—"

"Och, nay." Neill shot out an arm and grabbed him, pulling him back onto the bench. "You'll be staying put and telling everyone what you told Hughie and I not an hour ago."

To Jamie's surprise, Kendrick looked uncomfortable. But he sat back down and took a long sip of wine. "You've been using my bedchamber, I hear?" he asked, glancing at Jamie and Aveline. "Did you e'er see the little hole recessed in the side of one of the window arches?"

Jamie and Aveline exchanged glances.

Jamie nodded, remembering how he'd noticed the hole the night Hughie had regaled everyone with the tradition of the MacKenzie Marriage Stone and its ceremony.

He'd thought the hole was caused by fallen masonry.

"Aye, we noticed it," he admitted, waiting.

Kendrick hesitated, then tossed down the remainder of

his wine. "Ach, see you, there's a wee lever inside that hole in the window arch," he said, the color in his cheeks deepening. "I discovered it by accident a few years ago and quickly found out that it triggers the door to a secret passage Da and everyone else must've overlooked."

Munro half rose from his laird's chair. "And you ne'er told me?" He narrowed his eyes on his son as he sank back into his seat. "Dinna tell me the passage opens into my bedchamber?"

Kendrick shook his head. "Nay, it opens into the little anteroom between your bedchamber and mine." He looked down, running a finger around the rim of his wine cup rather than meet his father's eye. "The other end exits next to Mother's tomb, right inside St. Maelrubha's."

He glanced up, his flush an even brighter red. "I would've mentioned it as soon as we learned of the bogle goings-on, but"—he touched his bandaged head—"I haven't been conscious all the while since . . . since the Garbh Uisge. Once the pains in my head started lessening, I remembered the passage."

Munro arched a brow, looking anything but an auld done man. "And why did you not tell me before the Garbh Uisge?"

Kendrick squirmed on the trestle bench. "I kept it secret for my own purposes."

Neill laughed and clapped him on the back. "Soft, warm, and accommodating purposes," he said, wriggling his brows as he glanced round the table. "The sort Kendrick didn't want attracting Morag's attention when they passed through the hall on their way to his bedchamber!"

"That's enough, you." Kendrick tossed his older

brother a warning look, but Neill only laughed all the more and slapped the table.

"Och, aye, Kendrick used the secret passage to entertain the ladies," he went on, his eyes dancing with mirth. "Accommodating ladies. Including one fair damsel twice his age!"

Kendrick flushed scarlet. "She was five summers older than me," he blurted, his eyes shooting daggers at Neill. "Not a day more."

"Ah, well, whate'er you say." Neill let it go.

Kendrick pressed his lips together. "My business is my own," he finally said, looking relieved when Morag appeared with a platter of fresh honey cakes.

Grabbing the largest one, he plunked it onto Neill's trencher. "Eat and quit telling tales no one wishes to hear."

"But it's a tale that explains how Sorcha managed her way in and out of here," Neill couldn't resist adding as he reached for a honey cake. "She must've seen you sneak in one of your lady loves. Some might say *you* showed her the way."

"And I'll show you the edge of my blade once we're fully mended," Kendrick shot back at him. "Mayhap my fist in your nose as well."

"Pigs will fly that day," Neill returned, and bit into a honey cake.

"I'm wondering how we could have e'er missed such bickering," Morag declared suddenly, though the twinkle in her eyes and the wobble in her voice took quite a bit of the sting out of her words.

"And I'm wondering about *your* lady love," Munro announced, cocking a brow at Neill. "An Ulster lass if we caught the rights of it?"

This time Neill looked discomfited. "I meant to tell you," he said. "The day the footbridge . . . ach, you know what happened. She is Oonagh, daughter of O'Cahan of Derry. I met her at Lough Foyle and—"

"You'll be bringing her here, to wed." Munro pushed to his feet, looking around as if to dare anyone present to contradict him. "Like as not as soon as you're fit enough to cross the Irish Sea?" he added, eyeing the great hazel walking stick propped so noticeably against the trestle bench.

Neill nodded. "That is what I've planned, aye. Kendrick agreed to go with me. Though"—he shot a glance at his brother— "I'm no longer sure I desire his company."

Munro hooted. "You'll both go and be glad of the journeying. And your mission," he declared, starting to grin. " 'Tis time our house is put to rights.'

"Put to rights?" Neill stared at him.

Everyone did.

Something in his tone and the glint in his eye caused breaths to catch and hearts to still.

Aware of the stares, Munro glared around the high table. "Dinna gawp at me like a bunch o' dimwitted muckle sumphs! I've walked an ill path these years and now"—he paused to look at Jamie—"now, by God, I mean to set things aright."

Jamie swallowed.

Ne'er had he expected an apology from his da. He'd only hoped for acceptance. And mayhap someday, his

love. Sliding an arm around Aveline, he drew her close.
"He's overwrought by the day's doings," he said, speaking low. "He—" He broke off, his eyes widening when Munro stepped away from the table and turned to the Horn of Days, the clan's sacred relic, e'er watching o'er the hall from beneath a swath of ancient Macpherson plaid.

An heirloom Munro now lifted off the dais wall.

He held it high, letting all see and admire the elegant curve of the ivory drinking horn, the gleaming jewels embedded in its finely carved sides.

It was truly lovely.

A wonder to behold.

And proof that Jamie had misunderstood. His da hadn't meant to make peace with him at all. Something inside Jamie broke and tightened. A hot, stabbing flash of pain, but one he knew and was well used to squelching. Doing that now, he took Aveline's hand in his, lacing their fingers.

Needing her warmth.

"He is about to laird Neill," he told her, his voice discreetly low. Pleased, too, for Neill deserved the honor.

But no Clan Macpherson lairding vows rang out at the high table.

Indeed, a thick silence fell as all eyes turned on Jamie. Wide, awe-filled eyes boring into him until he, too, noticed that Munro had stopped behind him and not Neill.

Realization sweeping him, Jamie leapt to his feet. "You canna laird me," he objected, shaking his head. "Neill is—"

"Neill is my firstborn, aye," Munro agreed, his voice

catching on the words. "And 'tis Neill who'll be the next Macpherson chieftain—someday. This day I mean to start a new tradition. You—"

" 'A new tradition'?" Jamie stared at his father, glancing, too, at the curving ivory horn still clutched in Munro's hand.

"Call it what you will," Munro ceded. "The Horn of Days is our clan's most prized possession and I want you to have it. I can think of naught else worthy enough to express my joy in having you back with us. With me"—he cut a glance at Neill and Kendrick—"your brothers and everyone else at Baldreagan."

"But, I—" Jamie couldn't speak further. Not when his father thrust the fabled horn into his hands and then hugged him, clutching him tight.

"You keep the horn," Munro said, stepping back at last. "Neill and his Irish bride can start their own traditions at Baldreagan. I just hope I can prove to you how much you were missed, laddie."

And how much I love you, Jamie thought he heard him say.

An ear-splitting tumult had erupted all around them and amidst the confusion, Munro was suddenly gone. Swept away by shoulder-thwacking, grinning kinsmen, their boisterous calls, salutes, and foot-stomping drowning out all but the thundering of Jamie's heart, the Horn of Days, its smooth ivory and gemstones already warming in his hands.

And above all, the glow on his bride's face as she beamed up at him. "I always knew he'd missed you," she said, her voice hitching. "He loves you, too. In time, you will believe it."

Jamie leaned down and kissed her, pleased by her words.

But something troubled him and needed airing.

Namely, his lady's heart.

Setting her from him, he put back his shoulders. Then he cleared his throat. "Lass, I must ask you—do you mind being bride to a third son? You have heard that Neill will be the next laird. And Kendrick will surely wish to have his bedchamber returned. My own old one is not near so fine."

He looked at her, arching a brow. "I will understand if you'd rather—"

Aveline pressed her fingers against his lips. "Do you mind if we move to your old bedchamber?" she returned, knowing his answer already, but wanting to show him how foolish his worries were.

She lifted her chin. "Would you still rather be in line for the lairdship? And not have two of your brothers safely returned to you?"

Jamie shook his head. "Saints, no," he vowed, meaning it. "I'd walk naked to the edge of the world and back if I could be the tenth son again. The saints know, I'd even beggar myself if doing so might bring back my other brothers as well."

Aveline smiled.

She touched her fingers to his plaid, her violet scent drifting up to enchant him.

"I knew you'd say that," she said, unable to keep a note of triumph out of her voice. "Then you'll understand when I say that I would walk past a line of all the future lairdlings in the realm and not even glance at them if I knew you were waiting at the end of that line."

Jamie looked at her, certain his heart was bursting.

Then, heedless of staring, long-nosed kinsmen and a certain teary-eyed old nurse, he pulled his bride against him and kissed her. Long, hard, and deep.

But not near as deep as the feelings welling inside him. Good feelings. The likes of which he'd ne'er dreamt to experience.

"Past so many someday chieftains?" He kissed the tip of her nose, her cheek. "You love me that much?"

"I love you more than that," she answered, sliding her arms around him. "More than you will ever know."

Epilogue

✦

BALDREAGAN CASTLE, THE GREAT HALL
IN THE SPRING

Did I no' tell you she'd be here?" Jamie slid a glance down the high table at a tiny, black-garbed woman. A grizzle-headed, ancient-looking woman whose bright blue eyes sparkled with mirth.

"Aye, you did," Aveline agreed, her heart warming to have the far-famed Devorgilla of Doon present at their wedding feast revelries.

Taking Jamie's hand, she squeezed it. "I'll vow even you are surprised she brought along her special friend," she added, her gaze lighting on the little red fox sitting quite contentedly on the cailleach's lap.

Looking proud.

And happily accepting the accolades and edible treats many of the guests pressed upon him.

Jamie gave a good-natured shrug. "From all we've heard, Somerled earned his place at this high table and many others as well," he said, smiling as Beardie dropped to one knee beside the crone and, after doffing his Viking helm, began feeding the little fox a handful of sugared sweetmeats.

"As for surprises"—he broke off to sling an arm around his wife, drawing her close—"I dinna think aught under the sun will e'er again surprise me."

"Say you? I would not be too sure." Aveline lifted a teasing brow, her mind on a certain lumpy leather pouch hidden beneath the high table.

More specifically, beneath Munro's laird's chair.

But for the moment, she let Jamie hold her and simply savored the day.

And it *was* a day like no other.

Full to bursting, the torch-lit, gaily-festooned hall shook with horn-blowing and trumpet blasts, the whole of Baldreagan teeming with well-wishers. Good Highland folk from near and far, all beaming smiles, lusty humor, and good cheer.

One supposedly lusty guest drew Aveline's especial attention, Gunna of the Glen having arrived quite modestly dressed and proving to be of a pleasing, unassuming demeanor far different than Aveline would have expected.

Surprised by the woman's warmth and friendliness, Aveline watched her now, looking on as she danced and flirted with Kendrick in the middle of the hall. Neill and his soon-to-be Irish bride, Oonagh, appeared to be enjoying themselves as well, the clearly besotted pair not leaving out a single fast and furious whirl across the broad space cleared for dancing.

The MacKenzie girls danced as well, each one full of laughter and delight—even if partnered only by their father.

"I swear he ne'er ages," Jamie said, watching the Black Stag deftly maneuver his girls away from a hopeful new partner—a young MacKenzie guardsman who thought perhaps the day's merrymaking might relax Duncan MacKenzie's hawk-eyed watch o'er his lovely daughters.

The Black Stag's wife, sitting next to Jamie, leaned close. "And I vow I have ne'er been so pleased as I was when I heard you'd survived the Garbh Uisge," she said, touching a hand to his arm. "I ne'er thought to see this day."

"Nor did I," a gruff voice said from behind them and Jamie twisted around to see his father standing there, a bulky looking leather pouch clutched in his hands. "But today seems as good a day as any to put this behind me."

Jamie cocked a brow, something in his father's expression warning him something of great significance was about to transpire.

"Put what behind you?" he asked, his throat already thickening with emotion.

A grumbled *humph* answered him.

But then Munro looked down and fumbled with the pouch's drawstring, opening it wide before he unceremoniously plunked the thing into Jamie's lap.

"Have a look in there," his father said, stepping back and folding his arms. "But once you do, you'll keep the contents between ourselves, I'm a-warning you."

But Jamie's fingers froze on the well-worn leather and much to his horror, heat began pricking the backs of his eyes. This was the surprise Aveline had hinted at earlier.

His father's proof that he loved him.

Jamie knew it so sure as he knew the sun would rise on the morrow.

"Well, go on," Munro grumbled, nudging the pouch. "Or would you have me standing here like a fool gawping until all the long-noses in the hall notice?"

Jamie drew a deep breath.

Then he looked into the pouch.

It was crammed full with yellowed scrolls, the wax seals broken, each binding string untied. Jamie's heart clenched, then began thundering out of control when Aveline gave a little sob beside him.

"You must read them," she said, reaching into the pouch and retrieving one, thrusting the brittle parchment into his hands. "As soon as you do, you'll understand."

But, saints preserve him, he already did.

Leastways, he had a good guess. And the knowledge was making his throat so tight he could scarce breathe.

"God in heaven," he managed, unrolling the first missive and scanning the squiggly, faded lines.

Lines that told all about Jamie's safe arrival at Eilean Creag Castle in Kintail, his acceptance as junior squire to Duncan MacKenzie.

A second scroll detailed the time he'd fallen from a horse, breaking his arm, while a third extolled his skill at the quintain.

"God in heaven," Jamie said again, tightening his fingers around the scrolls.

He threw a glance at his da, not surprised to see tears streaming down the old man's face.

His own cheeks were damp, too.

As were everyone else's at the high table.

"Do you believe me now, son?" Munro placed a hand on Jamie's shoulder, gripping hard. "Can you e'er forget and forgive the past?"

Jamie swallowed, unable to answer in words.

Instead, he set aside the leather pouch and jumped to his feet, throwing his arms around his da and letting the fierceness of his embrace speak for his heart.

Others on the dais discreetly looked aside or cleared their throats, while some busied themselves flicking invisible specks of lint off their clothes or finding a variety of ways to avoid intruding on such a private moment.

Even Morag held her peace, bustling about the dais and replenishing emptied ale cups, a telltale brightness in her carefully averted eyes.

E'er congenial guests, Alan Mor and his contingent of Pabay men chose that moment to stretch their legs and enjoy some welcome fresh air in the bailey.

Aveline gave them privacy, too, turning her attention on the dancing until three of Lady Linnet's words echoed in her mind and she near choked on her wine.

See the day, Lady Linnet had said, the words lifting the fine hairs on Aveline's nape.

Her gaze shot to Hughie Mac, fiddling away with fervor, and then to Neill and Kendrick, dancing so vigorously at the heart of the tumultuous throng.

"Dear Saints," she gasped, clapping a hand to her breast. "I *have* seen this day—at the churchyard, near the Na Clachan Breugach stone!" She leapt to her feet, grabbing Jamie's arm. "You'll remember, I told you I saw Neill and Kendrick dancing there, to Hughie's fiddle music."

Awe washing over her, she shook her head. "I wasn't seeing ghosts or bog mists, but this very day."

"To be sure, you were," a sage voice chimed as Devorgilla of Doon shuffled near. "Had anyone asked me, I could have told them the Na Clachan Breugach stone was indeed one of the ancient Stones of Wisdom, able to foretell the future."

Stepping closer, she tapped a knotty finger to Aveline's chest. "Leastways, for those able to see with their hearts."

Aveline swallowed.

She slid a glance at Jamie and his father, her heart squeezing at how much at ease they looked. As if there'd never been a rift between them.

Turning back to the crone, she lowered her voice, "Tell me, do you think the Na Clachan Breugach stone will show me the future for Jamie and me? Perhaps let me know what awaits us?"

Devorgilla shook her head. "Ach, nay, lass, I truly doubt it," she said, reaching down to pet Somerled when he sidled up beside them. "Such magic only works when there is a need."

" 'When there is a need'?"

"So I have said." The crone dipped into a pouch at her belt, offering the little fox a bit of fine, dried beef. "You have no further reason to see into the future. You—"

"What she means," Jamie cut in, "is that you should already *know* our future, sweetness." Sliding an arm around her, he pulled her close and smiled at the wise woman. "Is that not so, Devorgilla?"

And the crone nodded, clearly agreeing.

"Then what is our future?" Aveline probed, her gaze

flitting back and forth between the two of them. "Is it as bright and filled with love as I imagine?"

"Our future is all that and more," Jamie promised, leaning down to kiss her brow. "And our love will last for time and eternity."

Aveline sighed, melting at his answer.

Devorgilla looked pleased, too.

Dashing a spot of dampness from her cheek, she smiled. "Aye, that is the way of it, my hearts. For time and for eternity."

About the Author

SUE-ELLEN WELFONDER is a dedicated medievalist of Scottish descent who spent fifteen years living abroad, and still makes annual research trips to Great Britain. She is an active member of the Romance Writers of America and her own clan, the MacFie Society of North America. Her first novel, *Devil in a Kilt*, was one of Romantic Times's top picks. It won RT's Reviewers' Choice Award for Best First Historical Romance of 2001. Sue-Ellen Welfonder is married and lives with her husband, Manfred, and their Jack Russell Terrier, Em, in Florida.

Chapter One

❖

EILEAN CREAG CASTLE
THE WESTERN HIGHLANDS, AUTUMN 1348

Let us speak plainly, my sister, what you would have us do is pure folly."

Lady Gelis MacKenzie dismissed her elder sister's opinion with an impatient flip of one hand. Scarce able to contain her own excitement, she ignored the other's lack of enthusiasm and stepped closer to the arch-topped windows of their tower bedchamber.

A bedchamber she hoped she wouldn't be sharing with Lady Arabella much longer.

Not that she didn't love her sister.

She did.

Just as she adored their lovely room, appointed as it was with every comfort and luxury their father, the Black Stag of Kintail, chose to lavish on them. Elegant trappings met the eye no matter where one gazed and those trusted enough to gain entry to the room, saw immediately that its sumptuous finery rivaled even the Black Stag's own privy quarters. But Gelis cared little for the splendor of the hooded fireplace and matching pair of carved oaken armchairs. The jewel-toned tapestries and extravagant bed hangings of richest brocade, each costly thread glowing in the light of fine wax candles.

Flicking a speck of lint off her sleeve, she cast a glance at her sister. Even if some stubborn souls refused to admit it, *she* knew that life held greater treasures.

Wax candles and hanging oil lamps might banish shadows and a well-doing log fire surely took the worst bite out of a chill Highland morn, but such things did little to warm a woman's heart.

Enflame her passion and make her breath catch with wonder.

Wonder, and love.

Such were Gelis's dreams.

And all her sister's pursed-lipped protestations weren't going to stop her from chasing them.

Apparently bent on doing just that, Arabella joined her in the window embrasure. "Such nonsense will bring you little joy," she contended. "Only a dim—"

"I am not light-minded." Gelis whipped around to face her. "Even Father wouldn't deny Devorgilla of Doon's wisdom."

Arabella sniffed. "There's a difference between spelling charms and herb-craft and expecting moon-infused water to reveal the face of one's future mate."

"Future *love*," Gelis corrected, unable to prevent a delicious shiver of anticipation. "Love as in a girl's one true heart-mate."

Looking unconvinced, Arabella moved closer to the window arch and peered down into the bailey. "Och, to be sure," she quipped, "we shall hasten below, stare into the bowl you hid in the lee of the curtain wall last night, and then we shall see our true loves' faces there in the water."

"So Devorgilla said."

Arabella lifted a brow with predictable skepticism. "And you believe everything you are told?"

Gelis puffed a curl off her forehead. "I believe everything *Devorgilla* says. She has ne'er been known to err. Or can you prove otherwise?"

"I—" Arabella began, only to close her mouth as quickly. Turning aside, she trailed her fingers along the edge of a small table. "'Tis only that you've so much fancy," she said at last, a slight furrow creasing her brow. "I would not see you disappointed."

"Bah!" Gelis tried not to convulse with laughter. "My only disappointment is when Father refuses a bonny suitor! I do not mind him naysaying the toads, but some have been more than appealing."

"Then why bother to peer into a scrying bowl if you already know Father isn't about to let you wed?" Arabella dropped onto the cushioned seat in the window embrasure, a frown still marring her lovely face.

"Isn't about to let either of us wed," Gelis amended, grabbing her sister's arm and pulling her to her feet. "He shall claim we are both too young even when we are withered and gray! Which is why we must use Devorgilla's magic. If the scrying bowl shows us the faces of our future husbands, we shall have the surety that there will *be* husbands for us. I will go mad without that certainty."

You already are mad, Gelis thought she heard her

sister grumble. But when she shot a glance at her, Arabella wore her usual look of eternal composure.

An expression that could needle Gelis beyond patience.

Choosing to ignore it, she tightened her grip on Arabella's arm and dragged her towards the door. "Come," she urged, triumph already surging through her, "there is no one in the bailey just now. If we hurry, we can test our fortune before anyone notices."

"We will see naught but the bottom of the bowl," Arabella decided as they made their way belowstairs and out into the empty courtyard.

An emptiness so stifling its heavy quiet threatened to dampen Gelis's confidence. Brilliant autumn sunshine slanted across the cobbles and nothing stirred. The whole of the vast enclosure loomed silent, the thick curtain walls seeming to watch them, looking on in stern disapproval of their frivolous pursuit.

Gelis paused and took a deep breath. She also lifted her chin and straightened her shoulders. Better to feign bravura than give Arabella the satisfaction of sensing her unease. So she glanced about as unobtrusively as she could, trying to dispel the day's oddness.

But the morn *was* odd.

And unnaturally still.

No sounds reached them from the nearby stables. No birdsong rose from the rowan trees beside the chapel and not a one of their father's dogs darted underfoot as they were wont to do, eager as they were for scraps of food or simply a quick scratch behind the ears. Even Loch Duich lay silent, with nary a whisper of lapping water coming from the other side of the isle-girt castle's stout walling.

The water in the scrying bowl glimmered, its silvery surface beckoning, restoring Gelis's faith as she knelt to peer into its depths.

"See? There is nothing there," Arabella announced, dropping down beside her. "No future husbands' faces and not even a ripple from the wind," she added, poking a finger into the bowl and stirring the surface.

"No-o-o!" Gelis swatted at her sister's hand. "We mustn't touch the water!" she cried, horror washing over her. "Doing so will spoil the magic."

"There wasn't any magic," Arabella scoffed, drying her fingers on a fold of her skirts. "You saw yourself that the bowl showed nothing."

"It was glowing silver," Gelis insisted, frustration beating through her. " 'Twas the light of the full moon, caught there and waiting for us."

Arabella pushed to her feet. "The only thing waiting for us is the stitchery work Mother wishes us to do this morn."

"The embroidery she wishes *you* to help her with," Gelis snipped, tipping the moon-infused water onto the cobbles. "I ply my needle with clumsier fingers than Mother, as well she knows."

"She will be expecting you all the same."

Gelis clutched the empty scrying bowl to her breast, holding fast as if it still shimmered with magic. The face of her one true love, a man she just knew would be as much a legend as her father.

Bold, hot-eyed, and passionate.

Arrogant and proud.

And above all, he'd be hers and no one else's.

"Let us be gone," Arabella prodded. "We mustn't keep Mother waiting."

Gelis splayed her fingers across the bottom of the bowl. It felt warm to the touch. "You go. She won't miss me. Nor would she want me ruining her pillow coverings," she said, distracted. Faith, she could almost feel her gallant's presence. A need and yearning that matched her own. "I'll help her with some other task. Later."

Arabella narrowed her eyes on the bowl. "If you persist in meddling with such foolery, she will be very annoyed."

"Mother is never annoyed." Gelis pinned the older girl's back with a peeved stare as she left Gelis to stride purposefully across the cobbles, making for the keep and hours of stitching drudgery.

"Nor will I be meddling in anything," she added, blinking against the heat pricking her eyes when the bowl went cold and slipped from her fingers. "The magic is gone."

But the day was still bright, the light of the sun and the sweetness of the air too inviting for her to give in to the constriction in her throat. Across the loch, the wooded folds of Kintail's great hills burned red with bracken, their fiery beauty quickening her pulse and soothing her.

She loved those ancient hills with their immense stands of Caledonian pine, rolling moors, and dark, weathered rocks. Even if she wouldn't venture that far, preferring to remain on Eilean Creag's castle island, she could still slip through the postern gate and walk along the shore.

And if her eyes misted with unshed tears, the wind off the loch would dry them. Not that she'd let any spill to begin with. O-o-oh, no. She was, after all, a MacKenzie, and would be until her last breath. No matter who she married.

And she *would* marry.

Even if the notion put a sour taste in her father's mouth.

Swallowing against the persistent heat in her own throat, she glanced over her shoulder, assuring that no one was watching, then let herself out the gate.

It was colder on the lochside of the curtain walls, the wind stronger than she'd realized. Indeed, she'd gone but a few paces before the gusts tore her hair from its pins and whipped long, curling strands of it across her face. Wild, unruly strands as fiery red as the bracken dressing her beloved hills and every bit as unmanageable as Arabella's sleek midnight tresses ever remained in place.

"*She* would look perfectly coiffed in a snowstorm," Gelis muttered, drawing her cloak tighter as she marched across the shingle.

Marching was good.

She wasn't of a mood to amble. And she certainly didn't feel like gliding along gracefully as was her sister's style. Truth be told, if her frustration didn't soon disappear, she might even do some stomping. Great sloshing steps straight through the shallows of the loch, heedless of sea wrack and rocks, needing only to put her disappointment behind her.

It scarce mattered if she looked a fool.

No one could see her.

Only the lone raven circling high above her.

A magnificent creature, his blue-black wings glistening in the sun as he rode the wind currents, sovereign in his lofty domain, impervious to her woes. Or, she decided, after observing him for a few moments, perhaps not so unaffected after all for unless she was mistaken, he'd spotted her.

She could feel his sharp stare.

Even sense a slight angling of his head as he swooped lower, coming ever closer, keen interest in each powerful wing beat. Challenge and conquest in his deep, throaty cries as, suddenly, he dove straight at her, his great wings folded, his piercing eyes fixed unerringly on hers.

Gelis screamed and ducked, shielding her head with her arms, but to no avail. Flying low and fast, the raven was already upon her. His harsh cry rang in her ears as his wings opened to enfold her, their midnight span blotting the sky and stealing the sun, plunging her into darkness.

"Mercy!" Gelis fell to her knees, the swirling blackness so complete she feared she'd gone blind.

"Ach, dia!" she cried, the bird's calls now a loud roaring in her ears. The icy wetness of the rock-strewn shore seeped into her skirts, damping them, the slippery-smooth stones shifting beneath her.

Nay, the whole world was shifting, tilting and spinning around her as the raven embraced her, holding tight, his silken, feathery warmth a strange intimacy in the madness that had seized her.

Gelis shivered, her entire body trembling, her breath

coming in quick, shallow gasps. Mother of mercy, the raven's wings were squeezing her, his fierce grip and the pressing darkness cutting off her air, making her dizzy.

But then his grasp loosened, his great wings releasing her so swiftly she nearly choked on the first icy gulp of air to rush back into her lungs. She tried to push to her feet, but her legs shook too badly and her chill-numbed fingers slid helplessly across the slick, seaweed-draped stones.

Worse, she still couldn't see!

Impenetrable blackness surrounded her.

That, and the unnatural stillness she'd noted earlier in the bailey.

It crept over her now, icing her skin and raising gooseflesh, silencing everything but the thunder of her own blood in her ears, the wild hammering of her heart.

Her well-loved hills were vanished. Loch Duich but a distant memory, the hard, wet coldness of its narrow shore barely discernible against the all-consuming darkness. The raven was gone, too, though his breath-stealing magnificence still gripped her.

She hadn't even seen him speed away.

Couldn't see . . . anything.

Terror pounding through her, she bit her lip, biting down until the metallic taste of blood filled her mouth. Then, her legs still too wobbly to merit the effort, she tried to rise again.

"*Please*," she begged, the nightmare of blindness a white-hot clamp around her heart. "I don't want—"

She broke off, losing her balance as she lurched to her feet, her gaze latching onto a dim lightening of the shadows. A slim band of shimmering silver opening ever so slowly to reveal the towering silhouette of a plaid-draped, sword-hung man, his sleek, blue-black hair just brushing his shoulders, a golden, runic-carved torque about his neck. A powerfully-built stranger with a striking air of familiarity, for even without seeing him clearly, Gelis knew he was watching her with the same intensity as the raven.

An unblinking, penetrating stare that went right through her, lancing all resistance.

Claiming her soul.

"You!" she gasped, her voice a hoarse rasp. Someone else's, not hers. She pressed her hands to her breasts, staring back at him, her eyes widening as she sank once more to the ground. "You are the raven."

The bright silver edging him flared in affirmation and he stepped closer, the gap in the darkness opening just enough to show her his glory. And he *was* glorious, a man of mythic beauty, looking as if he could stride through any number of the legends of the Gael. Dark, pure Celt, and irresistibly seductive, it almost hurt to gaze on him. So great was his effect on her. A Highland warrior ripped straight from her dreams, Gelis knew he'd be terrifying in the rage of battle yet insatiable in the heat of his passion.

She also knew he wanted her.

Or, better said, *needed* her.

And in ways that went far beyond the deep sensual burning she could sense rippling all through his powerful body. His eyes made him vulnerable, dark as the raven's and just as compelling, they'd locked fast with hers, something inside them beseeching her, imploring her to help him.

Letting her see the shadows blackening his soul.

Then, just when he drew so near Gelis thrust out a shaking hand to touch him, he vanished, disappearing as if he'd never been.

Leaving her alone on the surf-washed little strand, the high peaks of Kintail and the shining waters of Loch Duich the only witnesses to all that had transpired.

"Oh-dear-saints," Gelis breathed, lowering herself onto a damp-chilled boulder. Scarce aware of what she was doing, she dashed her tangled hair from her brow and turned her face into the stinging blast of the wind, letting its chill cool her burning cheeks, the hot tears now spilling free.

Tears she wasn't about to check, regardless of her proud name.

The blood-and-iron strength of her indomitable lineage. A heritage that apparently held much more than she'd ever suspected.

More than she or anyone in her family would ever have guessed.

Still trembling, she tipped back her head to stare up at the brilliance of the blue autumn sky. To be sure, the raven was nowhere to be seen and the day, nearing noontide now, stretched all around her as lovely as every other late October day in the heart of Kintail.

But this day had turned into a day like no other.

And she now knew two things she hadn't known upon rising.

Her heart full of wonder, she accepted the truth. She

was a *taibhsear* like her mother, inheriting more than Linnet MacKenzie's flame-colored tresses, but also her *taibhsearachd*.

The gift of second sight.

A talent that had slumbered until this startling morn only to swoop down upon her with a vengeance, making itself known and revealing the face of her beloved.

Her future husband and one true love.

There could be no doubt, she decided, getting slowly to her feet and shaking out her skirts, adjusting her cloak against the still-racing wind.

"I was wrong," she whispered, thinking of the scrying bowl as she turned back toward Eilean Creag and the postern gate. The magic hadn't disappeared.

It'd only gone silent.

Waiting to return in a most wondrous manner.

A totally unexpected manner, Gelis owned, slipping back into the now-bustling bailey. *She* possessed her mother's gift and knowing how accurate such magic was, she need only bide her time until her raven came to claim her.

Then true bliss would be hers.

Of that she was certain.

THE DISH

Where authors give you the inside scoop!

♥ ♥ ♥ ♥ ♥ ♥ ♥ ♥ ♥ ♥ ♥ ♥ ♥ ♥ ♥ ♥

From the desk of Sue-Ellen Welfonder

Dear Reader,

Anyone familiar with my books knows I enjoy weaving Highland magic into my stories. Scotland is rich in myth, legend, and lore, and it can be difficult to decide on the ideal tradition to use. Sometimes the choice comes easy, the answer appearing out of nowhere, almost as if by magic.

This is the fairy dust that gives writers those amazing ah-ha moments and makes the process so wondrous. Also called serendipity, this phenomena is something I definitely believe in and have seen happen time and again.

It happened to me most recently in Scotland, during the writing of BRIDE FOR A KNIGHT (available now). This book's hero Jamie Macpherson is a special character, larger-than-life, full of charm, and deserving more than his lot in life. I wanted to help him find happiness.

To do that, I needed something unique—a talisman—that would mean everything to Jamie. Something significant and life changing. But nothing felt right until I visited Crathes Castle and saw the Horn of Leys proudly displayed in the great hall. A medieval drinking horn of ivory and embedded with jewels, this treasure was presented to the Burnett family in 1323 by none other than Robert the Bruce.

When I saw the horn and learned its history, I knew Jamie would be well served if I included a Horn of Days in his story. As for serendipity, I hadn't planned on visiting Crathes. I didn't have a car that day and getting there meant walking six miles each way. So I walked. Something just compelled me to go there. I believe that something was Highland magic.

I hope you will enjoy watching Jamie discover the powerful magic of love and forgiveness. Readers wishing a peek at his world, might enjoy visiting my Web site at www.welfonder.com to see photos of Crathes Castle and even its famed Horn of Leys.

With all good wishes,

Sue-Ellen Welfonder

♥ ♥ ♥ ♥ ♥ ♥ ♥ ♥ ♥ ♥ ♥ ♥ ♥ ♥ ♥ ♥

From the desk of Elizabeth Hoyt

Gentle Reader,

Whilst perusing my notes for THE SERPENT PRINCE (available now), I noticed this preliminary interview I made with the hero, Simon Iddesleigh, Viscount Iddesleigh. I present it here in the hope that it may amuse you.

Interview With The Rakehell
Lord Iddesleigh sits at his ease in my study. He wears a pristine white wig, a sapphire velvet coat, and yards of lace at wrist and throat. His right leg is flung over the arm of the chair in which he lounges, and his foot—shod in a large red-heeled shoe—swings idly. His ice-gray eyes are narrowed in faint amusement as he watches me arrange my notes.

Q: My lord, you have been described as a rakehell without any redeeming qualities. How do you answer such an accusation?
Simon: It's always so hard to reply to compliments of this kind. One finds oneself stammering and overcome with pretty blushes.

Q: You do not deny your rakehell tendencies?

Simon: Deny? No, madam, rather I embrace them. The company of beautiful, yet wholly unchaste ladies, the exchange of fortunes at the gambling tables, the late night hours, and even later breakfasts. Tell me, what gentleman would not enjoy such a life?

Q: And the rumors that you've killed two men in separate duels?
Simon: (*stops swinging his foot for a second, then continues, looking me frankly in the eye*) I would not put too much stock in rumors.

Q: But—
Simon: (*admiring the lace at his wrist*) Is that all?

Q: I did want to ask you about love.
Simon: (*sounding uncommonly bored*) Rakehells do not fall in love.

Q: Never?
Simon: Never.

Q: But—
Simon: (*now sounding horribly kind*) Madam, I tell you there is no percentage in it. In order for a rakehell to be foolish enough as to fall in love, he'd have to find a woman so extraordinarily intelligent,

witty, charming, and beautiful that he would for-
sake all other women—and more importantly their
favors—for her. What are the odds, I ask you?

Q: But say a rakehell did fall in love—
Simon: *(heaving an exasperated sigh)* I have told you
it is impossible. But if a rakehell did fall in love . . .

Q: Yes?
Simon: It would make a very interesting story.

Yours Most Sincerely,

Elizabeth Hoyt

www.elizabethhoyt.com